MW01486954

THE CONTRACT

A Cowboy's Promise
and a Mother's Love

BOOK 8
HOME ON THE RANGE SERIES

THE CONTRACT

A Cowboy's Promise
and a Mother's Love

Rosie Bosse

Cover illustrated by Cynthia Martin

**POST ROCK
PUBLISHING**

The Contract
Copyright © 2023 by Rosie Bosse

ISBN: Soft Cover – 978-1-958227-08-4
ISBN: eBook – 978-1-958227-09-1

**POST ROCK
PUBLISHING**

Post Rock Publishing
17055 Day Rd.
Onaga, KS 66521

www.rosiebosse.com

Oh, the Stories You Lived!

What was your name? Where did you go?
You who lived in this house, now broken and old.
Did you just move away to follow your dreams
Or are you buried here somewhere, under the trees?
Did you till this land with your sweat and your plow?
Did you plant all these trees that shade this house now?
Did you laugh and plan, talk and share dreams—
Did you scrub all your clothes and hang out your jeans?
Did you bathe in the creek or haul water in here—
That rusty old tub sure worked through the years.
Charred wood in the fireplace, a broken plate on the floor;
The windows are gone and the doors hang ajar.
I listen for laughter—I can almost hear feet;
They rush down from the loft in a giggling heap.
The porch boards are broken and small animal eyes
Look up through the holes where they now live their lives.
When I touch these old walls, I feel life—I feel love;
Where did you go—do you look down from above?
Oh, the stories you lived, if you could just share them with me.
What would you tell—what did you see?
What was your name? Where did you go?
I touch these old walls and I'd like to know.

— RB, Feb. 6, 2018

I dedicate this book to my sweetheart, the man I married more than forty years ago. A man who has never read one of my books but listens to every one as I read them to him. The man I laugh with and work beside—the man who is my other half. To JR for all your encouragement, suggestions, and time spent alone while I "talk to my friends!" Thank you, Sweetheart!

PROLOGUE

Enjoy this eighth book in my Home on the Range series, *The Contract, A Cowboy's Promise and a Mother's Love*. It is set in the Bitter Root Valley in 1879.

The prologue is where I lay out the history. That history is then woven through the story. May you enjoy reading this novel as much as I enjoyed writing it, and may you learn a little history trivia along the way too.

Appaloosa Horses

Appaloosa horses are known for their colorful, spotted coats. Colors and patterns vary widely, and each color pattern is the result of that horse's genetics. Most of these horses will also have striped hooves, mottled skin color, and white (sclera) visible around the irises of their eyes. Color patterns on Appaloosa foals don't necessarily determine the color the horse will be as an adult. Patterns sometimes change as the horse ages. Each pattern has a name and specific coloring characteristics.

In America, the Nez Percé obtained their first horses from the Shoshone in the early 1700s. The nearly secluded location of the Nez

Percé people was conducive to horse breeding as it kept them somewhat safe from the raids of other Indian tribes. The Nez Percé or Nimíípu are credited with developing this distinctive American breed. However, prehistoric paintings of horses show the characteristic leopard spotting of the Appaloosas painted in old caves in Europe. They are also found in ancient Greek and Chinese art.

The French-Canadian fur traders are believed to have named the Palouse River where the Appaloosa name originated. That river runs through current-day Idaho and Washington, the homeland of the Nez Percé people. The French word pelouse means "land with short and thick grass" or "lawn." The spelling eventually changed to Palouse.

The name Appaloosa is credited to the early European settlers who came to the Pacific Northwest. They called the breed Palouse horses, most likely because of their location near the Palouse River. The spelling and names of these horses changed often over time. Old documents spell the name as Apalousey, Appaloosie, Appalucy, and Apalouse. Of course, the spelling of the word would have followed the pronunciation since there was no definitive name or spelling. Finally, the breed's name evolved to Appaloosa which is the name used today.

Appaloosas are found in a wide range of body types because of the multiple breeds of horses that have influenced their conformation over time. Different body structure benefited specific activities, and the horses were bred to perform specialized tasks.

The early breeds were tall and narrow-bodied horses. These rangy animals reflected the influence of the Spanish horses introduced on the American plains before the 1700s. The Spanish likely traded for the spotted horses before they came to the New World since southern Austria and Hungary were known to have had the patterned horses.

The Nez Percé were some of the first horsemen to geld (castrate) their horses to improve their breeding stock. Less desirable male horses were castrated so more desirable traits could be passed on through breeding. This led to their reputation as excellent horse breeders by the early 1800s.

While other horses might be purchased for much less, some mid-1800 cowboys who purchased or traded for Appaloosa horses from the Nez Percé were said to have refused offers to buy as high as $600 for one horse.

The Nez Percé War of 1877 resulted in the extermination of many of the tribal horses. The United States Army killed the captured horses they could not use when Chief Joseph surrendered just south of the Canadian border. They did this because the horses were the lifeblood of the Nez Percé people. By destroying the Nez Percé's livelihood and their way of life, the American government believed the native people would be easier to control. In addition, some of the surviving Appaloosa horses were crossed with heavy breeds of draft horses to create animals useful for farming. As a result of these actions, the Appaloosa breed was nearly destroyed.

Of course, some horses were left behind in the Wallowa Valley in Oregon when the Nez Percé retreated. More escaped or were abandoned along the way. With these surviving animals and a few dedicated horse breeders, a fight for the survival of the breed was begun.

It was a hard-won success. In 1938, over sixty years after the breed was decimated, the Appaloosa Horse Club (ApHC) was created for the breed's registry. Those registration records showed the breed had grown to one of the largest light horse breeds by 1978. The Appaloosa is now the state horse of Idaho.

John Mullan and the Mullan Road

The Mullan Road was the first northwest wagon road to cross the Rocky Mountains. It connected Fort Benton in the Dakota Territory to Walla Walla in the Washington Territory. (As territories changed, Fort Benton became part of the Idaho Territory and finally, the Montana Territory. Today it is in north central Montana.) Before the exploration of the Mullan Road, little detail was recorded about the land between that fort and the West Coast.

In the spring of 1853, an army expedition led by Isaac Stevens was given the authority to chart the area. In the group of engineers and explorers assigned to that expedition was a young man by the name of Lieutenant John Mullan. Mullan was placed in charge of surveying.

John Mullan was born in Norfolk, Virginia on July 31, 1830. He was one of ten children born to his immigrant father and his Virginian mother. John graduated from college at age sixteen and applied for entry at West Point. Mullan was a small man of five feet, five inches. During his entrance interview, President Polk noted his small stature. Mullan replied that the service could use small men as well as big ones. This must have impressed Polk because Mullan's appointment arrived about six weeks later.

At West Point, Mullan finished fifteenth in his class with other well-known future officers including Philip Sheridan. After graduation, he was commissioned second lieutenant of artillery. Mullan was twenty-three years old.

The Mullan Road was built under the command of Lieutenant Mullan between the spring of 1859 and the summer of 1862. It was started at old Fort Walla Walla on the Columbia River and built east. Mullan supervised a workforce of over two hundred. They included surveyors, engineers, and soldiers. Those men carved a twenty-five-foot-wide, six-hundred-eleven-mile-long road through dense forests, over mountains, across marshlands, and through difficult rivers. In some places, the road was even wider as Mullan deforested sixty feet to allow for the runoff from melting snow as well as room for fallen trees.

Mullan was said to be considerate, honest, and even-tempered. He also was respected by the Indians through whose land he had to build his road. He learned and communicated with them in the language of the Flathead and the Pend d'Oreilles. He also took an Indian wife during that time. Mullan was promoted to captain when the Mullan Road was completed.

Flooding in 1860 wiped out large portions of the new road. Those parts were moved and rebuilt in 1861. However, when more floods and winter weather damaged the new road after completion, repairs were done by the travelers themselves. The army did not allow manpower or money to maintain the new route.

Twenty thousand people were estimated to have used the Mullan Road the first year. They crossed with six thousand horses and mules. Those animals were used mostly to pull heavy freight wagons. Thousands of head of driven cattle, over fifty light wagons, and thirty-plus heavy immigrant wagons also traversed the rough road.

Even though the road was only used for three years before it was abandoned, the army considered it a success. The military road opened the Northwestern United States for settlement.

Interstate 90 follows the old road through some of its roughest parts. As with many of the old trails, much of the Mullan Road is now covered by paved roads and highways.

White Bronze Monuments

The Monumental Bronze Company of Bridgeport, Connecticut made most of the zinc carbonate markers that were sold across the United States beginning in the 1870s. Those tombstones were marketed as "white bronze," a name that made them sound elite. However, they were also known as "zinkies" because of their zinc composition. They were sold first through sales agents and later by catalog. Standard monument sets could be ordered. However, intricate monuments could also be custom designed.

The zinc alloy gravestones were cast from a mold. This made the lettering protrude on the metal plates rather than be indented. The casting process could be done in one step for simple stones keeping the cost as low as $6. These individual slabs were then bolted together. If a more elaborate design was created, the metal panels could be zinc-welded at the foundry. This was done by heating molten zinc higher than its melting point and then pouring it into the joints between the cast pieces. This melted the surface of the edges and fused them together. It was a technique that held up well over the years. Finally, decorative plaques were then bolted to the metal. Those removable plates could be updated when desired.

Once the zinc markers were completed, they were treated to give them a finish that simulated the rough appearance of stone. Although they were hollow, the final products were still heavy since zinc weighs more than iron.

Besides being cheaper to make than a stone marker and easier to customize, the zinc also didn't turn green when exposed to the elements. In addition, their metal surfaces warded off moss and lichen which were attracted to the granite stones.

Some potential customers were concerned the zinc markers wouldn't last as long as stone monuments. However, after one hundred fifty-plus years, many zinc markers are still standing. Weight can be a problem though. The heaviness of the large monuments has caused some bases to crack over time.

White bronze markers are more common in old cemeteries in the east than they are in the western states because of early accessibility. However, they are scattered over much of the United States and are fairly easy to identify if one knows what to look for.

Legend has it that the hollow markers were used to hide messages and contraband. That would have been especially helpful during the prohibition years. The friend who first inspired me to search for these markers told me that he and some of his high school friends stashed their liquor inside them at our little local cemetery—and he showed me the specific markers! (Thank you, Roy Arasmith!) I'm guessing that was a purpose the creators didn't anticipate.

White Bronze monuments were sold for around forty years. In 1914, the United State government mandated that the Connecticut plant manufacture munitions for World War 1. Since zinc was a key ingredient of brass, the price of zinc tripled. Those factors, combined with limited marketing, contributed to the end of the zinc monuments.

Incense

Aromatic relics dating back thousands of years have been found all over the world. Early civilizations quickly recognized that different types of wood and fibers not only burned differently—they also created different aromas. Today, incense still has ties to religious and medicinal purposes in many cultures. In fact, the name itself is derived from the Latin word incendere which means "to burn."

All the scents we have ever smelled as well as our reactions to them are stored in the limbic system of our brains. Burning incense stimulates those olfactory nerves. The resulting stimulation dictates how we react to specific scents.

Of course, incense may also be used to mask odors. Bathing in the 1800s was neither as common nor as easy as it is today. My nose and imagination tell me that incense was likely a beneficial addition to the smells emanating from inside the brothels.

George T. Baggs

George Baggs was born in Smyrna, Delaware on January 1, 1857. He attended various schools in Delaware and taught in his home county until age nineteen. However, he longed for the excitement of the West. By 1887, he was in the Bitter Root Valley, Montana Territory. He worked around Stevensville as a cowboy, a laborer in the lumber camps, and even in the grist mills. He made and saved little but gained skills and experience. He also became well-liked.

Baggs returned home at the request of his father. He studied law and completed a three-year program in one. He then practiced law in the East for over ten years, including an appointment by President Harrison as consul to New Castle, New South Whales. Being a staunch Republican, he resigned his post when Grover Cleveland was elected president.

That election gave him the perfect reason to return to Stevensville in the new state of Montana. There he received a warm welcome and soon had his own law practice. He was liked and respected in Stevensville both socially and politically. He married a local girl in 1895 and they had three children. In 1910, he became vice-president of the First State Bank of Stevensville.

George T. Baggs would have settled in Stevensville later than the timeline of this book. However, I decided to include him in this story. He wasn't flashy or boisterous. However, he created a name for himself as an excellent lawyer, not only in Stevensville, but in Ravalli County as well. He was known for his public speaking skills and was sought after both professionally and socially. He is another small piece of the history of Stevensville, Montana.

Music of the West

Songs that reflected the life and heritage of the West began to emerge in the mid-1800s. The trail drives added to that music since it drew young men from all over. The cowboys remade old songs and created new ones, often adding to the lyrics and even creating their own versions. Some were serious and others were comical. Many songs were about their lives on the range.

The Western frontier produced distinctive dance music as well. Mexicans adapted the accordions played predominantly by the Germans and Bohemians. They gave the old waltzes and polkas a distinctive Spanish twist. Texas fiddlers added their own touches too. They preferred tunes with three or more parts in contrast to the two-part tunes that were favored in the Appalachians and other fiddling areas of the east.

The cowboy was viewed as the "Knight of the Plains" even after the trail drives ended in the 1880s. Because he often worked away from civilization, music became a way to pass the time. Harmonicas, accordions, guitars, and fiddles were played at dances and social gatherings. Vocal music was common as well. Although not everyone who participated was talented, music was a big part of social gatherings.

"The Bonnie Banks O' Loch Lomond" is a traditional Scottish song. A loch is a body of water completely or almost surrounded by land. Loch Lomond is the largest Scottish loch.

The original composer is unknown. According to historian Murray G. H. Pittock, the song is an adaptation of an eighteenth-century song. The lover dies for his king and takes the "low road" of death back to Scotland.

"Loch Lomond" has been arranged and recorded many times over the years. Our grade school sang it for a concert when I was in fourth grade. Even though I didn't understand the meanings of all the lyrics, I always loved the lilt of the music.

"Oh! Susanna" was written by Steven Foster. Although it is believed to be among the first songs he wrote, it was first published in 1848. It is still among the most popular American songs ever written and is counted in the top one hundred of all Western songs.

It is an unusual song because while the first line refers to "a banjo on my knee," the song is played to the beat of a polka. Some of the lyrics contradict themselves as well. "It rain'd all night the day I left, the weather it was dry. The sun so hot I froze to death…"

To get his music in front of the public, Foster distributed his sheet music to minstrel shows as they passed through his town. The song was first performed in Pittsburgh, Pennsylvania. A local quintet sang it at a concert in Andrews' Eagle Ice Cream Saloon on September 11, 1847.

Some of the minstrel troupes who performed the song registered Webster's song for copyright under their own names. In addition, unscrupulous music publishers sold Foster's sheet music without compensating the songwriter at all. As a result, "Oh! Susanna" was copyrighted and published at least twenty-one times between 1848 and 1851. Foster earned just $100 for his popular song.

In 1849, the publishing firm of Firth, Pond, and Company offered Foster a royalty rate of $.02 per copy of his sheet music sold. That made him the first fully professional songwriter in the United States.

Steven Foster died in poverty at the age of thirty-seven. Though he wrote over one hundred songs in his final years, most of them were never published and are lost.

"Lorena" is a pre-Civil War song. Henry D. L. Webster wrote the lyrics in 1856 after a broken engagement. The poem was about his ex-fiancée. Webster was a poor preacher when he fell in love with Miss Ella Blocksom. However, her wealthy brother-in-law did not approve of the relationship. Because of that influence, Ella broke off their engagement. The line in his song, "If we try, we may forget," was in the letter she gave Webster.

Webster first made his lover's name in the song Bertha. He later changed it to Lorena since a three-syllable name was needed for the music. A friend by the name of Joseph Philbrick Webster wrote the music, and the song was first published in Chicago in 1857. It became a favorite of soldiers on both sides of the Civil War and was soon known across America.

Alfred Tennyson

Alfred Lord Tennyson was born in England in 1809. He began writing poetry as a boy and penned his first poems at age eight. He published his first poem at the age of eighteen. However, it was not until he was in his thirties that he became known.

In 1842, he published a two-volume book called *Poems*. It contained "Ulysses" which ends with the often-quoted line, "To strive, to seek, to find, and not to yield." That was followed by "The Princess" in 1847 and "In Memoriam" in 1850. The latter includes the line, "'Tis better to have loved and lost than never to have loved at all." The long poem was hugely popular and launched him on his road to success.

Tennyson was the leading poet during his lifetime. However, by the end of the Victorian age, his popularity faded. He may never again be as widely read as he was in the mid-1800s. However, many poets and literary experts still hold him in esteem.

I bought a well-worn copy of *Tennyson's Poems* in 2016. Louis L'Amour often wrote about cowboys carrying books such as *Tennyson's Poems* in their saddlebags. Reading material was hard to acquire, and many cowboys who were in cow camps by themselves memorized anything they could out of boredom. When I look at that old book, I wonder where it has traveled and how many lonely souls have held it in their hands.

Jesse James

Jesse Woodson James was born September 5, 1847, near present-day Kearney in western Missouri. Because so many of the residents of the area were from Kentucky and Tennessee, his home area became known as Little Dixie. The son of a preacher, James eventually became known as an outlaw, robber, guerilla, and leader of the James-Younger Gang.

Jesse's father, Robert, was a Kentucky farmer and a Baptist minister before coming to Missouri. After his marriage to Zerelda, he purchased six slaves and farmed over one hundred acres of land. Robert traveled to California during the Gold Rush to minister to the miners. He died there leaving his wife with three small children: Frank, three-year-old Jesse, and a younger sister, Lavenia.

Zerelda married two more times, once in 1852 and again in 1855. She had four more children with her third husband, Dr. Reuben Samuel.

Missouri was a border state and was proslavery. In Clay County where Jesse was raised, slaves accounted for twenty-five percent of the population, higher than the rest of the state. Tensions between pro and antislavery militias were high. The years leading up to and through the Civil War were violent. Confederate guerrillas or Bushwhackers and Union Jayhawkers battled each other. Civilians on neither side were safe although it is said that Jesse James was always polite to women. Frank was first caught up in the fighting. Jesse followed.

Jesse suffered a second severe chest wound when he was eighteen. He stayed with an uncle north of the City of Kansas (Kansas City) and was nursed back to health by his first cousin, Zerelda "Zee" Mimms. The two fell in love. Nine years of courting eventually led to their marriage.

The James brothers were credited with robberies and killings all over the country. While some of these crimes were their work, others were not. However, it was their robbery of the Daviess County Savings Association in Gallatin, Missouri that made them famous. Although they netted little money, they killed the cashier and made a bold escape when they rode through the middle of a posse formed to catch them. That 1869 robbery made Jesse James an official outlaw and the most famous surviving bushwhacker.

Shortly after the 1869 robbery, the James brothers joined with Cole Younger and his brothers. All former Confederates, they called themselves the James-Younger Gang. While Jesse is often considered a Robin Hood-type outlaw, there is no written evidence of the James Gang ever sharing their bounty outside their personal circle. Even so, he is still considered by some to be both a hero and a villain.

Killer and outlaw, father and friend, Jesse was a product of his time and upbringing. He didn't have to become an outlaw, but as a man who believed both his family and the South were severely wronged, he chose that life. He fought for revenge and that revenge consumed his life.

While there is no record of the James-Younger Gang in Wyoming, there is a written account of Father Cummiskey's experience with one of the Youngers around Laramie, Wyoming in the 1880s. With that information, I made them part of this story. After all, we likely don't know the locations of all their hideouts.

Sleigh Bells

Bells of all kinds have been used to adorn horses for hundreds of years. A few old Roman horse bells were found in Britain, left over from the Roman occupation. Horse bells were used for protection against disease and injury, to ward off evil and attract good luck, and to flaunt their owner's wealth. They were also used by street vendors to alert their customers.

In the 1800s, horse bells were used for winter pleasure on sleighs as well as for work. The correlation between horse bells and Christmas, as well as winter fun, led to those bells being called sleigh bells. In fact, James Lord Pierpont wrote the song "One Horse Open Sleigh" in 1857, a song which we know as "Jingle Bells."

In the United States, the sleigh bell industry began in earnest around 1810. William Barton is credited with starting the industry here. His willingness to share his knowledge and teach others the sleigh bell trade earned East Hampton, Connecticut the names of "Belltown" and "Jingletown."

By the late 1800s, bells were stamped from sheet metal. This process could produce twenty-five thousand bells in one day versus five hundred when they were cast. During this time, bell foundries sprang up throughout the East and Midwest.

Nearly all bell manufacturers in the United States went out of business in the early 1900s. Henry Ford's Model T automobile led to the disappearance of the horse as a necessary means of transportation. Horse bells disappeared as well.

Thanksgiving Day

Today, the United States celebrates Thanksgiving Day on the fourth Thursday of November. However, that is not how it always was. For a time, Thanksgiving was celebrated on the last Thursday of November. Of course, that was a problem when there were five Thursdays in the month. Politicians through the years attempted to address this.

The first Thanksgiving in America took place in 1621. The Plymouth colonists and the Wampanoag Indians shared an autumn feast. Following this tradition, for over two hundred years, days of thanksgiving and prayer were celebrated in the United States by individual families, groups, and states.

Days of Thanksgiving were designated by the Continental Congress during the American Revolution, and in 1789, President George Washington issued the first Thanksgiving proclamation by the national government of the United States. He called for Americans to "express their gratitude for the conclusion of the War for Independence and the successful ratification of the Constitution."

Sarah Josepha Hale, author of "Mary Had a Little Lamb," pushed for a national holiday beginning in 1827. Her thirty-six-year campaign earned her the nickname, "Mother of Thanksgiving."

Perhaps President Lincoln heeded that request because in 1863, during the Civil War, he proclaimed that a national Thanksgiving Day would be held the last Thursday of November. He invited all Americans to ask God to "commend to his tender care all those who have become widows, orphans, mourners or sufferers in the lamentable civil strife" and to "heal the wounds of the nation."

The year of 1876 brought another five-week November. George W. French was acting governor of the Wyoming Territory at that time. He issued a proclamation in accordance with President Ulysses S. Grant to designate Thursday, November 30, 1876, as a day of Thanksgiving and Prayer.

President Franklin D. Roosevelt moved the holiday to the second to last Thursday of November. He hoped to increase retail sales during the Great Depression. His plan, called by critics Franksgiving, was not widely accepted. Thirty-two states agreed while sixteen states refused to accept the change. Those sixteen states proclaimed Thanksgiving to be the last Thursday of November. In 1941, Roosevelt reluctantly signed a bill making Thanksgiving the fourth Thursday in November. That law stands today.

The Loretto Chapel and Its Mysterious Spiral Staircase

The Loretto Chapel Staircase is in a small chapel in Santa Fe, New Mexico. It rises twenty-two feet to the choir loft and makes two, three hundred sixty-degree turns. There are no center supports, and it is held together by wooden pegs. No glue, nails, or other hardware were used in the construction. There are thirty-three steps from the floor to the loft. The original staircase had no railings—those were added later.

In 1872, Our Lady of Light Chapel was begun in Santa Fe, New Mexico Territory. The Sisters of Loretto were to use and maintain the little chapel.

Construction was started by a talented French architect named Antoine Mouly. Mr. Mouly passed before the project could be completed in 1878. Unfortunately, plans had not been laid for the stairs from the chapel to the choir loft. The area where the stairs needed to be built was too small for a standard staircase, and a twenty-two-foot ladder was deemed unacceptable. Numerous suggestions and ideas were considered. No solutions were found.

The nuns were undeterred. They began to pray a nine-day novena of prayers. They asked Saint Joseph, the Patron Saint of Carpenters, to help them. On the ninth and final day of the novena, a gray-haired man arrived with a donkey and a tool chest. He was looking for work.

According to those nuns, the only tools he carried were a saw, a T-square, and a hammer. The nuns showed him their chapel and their obvious problem.

The old man accepted the job. He provided his own wood, and the nuns were not billed during the construction process. The man only worked when the chapel was empty to avoid disturbing the nuns' prayers. Months later, when the beautiful staircase was completed, the man disappeared. He was never paid, and the nuns never heard from him again. After searching unsuccessfully for the man or someone who knew him, the good sisters decided their carpenter must have been Saint Joseph himself.

Over the years, there have been unresolved theories about who the carpenter was. The wood is said to be spruce of an unknown species but has never been identified. The construction design has also been studied. Some experts believe the unsupported staircase should have collapsed the first time it was used. Yet it was used daily for almost one hundred years.

Regardless of what you think or believe, the staircase is truly a work of art. The old chapel is now privately owned and may be toured. When we visited, we were unable to get close to the staircase. Even from the back of the little chapel though, it was beautiful. I'm sure it would be even more impressive to the eye of a trained craftsman.

Thank you for choosing to read my novels. May this story become another favorite. Please connect with me on Facebook: Rosie Bosse, Author. Your comments and reviews are welcome as well.

Additional novels may be purchased through my website or through your local bookstore. They are also available through various online suppliers. Of course, they may be requested at your local library as well.

Rosie Bosse
Living and Writing in the Middle of Nowhere
rosiebosse.com

Slash B Ranch
Bitter Root Valley,
Montana Territory
Tuesday, September 30, 1879

CHAPTER 1

THE CONTRACT

SPUR ROLLED OVER AND LOOKED UP AT THE CEILING of the bunkhouse. His mouth was dry, and his breath made him choke. He sat up and ran his fingers through the dark, black hair that curled around his head.

He frowned as he thought about the conversation he'd had with Clare the night before. He cursed and grabbed his hat.

"Clare, what are you thinking? This marriage idea is a terrible one. Yeah, we are friends but after a month, we'll hate each other. Folks are supposed to marry someone they love. They shouldn't marry just to give kids a pa. We'll both live to regret this." He slammed his hat down on his head and stood up, still muttering.

"I'll go ahead with this sham since you are so determined. I sure don't want you to offer the deal you offered me to some other fellow. He might take advantage of you or hurt those little ones.

"I'm not happy about it though, and I doubt this is something Rock would want you to do."

His mind went to the cattle drive from Cheyenne through the Wyoming Territory. They had trailed through the southern part of the Montana Territory west to the Bitter Root Valley. That drive had just ended. In fact, the herd had arrived in Stevensville the day before. Spur shook his head.

"Rock, you were so darn excited about getting black cattle started up here. You came down to Cheyenne and bought a herd from William Sturgis. It wasn't a bad drive either although we all hated to lose Rufe.

"He was a heck of a nice fellow who was beaten to death for defending a woman. We got him out of that saloon, but it was too late. He didn't make it. Then we lost you shortly after that.

"You died less than two weeks before that drive ended. You left Clare a widow with three little ones and a baby on the way.

"Shoot, she's barely twenty-one. She had Zeke when she was sixteen. Annie was your child with your first wife, Suzanna. She died shortly after Annie was born.

"You were a widower for four years and Clare a widow for about six months when you married her. Then you took in little Nora. She looks enough like Clare to be her own child. But then she is a niece, so that's normal I reckon.

"Four little ones plus a ranch to run just overwhelmed Clare, I guess."

Spur rolled up his blanket and picked up his warbag. Both the contract Clare had given him and the sheet with the ten items he added were laying on top. He picked up the single sheet of paper he had written the night before after an evening of drinking and read his expectations. He studied Clare's signature at the bottom and frowned as he read the list.

1. Marryin is forever. It don't end after ten years.
2. I aint sleepin in the bunkhouse. This here marriage aint a sham even if ya think it is. An I'll be havin my husbandly rights after the baby comes.
3. There won't be no money paid. I aint the kind a feller who does this sort a thing fer money.

4. We're hirin Stub an Tuff back.

5. We'll be married down to the mission by Father Ravalli. I like that priest. Course I'll probably have to go to confession some fore we consummate this here marriage cause of impure thoughts.

6. I won't cut off my mustache an don't ya be askin me to.

7. Those kids will be my kids too so don't ya be callin them yores.

8. I cin call ya Darlin if I want an I cin kiss ya of a mornin.

9. I git to be there fer the birthin of all our babies.

10. An next summer, we're a goin swimmin alone an I git to see what ya wear in the water.

Spur was silent a moment and shook his head as he growled, "This whole setup sounds like an even worse idea sober than it did last night when I was drunk." He looked toward the dark house and cursed under his breath.

"What are you doing, Clare? You don't want this marriage any more than I do." Spur was silent a moment. He jerked off his hat and slapped it against his leg before he pulled it on a second time. He cursed again and strode across the ranch yard to the barn.

"Rockefeller, you have been on vacation long enough. It's time to get back to work." He was saddling his horse when Angel sauntered into the barn.

"Good morning, my amigo. Are you ready to become a married man? I think 8:00 this morning is not so far away."

Spur glared at his friend and didn't answer.

Angel's voice was serious when he spoke again. "I think, amigo, it is a good thing that you are marrying the señora. I think her heart is broken. Perhaps our Dios sent you to make her smile again."

Spur looked up in surprise. He studied Angel's face and shook his head. "I don't think anyone should ever marry except for love. We are starting this whole deal the wrong way, and it could blow clean up. Marryin' someone so the kids have a pa ain't right."

Angel was quiet a moment and asked softly, "Would it be so hard to love the señora? She is a beautiful woman, not only on the outside but on the inside as well. She loves her family enough to make a great sacrifice for them."

Spur's hands went still for a moment before he looked up. The pain that showed on his face was easy to read.

"I'm not worried about me, Angel. I've had plenty of chances to love. I threw them all away.

"Clare is barely twenty-one. She has lost two husbands already, and now she is settling for a loveless marriage.

"She doesn't know but someone will come along who will make her heart sing again. And then what? She will be tied to me and will never find happiness again."

Spur dropped the stirrup down over the tightened girth and growled, "I am going to find some flowers. A woman ought to have a few flowers on her wedding day even if she *is* marrying the wrong man."

He mounted his horse and rode east toward an open pasture. Small flowers were just visible in the early morning light. Angel watched as Spur stopped and picked them. When the tall cowboy mounted again and rode further into the pasture, Angel turned away with a smile.

"Sí, I think our Dios sent just the right man. I think my amigo will help the señora's heart to mend. And just maybe the two of them will find amour."

CHAPTER 2

CLIMB ON UP HERE

SPUR PICKED A HANDFUL OF FLOWERS AND THEN followed the scent of lilacs to a little corner of the pasture. His horse snorted and shied as he rode up. Spur's gun slipped easily into his hand.

"Come on out of there, whoever you are. And don't take too long. My finger is a little touchy this morning."

A gasp sounded from inside the lilacs and a woman's face appeared. Her blue eyes showed surprise as she stared at him.

"Clare! What are you doing out here?" Spur looked a little closer and frowned. "Are you in your nightgown? You slept out here?"

Clare was quiet as she pulled her shawl tighter around her body.

Spur reached out his hand. "Come on. I'll give you a ride back to the house."

Clare glared at him. "I am not riding astride in a nightgown, and I am certainly not going to sit on your lap."

Spur pushed back his hat and scratched his head as a slow grin filled his face. "Well, I reckon I'll just follow you back to the house. 'Course the mornin' sun is shinin' right through that nightgown, and it ain't leavin' much to a man's imagination."

Clare's eyes opened wide, and she turned a deep red. She turned to look at the rising sun and glared again at Spur.

"I swear, Spur. You have no muzzle whatsoever."

Spur chuckled. "That could be, but you might want to rethink that offer." He pointed his thumb over his shoulder toward the house. "I reckon most of the hands will be up by now, so you can go ahead and walk on up there...or you can ride back with me."

Clare looked up at him skeptically. "And how do you propose I get on that horse?"

Spur chuckled as he reached down his right hand. "You just take my hand and put your right foot up on my boot. Once you are up, turn around like you are doing a dance and I'll waltz you right onto my lap."

Clare stared at Spur a moment before she took his hand. He pulled her up easily and turned her onto his lap. His left arm circled her waist, and he pulled her tight.

"Now wasn't that easy? No effort at all."

Clare looked up at him. Her blue eyes were sparking fire. "Release your arm. I can hold on by myself."

Spur laughed softly. "I reckon not. I wouldn't be much of a man if I didn't take advantage of a woman on my lap to do a little cuddling. Nope, my arm is going to stay right there. We sure don't want you to take a nosedive off this horse."

Clare pushed his arm down and commented dryly, "You did that quite smoothly. I believe you have waltzed many women onto your lap."

Spur laughed. "Sure have. I've had lots of practice with the ladies. You are a whole different deal though. I don't recall ever giving a woman a ride in a nightgown." He pulled his arm tighter and whispered, "I ain't complaining though."

Clare's elbow hit him in the stomach. Spur let out a grunt followed by a chuckle. He relaxed his arm and leaned back in the saddle.

"So, Miss Clare, do you want to take a bath before we marry? I can bring some water in if you do."

Clare's eyes were shooting sparks again as she looked up at him.

"Are you saying I smell? You are a bold man, George Spurlock."

Spur leaned forward and took a deep breath. His arm tightened around her full waist again as he whispered, "You smell like lilacs, and they are my favorite flower."

"Nope, I just thought maybe you would like to take a bath. I don't know how often women do that sort of thing."

Clare was quiet a moment. She answered softly, "A bath would be wonderful, and I would love to have some water carried in."

Spur nodded with a smile on his face. His arm remained where it was as they rode the rest of the way to the house.

He turned Rockefeller parallel to the porch and said, "Down, Feller. Get down."

His horse dropped to its front knees and Spur slid Clare out of the saddle. "There you are, Miss Clare. Delivered to your own front steps."

Clare stared up at him a moment. Her eyes were bright, and she commented dryly, "And you couldn't have knelt your horse down to let me mount instead of grabbing me?"

Spur's grin was big. "Shore enough I could have, but what would the fun in that have been?" He was still chuckling as he dropped to the ground and followed her into the house. When she glared back at him, he pointed at the fire where a large kettle hung.

"Buckets? And how do you want to go to town? It's a nice morning for a ride."

Clare handed him two buckets. She thought for a moment before she answered. "By horseback will be fine and thank you." Then she disappeared quickly into her bedroom.

Spur was still grinning as he brought in two buckets of water. He poured one into the tub and dumped the other into the large kettle. He left two more full buckets setting in the kitchen.

He had stashed the flowers in his saddlebag when he lifted Clare onto his horse. They were a little crushed, but he laid them on the table before

33

he headed back to the barn. He was brushing the palomino Appaloosa when Angel wandered in.

The lean vaquero was quiet a moment and then asked, "The señora. She spent the night by the rock bench, yes?"

Spur nodded as he continued to curry the horse.

"That is where señor Rock asked her to marry, I think. The señor built that after his first wife died. It was special place for Rock. For Clare too."

Spur's hands paused for a moment. He cursed softly. "I should have figured that out." He looked over at Angel. "I am swimming blind here. I have never stuck around long enough to understand women beyond a first date or two. I'm not sure I'll be able to tell what Clare needs from me."

Angel's dark eyes danced, and he laughed. "No man will ever understand the women, amigo. Sometimes we get lucky and sometimes, it is poof. No good." Angel waved his hands and rolled his eyes as he spoke.

"Come. Let us eat and then we can both take a bath." His eyes were mournful as he looked at his friend. "I think if my amigo had not been so angry last night, we could have taken a bath in a tub with warm water maybe."

Spur laughed out loud and slapped Angel on the back. He left his arm draped over the smaller man's shoulders.

"Angel, you are a good man. I am going to miss you, my friend."

CHAPTER 3

SOME ORNERY COWBOYS

THE MEN GATHERED IN GROUPS AND TALKED AS THEY
waited for Clare to appear. Spur looked over to where Tuff and Stub
were talking. It looked like they were arguing, and he strolled that way.

"Morning. You boys riding down to the Mission with us this morning
or were you hoping to be put to work on this fine day?"

Stub glared at him while Tuff frowned. "We don't work here anymore.
Clare fired us yesterday. I am trying to talk Stub into letting me go on
down south and work for Gabe. We have to find a new job anyway."

Spur's dark eyes twinkled as he shook his head. "Nope, that ain't
necessary. We had a talk when I got home last night, and she hired you
back." He slapped Stub on the back. "We can't be letting our foreman
and one of our best hands leave now, not when we need them the most."

Stub eyed Spur carefully. "Clare was mighty clear yesterday. She
handed me a deed for Smitty's place and sent me down the road."

Spur was quiet a moment as he looked toward the house. He frowned
before he spoke.

"Clare isn't quite herself right now. She is making some brash
decisions she may regret." He squeezed Stub's shoulder as he added,

"But you two boys aren't going to be one of them. I only agreed to this deal if she kept you on, and a deal is a deal."

Stub slowly grinned. He walked over to his horse and untied his bedroll. "Come on, Tuff. Throw your things in the barn. We'll take them home with us tonight."

Tuff frowned. "Durn it, Stub. I want to go south."

"You aren't going anywhere until you are at least fifteen, and that is nearly a year away. Besides, Spur is going to need some help getting Rock's horse-breeding venture started. Maybe you can help him."

Tuff's eyes lit up and he looked over at Spur with excitement.

Spur nodded. "That's right. I don't know how this operation works at all, so I need both of you fellows." He grinned at Tuff.

"Why don't you and your two buddies ride on ahead. Tell Maggie to meet us at the church tomorrow morning at nine for the wedding. I'm certain they'll all want to be there."

Tuff's eyes lit up and he mounted his horse quickly. It was already running when he passed his friends, calling for them to follow. The rest of the riders watched as the three young men raced down the trail towards Stevensville.

Spur looked over at Gabe and chuckled. "That will be a fast trip to town. And I'm guessing they will find a reason to stop in the eating house so that young waitress can flirt with all of them."

Stub glared at him. "Not Tuff. He's too young. Shoot, he doesn't even think about girls. He just wanted to head south to hang out with his buddies this winter…and fish all summer."

Angel's eyes were innocent as he nodded his head. "Sí, and what of his brother? Señorita Adelia would be so lonely if you left. I think it is good that you stay here and keep her company this long winter." His eyes danced as he added, "But then, you barely spoke to her. Perhaps you did not like her so much after all."

Stub's neck turned a deep red. He stared at Angel and then turned his horse down the trail. He hollered back at the men as he spurred his horse, "I think I'll catch those boys. They need some supervision."

The rest of the men began to laugh. Their laughter quieted, and they turned as one toward the house when they heard the door open.

Clare appeared and the cowboys shifted their feet quietly as she approached. Her riding skirt was dark blue, and a light blue blouse showed through her open jacket. The jacket was fitted in the back but was cut fuller in the front. A row of silver buttons lined one side.

A small donkey charged out of the house behind her and brayed as it rushed into the hills. The men stared and several chuckled.

Spur stepped forward and took her arm. "You sure look pretty this morning, Miss Clare," he commented softly.

Clare looked up at him expecting him to be teasing but blushed softly when she realized that he meant it. He gave her a leg up and the rest of the riders mounted.

Spur looked around at the group and waved his arm. "Well, let's get this done. I never have been one to waste around, especially when a pretty woman is involved."

The riders laughed and the small group headed down the trail.

CHAPTER 4

Good Conversation

CLARE WAS QUIET ON THE TRIP TO STEVENSVILLE. SHE laughed at some of the stories the men told though. They were all trying to be careful and not mention Rock's name.

Finally, she looked around at the group of cowboys and stated, "If you have stories about Rock, I would love to hear them. Please don't be afraid to talk about him just because I am here."

Several of the riders looked uncomfortable but Angel nodded.

"Señor Rock was a fine man, señora. He made it a point to ride with each man. He wanted to know all of us who had joined him on the drive. He made sure too that none of the young men rode any horses he himself had not ridden first." He smiled at Clare. "He wanted to ensure that all of them made it home safely."

Clare was quiet as she studied the group of riders. Her face was pale as she spoke.

"Who of you is going to tell me how Rock died? No one has told me yet. Spur said Stub would, but Stub won't talk about it."

The men faced forward awkwardly. Angel spoke softly. "I think señor Spur should tell you, Miss Clare. Perhaps he can tell you later. I don't think we should talk of sad things now. Let's talk of things that make you smile. This should be a day for happy memories, yes?"

Clare was quiet and Spur touched her hand. "I'll tell you later. Maybe this evening after the kids are in bed." His dark eyes were soft as he studied her face. Then he smiled.

"Why don't you tell these fellows how you came to have Gomer. I don't think any of them have seen a donkey that sleeps in the house and thinks he's a dog."

The men stared at Clare in surprise. They laughed as she told them the story of how Gomer adopted Rock.

"I don't think Rock was too pleased in the beginning, but Gomer is quite the little protector. He brays if a stranger comes, and he tries to herd the kids to the house."

"Rock told us how one of his bosses up here tried to throttle that donkey. I think I would have enjoyed seeing that." Gabe was chuckling as he looked at Clare.

She laughed softly. "Yes, that is how Rock acquired Georgia. Gomer bred the boss' fancy mare, and that rancher wasn't pleased. Rock told me that was when he worked on the 3T by Helmville. I never met Mr. Slate or his wife, but Rock gave a colorful description of that incident.

"Georgia is a beautiful little gray mare mule. I wish mules weren't sterile. I would love to pair her with one of those Appaloosa studs."

The talk turned then to horses and the cowboys discussed the Appaloosas. They weren't that common down by Cheyenne although more of them were showing up all the time.

"According to Tall Eagle, they are one of the smarter horses out there. Tall Eagle says they are his favorite breed." Spur chuckled as he added, "He likes them because they keep him on his toes.

"I know they for sure have lots of stamina.

"The Nez Percé are quite the horsemen. They are one of the few tribes who gelded the male horses they didn't want to breed their mares. That helped increase the quality of their bloodlines. Shoot, some of the cowboys I know who traded with the Nez Percé for their cow ponies turned down offers over $500 from folks who wanted to buy them."

The riders looked at Spur in surprise. Gabe whistled.

"I think you had better get that breeding program started. You just might make more money off those horses than you do off cattle."

Tobe listened quietly and then commented, "I heard the cavalry took most of their horses when Chief Joseph surrendered in '77. I talked to some of those boys in the Seventh Cavalry shortly after that. They told me they were ordered to shoot a lot of the captured horses."

The men were quiet and then Gabe looked over at Spur. "How do they have enough to sell if the military took most of them?"

Spur chuckled. "The soldier boys didn't get all of them. Chief Joseph left some behind in the Wallowa Valley. More escaped as his people tried to escape to Canada. Some were just abandoned.

"The braves sneak off the reservation from time to time. They bring them in or arrange trades. There are all kinds of canyons and natural corrals to gather them in." Spur's smile changed to a frown.

"Darn shame to cross them with draft horses though. That is changing their blood lines, and the Nez Percé worked hard to develop those."

Spur's eyes twinkled as he added seriously, "'Course, lots of those soldier boys don't know much about horses. Half the time the braves in charge of the horses are pairing their mares with geldings. That or big mules."

Even Clare laughed at that. She looked curiously at Spur.

"How did the Appaloosa horses get their name? Appaloosa is a rather unusual word. Is that an Indian name?"

Spur shook his head. "No, the settlers started that. They called them Palouse horses, probably because the Palouse River runs right through the heart of the Nez Percé lands. There's a productive valley there they call the Palouse too. Somehow, that name eventually became Appaloosa.

"The government thinks the Nez Percé should become farmers since the land they are on is good farmland. You just can't make men be farmers if they don't want to though. A good farmer almost needs to have dirt in his veins." He looked around at the riders and added, "Like you fellows think and live cows." The conversation turned to cattle, and it wasn't long before they halted their horses in front of St. Mary's Mission.

Angel took Spur's and Clare's horses. Spur wanted to talk to Father Ravalli and make sure there would be no problem with the chosen wedding time.

"We don't have to do this, Clare. You can change your mind now if you want," Spur whispered as they knocked on Father Ravalli's door.

Clare paused a moment and then shook her head. "No, this is what I want to do. I'm not sure we should have asked Maggie and Ike to come though—or the children."

Spur stopped and took Clare by the shoulders as he stared into her face. "Clare, this is the real deal for me. If it isn't for you, we need to stop it now."

She stared up at him with a pale face and then whispered, "I am just so afraid."

Just then, Father Ravalli opened the door. He looked at the couple in surprise.

He opened the door. "Clare. Spur. Please come in. What can I do for you today?"

Spur twisted his hat and finally said, "We have come to be married. We were hoping you would have time this morning."

CHAPTER 5

A Determined Bride

FATHER RAVALLI STARED AT SPUR FOR A MOMENT AND then frowned. He looked intently at Clare. "Are you in agreement with this, Clare? It is quite soon after Rock's death."

Clare's voice was soft but firm. "My children need a father, and Spur has been wonderful with them. I know we are not entering this marriage with love for each other, but we both love the children. I hope that will be enough for you to marry us."

"Marriage is a lifetime commitment, you know. It is not something you walk away from when it gets hard. You are making a covenant with God." Father Ravalli's voice was quiet as he spoke. He looked intently at Clare. "Are you sure you want to do this?"

"I'm sure, Father. I don't ever expect to fall in love again. Spur wasn't willing but we have come to an agreement." She took a deep breath. "Yes, I want to do this."

Father Ravalli slowly nodded. "And Spur, you are in agreement that this marriage is forever?"

"Padre, I don't think Clare should do this and I told her so. Since she is determined to go through with it, I'll do it for the little ones."

Father Ravalli studied both of their faces a moment longer. Finally he smiled. "Come in. I have a small window between now and 9:30 this morning. I can't do a wedding Mass during that time, but I can marry you."

Maggie and Ike arrived with a clatter of hooves and excited children. The little ones tumbled out of the wagon and raced toward Clare.

Nora was the last to arrive. She smiled up at Spur and tugged on his hand. "Hi, Spur. Auntie Maggie said that when you marry our mama, you will live at our house. Then you can play with us every day!"

Spur chuckled as he looked down at her. He lifted her up and hugged her. "I reckon that's true, Nora," he whispered. She smiled at him and wrapped her arms around his neck.

"I'm glad you are going to marry Mama. Maybe she won't be so sad now."

Spur was quiet as he set her down. Annie charged him and he grabbed her as he swung her around.

"What do you think, Annie? You want me to be your papa?"

Annie shook her head soberly. "No, I want you to be a kid and play with us. Sometimes papas spank, and I don't want you to spank me."

Spur laughed out loud. He dropped down in front of Zeke.

"How about you, Zeke? Think it will be all right if I marry your mama?"

Zeke's face was somber as he studied Spur. "I reckon that will be all right if Mama says so. She's been mighty sad since Pa died. Do you think you can make her laugh like Pa did?"

Spur's heart squeezed and he hugged Zeke. "I'll sure try, Zeke," he whispered. "Things will be different, but I'll sure try to make your mama happy."

Clare's face was pale as she watched Spur interact with the children. *Even if we don't love each other, the children will love him. I hope that is enough.*

Spur stood and took Clare's hand. He smiled down at her.

"Well, let's get this done. No point in wasting any more time. Gabe needs to get his riders back home, and they should have left three hours ago."

The cowboys gathered in the front seats of the little church. Gabe and Angel stood on each side of Spur while Maggie and Adelia were next to Clare.

The ceremony was private and simple. Even the children were quiet.

When Father Ravalli asked for the ring, Spur pulled a small, gold band from his pocket. Clare still wore the wedding ring Rock had given her. Spur paused just a moment before he slipped the ring on the third finger of her right hand.

Once the priest finished, he smiled at the couple in front of him. He turned them around to face their friends.

"I present to you Mr. and Mrs. George Spurlach. Spur, you may kiss your bride."

Spur's eyes were intense as he looked down at Clare. It pained him to see the tears in her eyes and he gently kissed her cheek. Then he put his arm around her waist and grinned at his friends.

"Well, Boys. You have a safe trip back home." He handed Gabe a letter.

"Give this to Rowdy. Tell him I'm sorry to bail on him. He's just not as easy to look at as Clare." He winked at his bride and the men laughed.

The men all shook hands with the newlyweds before they filed out of the little church. As they mounted up and turned their horses south, Spur watched them go with a touch of apprehension. It was the first time he had stayed behind when his friends had ridden away. The children followed the riders outside and were calling to them as the cowboys waved.

Spur squeezed Clare a little tighter and took a deep breath as he smiled down at her.

"Now it's just the five of us. This is going to be a big change for everybody." His dark eyes glinted as he studied her face. "Any regrets?"

"Not yet but the day just started," she replied dryly. She didn't look at Spur but waved at the riders as they turned in their saddles.

Angel's voice carried back to them.

"Until we meet again, señora! And you, señor Spur—may you make many chicos to help you on your ranch!"

Angel waved his hat, and the riders spurred their horses south.

Spur's smile turned to a laugh. "Let's get these kids back home. They have been running loose here long enough.

"Do you need any supplies while we are down here? We just as well pick up what you need since Maggie and Ike brought our wagon over."

Clare pulled a list out of her bag. "I know we need these things." She paused before she looked up at him.

"Any certain kind of food you want me to make for you, Spur? I bake quite a bit but I'm not sure what you like."

Spur chuckled. "My standards are low, Clare. I appreciate good food, but I'll eat anything—even if it tastes bad. It's been a long time since I have eaten food cooked by a woman other than a meal here and there. You just keep cooking the way you have been, and I'll be tickled with whatever you set in front of me."

His smile slowly faded, and he cleared his throat. He lifted her into the wagon as he spoke seriously. "I would like to look at your ranch records and your accounting though.

"I want to see where Rock was taking things. He mentioned to me on the drive that he wanted to start selling some horses, and I can get started on that right away.

"I heard him tell Tall Eagle on the drive that he wanted more Appaloosas next spring. I want to make sure Tall Eagle knows that hasn't changed." He paused and then turned a little red as he added, "If you are all right with that."

Clare took a deep breath and then nodded. "I want you to run the ranch. We can talk about day-to-day decisions, but I want you to handle management of the ranch." She paused and added firmly, "I want to keep things as much the same as possible. Include me in the decision-making but don't make the management of the ranch my responsibility." She looked away and finally looked back at Spur.

"We added onto the house while you were on the drive. Rock wanted to add some bedrooms and I added an office for him." Tears filled her eyes, and she took a shaky breath. "It was going to be a surprise for him, but he never saw it. I moved the ranch records in there. Rock hated bookwork so I added a bunk as well. He would have appreciated taking a break when he became tired."

Clare's face colored lightly. "I thought maybe you would sleep in there until…until after the baby comes."

Spur glanced down at her and started to make a joke. Then he looked away.

He called over to where the children were racing back and forth.

"Come on, you little hooligans. Load up in this wagon. The hands are getting tired of doing your chores."

Ike lifted Maggie up before he climbed into the wagon.

"Now that thar was a fine ceremony." He grinned at Spur. "Ya always travel with a weddin' ring? Been hopin' to snag ya a bride fer some time, have ya?"

Spur chuckled as he tied Clare's horse to the back of the wagon.

"Nope. An old nun I loved a lot gave me that ring just before she died. It belonged to her folks, and she was the only girl. I didn't think it would ever be used again, but I kept it because it was hers. It has been laying around, waiting for the right gal for most of ninety years." He grinned at Clare.

"Then Clare here begged me to marry her. I figured Sister Eddie must have had a hand in this deal, so I dusted it off and gave it to the prettiest gal in the Montana Territory."

Maggie and Ike laughed. Clare looked up at Spur in surprise. She dropped her eyes to her hand and turned the small ring. The storm of emotions inside her almost pushed their way out. She forced a smile.

"Thank you, Spur. It is lovely. I wish I could have met your Sister Eddie."

"You would have liked her, and she would have liked you. Sister Eddie was all about efficiency and logic. She loved with the fierceness of a mother grizzly, and she could smack like one too."

"Ike, we'll drop you and Maggie at your house unless you need to go to the dry goods store. I think we'll head on home. It's about time we tightened up this outfit and tended to business on that ranch."

CHAPTER 6

SETTLING IN

FALL ROUNDUP HAD BEEN COMPLETED WHILE THE drive was taking place, but Spur wanted to see what the cattle looked like.

He rode out with Stub and the men every day for the next four days. Stub and he decided which cows needed to be culled and how many head were ready to drive to market.

"How do you usually market your cattle?"

"In the past, we have been able to sell most of them to the mining camps. We will have more calves to sell though with all the cows Rock bought these last two years.

"Not much for trains unless you go south. The tracks are moving north but they are barely into the Montana Territory. I think we'd be better to try to work with the government boys. Lots of soldiers up here who need meat."

Stub pointed north. "I think I'd rather take cattle north than try to cross over that pass to the south. 'Course, if that's what all the other ranchers are thinking, then maybe we should try it."

Spur looked south down the valley. "I've taken horses over that pass. It's a steep one but I think it can be done. I want to make sure we have a market for them though before we tackle that.

"Maybe Monday, I'll ride down that way. I might even get lucky and run into a cavalry unit while I'm at it.

"Later on this week, I can head north. I need to ride up to Helena anyway. Clare said Rock always banked there. I think I'll see if she wants to move things closer. I could close out his account and see what the market options are while I'm up that way.

"Stevensville has a bank now. Even Missoula would be easier than Helena."

Spur turned his horse and looked out over the ranch. "This sure is a pretty place. A fellow could get used to this view."

Stub chuckled. "Well, you'd better get started. Father Ravalli doesn't take marriage vows lightly." He looked toward the bunkhouse and then back at Spur.

"The boys were wondering if they could take the afternoon off. There is a dance in town tonight, and they are itching to shine up their belt buckles."

"That would be fine." Spur chuckled and added, "I think I'll take Clare to that dance. I haven't attended a dance in some time, and it would do Clare good to get out." He looked over to where the children were playing and laughed out loud.

"Those little girls too. Every night, I have to dance with them. We are working up some fancy moves. Maybe we'll just put them in motion tonight."

Clare had dinner ready when Spur walked into the house. He could smell the roast beef and his mouth started to water as soon as he opened the door.

"I don't know what you used to season that meat, Clare, but it smells so darn good that my stomach is chewing on its own sidewalls."

Clare laughed. "There is plenty so eat up.

"Did you finish riding the pastures this morning? Everything looks all right?"

"The graze on the winter range looks good and the cattle do too." He stopped washing for a moment and looked over at her.

"What would you think of moving your banking closer to home? I don't have a relationship with that banker in Helena like Rock did, and I'd just as soon deal with one closer. Stevensville would be mighty handy. Even Missoula would be more convenient."

Clare looked up from setting plates on the table. Her surprise showed on her face.

"I've never considered doing that. Rock banked there when he first took this place over. I guess I just assumed we'd be there forever."

"Rock probably would have. You and I can make a change though if you want."

Clare studied Spur's face and slowly nodded.

"Let's do that. Since we are going to change, let's make it as easy as possible. Put everything in Stevensville. George Baggs is the lawyer in town, and you should get acquainted with him as well.

"I will give you a letter stating that your name is to be added to all the accounts. He can draw up a legal form to make it easier for you to close our account in Helena."

Clare took a deep breath and added, "I am cleaning out Rock's clothes. I have a couple of shirts I am keeping, but you are welcome to the rest of Rock's things. If you don't want them, share them with the men."

Spur was quiet as he sat down at the table. He put his hand over Clare's and said quietly, "You don't have to do that yet, Clare. Don't push yourself so hard."

CHAPTER 7

ANSWERS TO QUESTIONS

CLARE PULLED HER HAND AWAY AND TURNED HER back. Spur could see her shoulders quiver as she tried to control a sob.

Just then, the kids came rushing into the house. Spur pointed at the wash basin.

"No dirty hands at this table. You get washed up and then sit down quietly. Your mother worked hard on this meal."

Annie frowned and Spur winked at her.

"How about I take my three favorite gals to a dance this evening in town? Maybe your mother will pack us a bait of food so we can have a picnic on the way down. And Zeke, you can try out all that fancy footwork you have been working on, this time to music."

The noise level in the house ramped up and the children began talking excitedly. Clare looked around at Spur in surprise and then slowly sat down.

Spur led the family in a blessing, but that was the only quiet time for the rest of the meal. The children ate as fast as they could and raced back outside. Spur ate slowly and enjoyed every bite.

Clare poked at her food. She finally looked up at Spur. Her chin was set stubbornly, and her blue eyes glinted.

"I haven't danced in years. I don't even know if I remember how."

Spur grinned at her. "You don't have to do a thing. I'll keep you moving so fast your feet will barely touch the floor. And wait until you see the moves these kids learned!"

Clare's pretty face drew down in a frown. "I don't think we should be running off to play. We have too much work to do around here."

Spur looked up at her and laughed. "Work will always be here, Clare. We will never get it all done. It is important to play too, or eventually you won't enjoy your work." He squeezed her hand and then released it.

"Let's play a little, Clare. It will be good for the kids."

Clare stared at him a moment. She slowly laughed as she looked at the excitement on Spur's face.

"Okay, but I am not keeping these kids out all night. When they start to get tired, we are going home."

Spur chuckled and pointed out the window. Zeke was in the top of a tree and Annie was on her way up to join him. She was climbing so quickly that she looked like a little monkey. Only Nora was at the bottom. As the other two called to her, she slowly began to climb. Soon all three of them were sitting on a branch, high up in the tree.

"I think we will be tired long before they will, so I am going to hold you to that. You be ready to leave at 3:00. And let's have a picnic. That would be a fine way to start an enjoyable evening."

He strolled out of the house with a whistle deep in his throat. Clare frowned as she watched him walk away. When he stopped at the tree and called up to the children, she smiled.

"Rock," she whispered, "did you send this man to help us all smile? It surely seems to be working on the children."

She went to the door and called, "Spur, if you will bring some water in, I will bathe the children. And I'll have everyone ready to leave by 3:00 this afternoon."

Clare hurried back to pick out clothes. "Annie is not going to like it, but I am going to make her wear a dress. I made her pantaloons. She has to wear them under her dresses because she is upside down all the time. Nora loves hers but Annie will throw a fit." She sighed and her hands went still for a moment. "Rock, your little girl is a handful. She has so much of you in her that she makes me cry and laugh at the same time."

She fingered a red shirt that was laying on her bed. She touched the little heart sewn in the back of the neck and sank down on the bed with the shirt in her hands.

"I went through our closet last night when I couldn't sleep, Rock. I packed all your clothes except for the green shirt I made you right after we married." Clare's bottom lip trembled a little. She pushed her shoulders back.

"In fact, I'm going to let Spur wear this shirt tonight—the one that Susannah made for you. It still looks new because you hardly wore it." Tears filled her eyes, and she hugged the shirt to herself.

"I miss you so much," she whispered.

She heard Spur come into the kitchen. He pulled out the tub and dumped a bucket of water in it. She could hear the water hissing as he poured the second bucket into the kettle over the fireplace.

"I am dreading this dance because I know people will think poorly of me for marrying so quickly." She kissed the shirt and carried it into the kitchen. She smiled at Spur as he set down the second round of buckets.

"Thank you, Spur. I'll hang this shirt here. You may wear it tonight if you'd like."

Spur picked the shirt up and held it in front of him. "It looks like it will fit." His eyes caught the small heart, and he touched it with his thumb. "You make this?" he asked casually.

"No, Suzannah did." Clare's voice caught as she spoke. "Rock loved that shirt, but he hardly wore it." Her eyes were large as she looked up at Spur and whispered, "I wanted to bury him in it, but you wouldn't let me see him." Clare was twisting her hands and tears were leaking from her eyes.

"Why won't you tell me how he died? I think my imagination may be as bad as what happened."

Spur hung the shirt over a chair back and sat down. He took Clare's hand and pulled her toward him. She tried to get up when he slid her onto his lap, but he shook his head.

"If I am going to tell you this, you are going to stay right here in case I need to hold you while you cry."

Clare stared at Spur a moment before she slowly nodded her head. She kept her hands on her lap as she twisted them. Spur's left arm was around her waist. He covered her hands with one of his.

"We were a little over a day out of Butte in a pretty place called Deer Lodge Valley. Rock had worked in that area some time before, and he had arranged with a man by the name of Conrad Kohrs to graze his herd across that valley.

"Kohrs owns that entire valley, and more land on top of that according to Rock. I have never met Kohrs, but Rock seemed to think a lot of him.

"Anyway, we were going to take it easy as we crossed since Rock had paid Kohrs for six days of graze." Spur's arm tightened and he pulled Clare a little closer as he continued.

"It was a fine day. We had made good time and the drive had been easy for the most part. Oh, there had been a few situations. Losing Rufe was a bad deal, but overall, the drive was a good one. We were about ten days from home and there was a lot of joking. The riders were looking forward to six easy days.

"There was a big bluff overlooking the valley, and Rock decided to ride up on top. Like I said, he knew the area and he was reminiscing that day.

"We were all pretty relaxed. The cattle were grazing well, the sun was shining, and everyone was happy.

"We heard a shot from the top of the bluff. That's all. Just one shot and then silence. Gabe, Angel, and Stub took off. They were racing their horses toward the bluff. I followed them.

"When we got there, Rock was on the ground. His horse had been shot. When Red went over backwards, he landed on top of Rock. The saddle horn crushed Rock's chest.

"Little Bear and his braves were there. They had been following the man who did the shooting. He had taken an Indian girl who was a sister to one of the braves about a month before. They had been tracking him since then."

Spur shifted his knees and pulled Clare against him. She was sobbing and he held her as he talked.

"Rock didn't last long. He was concerned about Red. He didn't want his horse to suffer." Spur's voice was barely a whisper as he added, "His last words were for you and the kids. He said to tell you that he loved you."

Clare cried quietly for a bit and then she sat up. She looked directly at Spur.

"Why did the man shoot Red? Why would a man shoot a horse?"

Spur frowned and shook his head. "I'm not sure. I think he was trying to spook Red but he turned. Instead of grazing Red, the bullet hit him in the side."

Clare's body became stiff, and she stared at Spur.

"What was his name? Who was the man who shot Red?"

Spur squirmed uncomfortably. "Clare…I didn't know the man."

"But you knew who he was."

"Most of us didn't know him. Stub said if there was anything left of him when Little Bear's braves finished, he was going to hang him."

Clare turned to look directly at Spur. Her voice was almost a whisper as she asked, "Did he try to steal Rock's boots?"

Spur stared at her, the answer on his face. Clare collapsed against him sobbing. She hung onto Spur tightly as she cried. Finally, the sobbing subsided. Clare sat up. Her voice was bitter as she spoke.

"He took everything from me. He took my life as a young woman and now he took my husband. Pony Dixon was an evil man." She wiped her eyes. Her voice was barely a whisper as she added, "And he was Zeke's father."

Spur stared at Clare before he pulled her close again. He was quiet as she sobbed. When she quieted, he put her face between his hands and smiled as he rubbed her tears away with his thumbs.

"Clare, Zeke is a fine boy. He will never know this story. The first two men you married showed him a father's love, and that won't change.

"The Good Lord doesn't make mistakes, and you remember that. What happened to you was evil and terrible, but from that, you were given a great gift. I just don't know that I have met a finer boy." He smiled at her and added, "I think I'm a lucky man all the way around."

As Clare stared into his soul, Spur knew then he was falling in love with this woman. He pulled her against him and silently cursed. *This wasn't supposed to happen. We were only supposed to be friends.*

Clare slipped off Spur's lap and straightened her dress. She wiped her face as she backed away. Her blue eyes were wide, and a flood of emotions rushed through them, too quickly for Spur to track. She waved her hands at him.

"Give Zeke a job while I bathe the girls. I need about a half an hour before you send him in." She smiled tremulously and added, "And thank you, Spur, for all you have done for us…and for being honest with me."

Spur nodded. He was quiet as he strode from the house.

"Girls! You need to take baths. Get on in the house now." Spur stopped and stared at Annie as she shook the kitten she was holding. She put it down gently and lifted another one to shake it wildly.

"Annie, what are you doing?" Spur asked carefully. "You could hurt your kittens shaking them like that."

"We can't tell which of these kittens are girls and which are boys. We asked Cookie and he said to shake them. He said if their nuts rattle, they are boys." Annie frowned as she looked up at Spur. "We didn't hear any nuts rattle so they must all be girls."

Spur bit his tongue to keep from laughing. He looked over at the old cook. Cookie just shrugged his shoulders.

"That's what my ol' pa told me." He grinned and added, "I ain't never said I was good with kids." Cookie was still chuckling as he walked into his kitchen.

Spur cleared his throat and coughed. His voice was gruff when he spoke again. "I don't know about that, but I don't think their mama will like you shaking them. She might move them away from here and then you won't have any cats to play with.

"Now get up to the house and take your baths.

"Zeke, you come with me. I am going to trim Rockefeller's hooves, and you can help."

When Annie immediately began to complain, Spur grabbed her and swung her around.

"You have to smell pretty, Annie. We are going to dance. I don't want to swing a stinky girl around." He pretended to drop her and started gagging as he grabbed his nose, staggering across the yard.

Annie watched him a moment with a big smile.

"You are funny, Spur!" she exclaimed as she giggled. She dropped her kitten as she turned around and raced for the house. "I'm coming, Mama! Make me smell pretty for the dance!"

CHAPTER 8

A Brazen Man

THE PICNIC WAS QUICK. THE CHILDREN WERE TOO
excited about the dance.

"Wait till you see what Spur taught us, Mama! He makes me fly and Nora stands on his shoulders!"

Nora nodded excitedly. "And Zeke moves his feet really fast, just like Spur."

Clare looked in surprise from one child to the next. Her eyes moved to Spur and then back to her children.

"Spur taught you dance moves?"

"Yes, and he takes us swimming. Zeke can already swim from the rope to the creekbank. Nora can almost, but I keep drowning." Annie frowned as she talked. Then her face brightened.

"He is teaching Nora and me to jump and dance. He swings us around really fast."

Clare tried to keep from frowning as she looked over at Spur. He just grinned and shrugged his shoulders.

"I haven't hung around a ranch this long in some time. I am usually on the trail. I have to do something with my extra time." His grin became bigger, and he winked at Clare. "Their mother won't play with me, so I have to play with the kids."

Clare blushed a deep red and looked away. Spur chuckled as he loaded the remaining food and the blanket into the wagon. He helped Clare in and called for the kids.

"Load up. We have a dance to get to!"

The kids tumbled into the wagon and Spur headed the noisy family on down the trail. As they bounced along, he commented, "I think we should get a surrey. A two-seated buggy would be more comfortable to ride in than this darn wagon. The bones in my bottom hurt after I am in this for an hour, let alone two. He looked over at Clare and grinned.

"How's your bottom, Clare? Any bruises?"

Clare stared at him and as her face began to turn red, she looked away.

"Good grief, Spur. That was an inappropriate question."

"Not when you're married."

"Well, we…we…It still is not acceptable."

Spur chuckled and was quiet for a moment. Then he looked over at Clare. Her face was still slightly pink, and she was holding herself stiff to keep from bumping into him.

He scooted a little closer to her. "You might want to hang onto me. If we hit a bump, this wagon could dump you right out."

Just then the right wheel hit a large rock and the wagon tilted to the left. Clare's body slammed into Spur's, and he grabbed her to keep her from falling back the other way.

"It would be easier for both of us if you just held onto my arm."

Clare straightened herself up and looked at him coolly. "And if you would stay on the trail instead of wandering toward the side, we wouldn't hit all the big rocks."

Spur grinned at her. He turned the mules to the left toward another rock and she grabbed his arm. He began laughing as he straightened the wagon.

"See? That wasn't so hard, was it?"

Clare glared at him. She loosened her grip on his arm and he immediately headed the wagon toward another rock. She grabbed his arm again.

"I declare, Spur. You are a most annoying man."

Spur just grinned at her. "Could be but I did get you to hang onto my arm. Now if I could just get you to smile."

Clare stared at him for a moment. Finally, a laugh bubbled out of her. "You win. I will sit here quietly if you drive more carefully. The children usually fall asleep around this time, and I would love for them to take a nap."

The wagon was getting quiet. Spur glanced over his shoulder. All three little ones were finally sleeping. He looked at Clare in surprise.

"It's almost like you told them to go to sleep and they did it."

Clare laughed. "Well, we have traveled this trail many times. I know about where they finally wind down.

"About these dance moves. What did you teach them?"

Spur grinned at her. "Mum is the word. You are going to have to wait and see. But if you see something that looks fun, I can teach you too." As Clare stared at him, he bumped her.

"How about it, Miss Clare? You want me to show you some of my slick moves?"

"Spur! Stop talking like that! Someone might hear you."

"Out here? We are the only ones on this trail. Shoot. We are the only ones who live on this trail. The kids are all asleep, so just who are you worried about?

"I reckon a man can talk that way to his wife if he wants." He was grinning as he spoke. "I have never been married before though, so maybe that's not how all men are.

"Of course, if you wanted a man who was all buttoned up, you should have asked another fellow to marry you."

Clare banged him with her elbow.

"You are so brazen, Spur. If someone was to hear you, I would be mortified."

"And yet, you are still hanging onto my arm."

Clare loosened her grip and the wagon immediately started drifting to the left side of the trail. She grabbed his arm again and Spur laughed.

"You sure make a long ride in a wagon fun, Clare…even if the bones in my bottom side do hurt." He chuckled as she looked at him skeptically, waiting for his next comment.

"If you are through bothering me though, I'd like to talk to you about my plans for this next week." He glanced sideways at Clare and she nodded.

"We need to find a market for our beef. I thought I might head south on Monday. There is an army camp just south of Lost Trail Pass and I can talk to them. That will probably be a two-day trip. I could leave for Helena on Wednesday. That will be a longer trip, probably at least six or seven days. That will put me gone over a week though. Are you all right with that?"

Clare's eyes were large as she looked at him. Staying at the ranch alone had always made her anxious. Since Rock died, it was even worse.

Spur patted her arm. "It will only be a week and all the hands will be around. Stub can keep them lined out."

Clare's face was pale, and her breath came rapidly.

"What if you don't come back?" she whispered as she stared at him. Her eyes were wide with fear.

Spur pulled the wagon to a stop and put his arms around her.

"Here now. No cause to be worried. How about I go north first? We have to close your account in Helena. If I can market the beef that direction, I won't need to go south. How would that be?" His voice was soft and soothing.

Clare could feel her heart pounding. She pinched her eyes shut and nodded. She let Spur pull her close and the beat of his heart calmed her.

When her breathing slowed down, she pulled away and looked up at him.

"I'm sorry. Sometimes I just panic." She looked away before she looked back at Spur. "That happened some before Rock passed. Now, it seems I am always afraid.

"And I hate being afraid. I want to be brave, and I do try. It is hard though."

Spur gazed at Clare for a moment. He quietly clucked to the horses. He looked over at her again as the wagon once more started to move.

"Clare, I think you are one of the strongest women I have ever met. You have been through a lot in your twenty-one years. If you panic now and then, well, so be it. Even a well-trained horse bolts if it's put under too much pressure."

Spur's eyes began to twinkle again as he added, "I would tell you that you are a mighty fine filly but looking at this wagonful of kids, I think you moved into the mare category some time ago—and that just doesn't sound as nice as a filly."

Clare sputtered a couple of times. She shook her head and laughed. She finally slid closer and took his arm.

"Spur, you are a bold and blunt man. I don't know how your talk calms me down, but it does. And then you make me laugh."

Spur chuckled and they visited the rest of the way to Stevensville.

CHAPTER 9

A COUNTRY DANCE

THE DANCE WAS IN A BARN ABOUT TWO MILES NORTH of Stevensville. By the time they arrived, the crowd was already large. As soon as Spur stopped the horses, the kids jumped out of the wagon and raced off to play with their friends. Spur helped Clare down and she grabbed a covered pan out of the back. He looked at it in surprise. He smiled as he took it from her.

"I always wondered how we came to have food at all these shindigs. I never heard anyone plan for it, but there was always a table of food."

"It's called a potluck, Spur. Every family brings a little something to eat. And there is nothing to plan. You just bring what you want." She pointed toward a covered basket.

"Please hand me that basket. It has all our plates and the rest of our table service.

"I see Maggie and Ike. If you will set that pan on the food table, I will see if there is room for us to sit beside them."

Clare hurried across the floor with a smile on her face. Ike stood and scooted down. Spur watched them for a moment before he headed for the food table. *I sure am glad Ike and Maggie are around. They have been almost like parents to Clare and for sure grandparents to all those kids.*

The musicians were warming up. The sounds coming from their instruments made Spur smile. *This is shaping up to be just a fine evening.*

He spotted Smitty across the room and strolled over to say hello. Smitty's wife had passed away some time ago and he had never remarried. The old man was pushing seventy years. He had sold Rock his ranch the year before and bought a little house in town. It was his ranch headquarters that Rock had gifted to Stub.

"Howdy, Spur. Good of you to bring the family out. I didn't know Clare was expecting. When is that little one supposed to arrive?"

"In December. I'm not sure exactly when." He watched as Clare laughed and then rubbed her back. "I hope there is no trouble. December could be a bad time for a wagon ride to the Mission."

Smitty nodded and laughed. "Well, it will come when it wants, I guess." His eyes twinkled and he added, "Maybe you should read up on birthing babies. You just might be on your own if the weather does get bad."

Spur's body went still. He could feel the panic well up inside him. He forced himself to smile before he looked up.

"Clare's done this before, so hopefully, it will go smoothly. I'll talk to you later." He paused and looked back with a smile. "Clare wants you to come over for supper sometime. Be thinking when that will work for you. I'm sure she will be asking you this evening."

As he strolled across the floor, the musicians started. Their first song was "Lorena." Spur reached for Clare's hand.

"Come on, Miss Clare. Let me waltz you around this floor once or twice."

As they spun across the floor, Clare whispered, "You are holding me too tightly."

Spur ignored her as they swung around the dance floor. Her feet barely touched the floor, and she was laughing by the time the song was over.

He grinned down at her. Clare laughed again as she whispered, "You are so inappropriate. I don't know why I laugh at your bad behavior."

Spur's dark eyes danced as he laughed. "I reckon it's because I'm so charming. Irresistible is what the ladies tell me.

"How about you, Miss Clare? I'd sure like to be irresistible to you."

Clare blushed. "Stop talking like that," she hissed. "Someone will hear you here for sure." She walked quickly away from him. Spur watched her go.

He looked around and finally wandered over to the table where the punch bowl sat. Two cowboys were trying to pour whiskey into the punch bowl and Spur grinned.

"Boys, there was a time when I would have helped you do that. Now I have kids, so I am going to ask you to refrain. Those kids are wild enough and loud enough without getting them drunk too."

The young cowboys looked at Spur in surprise. They stared at each other and set the bottle down. The tallest one grinned.

"Shoot. We didn't think about the kids. I tell you what. You get that fellow on the accordion to play something we can stomp to, and we'll forego spiking this punch."

Spur chuckled and nodded. He strolled over to the musicians and whispered to the one playing the accordion. The man nodded and Spur raised his hands as he hollered.

"Folks, Emil over here on the accordion is going to play 'The Military Polka.' Now that song was written in New Orleans back in 1861. As a Louisiana cowboy myself, sometimes I just get a hankering for home.

"You couples who want to dance, get out on that dance floor. And the rest of you cowboys, grab you a gal and swing her around. Everybody can polka." He bowed before Maggie.

"Mrs. Clampant, will you do me the honor of dancing this polka with me?"

Maggie's face lit up. "Why I haven't danced in years. Paddy always loved that song. I'm a little rusty but you lead me where I need to go."

Spur guided Maggie onto the dance floor and swung her around like they had danced together for years. He managed to dodge the many cowboys who were stomping and hollering as they tried to keep up with the fast beat. Once they reached an open spot on the floor, he spun Maggie around and around, never missing a beat. When the dance finally ended, they were both laughing. Maggie was dizzy and out of breath, but she was happy.

"Spur, I think I am going to like having you around. I haven't enjoyed a dance like that since my Paddy died. Now you take Clare out there and you make her smile." Maggie beamed at him, and Spur chuckled.

"I believe I will. Thank you, Maggie." He added with a whisper, "And thanks for all you and Ike have done for that little family."

Maggie smiled and Spur guided her back to her seat. "Home on the Range" was just starting and Spur put out his hand to Clare.

"Dance with me, Clare. Let's take advantage of this music before those kids wear out." He winked at her and she laughed.

The cowboy song was played as a waltz and Clare felt like they were floating. Once again, Spur held her too close. She finally put her elbow between her chest and his. He chuckled and relaxed his hold, so she removed her arm. When he tightened his hold again, she moved her elbow back up.

Her eyes were sparking as she commented dryly, "We can both play this game."

Spur laughed out loud. "You know, Clare. I can't think of a time I have enjoyed dancing more than this evening. You are light on your feet and sassy to boot."

Clare rolled her eyes and Spur began to spin her. When they finished, she was out of breath and needed to hang on to keep her balance.

They were both laughing as they took their seats. The musicians announced the Mexican Hat Dance would be played after their break. Spur stood.

"I have to find those kids. Now you pay attention, Clare. Your young ones have worked hard on this."

He sauntered across the floor talking to people as he went. He was soon back with all three kids. He whispered to Clare, "You might want to take the girls to the bathroom. They are going to be doing a lot of jumping."

Clare looked startled but she hurried the little girls toward the outhouse. They were back quickly. She had washed their hands in the horse tank, and they were still dripping with water.

He grinned at them. "Wipe your hands on my britches and remember how we do this. Don't worry about all these folks either. We are doing this for fun. Remember, the first part I will do with Zeke. When he goes down on his knees, you girls need to be ready."

Both girls nodded excitedly. Clare shook her head as she watched them. Annie's dress was soiled, and her face was dirty while Nora looked the same as when she had left home.

"I just don't understand how Annie can get so dirty," Clare muttered. "They play the same games and with the same kids. Somehow, Annie gets filthy and Nora doesn't."

Spur chuckled. He leaned over and whispered to her. "Because Annie is a wild little tomboy while Nora wants to be a lady. And I think you have a little of both in you."

Clare glared at him, and Spur chuckled again. He led the three children out onto the dance floor. Not many were dancing the Hat Dance, so they had plenty of room.

Zeke took his position beside Spur. He hooked his thumbs in his belt, cocked his hat at a rakish angle, and grinned at his mother.

Clare began laughing. She wanted to clap before the song ever started. When the music began, she was amazed. Zeke kept the beat. His feet weren't always where they were supposed to be, but they were close. He alternated from watching Spur to grinning at his mother.

Suddenly, he slid across the floor and dropped down on all fours. Spur stopped about four feet from him, and Annie raced toward them. Both girls had on moccasins and Annie's little foot hit Zeke in the middle of his back. She propelled herself into the air and Spur caught her. He spun her with her feet flailing wildly, his hands moving quickly around her wrists. He tossed her between his legs and caught her again as she slid out. Finally, he swung her up into his right arm and pushed his left leg forward.

Nora raced from the side. She hopped up on Zeke's back and then raced up Spur's leg and chest as he held onto her hand. He dropped his hand when she reached his shoulders and hung onto her ankle. She stood on his shoulders with her hands in the air until he raised his arm. Then she jumped.

Spur caught her as she slid down his shoulder. He held both little girls, one in each arm as the song was ending. Zeke stood and rushed up to stand beside him. Spur and Zeke bowed deeply to Clare when the music ended while the girls waved.

Clare stood with the rest of the crowd and cheered. Her heart was beating quickly. She had nearly quit breathing when the girls had started their part of the performance. She patted her chest as she whispered, "Oh, my heart! That was wonderful and terrifying at the same time."

All three of the children charged toward their mother. She laughed and hugged each of them.

"That was wonderful! You all did amazing. And girls, let me see those shoes. Where in the world did you get moccasins?"

"Spur made them for us. He said we might get splinters on the floor. But at home, we don't wear any shoes at all." Annie's eyes were shining as she talked. Nora grabbed Spur's hand and smiled up at him. He lifted her up and whispered something in her ear. She smiled and kissed his cheek before she slid down again.

He dropped into the chair beside Clare. "Those kids about wore me out. Who taught them to dance that wild anyway? Must have been their mother."

Clare's eyes were bright and she was laughing. "I'm not sure who is more of a kid, you or them. And I have never seen Zeke look so proud and ornery at the same time. Did you tell him to cock his hat like that?"

Spur shook his head. "Nope, that was all Zeke. He notices things though. He probably saw some cowboys do that and copied them.

"Now if my wife would just bring me some punch, I could maybe recuperate enough to dance with her a little more." He grinned over at Clare as he stretched out his long legs.

She laughed and stood. "I will do that."

CHAPTER 10

AN UNWELCOME STRANGER

SPUR WAS STILL SMILING AS HE GLANCED TOWARD THE door. His smile slowly faded as a dark-skinned cowboy stepped through the door. The man quickly scanned the room. His eyes rested on Spur, and his lips lifted in a smirk. He put his fingers to his hat and gave Spur a salute. Spur never responded, but he continued to watch the newcomer.

Clare was returning with the punch and the cowboy tried to grab her arm as she walked by. She jerked away, spilling one cup of punch. She threw the other one in his face and calmly walked back toward her table.

Spur pushed out of his chair and strode quickly toward the cowboy. When he reached the stranger, he grabbed the man's gun arm and drug him out the door. He threw him up against the side of the barn.

"What are you doing here, Slade? We don't need your kind in this valley."

Slade calmly watched Spur. He jerked his arm loose and rolled a cigarette. "I heard ya was up this way. Heard ya married. I knew that warn't true, so I didn't know if ya was here or not."

Spur's dark eyes were angry, and he glared at the man. "Both are true. Now why are you here?"

"Gettin' in the cattle business. Thinkin' on buyin' a herd. Thought I'd come south an' see what the grass is like."

"You never owned more than ten cows in your life, Slade. If you have a herd, it's someone else's or it's stolen.

"And there isn't any open range here. This land has all been bought up or homesteaded. This valley is less than a hundred miles long and it's all settled.

"You want land, you can buy it like all these hardworking folks had to do."

"Or I could marry it. Maybe that's what you done. Word is that you was shinin' up to a widow woman an' a wealthy one at that."

Spur hit him. The punch was a long one, and it contained all the anger Spur felt.

"Get out. If I see you in this town again, I'll cut you down. I have no use for back-shooters or men that kill their own family out of greed… and you are both."

Slade rubbed his jaw as he slowly climbed to his feet. Spur wasn't wearing a gun and Slade thought about cutting him down right there. Several men were lingering close by though. Slade knew he would never get away if he shot an unarmed man. He cursed softly.

"I'll kill ya for that, Spur. Ya always thought ya was too good fer us boys, an' we was even family.

"We aren't family, Slade. Madam Bella told you that to mess with your head. She had no brothers or sisters…I doubt she even knew who my pa was. If she did, she never told me.

"As far as looking down on you, maybe I did at that. I certainly wasn't going to join you in stealing cows."

Slade slowly smoked his cigarette and blew the smoke toward Spur. He nodded inside where the dance was still going.

"When I heard that polka, I knew ya was around. Ya always git sentimental at shindigs like this.

"Those that widow woman's kids ya was dancin' with? Heard she's a good-lookin' woman." He sneered at Spur as he added, "The word is though that she has ice water in her veins."

"I'd like to tangle up with a woman like that. See if I could warm up those veins."

Spur's voice was low and deadly.

"Slade, you have two minutes to clear out of here—two minutes because that is how long it is going to take me to get my guns out of my wagon. And we both know I can beat you to the draw even if I give you an edge.

"Now you clear out. I don't want to see you or any cattle you claim anywhere close to Stevensville.

"And you'd better not even think about messing with my family. I can and will hunt you down like the snake you are." He jerked Slade around and kicked him.

"Now get."

Slade cursed as he staggered. He threw down his cigarette and stumbled toward his horse. Spur watched him a moment before he strode to the wagon. He belted his guns on and walked in the direction that Slade had taken.

Slade took his time. He finally mounted his horse and headed north. He looked back once. When he saw Spur watching him, he kicked his horse to a run. He muttered angrily as he rode.

"I'll be back. I'll shoot 'im down for what he done to me tonight. An' I'll take his woman jist fer fun."

CHAPTER 11

AN ENTERTAINING MAN

CLARE LOOKED UP AS SPUR WALKED THROUGH THE door. She noticed his guns, but she said nothing.

He stopped to fill two empty cups with punch and carried them toward her table with a smile.

"I noticed you spilled our punch so I thought I might just get some myself." He was smiling as he set the cup down in front of her.

He leaned over and whispered, "I told you there was a little wild tomboy in you." Clare's face was pale but she laughed.

"Maggie and Ike offered to take the kids home with them. We can pick them up in the morning at church. They will take our wagon, and we can take their buggy home.

"Are you okay with that?" Clare watched Spur as she waited for an answer.

Spur nodded. "That sounds fine." He grinned at Clare. "They are worn out, huh? Does that mean you and I can play a little tonight?" He covered his ribs and dodged the elbow she threw his way.

"I swear, Clare. You throw a wicked elbow. You look so pretty and sweet, but you hit like a fellow."

Clare's eyes were sparking but Spur pulled her up. "Dance with me, Clare. This song always makes me melancholy. Let me hang onto you while I remember."

Spur was quiet as he listened to the lyrics of "The Bonnie Banks O' Loch Lomond." As the song continued, he began to sing along. Before long, he was singing it in her ear. "Oh ye'll take the high road and I'll take the low road, and I'll be in Scotland a'fore ye. But me and my true love will never meet again, On the bonnie, bonnie banks of Loch Lomond."

Clare listened as Spur sang. When he became quiet, she looked up at him.

"Why does this song make you sad?"

Spur thought a moment as he swung her around.

"When I was a little tyke, I used to pretend I knew my father. I was convinced he was a Scottish highlander. I'm not sure where that idea came from. Someone might have read me a book. Maybe I heard someone talking one time. I'm not sure.

"It always reminds me that I have no idea who my pa is, and that makes me a little sad." He was quiet a moment. He finally looked down at Clare and his dark eyes glinted.

"Unless I am dancing with a pretty woman...then I use it as an excuse to hold her tighter," he added with a grin.

Clare's eyes had been soft as Spur talked about his father. Then they shot fire. Her elbow started to come up, but Spur pulled her closer.

"Not on this song. This song we are going to cuddle a little," he whispered.

When the song finished, Spur spun Clare away from him and spun her back. He looked down at her intently for a moment. Finally, he took her hand and led her back to her seat.

Spur pointed toward the door. "I see Stub, but I don't see any of the other men. Did you see them this evening? I never noticed any of them dancing."

Clare shook her head. "Stub has been in and out. I think he was watching for Adelia.

"She's not coming though. Maggie said they took her to Missoula and put her on the stage to Helena. She wants to work with the nuns up there and maybe join their order."

Spur looked at Clare in surprise. "And Stub doesn't know that?"

"Not unless he talked to Maggie or Ike. They just put her on the stage yesterday."

"I wondered what was going on. I thought maybe something would spark with the two of them. She just kind of disappeared though after the herd arrived. Now it all makes sense.

"Darn. All your hopes of having another young woman to talk to just went up in smoke. Guess you'll have to talk to me." Spur winked at her, and Clare rolled her eyes.

"As much as you talk, Spur, it's a wonder that anyone can work in another word."

Spur laughed and pulled her up. "Let's dance one more time before we head for home." He paused and looked down at Clare. "Unless you would rather stay in town with Maggie. That way, you wouldn't have to come back in for church. I could pick you up on the way."

"No, I would rather go home. If you will bring some water in, I'll take another bath tonight. Besides, I'd rather sleep in my own bed."

Once again, Spur sang along with the song, swinging and dipping Clare to the lilting music. When it ended, he smiled down at her.

"Now aren't you glad you agreed to come this evening. A good dance is always fun, and you have some fine musicians in this valley."

"And if any of them ever lose their voices, you can step in," Clare commented dryly. "I think you knew the words to every song that was sung this evening."

"Sister Eddie used to say, 'He who sings prays twice.' She made all of us sing, especially at Mass. I enjoyed it though so that was the one thing I didn't argue with her about." His eyes twinkled as he looked sideways at Clare.

"Although my repertoire of songs has increased quite a bit since then. And for sure, all the songs I know wouldn't be appropriate for church or for Sister Eddie."

"There is a lot about you that is not appropriate, Spur."

"And yet I make you smile."

Clare laughed and nodded. "Yes, you do. I shouldn't either because it just encourages you."

CHAPTER 12

A Trip in the Dark

SPUR LIT THE LAMPS ON EITHER SIDE OF THE BUGGY and turned the team south out of town. They rode in silence for a time. Clare finally commented softly, "Rock would never have stayed this late. He hated driving that trail in the dark."

Spur nodded. "He told me that. He said he had burned his eyes one time working in the snow. Afterwards, he had a hard time seeing at night. He said this drive always made him a little leery since there are places where the water washed the trail out."

Clare was quiet for a moment before she spoke.

"You looked terrible when you brought Rock's body home. Was that a hard ride?"

Spur shifted uncomfortably in his seat. He finally nodded.

Clare waited for him to speak. When he didn't, she asked, "Did you come over Skalkaho Pass?"

Spur looked over at her in surprise as he nodded.

"In the dark?"

Spur flicked the lines across the rumps of the horses before he looked at her. "Clare, that was a hard ride and a sad time. I don't really want to talk about it tonight."

"I'm guessing you volunteered to do it though, and you didn't even know Rock that well."

Spur looked at Clare in surprise. "I did it because I could. I knew that area and that pass better than any of those other riders.

"Any one of those boys would have brought Rock home, but Skalkaho Pass is dangerous. It's high and steep as well as rough. It's a tough trail and a little scary even if you are familiar with it. Rockafeller, he's been over that pass as many times as I have, so he was familiar with it too. We put a travois behind Angel's little mountain-bred mustang, and I took off.

"I didn't do anything amazing. I just did what I could."

"I don't remember if I even thanked you. I should have." Clare's voice broke and she gripped Spur's arm tightly.

Spur put his arm around her.

"Clare, you did thank me, but I didn't expect you to. That was a hard time." He was silent a moment before he continued.

"I asked Father Ravalli how the Good Lord picks and chooses who lives and who dies. Of course, he couldn't tell me." Spur flicked the lines as he gazed down the dark trail.

"I told him I should have been taken instead. Rock was such an important part of this family, and in fact, the whole community. If I could have traded places with him, I would have."

Clare sobbed and Spur pulled her closer.

"The Good Lord didn't let me do that, so I guess He sent me here to help you heal your heart. You go ahead and mourn however you need to, and I'll try to make you laugh from time to time." His voice was a whisper and Clare didn't answer.

They rode in silence for a time and then Clare sat up. She dried her eyes and smiled at Spur.

"You are a good man, George Spurlach. I think my children chose well."

CHAPTER 13

THE LETTERS

SPUR WAS UP EARLY ON MONDAY. HE WANTED TO LEAVE by 6:00. Clare was quiet as she fixed him breakfast.

"You didn't have to get up, Clare. I could have eaten hardtack on the trail."

Clare's face was pale, but she smiled as she shook her head.

"You have a long week in front of you. I want you to leave with a full stomach."

Annie stumbled out of her room, rubbing her eyes.

"I heard you talking, Mama." She stopped and stared at Spur a moment. Her eyes went from him to the heavy coat and war bag sitting on the floor beside his chair. She ran across the room and grabbed his arm.

"I don't want you to go, Spur. My papa went on a trip, and he didn't come home." Annie started to cry. Soon, the other children were up.

Spur picked Annie up. "I won't be gone long, Annie. Just about a week. I am only going to Helena. Your papa went there every year, and he always came home."

Annie's blue eyes filled with tears again and she began to sob. "I miss my papa. I don't want him to live under the dirt anymore. I want him back in the house with me."

Nora's big brown eyes were sad. They slowly filled with tears and Spur reached for her. He lifted her on his lap as well. "You too, Zeke. Come over here. I have something to show the three of you."

He pulled three letters out of his vest pocket and showed them to the children.

"Now who can tell me the names on these letters?"

Zeke pointed at them. "That one says Annie, this one says Zeke, and the one over there says Nora."

Spur's eyes were soft as he nodded his head. "And do you know what that word is?" he asked as he pointed at the upper left side of each letter. All three children shook their heads.

"That says Heaven. I think your papa sent you these letters from Heaven."

Each child reached for their letter, holding it carefully.

Clare dropped her spoon. One hand clutched the table, and the other hand was over her mouth. Her breath was coming rapidly.

Annie stared at her letter before she looked up at Spur. "Are you sure this letter is from my papa?"

Spur squeezed the three of them and smiled. "I *know* these letters are from your papa. Would you like me to read them?"

Zeke and Annie both nodded their heads, but Nora shook her head. "I don't want you to mess my letter up. I want to keep it just like it is."

Spur's heart clutched for the little girl as he nodded. "That's fine, Nora. You can listen while I read Zeke's and Annie's letters."

Zeke pointed to Annie's letter. "Read Annie's first."

Spur carefully opened the letter and unfolded it. His eyes skimmed the page, and he cleared his throat. *Lord, help me to handle this right.*

My Precious Annie,
    I have gone to Heaven to be with Jesus. I guess He needed another cowboy up there to ride all his horses. I want you to know that I love you very much.

You won't see me, but in the mornings, before you wake up, I will hug you. I will even hug you when you get big because little girls are never too big for their papa to hug.

Now you be a good girl for your mama. You help her and give her hugs too. Mama will need lots of hugs since I won't be there to make her smile.

When you feel sad and you want to cry, you just remember that I can see you even though you can't see me. When the sun shines and makes your face feel warm, that is me kissing you. I love you, Annie, and I always will.

Love Papa

Annie stared at Spur for a moment and then she climbed down from his lap. She ran around the table and hugged Clare.

"I love you, Mama. And Papa does too. He said for me to hug you for him."

Clare dropped down on the floor and hugged the little girl smiling up at her. "Oh, Annie. My precious Annie." Clare was trying hard not to cry. She whispered, "Your papa loved you so much."

Annie handed the letter to Clare. "You keep this for me, Mama. I want you to read it to me *every* day. And someday when I can read, I will read it by myself."

Spur smiled at Clare and Annie. Then he looked down at Zeke.

"Ready to read yours, Zeke?"

Zeke slowly nodded and Spur carefully opened the letter.

Zeke,

I am so pleased that you and your mama came to live with Annie and me. This place needed another man. Girls are nice to have around, but a ranch needs a few fellows too.

You are the man of the house now. I want you to be strong for the girls. When you feel sad, you remember how brave Patches was when he tried to kill that bear. Even though he was afraid, he was still brave. If you need to cry, well, you go out to the barn and you talk to him. You hug his neck. And you remember that crying doesn't mean a fellow is weak. It just means that his love is leaking out through his eyes, and that happens sometimes.

I love you, Zeke. When you see an eagle flying over our ranch, you remember I am up there watching over you. Shoot, I might even be riding it. They do that in Heaven, you know. Now hug your mother and help your sisters. I know you will grow into a fine man.

Love your papa

Zeke was quiet. He looked up at Spur and his brown eyes filled with tears. He quietly folded up the letter and put it into his pocket.

"I am going to go talk to Patches," he stated softly. He quietly walked out of the house toward the barn.

Nora stared at her letter. She ran to the bedroom she shared with Annie. "I am going to sleep with my letter, and when Spur comes back, he can read it to me.

"I think I will go talk to Patches too."

She ran outside and Annie followed her.

Spur stood and walked over to Clare. He pulled her close and held her as she sobbed. "I miss him so much," she whispered. She dried her eyes and pulled away to look up at Spur.

"Those letters were in Rock's handwriting. When you told me you had letters for the children, I thought you had written them." She paused and then whispered, "It's like he knew he was going to die."

Spur sat down and slid Clare onto his lap. He pulled her head against his chest.

"Maybe. And maybe he wrote them one night when he missed all of you. Drives give you lots of time to think.

"I'm glad he wrote them. They will be something for your little ones to hang onto." He put her face between his hands and whispered, "And I still have the letter he wrote to you."

Clare's lips trembled and she sank back against Spur as she sobbed quietly. She stayed there for a time before she stood up. Once again, she dried her face on her apron.

"You hang onto it. Maybe you can read it to me when you get back from Helena." She straightened her dress and busied herself with breakfast.

Clare didn't sit down with Spur. Instead, she began to clean up the kitchen. When Spur finished, he stood and grabbed his war bag. He paused and looked at her.

"I should be back in a week. It will take me about four days to get there with all the stops I am making. The trip home should take about three."

Clare gripped the broom tightly and nodded. She followed him to the door and stood watching as he mounted his horse.

Rockafeller's feet were still a little tender, so Spur had decided to ride one of the Appaloosas he was working with. The horse was large. It was mostly white with a blanket of brown spots scattered over its rump. Spur called it Beau.

He sat looking down at Clare for a moment. Finally, he dismounted. He wrapped his arms around her and kissed the top of her head.

"Don't be afraid. I'll be back," he whispered.

Clare's eyes were wide as she looked up at him. She didn't answer but she didn't pull away either.

Spur grinned and chucked her under the chin. "I'll see you in a week," he said as he mounted Beau. He waved his hat and turned his horse down the lane.

"You kids be good now. Maybe I'll bring you a surprise if you help your mother."

All three children appeared in the doorway of the barn and waved at him.

"Bye, Spur!"

"Don't fall off your horse!"

"Ride really fast!"

Spur grinned at them and pushed Beau into a gallop. He raised his hat again and was gone.

CHAPTER 14

Spur's Trip

SPUR HAD THE PAPERS CLARE HAD SIGNED IN HIS saddlebags. He was stopping by George Baggs' office on his way through Stevensville to make sure everything was official.

He looked behind him. He couldn't see the ranch house because of the trees but he smiled. "I had hoped to leave by six this morning. Instead, it is after seven. Oh well. It has been a fine morning so far."

George Baggs was originally from back East, but he had lived in the West for some time. He had held just about every job available on the frontier when he had first arrived, even living for a while in the Bitter Root Valley. Finally, he returned to the East and studied law. Now he was back in Stevensville as the town lawyer.

Spur had met the man on several occasions and liked him. Baggs was a hard worker and was willing to take on difficult court cases, even those deemed unwinnable, if he believed in the cause.

Their meeting was brief. Spur showed him the papers Clare had given him, and Baggs signed his name along with his title at the bottom.

"I was sure sorry to hear about Rock. How is Clare doing?"

"Better. It's a hard thing to lose a husband anytime. When you have a ranch to run and three small children to raise, it adds to the stress."

Baggs studied Spur's face a moment before he leaned back in his chair.

"Be glad she has a ranch to fall back on. Many women who lose their husbands have little or nothing and no marketable skills to support their family either. When you add financial difficulties to the loss of a spouse, it makes the whole situation even more difficult."

Spur was quiet for a moment. "That happen often here?"

"More than you'd think and not just here. It happens everywhere. I'd like to set up a community fund of some kind to help some of the families around here, but I just don't know where to start."

Spur studied the man in front of him. He frowned slightly before he spoke.

"Let me talk to Clare when I get back. She just might want to get involved with something like that. She has a big heart and a fierce soul.

"I guess I never gave that much thought. When you are a bachelor, you just kind of float around. You miss all the down and dirty, everyday problems."

Baggs laughed. "But now that you are married, you get to experience all of those things."

Spur grinned and nodded. "It's a big change, but it's been a good one. Thanks for your time. I will talk to Clare and one of us will get back to you."

He stopped at three different mining camps on his way to Fort Missoula. The mining camps wanted beef, but they wanted it every month rather than a large herd delivered once every six months.

"I can do that but I need a contract for one hundred head every month, with the next month's beef paid for in advance."

The butcher in the last camp growled and complained but he finally agreed. Spur left with a smile on his face, and a third payment for one hundred head in his pocket.

"Three mining camps between Stevensville and Missoula. That won't be too bad of a drive. We can move three hundred head at a time and leave one hundred head at each location." He frowned and shook his head. "Winters here can drop a lot of snow. That is worked into the contract though, so we should be fine."

Spur pushed the contracts and payments into his saddle bags. His hand touched the letter Clare had sent with him. He stared at it.

Clare didn't tell him what was in it. She just asked that he deliver it to Delmonico's and leave it for Kit Saunders. If she didn't work there anymore, Colonel Black would know where she was.

"One more stop at Fort Missoula before I head on up to Helena."

Spur studied Fort Missoula as he rode up. "Crazy to have a fort with no walls. That is pretty common out here though. As soon as I find Captain Rawn, I can finish here and be on my way."

Captain Rawn shook his head. "The military has already contracted for beef this year. Now if you want to talk horses, that is a whole 'nother deal." The two men visited about horses and the captain took Spur's name.

"I will let you know as soon as I hear back from the brass. The units south of us have a contract with a Rowdy Rankin down by Cheyenne. We have used him some and he was good to do business with. However, if we could get horses closer, that would benefit all of us."

"I worked for Rowdy until just a month ago, so I know what kind of horses the military likes. I'd be glad to work with you on that." Spur put out his hand and the two men agreed to talk as soon as the captain heard back from his superiors.

Spur was excited when he left. "No beef contract, but a horse contract looks promising." He arrived in Helena three days later.

CHAPTER 15

CLARE'S FRIEND

SPUR DROPPED INTO A CHAIR IN DELMONICO'S. IT had been a long four days. He was ready for a hot bath, a good meal, and a real bed. Since it was nearly 8:00 p.m., he opted to eat first.

The little waitress was a bright-eyed girl with a wealth of brown hair. Her dark eyes were friendly, but she didn't flirt with the customers. She appeared to be in her early twenties. She was shapely and pert.

Spur grinned. "Just the kind of gal I would have flirted with before I married. Now I only have eyes for a tall, blue-eyed woman."

He ordered the special and then asked, "You know where I can find Kit Saunders? I have a letter here for her."

The young woman looked at him in surprise. "I am Kit. How did you know to find me here?"

Spur grinned and pulled the letter from his saddlebag. "A woman by the name of Clare down by Stevensville asked me to look you up. I was to make sure you received this, and I'm darn pleased I didn't have to work too hard."

Kit's eyes lit up. "Oh, how is Clare? I haven't seen her since she left. I know she came though her surgery in flying colors, but I haven't heard from her for nearly nine months.

"She used to work here. Rock took her riding one day and not long after that, Clare left Helena. A doctor down there had offered to examine her." Kit's eyes clouded. "She was so sick when she left, and so worried about little Zeke."

Kit's eyes were soft when she looked at Spur. "Clare thinks the sun rises and sets on Rock. I was so excited for her when they married. I think Clare has loved him her whole life.

"How is Rock? He was Clare's knight in shining armor. Mine too in fact." Kit giggled. "He punched a man who was sitting right over there for talking inappropriately to me. And then Clare married him.

"The morning after she went riding with him, she was walking on air. She was so in love with that man." Kit blushed and shook her head.

"Pardon me. I am just rambling on.

"I would love to talk to you more about Clare. Will you be back for breakfast? Maybe we could eat together. I don't have to work until 9:00 tomorrow morning since I am closing tonight."

Spur nodded slowly. "That should work. I want to meet with Tom Fox here at the bank, but it won't open before eight.

"I'll see you here around seven tomorrow morning if that's not too early for you."

Kit nodded happily and hurried away to wait on her next customer.

Spur's heart was heavy. *She will find out about Rock in that letter or else I am going to have to tell her. Either way, tomorrow morning may not be as enjoyable as she thinks it is going to be.* He glared down at the table and muttered, "Life was sure easier when I just picked up and rode whenever emotions got too high." Then he thought of the faces of the three children when they finished their special dance, and he laughed.

"Nope, my life is not easier, but it is sure satisfying. I just can't wait to get home, and it's been a *long* time since I said that."

His forehead drew down again in a frown. *I wonder what surgery Clare had. She never mentioned it. I hope it wasn't anything that will affect her birthing that baby she is carrying.*

Spur was still thinking about all that Kit had told him when he laid down. *Clare was right to make me marry her. I'm tempted to bail. I might not have gone back there if we hadn't married.* He frowned and rolled over onto his side. *I'm just not sure I should be any part of Clare's life right now. I don't even know what she needs from me.* Then he shook his head.

"Nope, I'm going home." He thought a moment and muttered to himself in surprise, "I've fallen in love with a woman who has sworn to never again share her heart. A woman who has only loved one man in her life, and that man is dead."

CHAPTER 16

A MESSAGE FROM SISTER EDDIE

KIT DIDN'T SHOW UP FOR BREAKFAST. SPUR WAITED to order until 7:30. When he did order, he ate slowly, but Kit never did arrive.

He frowned as he watched for her. Finally, at 8:00, he left and headed for the bank. A young woman stopped him on the street.

"Excuse me. Are you Spur? George Spurlach?"

Spur slowly nodded his head as he watched her carefully. The woman wore a long cloak but the fancy red dress that peeked from under it told Spur where she worked.

"Big Dorothy would like to see you. She said to use the special door. Give the man who is there this token." She pressed a token with Big Dorothy's logo stamped on it into Spur's hand and disappeared.

Spur looked at the token. He turned to stare toward Big Dorothy's House of Entertainment down the street.

"I am guessing this message has something to do with Kit. I'd better take care of my banking business first. Who knows what this message means?"

As Spur walked by the convent, he saw Sisters Rudolph and Casimir working in their garden. Sister Casimir had her long dress tied up while

Sister Rudolph wore an apron over hers. He walked over with a grin on his face.

"Good morning, Sisters. Find any young boys you had to help save lately?"

The nuns looked at him in surprise. Sister Casimir slowly smiled. "George? Is that you?" She looked back at Sister Rudolph and exclaimed excitedly, "Sister, it is little George Spurlach!"

Both nuns hurried to the small fence that surrounded their garden. "Why, George, we haven't seen you since Sister Edwina passed away. Are you living up here now?"

Spur nodded. "I am. I married a nice gal with three little ones. Her husband passed away and left her with a ranch down by Stevensville. I came up here to move her banking business closer to home." He chuckled.

"I don't think the two of you have changed at all. Of course, I thought you were old fifteen years ago, so that's not much of a compliment." His dark eyes were twinkling as he grinned at the nuns.

"The same ornery smile, George. The mustache is different but those black curls, that big smile, and those dark eyes look the same." Sister Rudolph laughed.

"I think often of Sister Edwina. She loved you so much. She always said you were her special boy."

Spur could feel his throat getting tight but he grinned.

"Sister Eddie had quite an influence on me. Even now when I start to step over the line, I can almost feel her shaking her finger at me." His voice was soft as he added, "I gave her ring to Clare when we married. I think she would approve."

Sister Casimir beamed, and Sister Rudolph took Spur's face in her hands. She kissed his cheek and smiled at him. "That is from Sister Edwina since she can't give you one from Heaven. My how we prayed you would grow into a fine man.

"Now you love those little children and your Clare too. And no running away when things get hard. You remember the love Sister Edwina gave you. You pass that on now."

Spur nodded and backed away from the fence. Both nuns waved at him. He smiled and turned back up the street toward the bank. He could feel tightness in his chest and he cleared his throat. Sister Eddie's face was clear in his mind and he laughed.

"You always said I was a runner, even when I was young. You just had to have Sister Rudolph pass that message on, didn't you?

"Well, I'll do my best, Sister Eddie. I owe you that." He was still smiling when he entered the bank.

"George Fox, please. I want to talk to him about closing Rock Beckler's account."

CHAPTER 17

A Friendly Banker

GEORGE FOX STOOD WHEN SPUR ENTERED HIS OFFICE. "Have a seat, Mr. Spurlach. What can I do for you?"

Spur laid his papers on Fox's desk. "Rock Beckler was killed in an accident. His wife has decided to move her financial business to Stevensville. We have a bank now, and it will be easier for her."

Surprise and then shock registered on George Fox's face.

"What—when—when did he pass away?"

Spur's face was tight as he sat down.

"A bushwhacker shot his horse, and it went over backwards on him. Crushed his chest. That was on September 18 so just about three weeks ago. He was bringing a herd of black cattle north from Cheyenne. We were about ten days from Stevensville."

George Fox sank back in his chair. "How is Clare doing? And the children?"

Spur looked away and then shrugged. "I think the kids are probably doing better than Clare. She is starting to smile again though, so that is good."

"Well, you give her my condolences, will you? Rock was a fine man. He will leave a large hole in their family and in the community as well."

George Fox was quiet a moment as he studied Spur's face. He finally cleared his throat and pulled a ledger from his drawer.

"Now how do you want to do this? Would you like to take cash, or do you want me to wire the money to the bank in Stevensville?" He glanced at a list of banks on his desk and asked, "Is that the First State Bank of Stevensville?"

"Yes, that's the one. You can wire it, but I'll need an accounting for Clare."

The banker nodded and quickly pulled out the papers he needed.

"Here is the amount that will be wired to your bank. If you'll sign under that amount, I will take care of this today."

Spur stared at the large number in front of him for a moment before he scrawled his name across the bottom of the statement.

Looking at that number, folks will for sure think I married Clare for her money.

George Fox quickly filled out the rest of the papers he needed. Spur signed them and stood.

"Thank you, Mr. Fox. I appreciate you making this process so easy. Clare said Rock always enjoyed his visits with you. I hope you understand she is doing this strictly for convenience."

Fox nodded. "I understand. We hate to see you take your business elsewhere, but it makes sense.

"I'll send Clare a note this week." He smiled as he leaned back in his chair.

"Rock always thought a lot of Clare. He told me on his yearly visit this past spring they had married. He said he just couldn't be happier. A darn shame he died so young."

George Fox studied Spur's face as he tapped his pencil. When he spoke, his voice was soft.

"You know, Rock was in here July of last year. He didn't know Clare was living in Helena until he spotted an envelope on my desk with her name on it.

"Johnny Braxton wasn't much of a husband to Clare, and he was an even worse gambler. He had run up tickets all over town before he died in May of that year, and the merchants were starting to contact me. I had over $800 in charge tickets in that envelope. I hated to do it, but I had to ask Clare to come by the bank.

"Rock took those tickets out of the envelope, and he slid $50 in. He told me to give it to Clare. He said to tell her that some cowboy had come through and paid back the money he owed Johnny. Then, Rock went around to every business and paid off those charges.

"Clare didn't believe me about the money of course. She knew Johnny borrowed from anyone who was foolish enough to lend to him. He certainly didn't ever loan money himself.

"She finally took the money. She opened an account here and began saving a little each month." George looked down at his desk and then back up at Spur.

"I didn't know Clare well, but Colonel Black down at Delmonico's thought a lot of her. She was quite sick when she left here later that year. I heard she was going to Stevensville to have some kind of surgery." He smiled at Spur.

"Good luck to you, Spur. Thank you for helping Clare work through her grief as well as all the headaches that go with handling a business. I'm sure she appreciates that."

Spur nodded as he shook Fox's hand. *No wonder Rock enjoyed coming up here. The two of them became friends over the years. I certainly hope Clare won't regret ending this relationship.* Spur took a deep breath and started down the street toward Big Dorothy's brothel.

CHAPTER 18

THE MESSENGER

SPUR WALKED AROUND TO THE SIDE DOOR OF BIG Dorothy's House of Entertainment. It was hidden from the street and was the most discreet of her three entrances.

He tapped on the door and dropped the token he held into the hand of the man who answered. The man stepped aside and nodded for Spur to come in. He led him down the hall to an elaborate sitting room without speaking and left him there.

Spur looked around and finally sat down on one of the fancy chairs. The room brought back memories of the house his mother had run.

"I don't even know if she is still alive. She'd be over fifty by now." He frowned. "Age is an enemy when you make your living this way."

Big Dorothy swirled into the room. She was a tall woman, nearly six feet. At one time, she had been shapely, but now her full body was stuffed into the clothes she wore.

Spur stood and put out his hand with a grin.

"Miss Dorothy. It has been some time since I've had the pleasure of your company."

Big Dorothy's hard face softened, and she smiled.

"Come with me, Spur. There is someone here you need to see." She led him through a series of halls and rooms until they reached a small room nearly hidden under a stairway. She opened the door and beckoned for him to come in.

"Kit, Spur is here. Tell him what happened."

The woman lying on the bed slowly turned toward him. Spur almost choked when he recognized Kit.

She had been savagely beaten. Both of her eyes were black, and her cheek had a large cut on it. Her lips were split, and one arm was in a sling.

Kit winced as she tried to sit up. Big Dorothy slipped an arm behind the young woman's back and steadied her.

Spur dropped down beside the bed. "Kit! What happened? Who did this to you?"

Tears slid from Kit's eyes as she whispered, "Slade. Dick Slade."

Spur's face hardened and he rocked back on his feet. "What does Slade have against you?"

Kit shook her head. "This was a message for you. He saw you talking to me in Delmonico's. He said what he did to me won't compare to what he is going to do to Clare.

"He hates you and Clare too. In his words, 'That high and mighty gal Spur was dancing with won't be so purty when I get done with her. I'm going to take her down a notch. Then we'll see how tough Spur is. I'll use her up and leave what's left for him to find.' He said you are related, but you think you are too good for him." Kit began crying.

"Go home, Spur. Find Clare before Slade gets to her. He is an evil man."

Spur was already moving. He paused at the door and looked back. "What about you, Kit? Are you going to be all right?"

Kit nodded and then winced. "I'll be fine. Clare sent me fare money to come down and visit. I'll take the stage as soon as I can move around. Dorothy has a doctor coming today. She said I can stay here until I am better."

"Please go, Spur! Slade left last night already. He intends to beat you home."

Spur was gone. He was running by the time he reached the side door. He yelled at the hostler to saddle his horse as he raced down the street. The man poked his head out the door and darted back into the livery. By the time Spur reached the livery door, the man was leading Beau out.

"I tied a bag of oats on the back there. I'm guessing you are going to be making a fast trip."

Spur nodded and threw the man some money. He mounted the horse and charged the Appaloosa up the street toward the Pacific Hotel. He slid off and raced into the hotel.

"The name's George Spurlach. Figure my bill. I'm leavin' on the run!" He took the steps two at a time. He had packed his bag that morning. He grabbed it and his rifle off the bed as he spun around. He raced back down the stairs and threw some money at the startled clerk.

"This…this is too much, Mr. Spurlach," the clerk stuttered as she grabbed the scattered money.

"Give the extra to the good sisters," he shouted over his shoulder. He tied on his war bag, thrust his rifle into the boot and raced his horse southeast out of Helena.

The Appaloosa liked to run, and Spur let it pick its pace for the first mile. Then he slowed down, walking, trotting, and galloping as they ate up the miles. He rested his horse briefly at Deer Lodge and gave it some oats. An hour later, he was back in the saddle.

The Phillipsburg Valley was lush with grass. Tall mountain peaks surrounded it. Spur had always enjoyed a slow ride through that valley, but today he took it on the run.

"Beau, this is going to be a hard trip, but I know you are up for it. After we get through this valley, we are going to start climbing. The trail leading up to Skalkaho Pass will be steep. Once we get over that, it will all be downhill. I'll rest you before we start that climb, so give me all you have."

Spur camped by a small creek. He chewed on hardtack while Beau grazed. "I should have shot Slade when I had the chance instead of letting him go." He cursed and threw down the stick he was whittling. He refilled his canteen and watered Beau again.

"Come on, boy. I know we've come close to ninety miles but we need to keep moving. And don't you go lame on me."

It was nearly 2:00 a.m. when they reached the base of Skalkaho Pass. The wind was coming up and Spur pulled on his heavy coat.

"Let's go, Beau. You and I both know this pass. That moon is playing with us tonight, so there may be places we'll have to feel our way."

The trip up the pass was slow. When they reached the top, the snowfall was heavy. Beau snorted as he picked his way across the flat top. Spur was almost ready to dismount when they pushed their way through. The snow stopped as they started down and the moon shined brightly for the rest of the night. They finally reached the Bitter Root Valley around eleven the next morning.

Beau was tripping with exhaustion. Spur petted him and talked softly. "Another twenty miles or so, old fellow. Then I'll turn you over to Ike, and you can rest."

It was noon when Spur rode into Stevensville. Beau was played out. His legs trembled and his head hung low when Spur dismounted.

Ike hurried out of the livery. He took one look at the horse and rushed back inside. He led a large, black Morgan out and switched Spur's rig over.

Spur's eyes were bloodshot, and his legs shook as he mounted.

"Any strangers come through here today yet?"

Ike nodded. "That feller what was causin' problems at the dance. He didn't stop here though. Rode right through town and on south."

Just then a rider raced into town. "Fire! There's a fire! It's burnin' toward the Beckler Ranch. I need help to start a backfire!"

A surge of men rushed toward the livery and Spur raced his horse toward the Sapphires. He didn't take the normal trail but turned the horse toward the narrow trail that led up from the Mission. "Come on, boy. I'm guessing Slade started that fire to draw the hands away from the house." He spurred the horse and they raced up the mountain, cutting back and forth on the crooked trail.

Spur could smell the smoke from the fire. He looked worriedly to the south. "I hope the boys have that under control. I'd sure hate to lose our buildings, especially this close to winter."

The horse was breathing hard when they finally reached the top of the trail and started down toward the ranch below. He paused the horse as he studied the scattered buildings.

Spur could hear Annie screaming.

"You get out of here, you mean man. You leave my mama alone!" There was the sound of a scuffle followed by children crying.

He slid off the horse and quickly worked his way down the side of the hill. Gomer met him and Spur petted the little donkey.

"Now you stay back, Gomer. I don't want you to get shot," he whispered. The small donkey was quiet as it watched Spur ease toward the house.

CHAPTER 19

FOR GRUDGE AND REVENGE

SPUR SLIPPED THROUGH A SMALL DOOR IN THE BACK of the house. He moved silently through the hall and slid into the back bedroom. He peeked his head through the doorway and began to inch his way toward the kitchen.

Slade held Clare with one arm around her neck. The other held a knife that was pushed up against her stomach.

"Ya move an' I'll cut that kid right out a ya. Now y'all an' me—we's a gonna go back in one a those rooms an' have us a little fun." He leered at the children and added, "An' ya jist stay out here. If ya come back an' try to help yore ma, I'll slit 'er from her chin to 'er knees."

Nora slid down to the floor. Her eyes were wide, and she was gasping for air. Annie was crying as she watched him. Zeke took each of his sisters' hands.

"When Spur gets back, he'll get you. You are a bad man, and he will hunt you down." Zeke's face was pale, but his voice was strong.

Slade laughed. "Well Spur ain't here an' by the time he gets here, I'll be long gone. Now y'all mind what I say."

Spur's voice was quiet and cold as it cut through the room.

"Slade, you put that knife down. Let's take this outside and finish it like men." He paused and added in a deadly voice, "And if you don't, I'll kill you here."

Slade pushed Clare so she was directly in front of him. He ducked down so her body nearly covered his.

"Zeke, you take your sisters outside. Go talk to Patches. Shut that door behind you."

Zeke watched Spur a moment. He didn't want to leave his mother, but he led the girls toward the door.

"Let's go find Gomer. Gomer will help," he whispered. His sisters followed him and the three children were gone quickly.

Spur moved his eyes back to Clare and the man holding her. Clare's face was terrified, and silent tears were leaking from her eyes.

It took a lot to make Spur mad, but he was white-hot with anger. He leveled his gun at Clare's shoulder. His voice was quiet and steady as he spoke.

"Clare, I am going to shoot him, and I may have to shoot through you. Now you hold still."

Slade jerked to the left with a curse and then he laughed. "Ya don't have the guts to shoot this here gal. Y'all always was a softie when it come to women." His voice was bitter as he added, "That whore ya helped down to Texas could a died an' no one would a cared. I cut 'er an' then ya come after me.

"I never fergot that pistol whippin' ya gave me. After that, I promised myself I'd get even, an' I will." His eyes narrowed down and he nuzzled Clare's neck. "'Cept I think ya care 'bout this here gal, an' that's why I'm fer sure gonna cut 'er."

Spur fired and caught the top of Slade's shoulder. The outlaw's mouth twisted into an evil grin.

"Y'all jist killed her." He turned the knife to cut Clare's stomach when Gomer charged through the door. The little donkey rushed toward Slade and grabbed the man's thigh in his open mouth.

Clare stomped on Slade's foot as the outlaw screamed. He let go of Clare and swung his knife at the donkey. Clare dropped to the floor and Spur shot him.

Gomer still had hold of Slade's leg and he drug the dying outlaw toward the door. Clare stood. She took the gun from Spur and walked slowly over to Slade. She fired four more shots into him before she let her hand fall by her side. Her body was shaking, and Spur grabbed her. He shoved his pistol back into his holster as he held her.

"Here now. It's all over. You sit down on this chair. Let me drag him outside and check on the little ones. I'll be right back."

He drug Slade's body to the side of the yard and tumbled him down a draw. All three little ones were in the doorway of the barn and Spur called to them.

"You kids stay there. I'll be down in just a bit."

He strode back into the house. Clare's head was on the table and she was sobbing.

Spur lifted her up. He sat down and pulled her onto his lap.

"It's all right now. You're safe and the little ones are fine," he whispered. He kissed her cheeks and wiped the tears away.

Clare slowly quit shaking. "I didn't think you were coming," she whispered. "I knew you weren't due home for two more days."

Spur pulled her tighter. "I left yesterday morning. Slade had Kit tell me he was headed here. He went through Missoula, and I came over Skalkaho Pass. It's a good thing I had a mountain horse because I wore him down." He was quiet a moment. "I might have ruined Beau but he carried me fast. I left him in Stevensville and picked up a fresh horse from Cappy.

"I came as fast as I could, Clare. I wish I had been here sooner." Spur's voice was soft, and his eyes were intense as he looked at her.

Tears filled Clare's blue eyes again and she wrapped her arms tightly around Spur's neck.

"I'm so glad you are here. I was terrified, for the children and for me."

Spur slowly grinned as he stared down at her. "Well, looking at how you handled that gun, I'm thinking Slade was lucky you didn't get hold of one sooner. You're a strong woman, Clare."

Clare looked up at him. She studied his face and slowly smiled.

"You always see the humorous side of things, Spur."

Spur chuckled and pulled her up. "I try. Now let's go get those wild kids of ours.

"Annie was mad. I'm glad she didn't see you shoot Slade. She might start taking lessons. Nora, on the other hand, probably needs a little hugging."

Spur opened the kitchen door and all three children raced toward the house. They pushed both Clare and Spur back into chairs as they clustered around them.

Clare lifted Annie up and Nora crawled onto Spur's lap. She snuggled up against him and he hugged her.

"You're all right, Nora," he whispered. "In fact, we are all fine."

Nora stared up at him and then wrinkled her nose. "You don't smell so nice, Spur. I think you forgot to take a bath again." She touched the thick bristles that covered his face. "And your face is all stickery."

Spur rubbed his face against hers and she giggled. "Feel Spur's face, Annie. He has stickers all over him."

"You were brave today, Zeke. You did a fine job and kept a cool head." Spur squeezed the young man's shoulder. "I'm proud of you."

Zeke's face changed from serious to smiling. "We called Gomer. We pointed at the door and said, 'Sic 'im!' like Mr. Boswell says to his dog!"

Clare looked startled. She laughed as she looked toward the door. "You know, I think Gomer could use a bath too. You take him down to the horse tank and scrub him. And don't forget to wash his face. You don't need to use soap, but brush him out when you are done."

The three children rushed back outside calling for Gomer. Clare watched from the kitchen window as they poured buckets of water over the little donkey. He seemed to enjoy it and even tried to drink from the buckets as they were lifted from the well.

"Gomer has been such a blessing." She looked back at Spur and her eyes sparkled.

"I just don't know who I would give up first, you or Gomer. It would be a toss-up."

Spur made a grab for her, and Clare dodged away laughing.

He chuckled and sat back down. "How about you fix me something to eat if I promise to leave you alone? After that, I'd like to sleep for a day or two."

The smoke smell was fainter and Spur pointed toward the window. "You don't see any fire out there, do you? It smells like the men might have gotten it stopped."

Clare looked out the window and shook her head. "I can smell smoke but not as much as earlier. Was it close?"

Spur shrugged. "I'm not sure. A fellow rode into Stevensville just as I arrived and rounded up a crew to fight it. He said it was southwest of town. It could have been on our range.

"Not anything I can do to fix that. The riders are all out, so I'm guessing Stub was on top of it. I'll check it later."

Spurs head was drooping before he finished eating.

"That was mighty tasty, Clare." He stumbled as he headed for the office and his cot. He was snoring almost as soon as he lay down.

Clare followed him in. She watched him a moment before she pulled his boots off. She stretched his legs out on the cot and drew a blanket over him.

"You are a good man, George Spurlach," she whispered. "I'm glad my children chose you." She paused to look back at him again before she quietly shut the door.

CHAPTER 20

A Tired Crew

THE HANDS SLOWLY DRUG IN FROM FIGHTING THE fire. They arrived at the ranch in time for supper. They had fought the fire since mid-morning and had missed their dinner.

Stub looked at Spur in surprise.

"We didn't expect you back for two more days."

Spur nodded and looked back toward the house.

"I was given a message by a nice little gal in Helena to get home fast. I left on the run yesterday morning and got here just after noon." His eyes were hard as he looked at Stub. "Good thing too.

"Was that fire started? I'm thinking it was a reason to get you fellows away from the ranch."

Stub frowned. "It appeared to be just the way it burned. We lost some of our winter graze so that isn't good.

"Boswell has been hinting he might be selling his ranch. His grass would sure help us out. Maybe you should talk to Clare. She has been going over there some."

Spur studied Stub's face and slowly nodded. "I think I will see if Clare wants to ride over there with me tomorrow."

Stub laughed. "You sound like Rock. He would be pleased." He grinned at Spur and added, "You might want to take a bath tonight. You are downright ugly after that long ride. I'm surprised Clare let you in the house."

Spur chuckled as he rubbed his face. "Maybe I should just grow a beard. Might be helpful with the winter up here."

The hands split off, some taking the horses and others finishing the evening work. When Spur and Stub were alone, Stub nodded toward the house.

"What happened up there?"

Spur frowned. "Let's go lean on the corral. I'm still tired."

The two men walked to the corral and leaned their arms over the top bar. Spur was quiet for a moment before he looked over at Stub.

"A fellow by the name of Slade came through here the night of the dance. I should have shot him then. I probably would have, but I had left my guns in the wagon.

"I pistol-whipped him down in Texas some years back for trying to cut up a working gal. He has been carrying a grudge around on me ever since.

"He must have seen me in Helena because he beat up a little gal there by the name of Kit Saunders. She is a friend of Clare's. It was a message to me of what Slade was going to do to Clare.

"Big Dorothy took Kit in and then sent one of her girls to find me. I came over Skalkaho Pass and rode it straight through." He frowned.

"I used to enjoy that route, but after these last two trips, that pass is becoming just downright distasteful." Spur cursed.

"Slade always said we were cousins, but we weren't related that I know of. He was always mean too. He enjoyed hurting women, and neither of those little gals deserved what he did.

"He intended to do the same thing to Clare today." Spur scowled and looked over his shoulder toward the house as he cursed under his breath. "Scared those little kids too."

"Slade was a low-down, miserable man and I'm glad he's gone." Then his face broke into a grin.

"I can't take all the credit today though. Gomer charged into the house and grabbed him by a leg. That was enough for Clare to get away and for me to get a clean shot.

"It was touchy for a bit there. I thought I was going to have to shoot through Clare, and I didn't want to try that." He chuckled as he looked at the scruffy donkey sleeping in the sun.

"Gomer doesn't look like much, but he sure comes through when he is needed."

Stub listened quietly before he asked, "Clare said she invited a woman friend of hers from up in Helena to come down for a visit. Think that's the gal who was beat up?"

Spur shrugged. "Could be. I'm not sure how many people Clare knew up there. Kit did mention that Clare had sent her fare to come and visit, but she might not be the only gal Clare invited.

"George Fox at the bank said Clare's boss at Delmonico's thought the world of her, but as for friends, I don't know." He grinned at Stub and bumped him with his elbow.

"You can always hope Kit comes and stays for a time. She's a good-lookin' little gal. 'Course that probably means she has a beau or is getting married."

Spur's grin became larger. His eyes were twinkling, and he added innocently, "If she meets you though, she might decide to become a nun. You seem to have that effect on women."

Stub glared at him and snorted.

"I'm swearin' off women. They're just too much effort. I always have to think on what I should say, and even then, it mostly comes out wrong.

"I'm done. I'm pushing thirty years old, and I've accepted the fact that I'll be single till I die." He grinned up at Spur.

"Unless some gal makes me marry like Clare did you." He began to laugh. "I read those contracts. Sounds like a fine way to start the rest of your life."

Spur frowned and growled under his breath. "Yeah, I s'pose the boys all got a good laugh in the bunkhouse."

"Well, let's see. Angel, me, Gabe. We all read them after you raised so much Cain at the house. You were passed out on your bunk, and the papers were handy-like there. Then I read them again the next morning just to see if they sounded different when I was sober." He grinned at Spur. "Your demands were just as funny as they were when I was drunk so I got to laugh again.

"By then, the rest of the hands were home. They might have read them too. Don't know. Sure was nice of you to negotiate my job back though.

"Maybe if that little gal makes it down here from Helena, you will be able to move into the bedroom instead of sleeping on a cot in the office—since she'll need some place to stay." Stub's eyes were twinkling, and he chuckled as he spoke.

Spur swung at him, and Stub ducked as he laughed again.

"Yessir, if your marriage is what they are all like, I think I'll stay single."

Spur laughed and shook his head.

"I think maybe Clare was wise to make me marry her. I sure would have bailed by now if I hadn't been tied down. I am starting to get used to the idea though. Before long, it won't bother me at all." He grinned at Stub.

"I'm living every cowboy's dream. A spunky, pretty little gal who can cook. I don't have much to complain about."

Stub almost added *and she owns a big ranch too*, but he stayed quiet.

He liked Spur. The man was a hard worker. He was savvy around the cattle and horses as well. Plus, the hands liked him. *Shoot, maybe someday Clare will be able to move on from Rock. If not, I hope they can at least be good friends.*

Spur slapped Stub on the back as he turned toward the house.

"I am going to ride down to Stevensville tomorrow. We'll go to church and then I am going to go check on my horse. I think I'll see if Clare wants to go see Boswell after that. Otherwise, I'll go on Monday.

"You start moving those cows toward the winter range. Hopefully, we'll have more grass after tomorrow."

CHAPTER 21

MAKING PLANS

SPUR CARRIED TWO BUCKETS OF WATER INTO THE house. "You need to give baths tonight?"

"I do. I want to take one too, so we'll need extra water. I want to get the children bathed as soon as supper is over."

Spur nodded. His dark eyes were twinkling. "You want to take a bath in the kitchen? I need one too. Maybe we could take one together."

Clare blushed a deep red. "Spur! Don't say things like that. The children might hear you." Her voice was barely above a whisper, but Annie looked up.

She looked from Spur to her mother.

"I don't think that will work, Spur. You are too big. Two big people can't fit in that washtub."

Spur chuckled and slowly nodded. "I reckon you're right, Annie. We will just have to take them separate. But maybe your mother will wash my back. Think that would work?"

Annie nodded. "Mama can do that. She washes our backs and it feels fine."

Spur leaned back in his chair with a grin. Clare's face was still a bright red, and she kept her back to the children. When she finally looked up, her blue eyes held just a hint of a twinkle.

"And maybe I will pour some cold water on you to cool you off a bit. I think you could use that."

Spur laughed out loud. He was still smiling when he led the family in a mealtime prayer.

When they finished eating, he pointed at the kids.

"You go ahead and start on baths. I can clean up here or at least get started." He winked at Clare as he grinned. "Besides, I smelled pie when I came in, and I don't see it anywhere."

The kids began to chorus about the pie, but Clare shook her head.

"That pie is for tomorrow. I invited Mr. Boswell over for dinner, and we will have it for dessert."

Spur looked at Clare in surprise and she shrugged.

"You said he was thinking about selling, so the children and I rode over there while you were gone. I invited him for supper on Sunday.

"I hoped you would be home but if you weren't, I figured I could talk about it with him myself." She added, "I asked Stub what I should offer."

Spur shook his head as he scraped the plates and stacked them.

"I say, Clare. You are a force to keep up with. Why in a few years, you won't need me at all."

Clare's hands stopped moving and she glanced at Spur quickly. He was smiling and color rose from Clare's neck up to her face. She turned away and began to fill the tub with hot water.

Spur filled the wash basin with water and began to wash dishes, singing as he worked. He started with "Clementine." By the time he reached the third verse, he was singing loudly, throwing back his head as he splashed water everywhere.

He had put on one of Clare's aprons and the pink ruffles around the outside reached about two inches down his legs.

Clare looked up at him and started laughing.

He turned around with a grin. "Don't you be laughing, woman. I'll make you dance with me."

Clare had both girls out of the tub. They were wrapped up in quilts and smiling at Spur. He grabbed Clare and began to dance around the kitchen, singing loudly.

The children loved it. Clare tried to protest but Spur was swinging her wildly and her feet barely touched the floor. Soon his song changed to "Buffalo Gals, Won't You Come Out Tonight!" By the time that song was done, Zeke joined them, and all the children were rushing wildly around the kitchen, singing with Spur.

Spur spun Clare around and dipped her low before he released her. He looked around at the kids with a grin.

"Now wasn't that fun? Maybe we should do that every night."

Clare pointed her finger at him and turned to the children. "Go get your nightgowns on. Then come out here so I can clean your teeth." She was almost out of breath when she added, "And you, Dancing Man, I need more water."

Spur chuckled. He picked up the two buckets and headed for the door, still wearing Clare's apron. The girls began to squeal, and he winked at them. He drew up two more buckets.

Several of the men hollered at him. Spur grinned and drawled, "Nothin' like a pretty apron to make a man feel useful."

Clare stared at him and then laughed.

"I declare, Spur. Nothing embarrasses you."

"Not much. And I'll do just about anything to make a pretty lady smile." He winked at her and Clare laughed again.

"Zeke, it's your turn. Jump in here while the girls are changing."

Once the kids were in bed, Spur dumped the water around some small trees and brought in more for Clare.

"Where do you want your wash tub?"

Clare looked closely at him.

"I want it in my bedroom, and I want the door shut. I don't trust you tonight."

He grinned at her.

"Call me when you are done. I want to take a bath too."

Clare called when she was done, and Spur strolled back into her bedroom. Clare was standing in the shadows, trying to keep from being seen.

"Now don't act all shy with me, Clare. I've already seen you in your nightgown. In fact, you even sat on my lap with it on." He grinned toward her and Clare almost gasped.

"You are a bold man, George Spurlach. You get out of here. I declare. You should be tired, but I think lack of sleep makes you even ornerier."

Spur chuckled as he carried the heavy tub into the kitchen. He added another bucket of hot water and then stripped down.

Clare could hear him walking around the kitchen, looking for something.

"What do you need, Spur?" she called.

Spur stopped and grinned as he looked toward the closed door.

"I was looking for some whiskey. You are sure welcome to come out here and help me look."

"I most certainly will not. I doubt you have any clothes on at all."

Spur chuckled. Clare was right. He was in his birthday suit. He finally found the whiskey, poured a glass, and sat down in the tub with a loud splash.

He sang "My Bonnie Lies Over the Ocean" as he scrubbed himself. After two verses, he looked toward the bedroom door.

"I'm ready to have my back scrubbed, Clare. Why don't you come on out and do that?"

He chuckled when he heard the bed squeak. Clare didn't answer and he sang softly until he finished his bath. He poured the water over Clare's mulched garden and hummed softly as he shaved.

"There is nothing like a bath and a shave to make a man sleep." He padded into the office and was almost instantly asleep.

Clare waited until Spur was quiet before she slipped back into the kitchen. She wiped up the floor and straightened her kitchen before she went back to bed. She tossed and turned for nearly an hour.

"That man just loves to mess with me. Now my mind is so full that I am hardly tired." She finally got up and made herself a cup of tea. She walked slowly to the window and watched as the first snow of the season began to fall.

"Pretty, isn't it?"

Clare muffled her scream and nearly dropped the tea.

Spur grabbed for the slipping cup and cursed as the hot water splashed on his hand.

"Did any of that get on you? I didn't mean to scare you."

She shook her head. Spur was standing close behind her and she whispered, "You had better have some clothes on."

He laughed out loud.

"Well, maybe I do and maybe I don't. Guess you had better not turn around."

Spur put his arms around her. His hands were warm against her thin nightgown.

"You are a beautiful woman, Clare. A distracting one too." He kissed her neck and was gone.

Clare shakily picked up the nearly empty cup and drank the last of her tea.

"You are a pest, Spur. You keep me rattled all the time. And I almost enjoy it," she whispered softly. She quietly set the cup in the washbasin and climbed into her bed.

CHAPTER 22

A WHITE SUNDAY

THE SUN CAME OUT BRIGHT AND CLEAR. SPUR RODE partway down the trail to see if they could get out.

Clare had just gotten up when he walked into the house.

"The snow has drifted over the trail. We aren't going to be able to get that wagon through it." He paused as he looked out the window.

"We need a buggy, Clare. They have higher wheels and aren't so cumbersome. We could almost make it to church in a buggy. I think a two-seater would be nice."

Clare was quiet a moment and then nodded. "Talk to Ike when you go to town. He can order one for us. Are you going to ride down today?"

"No, I'll wait until tomorrow now." He turned to look at her.

"Think Boswell will still come over? Does he get out much in the snow?"

Clare laughed and nodded. "Chas has no idea how old people act. He will try to come and none of his men will be able to stop him."

Spur frowned. "Why don't you pack up some of that pie, and I will ride over there. I don't want him out. I think we are going to get another snow." Spur pulled his heavy coat back on and strode down to the corral. He caught the large, black Appaloosa stallion he called Hell

131

Fire—at least that was what he called him when neither Clare nor the kids were around.

"Hell Fire, you and I have a tough trail to ride today. I want to get started because I think it is going to start snowing again. I hope I'm wrong, but I feel it in my bones."

The large horse snorted and looked back as Spur saddled him.

"And don't you go showing off for your mares this morning. I have so darned much coat on that I can hardly move my arms, let alone put up with your shenanigans."

Spur led the horse toward the house still talking to him. Hell Fire snorted again and shook his head. Spur chuckled.

"And that attitude is exactly why I chose you. I may need a cantankerous horse who wants to get back home today as bad as I do."

Clare came to the door. Her face was pale as she handed him the package.

"Be careful, Spur. And don't talk too long. I don't want to worry about you getting back home.

Spur grinned at her from the saddle as he dropped the package into his saddle bag.

"Shoot, Clare. You're already worried. I think I'm growing on you."

Clare's neck slowly turned pink. Then she glared at him.

"Spur, you are a bold man." She turned to go into the house and Spur called after her.

"But you didn't deny it!"

Spur could hear her laugh as she closed the door and he chuckled.

"Let's go, Hell. I have more reason to come back home every day."

Parts of the trail had blown clear while other places had drifted deeply. It was nearly noon when Spur arrived at Chas Boswell's ranch.

Four riders were changing horses and Spur rode towards them.

"How's your boss today? He's supposed to come over for supper this evening. We thought it would be best if he didn't get out."

One of the men answered dryly, "Well, you are too late. He was the first one out this morning, and we haven't seen him since. He said something about riding around the cattle in the South Pasture and trying to push them this way. He left without waiting for us.

"Nudge, he's the foreman. He took a couple of boys out to break ice. He said he would come home that way.

"I heard a rifle shot a while ago. I'm guessing they must have found him. They should all be coming back any time."

Spur looked toward the south. "I know where that pasture is. I think I'll mosey over that way—see if they need any help.

"You boys enjoy a nice afternoon in the house, all cozied up by that fire now."

Spur was grinning and the men chuckled. They paused to watch as he rode down the trail.

A rider they called Caine nodded toward Spur's departing back as he commented, "Heard Spur there married Mrs. Beckler. You boys know anything about that?"

Another cowboy who went by the name of Jake snorted as he tightened the girth on his saddle.

"That ain't likely. Most of the fellows I rode with down Texas way knew Spur. They said he was as wild as a painted pony. Shoot, he knowed ever' gal in ever' sportin' house down there. They all liked 'im too. Miz Beckler's purty buttoned up fer ol' Spur. Ain't likely."

"Heard his mom runned a sportin' house." Squirrel spoke softly as he saddled his horse.

Jake nodded. "I heard that too, but Spur never talked 'bout her. He'd talk 'bout some gal he called Sister Eddie when he was drunk. Seemed to think a lot a her. I figgered he must a had a little sister at one time. Never mentioned her when he was sober though."

A fourth cowboy who went by the name of Ladder listened quietly. He finally commented, "I hung around one a those dance houses in Cheyenne fer a time. Spur was always there. Those gals all liked 'im an' he danced with all of 'em. The one I danced with though said he didn't never take none of 'em upstairs. She said he was more like a brother to 'em. He's the one they all called on when some feller done 'em dirty.

"Spur was wild but he was always respectful of the ladies—no matter what they did for a livin'."

Caine scratched his head and looked up toward the big house.

"I wonder if the boss is thinkin' on sellin' out. He's gettin' up there in age. Rock would a been down here talkin' already. In fact, I'm a guessin' that was in the plans 'fore he died."

"Miz Beckler was down here while Rock was on that drive. She come again last week. 'Course she comes down here purty regular since she married Rock. She always brings those kids. Last time, she took ol' Chas on a picnic. I'm a guessin' he ain't been on a picnic in years." Jake chuckled as he dropped his stirrup and mounted his horse.

"'Course any feller who wouldn't go on a picnic with as good lookin' a woman as Miz Beckler ain't got no eyes.

"I thought on courtin' 'er my own self after Rock died, but I ain't a brave man. I like to look but when it comes to doin', I jist chicken out." Jake grinned at his friends. "'Sides, three kids an' one on the way is a lot fer a feller to take on, 'specially if he ain't been married before. I talked it over with my horse, an' we decided we ain't done movin' 'round jist yet."

The men mounted and rode away, still discussing if Spur had married his widow boss lady.

CHAPTER 23

A HEART-SHAPED BIRTHMARK

HELL FIRE SLUGGED HIS WAY SOUTHEAST. SPUR frowned as he looked at the burned spikes of trees that remained after the fire.

"That fire probably burned over five hundred acres. I should have killed Slade when I had the chance. It just doesn't pay to try to change your ways when men like him still roam around."

He found small groups of cattle and started them south.

"You girls get on out of here. You won't find anything to eat but burned ground under this snow."

Spur was nearly fifteen miles down the valley when he saw a horse standing with its reins dragging. The animal's eyes were dilated, and it was trembling as its sides heaved.

He rode slowly toward the horse.

"Easy, Boy. Don't you jump now. I am going to grab those reins. Let's see where you came from."

There was no one around that Spur could see. He turned Hell Fire to backtrack the deep prints the running horse had left behind. He had gone about a mile when he saw a man leaned against a rock.

Spur cursed softly and urged Hell Fire up the trail. He dismounted quickly beside the seated man.

"I reckon you're Chas. You all right?"

Chas looked up slowly and shook his head. Spur cursed quietly when he saw the old man was holding his side.

He lifted Chas' hand away gently and saw a gaping hole in his side. He looked around and saw a shattered stump of a small tree. The tree was broken off about ten inches from the base and a short, bloody shaft lay beside the shattered stump.

"We scared out a cougar and my horse spooked. I couldn't grab my gun with my heavy mittens. By the time I threw them down and got to my gun, that cougar jumped. My horse reared and I fell off. Landed right on the shaft of that tree. Probably wouldn't have been hurt too bad, but my horse went over backwards and rolled atop me." Chas nodded his head toward the broken stump. "Run that durn tree clean through me.

"My horse slid to the bottom of the hill there and raced off to the south. That lion took in after him. I finally got my rifle up and shot. I must have grazed that lion because it swerved and cut out of there like Hades was after it. My horse didn't slow down though." The old man looked up at Spur and swore. "I pulled that piece of tree out of my side and drug myself over here."

Chas relaxed slowly against the snow-covered rock. "Thought I'd die out here alone and then you come along." Pain showed in his eyes, but the old man smiled slightly. The sky had clouded over, and snow was starting to come down again.

"I need to get you to a doctor, Chas. Stevensville is only about fifteen miles up the valley. I can help you on your horse." He leaned back to rise but Chas grabbed his arm.

"Don't waste your time. I'm about done. That tree tore me up some going in and more coming out.

"Help me lean a little more to the right." His old eyes glinted with mirth for a moment. "I have a birthmark on my ass, and it gets cold before anything else does."

He gasped as Spur moved his legs. He took several deep breaths before he spoke again.

"Just talk to me. There is something about dying that makes a man look back over his life." He looked up at the man leaning over him.

"You Spur?"

When Spur nodded, the old man smiled.

"I've heard of you, but we haven't met yet." He put out his hand to shake. His old eyes twinkled slightly as he added, "Heck of a way to meet the new neighbor.

"Where are you from, Spur?"

Spur stared at the old man and then relaxed beside him. He took off his heavy coat and laid it over Chas before he shrugged.

"I've worked all over. Before I settled here, I rode for a rancher down by Cheyenne."

"You talk like a southern boy. You from Texas?"

Spur laughed and shook his head.

"Naw. I was born in a bordello down in New Orleans." His dark eyes glinted. He laughed again and added, "Born into a life of sin and iniquity. Probably would have stayed there but an old nun rescued me. She took me in and tried to raise me proper." He pulled his gloves off and he offered them to Chas.

"You want me to put these gloves on you, Chas? Your hands look mighty cold."

Chas' wrinkled hands were trembling. He took Spur's left hand and turned it over. He rubbed the small birthmark on Spur's wrist with his thumb.

"That's an interesting mark. Were you born with that?"

Spur nodded and chuckled. "Yeah, it's a birthmark. Heck of a thing for a fellow to have a heart-shaped birthmark on his wrist. I've taken a lot of ribbing for that over the years." His dark eyes glinted and he added, "Now I just tell the ladies it's because I'm a lover."

"Your folks still alive?"

Spur looked away before he answered. He tried to keep the bitterness out of his voice, but it was there.

"I never knew my pa. Madam Bella was my ma. She didn't like me much. She refused to talk about my pa. She wouldn't even tell me the date I was born.

"That old nun took me in when I was around six. She smacked me around when I misbehaved and made me straighten up.

"She was the first person who ever showed me love—tough love for sure. I grew to love her too. I left New Orleans when she died. I was fourteen. I've been back several times but I never stay long."

Chas gripped Spur's hands with his and tears leaked from his eyes.

"Your name is George, isn't it?"

CHAPTER 24

FATHER AND SON

SPUR LOOKED AT CHAS IN SURPRISE AND SLOWLY nodded.

"I've found you. I have looked my whole life for you, and here you are in front of me."

Spur stared at the old man in confusion. Chas was almost crying but he was smiling too.

"I'm your pa, Spur. Your mother wrote me after you were born. She wanted me to come and get you. And she wanted $5000.

"I should have done it. I've regretted not going ever since. Your mother was a cunning woman though, and I wasn't convinced you were mine. After all, she worked in a whore house.

"Besides, I didn't want to tell my wife what I had done. I wrote your mother back. I refused to pay her. I told her I doubted you were mine.

"She wrote a second time. She was furious. She told me someday I would want to find you, that I would be sorry.

"I showed my Agnes the second letter. We talked and we both cried. She agreed we needed to find you. We decided that even if you weren't my son, we would take you in." Tears filled Chas' eyes and he looked away. "I was so ashamed of what I had done. I was sure my selfishness had condemned you to a horrible life.

"Agnes and me, we looked and looked.

"Maebeline—that's what I called your mother—she didn't give me much information to go on though. I didn't know your name, just that I had a son born on April 9, 1850." The old man pressed his finger into Spur's wrist. "And that he had a heart-shaped birthmark on his wrist." Tears ran from the old man's eyes. "We hired a private detective. He found out your name was George.

"Forgive me, Son. I am sorry I didn't come to get you."

Spur stared at Chas in confusion. He finally smiled.

"I used to dream of what it would be like to have a pa. I always called you Pop in my mind." His smiled became bigger.

"Nice to meet you, Pop."

Chas' smile was huge. He pulled Spur's face down and kissed it. Then a spasm of pain shook him, and he collapsed against the rock gasping. He continued to grip Spur's hand. He alternated between crying and smiling as he stared at the man beside him. He finally let go with one hand and wiped his face. He took a deep breath and before he looked up at Spur again.

"You have any little ones, Spur? Besides Clare's kids I mean."

Spur shook his head. "Naw. I've always been a runner. When things start to get serious, I take off. I only was maybe in love one time before Clare came along, but I left her."

Chase's eyes were full of pain, but he gripped Spur's vest.

"Don't run this time, Son. The Good Lord has given you the real deal here. Clare's a fine woman, and she deserves to be loved."

Spur could feel the heat come up in his face. He rubbed his eyes before he looked directly at Chas.

"I'm head over heels in love with her," he stated simply. "I'm not sure when it happened, but she stole my heart.

"All she thinks of is Rock though. I'm just not sure she needs a love-sick cowboy around her."

Chas stared hard at Spur. He tried to cough, and Spur helped him to lean forward. He slowly leaned back against the rock. His chest rattled as he tried to breath. His eyes were intense as he stared up at Spur.

"Clare and I became close after she married Rock. He and I had always gotten on well, but Clare, she's special. She was always comin' over and bringin' me food. That or sending it with one of their hands. Usually, it was that young Tuff.

"She became the daughter we lost.

"And those three little ones. They are just as sweet as can be. Annie is a little dynamite miniature of Rock. She's a pistol. Nora is so sweet she just melts, and Zeke tries hard to be a little man. He's a serious little fellow." Chas' voice caught in his throat.

"Plumb broke my heart when Rock died. I told the Good Lord He should have taken me."

Spur stared at the old man and slowly nodded.

"I told Him the same thing. In fact, I've had several talks with Father Ravalli about that very thing since I settled here. I just don't understand how the Good Lord thinks."

Chas smiled and coughed again. His body shook and Spur gripped his hand.

"Easy, Old Timer. Take it easy now."

Chas looked up at Spur and grinned.

"Ike told me Clare had asked you to marry her. He wasn't sure you were going to agree till he heard about your additions to her contract. Old Ike must have studied that list because he was able to recite all ten of your requirements. He repeated them for me, and we both got a good laugh." Chas' old eyes glistened with humor, and he tried to laugh.

"I'm guessing you were a challenge for that old nun."

Spur was quiet. He studied the old man's face as a tear leaked from Chas' closed eyes. The dying man's voice was labored when he continued.

"Agnes and I only had one child. Our baby died shortly after she was born. It's a hard thing to watch the life drain out of a newborn child right before your eyes.

"Our little girl was born too early, and Agnes almost bled to death after she delivered. It was in the middle of a blizzard, and I couldn't do anything to help either of them.

"That's when I learned how to really pray and pray I did." He looked up at Spur.

"Agnes never conceived again. I guess something inside her wasn't working. But then, maybe I was being punished for not accepting the child the Good Lord had offered me so many years before." He tried to shift his body into a different position and groaned.

"When you get back to the ranch, look in my office. There's a will in there. Read it over and share it with my men." He tried to smile at Spur. "I left my land to you."

CHAPTER 25

A New Boss

SPUR STARED AT HIM IN SHOCK AND CHAS CHUCKLED. It turned to a groan and he grimaced.

"I don't have any family left but maybe a few distant cousins. Not anyone I want to leave my land to for sure. All they'd do is fight over it and then sell it off, piece by piece.

"I had Rock's name on my will originally. I was going to change his name to Clare's. When you and Clare married, I put your name on it. I decided any man who would marry a woman he barely knew just because she asked him to be the father of her kids…well, that man should have a little land with his name on it." His big hand gripped Spur's and his eyes were intense.

"I sure didn't know I would be leaving it to my own son though." A large tear leaked out of Chas' eye, and he shook his head.

"Here my son is right in front of me and I am dying." He slowly smiled as he looked up at Spur. "Well, I reckon the Good Lord answered my prayers. I prayed I would meet you before I died, and He made that happen." Chas' eyes clouded over with pain and he gasped.

He pulled Spur's head closer as he whispered, "You make her happy, Spur. You put that sparkle back in our Clare Ann's eyes." The old man's grip on Spur's shirt relaxed.

"Reckon you could call me Pop once again before I go?"

Spur was struggling to keep the tears in his eyes from leaking out, but he nodded.

"Pop, I sure wish we could have known each other longer. I'll try to be as good of a man as you are. Folks around here think a lot of you."

Chas' smile was large. His head rolled back against the rock, and he labored to get his breath.

"You find that will, Son. I have some good hands, and I want them taken care of.

"I'd like them to stay on for the winter. You tell them that. I won't have a rider put out this time of year with no job. And tell Clare I'm sorry I won't be able to meet that little one inside her. You tell her I love her since I won't be able to tell her myself." He gripped Spur's hand again and his eyes were intense even through the pain.

"I'm sorry, Son. I'm sorry for not being the father I should have been." Chas' body relaxed and his final breath eased out of him.

Spur rocked back on his feet. He stared at the old man's quiet body in front of him a moment. Then he pulled Chas toward him. His breath caught and his body shook with the sobs he wouldn't release as he hugged the lifeless body of his father.

"Durn it, Pop. I wish we'd had a little more time to talk," he whispered. "You couldn't find me, and I didn't know you existed. Too bad the Good Lord didn't hook us up sooner."

Spur held Chas' lifeless body until his own stopped shaking. He gently leaned his father against the rock.

"I'd better get you back to the ranch, Pop. Another hour and I won't be able to find my way."

The hands were riding in when Spur came up the trail leading Chas' horse. They stopped what they were doing and gathered in a loose group as they waited for Spur to arrive.

Spur pulled his horse to a stop and faced the quiet cluster of cowboys.

"Your boss scared out a lion. It spooked his horse and his mount went over on him. I found his horse a couple of hours south of here, down the valley a ways. I backtracked it and found Chas.

"I know it's cold and the ground will be hard, but maybe a couple of you can dig a hole." He turned Hell Fire toward the house but stopped after a few feet.

"Chas left a will and I'm supposed to find it. He said he wanted all you boys to stay on for the winter if you wanted." Spur studied their faces and his voice caught as he added, "I didn't know your boss well, but he seemed like a heck of a man."

Two of the cowboys lifted Chas from the back of his horse and they all turned toward the barn. Eight men with shovels and picks headed up the hill to the little cemetery where Chas' wife was buried.

The first two men wrapped Chas' body in a blanket. They gathered their tools and began to build a coffin. New wood had been hauled in a month before to replace some old boards in one of the stalls and the men used that. Caine was the younger of the two cowboys and he began to talk.

"Reckon I'll move on once the weather breaks in the spring. I liked old Chas an' I doubt I'll like another boss near as much. Never had one treat me like Chas did." The other rider was quiet and Caine continued.

"Nudge said the boss told 'im he was goin' to offer the place to Rock next spring. He said he'd ask that we all be kept on. That ain't gonna happen so who knows what now. Some durn relative will probably get it all.

"And if they want to sell, I doubt Miz Beckler 'ill want to take on any debt. She seems like a cautious woman when it comes to spendin' money." He paused and waited for the man working with him to talk.

"Durn it, Jake. Why cain't you talk more? I just have to listen to myself blabber on all the time."

He growled a little longer. Soon both men were quiet as they measured and sawed. Finally, Jake looked up at his partner.

"Caine, we don't have to worry 'bout nothin' till spring. Spur said we had a place through the winter, so I reckon we do. He seems to be a man of his word, an' the boss fer shore was.

"Come spring though, I might head back south. I been thinkin' on warm weather an' dirty rivers. I miss the Brazos. I jist might go home."

Caine grinned at his partner.

"I reckon I'll go along with ya, Jake. Ya talked once of yore little sister. She'd be 'bout seventeen now. Mebbie I'll settle in close to y'all an' do a little sparkin'."

Jake glared at his friend and muttered under his breath. Caine elbowed him and they both laughed.

The two men worked together while Caine talked, and they soon had the coffin finished. They gently laid their boss' body in it and nailed the lid on.

CHAPTER 26

A FINE MAN

SPUR ENTERED CHAS' HOUSE AND STOPPED IN THE doorway. The house was huge, and the large kitchen showed a woman's touch. The hand pump attached to the counter caught Spur's eye. He stared at it a moment and shook his head. "This kitchen doesn't look like it has been used for some time, but it sure has some conveniences a fellow doesn't see everywhere.

"I'm guessing you ate with your men, Chas," Spur commented as he looked around.

The big house was dusty but neat and tidy. Spur wiped his boots on the rug in front of the door. He tiptoed to a closed door he hoped led to the office.

The room held a large rolltop desk with a chair pushed up to it. The desk was worn and crumbles of dried mud lay under it. A bookcase packed full of books was across the room. The cot by the door was made precisely, almost military style. A large chair and small table sat between the cot and the desk. An old Bible lay on the table beside an oil lamp. There was a white doily under the lamp. The office was simple, efficient, and tidy.

Stacks of papers were piled neatly on the desk. Spur sifted through them. Beneath the second pile was a large envelope that read, "Last Will and Testament of Chas Boswell."

Spur lifted up the envelope and held it a moment. He frowned.

"I almost feel like I am sneaking around, digging through a man's private papers."

He heard a voice and stepped back to look through the doorway. A young man stood there. He had curly, blond hair and a large smile. He wiped his feet and tromped through the kitchen to the open office door. His smile became bigger as he put out his hand.

"Nudge Fuller, Chas' foreman. You must be Spur. The boss said he was going to be talking to you tonight." The smile left his face, and he shook his head.

"I told him last night not to help today. I could feel the snow coming, and I wanted him to stay home. Durned old man was already gone when the rest of us woke up. He was a tough man who refused to accept the fact that he was old." Nudge paused a moment and then added cautiously, "The boys said we are to be kept on through the winter."

Spur nodded. He held up the large envelope.

"We talked a little before he died, and he told me to find his will. I want to talk to your men once we get him buried. I'd better read through this quick to make sure I didn't get anything wrong during our visit." He gestured around the house.

"Nice big house."

"Yeah, but the boss only used this room. He took his meals with the men. Oh, he made a little coffee now and again, but that's about it. Once his missus passed, he just didn't go into the rest of the house. Shame too 'cause she's a beauty. He just finished building it about a year before Agnes died.

"She was from down south somewhere. I think they met around New Orleans. Her pop wasn't excited about her moving up here. Agnes had made up her mind though. Not sure when her ma passed. As long as the boss knew them, it was just Agnes and her pa.

"She was a real southern lady. Liked things nice and Chas wanted her to be happy. They were too. They were married about five years before Agnes became pregnant. I don't know what went wrong but she started bleeding one evening. She lost the baby and almost died too. It took some time, but she finally pulled out of it. They never did have any more kids though. She died about fifteen years ago.

"'Course all that happened before I signed on. He never talked about any of that with me. Cookie was the one who filled me in." Nudge gestured toward the large, curved stairway that led upstairs.

"I've never been up there or even to the back of the house, but it reminds me of one of those old southern mansions down Georgia way. I was raised down there, and this house looks a lot like some of the houses that were around us." His blue eyes sparkled and he grinned again.

"Not my house. My pa was a cowboy. He broke horses and ran a few cattle. Our house wasn't bad, but it was a shack compared to this." He jabbed his thumb toward the barn where the men were gathered.

"Chas was a good man. He treated us cowboys well. Kind of spoiled us if you want to know the truth. I have only been here two years. I was hoping this would be my last stop. Guess it won't be now." He was quiet as he looked up at Spur.

"Not sure how many riders will stay on now that Chas is gone, so you'd better ask if you are wanting them to."

Spur slowly nodded and pointed at the will.

"Let me read this and then I'll be out." He looked toward the cook shack. "Think your cook will stay on?"

"Most likely. He doesn't like to get out in the snow, so he for sure won't be leaving until spring. He's been here the longest. He started here with Chas as a cowboy, left awhile, and came back as a cook. He's cooked here fifteen, maybe even twenty years."

Nudge turned to leave. He waved his hand and spoke over his shoulder. "I'll tell the men you'll be out in a bit."

CHAPTER 27

THE GIFT

THE SNOW HAD STARTED AGAIN BY THE TIME THEY laid Chas down. One of the hands was a fine Irish tenor and he offered to sing "The Bonnie Banks O' Loch Lomond."

"The boss always liked that song. Said his family was from Scotland. I reckon that's the song we should sing," Ladder commented.

Spur could feel his chest tighten as the cowboy's voice lifted across the small valley. *That song is beautiful, but today it is even more melancholy.* Slowly he smiled. *Maybe that was the Lord's way of telling me I had a pa who was looking for me. I reckon that song will always make my heart hurt a little and make me happy at the same time.*

The ground had a second blanket of snow by the time they filled the dirt in. Chas was laid beside his wife, and the frozen dirt was soon white. They all turned away from the little hill and headed back down to the buildings.

Nudge fell in step beside Spur.

"I told the men to gather in the barn. I figured we'd be out of the weather that way." He looked out into the hills before he looked back at Spur.

"You might want to spend the night. This snow doesn't look like it is going to let up before morning."

"I appreciate that offer. I probably will do that even though I'd like to get home. Clare will worry, but I can't change the weather."

They trudged through the snow and stepped into the shelter of the barn. Spur was glad to see that someone had brought Hell Fire in and unsaddled him. The horse was eating hay and grain in one of the stalls.

Spur turned to face the men.

"Boys, I was with your boss when he passed, and he asked me to share what he had in his will with you." He looked over at Nudge.

"How many head of cattle do you reckon Chas has here right now?"

Nudge scratched his head.

"I'd say about twenty-five hundred. Closer to three thousand counting the calves that are on the ground. Plus or minus a few but that should be close."

Spur nodded.

"That's about how many Chas thought there would be when he wrote out this will.

"Fellas, your boss just gave each of you a hundred head of cattle. You are all to share and share alike when they are sold next year."

The men quit shuffling their feet and stared at Spur in surprise. They looked from one to the other and then watched Spur skeptically as he continued.

"Now if some of you decide to leave before the herd is gathered and sold, you forfeit your share. You will still get your winter wages but not your percentage of the herd." He looked over at the old cook who was leaning against the open door to the barn.

"Cookie, he gave you the same cut for putting up with all these fellows' complaining over the years. Again, you will get your share after they are gathered and sold." The cook's face tightened, and the man looked away.

"Putting today's market price on those cattle, you boys should each walk away next summer with an extra $3000, maybe more in your pockets." Spur stared out at the stunned cowboys.

"Your boss didn't have any family to speak of. His only love was this ranch and that woman we buried him next to. He thought enough of each of you though to give you a little nest egg, a start to get your own place." Spur's face was serious as he spoke and his eyes watered just a little.

"I have cowboyed a lot of years, and I have never seen this done. Maybe there were some cowmen out there who would have liked to have done it and couldn't. I don't know. I do know that I've never heard of it being done before.

"And if I were you, I'd put that money in a bank and not talk about it. Then have it wired to where you put down roots. Too much temptation to blow it or get it stolen if you keep it on you." He grinned at them and added, "Not to mention lots of broke friends looking for free beer or a loan." Spur chuckled as he watched the men's faces.

"Anybody have any questions?"

The men stared from Spur to one another in shock. Nudge's face turned pale.

"You reckon that will hold up legally? I sure don't want to be accused of stealing my dead boss' cattle."

"It's all done up legal. That lawyer down in Stevensville, Baggs, he signed it. It's official all right." He looked toward the little cemetery.

"I reckon ol' Chas wasn't a dummy. He knew you fellers would stay on after he passed if you held an interest here. Still, not many men would gift a herd of cattle to his drovers. I reckon Chas thought a lot of you boys."

Spur cleared his throat and added, "Chas gifted his land to Clare and me. I guess that makes me your boss." He looked from man to man and added, "I'll keep on as a hand any of you who decide to stay after the cattle are sold. If you want to leave, I'll understand that too.

"I'm going to spend the night since this snow is coming down heavier. I'll see you in the morning." Spur turned toward the house. He paused to look back at the quiet men.

"And thanks to whoever put my horse up for me. Hell Fire would have taken his poor treatment out on me tomorrow." He grinned at them and plodded through the snow to the house.

"Sure wish I could let Clare know I'm all right. I know she'll worry," Spur muttered to himself. A lamp was by the door and he lit it. He pulled off his boots and paused as he looked toward the back of the house.

"I think I'll wait to look around. I'm excited to show Clare this house. Shoot, she might like it so much she will want to move down here. I think she'd appreciate having water in the kitchen not to mention all the extra room."

There was plenty of wood by the fireplace and Spur lit a fire. He grabbed a packet of papers that had been with Chas' will and sat down to read. He grinned as the heat warmed his feet.

"A man could get used to this. Just sit around in the house and give orders." He chuckled and opened the pack of papers.

CHAPTER 28

CHAS' SECRET

THE PAPERS CONTAINED LETTERS AND LEGAL documents. Spur glanced at them and pulled the lamp closer to study them. His face drew down in a frown as he flipped through the battered envelopes.

Several were from New Orleans. They appeared to be old as the envelopes were yellowed and brittle. There were two in the same handwriting. The shape of the handwriting was large and dramatic, so he assumed they were from the same woman.

Spur looked around and frowned again.

"Pop, I feel like I am snooping through your life. I apologize for that. And if I find something that might smear your reputation…well, that secret will stay right here."

He pulled open the first letter and began to read.

April 12, 1850

Charlie,

I wanted to let you know that you have a son. He was born just three days ago. He has a birthmark on his wrist that looks like yours, and we both know where that one is. I haven't decided what to call him. If you don't claim him, I am going to give him a last name I found in a book. Or maybe I won't even give him a name. I'll just call him, "Déranger." That is French for bother, because that is what he is. None of the women who work for me know my true last name, and I intend to keep it that way.

If you want your son, send me $5000. When I receive the money, I will tell you where to find him. And you had better pay. I certainly don't need a bratty little boy running around here, messing up my life.

You know where to mail the money, and we both know you can afford it.

MB

Spur could feel his face heating up and he cursed at he stared at the letter again.

"Madam Bella, I knew you didn't want me but, I never knew how much you despised me."

A large envelope held a certificate of birth. It showed that a male child was born. The date was April 9, 1850. No parent or baby's name was listed, nor was there any address.

The next letter was in the same handwriting and the woman was angry.

September 24, 1850

I despise you, Charlie. I was sure you were too much of a gentleman to abandon your own kin. I guess you and I are more alike than you want to admit.

I refused to feed your son after he was born. I left him outside to freeze, but one of the girls here brought him in. I guess she couldn't stand his screaming. She has been nursing him. Silly woman birthed *a child and it died. She has been carrying on for days. Well, she can have this one. I tried to get rid of him before he was born. The potion I was given made me sick though and I threw it up.*

Say goodbye to your son, Charlie. You will never know him, and he will never know what it's like to be loved.

MB

Spur stared at the letter. He almost dropped it in the fire. Instead, he slowly laid it back on the pile. His chest was tight as he stared at it.

He remembered all the nights he had cried himself to sleep as a small child. He had just wanted someone to hug him and tuck him in at night. No one ever came. He cried until Madam Bella came and yelled at him.

"You were a mean-spirited woman, Maebeline. You didn't deserve a child. I am mighty thankful Sister Eddie came along."

The next stack of correspondence was dated 1865. Spur studied the date.

"I was fifteen by then. I was living in Texas and working on the Wagner Ranch. Life was getting better. I had met Gabe and we were pards."

Spur looked at the date on the first letter and frowned.

"Looking at that date, you must have met Agnes shortly after your tryst in New Orleans. No, I don't suppose you wanted Agnes's father or your new wife to know you already had a child—and with a painted lady at that."

The next paper Spur pulled out was Chas and Agnes's marriage certificate.

"May 21, 1850. Yep, you were a new husband when that first letter came. It probably took a couple of months for that letter to get up here. I'm guessing that was a shock." Spur shook his head.

The rest of the papers were receipts and letters from a private detective in 1870. The man had no luck finding Chas' son. After that, there was no more correspondence.

Spur started to stack the materials up and a letter fell out of the pile. It was not addressed or sealed. He opened it and stared at the words Chas had written. His handwriting was neat and precise even for an old man.

Son, I am an old man now. I let you down and I'm sorry. I should have come to get you as soon as I found out you were born. I was a chicken, and I have spent my whole life trying to make up for those early mistakes.

I decided to write you this letter even though you will never read it. There are some things I just needed to say.

I was forty years old when I met your mother. Ah, but she was a beauty. I had never seen a woman so handsome. She had the brightest eyes, and her black hair was thick and curly. She had a captivating smile that just drew a man in.

It was August of 1849. I had panned a little gold the winter before and had some money in my pocket. I had spent the previous winter sleeping in a cave up here in this valley not far from where I live now.

I traveled down to New Orleans that summer. My sister lived there, and I hadn't seen her since I'd left home at fifteen. I knew it was a mistake to go to that sporting house, but I told myself I deserved a little fun. I had worked hard and now it was time to play.

Maebeline was your mother's name. Her family was French. She told me that her mother named her Maebeline because it means goddess. She was a goddess too. She was a beautiful, intriguing woman. She could be as hard and cold as stone one minute and as tender as a kitten the next. I spent every night with her for three weeks. I thought I was in love.

Like the fool I was, I told her that I had found gold up here. I struck a little pocket right at the end of the winter. $5000 in gold was a lot of money back then. Shoot, it still is. I was carrying it in a money bag around my waist.

One evening when I arrived, one of the girls who worked at that sporting house met me outside. She told me that Maebeline was planning to kill me for my money. Maebeline said she had worked hard the last three weeks to get me to hand it over, and she was done waiting. Oh, I'd paid her for every night, but I

158

paid her the going fee-nothing more. That girl told me Maebeline was going to poison me.

I couldn't believe it, but the girl was almost crying. She begged me to leave. She said, "Chas, find yourself a nice girl and don't come back here. You are too fine of a man to be caught in Maebeline's web of evil."

It broke my heart but I left and never went back. I caught a riverboat on the Mississippi the next morning and rode it north. That's when I met my Agnes.

Agnes was every bit as beautiful as Maebeline, but where Maebeline was dark and seductive, Agnes was bright like sunshine. Talking with her made me feel like I had broken free from a spell.

We were on that boat together for over a month and we fell in love. Her father was headed to St. Louis. He was a trader and was planning to open a store there. We parted ways not too far south of St. Louis. The day before I left, I asked Agnes to marry me. She said yes and we agreed to meet at Fort Union on May 15 of the next year. That would have been 1850.

Fort Union wasn't really a fort. It was more of trading spot at the mouth of the Yellowstone River in the North Country. It was two thousand miles from St. Louis and was the most important rendezvous point in the West at that time.

Agnes's pa wasn't happy about her decision. He thought I was a rambler, and he didn't want his daughter marrying a poor cowboy. At first, he refused to take her with him. He said, "That cowboy was just blowing. He won't be there. He will have moved on with another woman by the time we get up there." Agnes was a persistent woman though and he finally gave in.

Looking back, I can't believe it all worked out. It did though. I arrived at Fort Union on May 10. I was so afraid Agnes wouldn't come. She and her father arrived on May 20. Waiting there for her were the longest ten days of my life.

We were married the next day, I had already been a daddy for over a month, but I didn't know it. Maebeline mailed her first letter in April, but I didn't receive it until June. I sent her one back denying that you were my son. Her second letter arrived in December.

I showed that one to Agnes and we both cried. I was so ashamed. Ashamed for what I had done and ashamed for not taking responsibility. Agnes forgave me and we began to search for you. We wrote letters to everyone we knew there. Some folks wrote us back and others didn't. I never heard from Maebeline again, and we never found you.

After we lost our little girl, it was even harder. I wanted to throw those letters away, but Agnes wouldn't let me. She was convinced that someday we would find you.

Now I am an old man. If you are alive, you would be nearly thirty years old. I will never know you, and the chances of you reading this letter—well, they don't exist.

I wrote this letter because I want you to know that I love you and that I am sorry. If I could go back, I certainly would make that long trip to get you.

Maybe, when you hear "The Bonnie Banks O' Loch Lomond," you will sit a little straighter and listen a little harder. I often sang that song to your mother. My family was Scottish, and I have always loved to sing.

Mae liked music and she loved it when I sang. In her gentle moments, she would tell me I was her Scottish Highlander.

The little gal who warned me away so many years before wrote me in '57. She said your name was George. She said you had been taken in by an old nun. She couldn't remember your last name or the nun's name. The letter came from San Antonio down Texas way. She said she was dying when she wrote it.

It took four months for her letter to get up here. It was beaten and battered when it arrived. We wrote her back, but we never heard from her again. I'm guessing she died before it arrived. Her letter finally fell apart and I had to throw it away.

So, Son, I will never know you. I'm not even sure that George is your actual name. But if by chance someone shares this story with you, know that I love you. I only wish that we had met. Mostly, I wish I could go back through the years and make things right for you.

Your Scottish Highlander Pa, Chas Boswell
You take the high road because I surely did take the low road.

160

Spur's hands shook when he finished reading the letter. He stared at the yellowed paper and rubbed his hand roughly across his face. He leaned back in the chair and smiled.

"We did meet, Pop. I'm proud to know you were my pa. I'll share this story with Clare, but I won't tell anyone else.

"The folks around Stevensville think mighty highly of you, and I don't want to put even a smudge on your good name. Just knowing you were my pa is good enough for me."

Spur closed his eyes. When he awoke, the fire was out, and the sun was rising in the east. He rose stiffly and gathered the papers together.

"I'll take these home with me so I can show Clare."

CHAPTER 29

THE BOSS HAS A SON

THE SUN WAS BARELY UP WHEN SPUR STEPPED INTO the bunkhouse.

"I'm headed home. Nudge, just keep doing what Chas told you to do. I'll plan to come back over tomorrow. Maybe you can show me around." He glanced around the bunkhouse and added, "There were still a few cattle down on that burned ground and they should be moved south." He nodded at the men. "I'll see you boys tomorrow."

As the door closed, one of the riders groaned.

"Another boss who likes to be up at the buttcrack of daylight. Why can't we find us a boss who likes to sleep in?"

There was more grumbling. As they all began to dress, one of the older riders asked quietly, "Any of you fellers notice how much Spur looks like that old picture of the boss hangin' in the sittin' room of that big house?"

The cowboys all turned around to stare and the man nodded. "I was in that sittin' room one time. The boss wanted me to give his missus a message. I knocked on the door an' Miz Agnes told me to come in.

"It took me some time to get my boots off. I was almost afraid to go any further, but Miz Agnes was jist real friendly.

"She saw me a lookin' at that picture an' she smiled. She said it was taken by a travelin' picture feller the day a their weddin'. The boss had a mustache just like Spurs. His eyes was blue but they are related fer sure. Even stand an' walk alike."

The men were quiet for a moment before another rider commented quietly, "I heard the boss had a son. There was a feller come through here one time shortly after the missus died. Said he had some information about that. He was kind of a shady-lookin' feller an' he didn't stay long."

The men all looked over at Nudge.

"Reckon we can go in the house an' look that picture over? Might behoove us to know if our new boss is family." Caine's question reflected what most of the riders were thinking.

Nudge stared at the men. He was almost irritated. He knew if he didn't allow it though, they would all sneak in at one time or another.

"We'll all go in. Boots are left at the door, and no one goes but where I lead. We'll look and then we'll come out. And we'll never go in again without an invitation. Agreed?"

The men nodded somberly, and the group was soon headed for the big house. Cookie came out of his kitchen and stared at them. He cursed once and then hollered, "When ya durn snoops git done lookin', breakfast is ready." He turned away still muttering.

"Reckon they're all curious if Spur might be the boss' son. Well, he is. I knowed that when Spur showed up here yesterday. The boss ain't worn a mustache since his early years on this place, but he used to. I worked here then fer a time too, an' they look jist alike. An' if the boss had met him 'fore today, he'd a known too.

"The boss spent lots a time an' money tryin' to track his son down. Now here that boy is an' the boss is dead."

"Well, I'm glad the two of 'em had themselves a talk 'fore he died. Guess they got that all figgered out. That means ol' Chas died happy." He smiled and walked back into his kitchen. His face changed as he looked around. He cursed long and loud.

"I don't know that I cin work here if Miz Clare moves in. I doubt she'll like my rough ways much. She's a re-fined lady, an' I'm a guessin' she ain't used to rough men."

He stomped to the door of his kitchen and jerked it open. A quiet line of men was just leaving the house.

"Well? Git it all figgered out? I could a told ya the answer without ya snoopin' 'round.

"An' now ya shut yore traps. It's Spur's job to let folks know. If he don't tell, we don't neither. We ride fer the brand." He glared around at the men. His eyes focused on Nudge. "This here deal ain't spoke of after today." The cook was holding his large rolling pin, and no one dared to disagree.

"Let's eat then."

CHAPTER 30

A Different Response

THE RANCH YARD WAS QUIET WHEN SPUR ARRIVED home. It was still early but he could tell the men were gone. He dropped Hell Fire's reins in front of the door and poked his head inside the house.

"I'm home, Darlin'!"

Clare was coming out of her bedroom, and she started to rush toward him. She slowed and smoothed her dress as she smiled.

Spur opened his arms. "Come on, Darlin'. Give me the greeting you almost did."

Clare paused a moment before she rushed toward Spur. She let him wrap her up as she struggled not to cry.

"I was so afraid," she whispered. "I just knew you were lost in the snow."

Spur hugged her a little tighter. He led her to a chair and pulled her onto his lap. He smiled down at her for a moment. His dark eyes became somber as he studied her. He slowly nodded.

"It was a rough day." A rush of emotions washed over Spur's face and his voice broke as he spoke.

"Chas is dead. His horse spooked at a lion and threw him. He landed on the stump of a burned-out tree." His stared at her a moment before he pulled her tightly against him.

"He loved you and the kids. He wanted you to know that."

Clare's blue eyes filled with tears as she stared up at Spur.

"He was such a kind man. The children loved to go there, and he seemed to enjoy them."

Spur hugged her tighter. "He gave us his land," he said simply. "He said he had no heirs. He was going to leave it to Rock, but after Rock died, he left it to us." Spur's eyes were red as he added, "We talked a while and…well…Chas is my pop."

Clare's eyes opened wide in surprise.

"Chas? How did—What? Are you sure?"

Spur chuckled as he turned over his wrist.

"That durn birthmark got me in more fights over the years than you'll ever know. Chas put things together when we talked. Once he saw the birthmark, he figured it out." Spur's face showed the happiness he felt.

"I have a pop, Clare. I know who my pa is!"

Clare smiled as she stared into Spur's excited face. She laughed quietly and kissed his cheek.

"Oh, Spur. I am so happy for you."

Spur hugged her again before he leaned back in his chair.

"We have some decisions to make. I'd like you to go over with me tomorrow to look at the house. I think you might want to live there. Chas built it for Agnes about a year before she died. It is two stories and has plenty of bedrooms. There would be more room for the kids to play and sleep, plus more conveniences for you.

"It is closer to the valley floor too. It would be about the same miles to town, but they would be easier ones." His smile became larger, "And it has a pump in the kitchen! No more hauling water in."

Clare stood up. Her breath was coming quickly, and she shook her head.

"No. I don't want to leave here. Rock is here. This is where I want to stay."

The smile left Spur's face and he slowly stood.

"Whatever you want." His voice was strained. As he turned quietly toward the door, he looked back at her.

"I am going to have to stay over there some. Nudge doesn't have much experience as foreman. He needs someone to give him a little guidance." His eyes were sad as he added, "I had hoped for a different response."

Clare didn't look up. She was gripping the table tightly and her breath was coming in short spurts. She felt the wind rush in as Spur opened the door. When it closed, he was gone.

She sank down onto a chair and sobbed.

"I was so afraid when you didn't come home yesterday, Spur. And today, I broke your heart."

The bedroom door opened, and Clare heard Nora's voice.

"Are you crying, Mama? Don't cry. Jesus promised to send Spur home."

Clare turned toward Nora in surprise. She laughed as she wiped her face.

"He was right because Spur is home." She picked up Nora and hugged her. "I love you, Nora. You are so precious," Clare whispered.

Nora's brown eyes shown with excitement.

"Should we make him a cake, Mama? Spur told me he *loves* chocolate cake with chocolate frosting. He likes to clean out the frosting bowl."

Clare laughed again and wiped her eyes one more time.

"We will do that, Nora. You eat your breakfast. When you are finished, we will make Spur a chocolate cake."

CHAPTER 31

A Bowl of Frosting

SPUR WAS QUIET WHEN HE CAME IN FOR DINNER, BUT the children were not. They rushed him and drug him to the table.

Annie and Zeke pulled him to his chair and Nora pushed on him until he sat down.

"We made you a cake, Spur! I told Mama you liked chocolate cake, and we even saved the frosting bowl for you!"

Spur looked at them in surprise. He glanced over at Clare and his face broke into a grin.

"A whole bowl of frosting? Who all is going to help me eat it?"

Three little voices created a loud chorus of "I will!" and Spur laughed.

"Well, that would take too many spoons. We should probably just use our fingers." He dipped his finger into the chocolate frosting and rolled his eyes. Soon, two little bodies were sitting on top of the table, and one was on his lap. They talked excitedly as they dipped their fingers into the frosting bowl.

"You know, there is a lot of frosting in this bowl. I am wondering if there is any on that cake at all." Spur had frosting stuck in his mustache and Clare laughed.

"I admit I did make a little extra after Nora told me you liked to clean out frosting bowls."

Spur looked up at Clare and commented quietly, "I believe I told Nora I would *like* to clean out a frosting bowl. I never had until today." He winked at Clare and stuck his finger back in the bowl.

The bowl was nearly empty when Spur leaned back in his chair. He smiled.

"We had better wash our hands. I'm thinking we might have already broken some rules by letting you sit on the table.

"Once you're done, go outside and grab those shovels. Scoop a path between the house and the chicken coop as well as another to the barn. I don't want your mother to get snow in her shoes."

Clare waited until the children were outside before she sat down at the table.

"Spur, I—"

"No, Clare. I was pushing too hard. You aren't ready to move on and you need time. Sometimes I forget that.

"I am going to go to Chas' tomorrow. I'll spend at least three days there, probably four. I'll be home by Saturday for sure so we can go to church on Sunday if the weather permits.

"I'll pack some things this evening and plan to leave first thing in the morning." His voice was quiet as he added, "I think me being here every day is making it hard on both of us. Me because I want more, and you because you want Rock." His eyes were sad as he looked at her and Clare's breath caught in her chest.

"I need to get back outside so I will just eat with the men." He pushed back from the table abruptly and strode to the door. His hand was on the latch when he looked back at her.

"Thank you for the bowl of frosting. That was fun and tasty too."

"Please, Spur. Come back and eat. I have it ready. You don't have to wait for the children. I fixed food I knew you would like. Please sit down." Clare's blue eyes were large as she watched him.

Spur turned around slowly and came back to the table. He looked long at her before he sat down.

"Clare, when we made this deal, my biggest concern was that we might hate each other within a month. Instead, I have fallen tail over teakettle in love with you. Because of that, my heart hurts when you push me away.

"I can't take that every day. I need to put some distance between us so I can breathe normal again. When you move around the kitchen—when you laugh or rub your stomach and smile, I want to hold you. I want to be part of what makes you happy.

"And I'm not part of that. I only make you happy when I play with the kids.

"Now we have a deal and I'll be back. For now, I think some distance between us would be good."

Clare nodded slowly and a sob caught in her throat.

"You will come back?"

"See? This is what I can't take! Five minutes ago, you didn't want me here."

Clare's lip trembled and Spur squeezed her hand as he winked at her.

"Of course, if you miss me too much, come on over. I'll always be glad to see you." He let go of her hand and ate without talking. When he was finished, he leaned back in his chair and rubbed his stomach.

"That was mighty tasty, Clare. I am working in the barn if you want to bring some of your cake out later. We are making a couple of those stalls a little smaller. If the rest of the men get back before dark, we are going to build a hay lift to take hay up and down from the loft."

He pulled on his hat and was quickly gone. Clare watched as he stopped to talk to the children. Soon, they were all in a snowball fight. Some of the hands joined in and the children were shrieking with excitement.

Clare laughed and shook her head. "You are a mess, Spur. You are growing on me and that terrifies me. Now you are leaving, and I will miss you terribly."

CHAPTER 32

SLEIGH BELLS

IT SNOWED MOST OF THE WEEK. SATURDAY AFTERNOON, Clare shooed the children outside.

"Go watch for Spur. He is coming home today." She wasn't sure when Spur was going to arrive, but the children were convinced it would be soon. They raced outside and ran sliding down the trail, tumbling in snowdrifts as they ran. Clare rubbed her back.

"Oh, for a nap. Maybe I will lie down for a bit." She was just turning toward the bedroom when she heard the sound of bells.

She frowned and hurried to the kitchen window. A sleigh was pulling into the yard. All three children were in it along with a grinning Spur. Two large horses were hitched to it, and Spur drove them up to the house.

"Anyone in there want a sleigh ride?" he hollered. He looked back at the kids. "You kids climb out and let me talk to your mother alone."

Clare grabbed her cloak and hurried to the door. Spur jumped down to help her in. She looked around at the sleigh before she commented carefully, "I thought you were going to order a buggy."

"I did. This one came with sleigh attachments. Ike and I put them on at the livery. A buggy in nice weather and a sleigh in the snow." He reached up with his whip and tapped the bells over the backs of each horse. "And bells just because." He grinned at her and swung the team around.

"You surely aren't going to leave those bells on tomorrow for church."

"Why, I reckon I am. And everyone will say, 'Here comes Mrs. Spurlock with her wild family. I hope they behave at Mass today.'" Spur's voice was high as he spoke, and Clare stared at him.

He bumped her with his shoulder and grinned.

"Miss me?"

Clare tried hard not to laugh. She shivered as she giggled, and Spur pointed at a blanket across his lap.

"If you scoot over closer, I'll share my blanket with you. Otherwise, you can just sit there and shiver. Your choice."

She slowly slid over a little and Spur moved part of the blanket. "You give a little, I give a little," he commented with a grin.

Clare's face slowly turned red, and she slid her bottom next to his.

He draped most of the blanket over her with a chuckle.

"Now isn't that better? A warm man and a warm blanket." He leaned over and whispered, "And if you'd let me share your bed, you'd be warm at night too."

"George Spurlach! You are a bold man." She moved away from him to the outside of the sleigh and Spur pulled the blanket back across his legs.

"A deal is a deal. Life is full of wonderful choices," he commented with a grin.

Clare glared at him and faced forward. She pulled her shawl closer. When her teeth began to chatter, Spur relented and tossed her the blanket.

She immediately stopped shivering and laughed.

"Two can play that game, and now I have the blanket."

Spur laughed out loud and waved his whip.

"What do you think? Smooth riding, isn't it? Much better than a wagon. Maybe we should take the long way home from church. You can see Chas' house from the valley if you look up in the right place.

"I rode around with Nudge these past three days and looked the cattle over. He has enough winter graze that we are going to move some of our cows over there. I might even add a few more gates between us."

Clare was quiet a moment before she asked, "Did you bunk with the men?"

Spur grinned at her and shook his head.

"Nope. Had a nice soft bed and it felt good. I tried every bed in the house until I found the one I liked. Kind of like that little girl and the three bears. What was her name—Curlylocks or something?"

Clare laughed. "Goldilocks and the Three Bears. So which bed did you pick? One upstairs or down?"

Spur grinned at her.

"Why I reckon you will have to come visit to find that out. That's kind of a personal question to ask a man you aren't sharing a bed with, isn't it?"

Clare sputtered and her flushed cheeks turned redder.

"I declare, Spur. You are so bold."

Spur chuckled. He looked at Clare seriously.

"Maybe a little, but mostly, I'm just lonesome. I missed all of you. I sure hope you will move down there with me."

He turned the sleigh around and headed back home.

"Ike just got these horses in. I didn't know if you wanted to buy them or if you wanted to use the mules we already have. The horses will eat more but they will move faster. Your call."

Clare was quiet and Spur put out his arm.

"Come on over here, Clare. My right side is freezing. It needs a warm woman."

She eyed him suspiciously but finally slid over just a little.

He whispered, "If I promise to behave, will you come closer?"

Clare laughed out loud. "Spur, you are impossible." She slid closer and took his arm. "Is that better?"

He patted her hand as he grinned, and he kept his hand over hers. "I don't know that it could be better. Now tell me what you did while I was gone."

CHAPTER 33

STUB'S STORIES

SPUR TOOK THE SLED DOWN TO STEVENSVILLE WHEN he left Monday morning. Ike was going to put the wheels back on if it warmed up, and Spur would pick it up on Saturday.

The weather broke and the sun shined all week. Clare found herself watching the trail for Spur more every day.

She rarely walked up the hill to visit Rock's grave. She preferred to go to the little lilac cove and sit on the bench. There she felt his presence. Her days were too busy to go every day though. She had started teaching the children, and their classes took most of the morning.

Spur had given half the hands the following weekend off before he left on Monday. They had been driving cattle to the mining camps all week, and the men were ready for a break.

Stub refused to be gone all weekend. A couple of hours in town were enough for him.

"I'll take Tuff down this afternoon. That boy is outgrowing everything he owns. And he can't borrow any britches from me because his legs are longer than mine already," Stub complained good-naturedly to Clare as he picked up her list. "You want to send the kids along? I can drop them off at Maggie's if you'd like."

"Are you sure you don't want to come along? It would do you good to get out and Maggie would enjoy the visit. Lots of folks come to town on Saturdays you know."

Clare shook her head.

"You take the children. I will go down for church tomorrow with Spur. He should be home before too long." She smiled at Stub and asked, "Why don't you bring the sled runners home with you though? That way, when it snows again, we will have them here.

"And thank you for picking up supplies as well as taking the children. Maggie doesn't need to make this drive so often, and she would. She can only go so long before they have to stay with her."

The noise coming from the wagon was loud. The children called back to Clare as Stub drove down the trail. They were soon clustered around Stub, talking excitedly.

"Tell us one of your stories, Stub. Tell us the one about how Jesse James robbed the train and how those bandits used dynamite to stop the engine."

Stub was usually a quiet man. However, when he was alone with the children, he told them stories. Those stories were so detailed that even the kids thought he must have been there.

"Do you know Jesse James, Stub? Is he your friend?"

Stub was quiet a moment before he answered.

"I've met Jesse James, but I wouldn't say he was my friend. We were never pards, not like your pa and I were.

"Jesse wasn't always a bad man though. He was just a common fellow before the War Between the States. He was from a little town down south of here in Missouri.

"I'd heard of him and his brother, Frank, during the War Between the States. We never actually met until '70 though. That war had been over for five years by then.

"I was kind of bumming around, looking for a place to settle down when I met him. That was in Kansas. He was robbing and stealing by then, and some of the members of his gang were vicious men.

"Jesse invited me to ride with them, but I headed back up here. By that time, he was known as a bad outlaw." He grinned at the kids and added, "Besides, if he had known I was a Blue Belly Yankee, he'd have wanted to hang me. That's because he was a Confederate—a Reb as we called them."

Zeke's eyes were serious as he listened to Stub.

"Were all of the Confederate soldiers bad?"

Stub shook his head.

"No, most of them were good men. We were just on opposite sides of some disagreements. Funny thing was, most soldiers in that war didn't even believe in all the things their governments promoted. Lots of the Rebs I met didn't believe in owning other folks—and some of our own men in the Union army did. It was a mixed-up time.

"Now let's talk about something else—like what you are going to do at Auntie Maggie's or if Grandpa Ike will take you ice fishing. I think I would like to go ice fishing if the ice is thick enough. Maybe Tuff and I will join you." Stub looked behind the wagon. "I think I hear his horse coming now."

CHAPTER 34

TALKING TO ROCK

CLARE WALKED UP THE SMALL HILL TO THE CEMETERY. She looked at Rock's grave in surprise. Someone had planted lilacs there. The blossoms were gone now but they would be back in the spring.

She sank down on her knees and stared at the flowers.

Rock had enclosed the little cemetery with a wooden fence after his first wife died. A stone marker showed where Rock's Suzanna and Darby McCune were buried. Arnica and the other flowers Rock had planted on his wife's grave were spreading. Even though it was now dormant, new growth could be seen on Rock's grave as well.

The wooden cross the men had carved the day Rock was buried was at the top of his grave.

Tears filled Clare's eyes as she knelt there.

"I miss you so much, Rock. I'm angry with you too—and I'm angry with Suzanna as well. I know it's unreasonable to say this, but she has you all to herself. And how does that work once I die?

"I don't understand life after death. Father Ravalli has tried to explain it to me. He said there will be no jealousy or anger in Heaven, but here I feel both." Tears trickled over Clare's cheeks as she looked down the trail. "You left me and now I am alone." She looked back again at Rock's grave.

"Spur should be home any time. He is spending more time at Chas'. This week he left on Monday. It is now Saturday afternoon, and he still isn't home.

"I have pushed him away, Rock. He isn't you, and I don't want anyone but you." A sob slipped out of Clare's throat as she touched the dirt that covered Rock's grave.

Rock's voice sounded clearly in her head and Clare looked up in surprise.

"My beautiful Clare. You know I would have stayed if I could have. I was a blessed man to have loved and been loved by two such wonderful women.

"Don't be angry. Life here is beautiful and Father Ravalli is right. No one is jealous. Every day is perfect." Clare could hear him laugh as he added, "I still take care of cattle, but they never get out or go where they shouldn't. The mama cows never have trouble calving, and they always claim their newborn calves.

"I am in charge of a herd of Angus cattle. Even if I wasn't already in Heaven, I would be because of that job.

"Only the men who enjoy putting up hay help with it. You know I don't help. I always hated pitching hay. I don't help build fence either. Our fences here never need fixed so the fellows who enjoy that job can just keep building new fence.

"I have met some old friends. Dally and Pete are here. Dally has his own herd of Jersey milk cows, and Pete is friends with the head carpenter. His name is Joseph.

"That Joseph is quite the carpenter too. He showed Pete a staircase he built down in Santa Fe in the New Mexico Territory. He built it for some nuns. Pete told me about it. It curves from the floor up to the loft but has no supporting parts. Some fool man designed a church, added a choir loft, and then forgot to allow room for a way to get up there." Rock chuckled but his voice was serious when he continued.

"Those nuns prayed for someone to come and build them a stairway. Joseph showed up but he never told anyone who he was. He just built the stairs and left." Clare could hear the smile in Rock's voice when he added, "I thought you might enjoy that story.

"Please don't be sad, Clare. I pray for all of you every day. I asked the Good Lord to send someone to help you smile. I had no idea that person would be Spur.

"He's a good man though. We can look down on things from up here, even things that have already happened. I was able to see Spur as a child. He had a hard life, but he never lost his sense of humor. Sister Eddie was the best thing that could have happened to him for sure.

"She is up here too, and she is still keeping an eye on him. She is quite the character.

"Every once in a while, I hear her scold him. I guess he hears her too because he looks up and smiles.

"Smile for me, Clare, and smile for our little ones. They need a happy mama. Keep talking to Father Ravalli too. He is a fine priest and a good man to have as a friend.

"And don't be too hard on Spur. He was your friend before you married, and he is still your friend." Rock's voice was soft as he added, "Let me go, Clare. I'm happy here, and I want you to be happy too."

Clare lay down on Rock's grave and sobbed. An eagle called from above. After its voice echoed away, the little cemetery was quiet again. She lay there for a time and listened. Rock never spoke again though. Clare's heart still ached but she felt some of the anger slip away. Joy took its place and she smiled.

"Thank you, Rock. Thank you for talking to me today and for watching over us. I don't think I will ever love another man like I loved you, but I will try to be kinder to Spur. He has been wonderful with the children. And me too. He has a gentle heart under all his teasing.

"He is so bold though. Such a contrast to your shyness." She kissed her fingers and touched the cross on Rock's grave.

"I will always love you, Sweetheart."

She was just walking down the hill when she heard Spur coming. He was singing "Shenandoah" at the top of his lungs and Clare smiled.

"You are a mess, Spur, but I'm glad the Good Lord sent you."

CHAPTER 35

An Evening Ride

SPUR PULLED HIS HORSE TO A STOP WITH A SMILE ON his face.

"Well, hello to the prettiest woman in this territory! Are you ready to go for a ride?"

Clare frowned and Spur chuckled.

"No, you don't need a horse. Just dance yourself right up here on my lap." His eyes sparkled with orneriness as he added, "Or you can put your nightgown on first. I did like that."

Clare's face blushed a deep red as she sputtered, "I declare, Spur! You are a bold man." She started to turn away but paused and turned back.

"Ride where? What do you want to show me?"

He rode Hell Fire over to her and nudged his front leg.

"Down, boy."

The horse dropped onto his knees and Spur put out his hand.

"Come on, Miss Clare. Waltz right up here. I want to show you something you will enjoy."

Clare studied Spur for a moment before she slowly walked toward him. She paused but finally lifted her hand. Spur swung her up in front of him and squeezed her.

"You feel nice and you smell good too," he whispered. His arm touched her stomach, and the baby kicked him. He looked at her in surprise.

"I think that little feller just kicked me!" He spread his large hand over her stomach and the baby kicked again as it slid away.

"I'll be durned. That baby is having a party of its own in there. Does he hurt you when he kicks?"

Clare laughed softly. "Sometimes. If he gets his foot in the right place, he can almost take me down. It must hit a nerve or something. What he did just then didn't hurt though. I like to feel him move inside me. When he is moving, I know everything is all right."

Spur was quiet a moment before he spoke again.

"Do things go wrong very often?"

"I have only had one child and I had no problems." She moved slightly in front of Spur before she continued. "Some women do though. Suzanna died shortly after Annie was born. Rock said she had lost two babies before that." She looked up at Spur. She smiled softly before she looked away.

"He was excited about this baby, but he was afraid too. He said he didn't want to lose another little one, and for sure, not another wife." A sob caught in her chest.

"I miss him so much. I rarely go up to his grave, but I decided to this afternoon." She was quiet a moment. Her voice was soft when she asked, "Do you ever talk to people after they die, Spur? Like you can hear someone's voice so clearly that he or she could be with you?"

Spur slowly nodded. "I hear Sister Eddie's voice a lot. She is really the only dead person I have ever loved that much. Oh, I have lost some folks I cared about over the years, but none I loved like Sister Eddie. I think about Chas some too. We had just met when he died though."

Clare looked up at him again. Tears sparkled in the sides of her eyes.

"Rock talked to me today. He told me he met Sister Eddie. He said she loves you a lot and that she watches over you. Sometimes she even scolds you."

Spur was startled. He stared at Clare and finally chuckled.

"I reckon that's right. I can hear her voice when I step out of line." He pulled Clare closer and whispered, "But she hasn't scolded me much since you came along. I think she likes you."

Clare let him hold her, but she didn't answer.

Spur pulled Hell Fire to a stop. "Look down there. Isn't that about the prettiest thing you have ever seen?"

The Angus cattle were grazing, scattered over a snow-covered valley. The valley was surrounded by ponderosa pines and fir trees. Further up the mountains, the ponderosas changed to lodgepole pine trees. A small creek sparkled at the edge of the valley.

Clare caught her breath. "That is so beautiful. The cattle are little dots of black scattered all over the valley. They look so close. They must be far away as small as they are though."

Spur nodded. "They are almost a mile away. Sure is a pretty sight." He looked down at Clare and grinned, "Almost as pretty as you today, standing there by the hill looking down the trail."

He added mournfully, "I had hoped you were watching for me but no such luck."

Clare elbowed him and he grunted as he chuckled. "At least you went on a ride with me. I have been dreaming about doing this since that first time. You sure looked fine on our wedding morning with the sun shining through your nightgown."

Clare leaned forward and glared back at him.

"Stop it, Spur. You have no muzzle whatsoever. You shouldn't talk like that."

"We are married, so I guess I can if I want." His dark eyes sparkled, and Clare shook her head.

"You are so bold. I am not used to a man who is so bold." She moved her head to get her neck away from his mustache. "And your mustache tickles my neck."

Spur rubbed his face against hers and rubbed his mustache around her neck. Clare was laughing and moving away. She almost fell off and Spur caught her. He pulled her up close to him again, still chuckling.

"This marriage business is more fun than I ever thought it would be. It is nice to come home to a pleasant woman." He wrapped his arms around Clare again and felt her shiver.

"We'd better get you home. You'll freeze to death in that light cloak." He shrugged out of his heavy coat and wrapped it around her. "That better?"

Clare snuggled into the warm coat and relaxed against Spur. She nodded.

"Now I am so warm and cozy I could almost fall asleep." She was quiet for a bit.

When she looked up again, she said softly, "Let's drive by Chas' house after church tomorrow. I want to see what it looks like on the inside. I have been thinking about what you said. It might be nice to have a larger house as well as one not so far up in the mountains."

Spur was quiet. He looked down at her and squeezed her lightly. "I reckon that would be fine. I have been doing a little work around there. Ladder showed me some peonies by one of the fences. Come spring, I am going to move them up closer to the house. They won't bloom until next June but with them and the lilacs, it will smell mighty nice around there come summer." He looked toward the southeast and added, "The ranch headquarters are closer to the center of our operation now too.

"Old Chas put some time into planning and building that house. He laid up a lot of clay and rock for the chimney and foundation. He built his house on top of that. The woodwork inside could use some polish, but it was smooth at one time. A big, curved staircase leads upstairs. Five bedrooms up there. Big ones too.

"His house reminds me of some of the houses down in New Orleans when I was small. I roamed the streets quite a bit before Sister Eddie took charge of me. I used to sneak into those big old houses and wander around. I wanted to see how those folks lived.

"The only house I had ever been in that big was Lady Bella's House of Entertainment. She never opened the windows though and I thought it smelled bad." He grinned at Clare. "She always had some kind of incense burning. She thought it made her customers more agreeable. I told her everything stunk. She didn't like it much."

Clare asked softly, "Is Madam Bella—your mother—is she still alive?"

Spur shrugged. "Don't know. I left New Orleans at fourteen and I have only been back a couple of times. I stopped at her house the last trip, but I didn't see her.

"I know lots of girls on the line. They all move around a lot. I talked to one in Cheyenne last year who used to work there. She said Madam Bella had closed shop five or ten years ago. They didn't know where she went.

"I don't really know how old she is—probably at least fifty by now. Age isn't a friend to a woman in that business. 'Course, the boss ladies don't usually work in the cribs or at least not as much as the younger girls. It's hard to tell.

"I heard some bigwig died in her house down in New Orleans some time back. The doctor who examined the body said the fellow had been poisoned. That wasn't good for business, for sure.

"I don't know if the city fathers shut her down or if she fled. Either way, she disappeared."

He looked seriously at Clare. "Madam Bella is an evil woman. Chas called her Maebeline DuFloure. I never knew her last name. I found it in his papers.

"I hope you never meet her, but if you do, don't trust her. She was wicked and conniving when I was small, and she's had lots of years to perfect that.

"She was a beauty though, and she knew how to make men do what she wanted. Chas was lucky he got away with his life.

"I'm guessing it was Little Nell who warned him. She kind of watched out for me. I think maybe she is the one who nursed me when I was a baby, but I'm not sure. I just know she was my favorite there.

"Madam Bella threw her out when I was three or four. They had a terrible row and Little Nell was gone after that. I never did know what it was about.

"I never called Madam Bella 'Ma,' and I avoided her as much as I could. When I was a little squirt, I was terrified of her. By the time I was five or six, I'd learned how to pull her strings. Then I made it my business to terrorize her. After Sister Eddie took me off the streets, I rarely saw her.

"Shoot, I didn't even know the date of my own birthday until I saw it in Chas' papers."

Clare was quiet as she listened to Spur talk. She could feel her chest tighten as she thought of him as a sad little boy. She smiled up at him.

"Next April, we will have a birthday party for you. You can tell me what kind of cake you want, and we will have a party."

Spur looked down at Clare in surprise and slowly smiled. "I reckon that would be just fine. And as far as cake goes, anything would be good—although a bowl of chocolate frosting would be nice."

They were both smiling when Spur had Hell Fire drop to his knees to let Clare off at the house.

"I'll put this horse away and then I'll be in. You need water for a bath?"

Clare nodded happily and hurried inside. She had made fried chicken earlier. She put some in a pot with potatoes and gravy. It was warming over the fire when Spur came in with two buckets of water. He carried the tub into Clare's bedroom. One bucket of water went into the tub and one into a pot hanging over the fireplace. He set two more buckets down inside the door. He dropped down into his chair with a smile. Clare set the warm food on the table and sat down beside him.

"Thank you for riding with me, Clare. I think you are about the easiest person to talk to I have ever met." Spur's smile was happy, and Clare smiled too. She put her hand in his and Spur led them in a prayer.

CHAPTER 36

A LIVELY CONVERSATION

STUB HANDED CLARE A LETTER THE NEXT MORNING as she was getting into the buggy.

"Good morning, Miss Clare. The fellow at the freight office gave me this. He said it came earlier in the week. He apologized for not getting it to you sooner."

Clare nodded and breathed a thank you as she ripped open the envelope. Her eyes lit up in excitement.

"Kit is coming to visit! She is coming down by stage. She will arrive in Missoula tomorrow." She read the letter a little further before she added, "If we can't pick her up, she will catch a ride with some freighters who will be coming down this way." She looked over at Spur and her eyes sparkled with excitement.

"May we pick her up? Oh, it will be so good to see Kit."

Spur slowly shook his head. "I can't make it. I am meeting with some cattle buyers tomorrow, but Tuff can take you up." He studied Stub's profile and his eyes twinkled. "Is this the Kit I met? If so, maybe we should send Stub."

Stub snorted and turned to walk away. Clare laughed out loud.

"Yes, she is the one. Kit is very pretty. She is a tiny, little brunette with big, brown eyes. They sparkle when she talks, and she walks so fast that she almost bounces."

Stub had slowed down when Clare began to describe Kit. When she finished, he turned around with a bland look on his face.

"I reckon I can make that trip to Missoula tomorrow, Boss. I'd be glad to take Miss Clare to meet her friend."

Spur chuckled as he jumped into the buggy beside Clare.

"You two can work that out." He was laughing and his dark eyes danced. He leaned over to Clare and whispered, "If we play our cards right, ol' Stub just might get married yet. Then you will finally have a girlfriend on this ranch."

Clare giggled and Spur tapped the horses. He called back to Stub, "I'll save you a place beside us in Mass. Father Ravalli was asking about you last week."

Stub frowned and Tuff grinned.

"I'll saddle our horses," Tuff called back to his big brother as he rushed toward the barn.

As they moved down the trail, Spur patted Clare's stomach.

"So when is that little fellow going to show up? You look like you could pop any time now."

Clare glared at the man beside her. Her back stiffened before she spoke.

"Spur, that is not how you talk to a pregnant woman. I already feel unattractive, so you don't need to point it out."

Spur looked at Clare in surprise. He shook his head and he frowned.

"I didn't say anything about you being unattractive. I think you're beautiful. Your belly is so tight and hard that it looks like maybe you might explode is all. It doesn't look to me like you can grow much more without that happening. I am just wondering when it is going to come out."

Clare's mouth tightened into a line and she faced forward.

"I am not going to discuss this with you, Spur. You don't know a thing about women."

Spur chuckled as he studied her profile. He nodded his head.

"I used to think I knew a lot about women—till I met you. You, I don't understand at all. When I am honest with you, you tell me I don't have a muzzle. If I don't tell you everything, you think I'm hiding something from you.

"And in my defense, I have never been around pregnant women much, certainly none that I lived with. I know how you get that way but that is the extent of my knowledge of babies. Maybe you just need to share a little with me so I don't keep horrifying you with blunt questions."

Spur's face was honest as he spoke. When Clare looked at him, he grinned and winked at her.

"Talk away, Miss Clare. Tell me how the rest of this deal is going to go. I plan to be there for the birthing, you know."

"I don't even want you in the same room."

"Well, too bad. That was #9 on my list of requirements before I signed up for this marriage deal. Besides, I have helped birth mules before. How different can it be?"

Clare turned to glare at him. As she opened her mouth to retort, Spur grinned and squeezed her. He chuckled.

"You are a fiery one, Clare. You are sure a lot of fun to tease.

"Now when is this little fellow scheduled to come out? I know it takes around nine months, but since I wasn't here for the conceiving, I'm not sure when those nine months started."

Clare's face blushed a deep red and she looked away. When she looked back at him, her face was calm although the fire was still in her eyes.

"Before Christmas. And Father Ravalli wants me to stop in this morning after Mass. I had gall bladder surgery last year, and he wants to make sure there is no scar tissue attaching to my uterus."

Clare looked away and Spur said nothing for a few minutes.

"That would be bad?"

"Yes, but I have had no pain or pulling, so I am assuming there is no problem." She glared at him and added, "And you are not coming in with me. Someone needs to watch the children."

Spur chuckled. He started to respond. Instead, he tapped the horses and faced forward. He laughed again and began to whistle, "Buffalo Gals, Won't You Come Out Tonight?"

Clare watched him for a moment, and her glare became deeper.

"I know what you were going to say."

"Can't, because I didn't say it."

"Well, I am sure I know."

"You want me to say it to see if you are right?"

"No!" Clare's voice was exasperated, and Spur began to laugh.

"See, this is why men don't understand women. You just don't track in a straight line. We can't keep up with all of your dodging and jumping around.

"How about you slide over here next to me, and let's talk about Chas' house. You can ask me any question you want because I have explored every inch of it. I have checked out all the buildings as well." Spur put out his arm. His dark eyes were twinkling and Clare slowly relaxed. She slid a little closer and he pulled her up next to him.

"That's better. Now, what do you want to know?"

Just then, Tuff and Stub rode up beside them. Tuff's face was excited.

"Stub told me you might be moving down to Chas' house, Clare." His eyes were sparkling as he looked at her.

"You will like that house. Chas tried to make things as easy as he could for Miss Agnes, and he sure did. An inside water pump, an icehouse, a root cellar under the house, and flowers everywhere. He even put a garden in behind the house not far from the clothesline. It's a real fine place for sure, and it's not far from the house down to the road that runs into Stevensville. Maybe a mile or two. From the yard, you can look right out over the valley. It's mighty pretty.

"You could invite all kinds of fancy ladies out and drink tea in little cups." Tuff mimicked what he thought that would look like. Clare laughed.

"Well, I don't have any fancy friends, so we don't have to worry about that." She looked at Tuff and Stub seriously.

"You don't think it would be an insult to Rock? Look at all he built. I would leave it and move away."

Stub studied her face before he shook his head.

"Rock was all about efficiency, Clare. Chas' ranch is more centralized to your operation now that you added his land. Rock built a mighty fine place, but you could put a foreman in that house. He'd have it right nice too." He grinned at her and added, "Ol' Nudge has been courting a girl down south. Giving him a place to live might be enough to keep him on—for a time anyway."

Clare was quiet as she listened to Stub.

"What about you, Stub? Would you like to live there?"

Stub looked away as he chewed on a toothpick he had carved.

"Two years ago, I would have. Now that you and Rock gave me my own little place down in a pretty valley, I want to stay there. I like things the way they are. I can work here for you, then go home and enjoy my own land. I add a few cows every year." He grinned at Clare and drawled, "Besides, I might just stick around a long time if I like the looks of your little friend."

Stub winked at Clare and Spur chuckled. Clare was surprised but she was pleased too.

"I know you will like her, Stub. Kit is a wonderful person. She was my first friend in Helena, and I'd love to have her move here. It would be wonderful to have her closer." Her blue eyes sparkled as she added, "So my intentions are mostly selfish."

Stub grinned and the conversation moved on to cattle. Clare thought about what Stub had said. *Rock, please don't think me ungrateful if I move. I love our home and I would stay here forever. It's just that…well…Stub had some logical reasons, and you did tell me to move on. This would be a big change, but it might be good for all of us.*

Clare was quiet the rest of the way to town. She looped her arm through Spur's and sat a little straighter. Spur looked down at her. He patted her hand and squeezed it before he took the reins in both hands again.

CHAPTER 37

CHURCH AND A CHECKUP

MAGGIE AND IKE HAD ALL THREE CHILDREN ON THE front row of the little mission church. Nora was sitting quietly, staring at the statue of the Blessed Mother. Annie was whispering loudly and fell off the seat just as Spur and Clare arrived. Spur scooped her up as he stepped into the seat behind Clare.

"Good thing you are a tough girl," he whispered as he winked at her.

Annie rubbed her head and eyed him carefully. Finally, she smiled and nodded. She started to climb down but Spur whispered, "Why don't you sit here for a bit and give your mother a chance to pray—before you fall off the seat again?"

The little girl stared at him before whispering loudly, "Don't you need to pray, Spur?"

"I reckon I do. Fold your hands and think about Jesus. We will both pray right now." Spur was struggling not to laugh, and Annie squeezed her eyes shut. She was muttering her prayer aloud when Stub and Tuff squeezed into the seat beside them.

Annie quickly climbed down the pew. She tugged Stub's arm. "Can you tell me a story about Jesse James?" Stub frowned at her and knelt down.

Spur leaned over and whispered, "Annie, if you are good, I will tell you a story about a saint who was a great warrior. His name was Sebastian. And maybe even a story about girl warrior saint named Joan of Arc. Only if you are quiet though."

Annie slid down in the seat and sat as quiet as she could. She was trying to remove her shoes when Clare made her kneel.

When Mass was over, Clare was exhausted, and Spur was trying hard not to laugh. She glared at him.

"Instead of making deals with Annie, you need to make her behave. She is old enough to be quiet in church."

"What do you want me to do?"

"A thump now and then wouldn't hurt. She riles the other two up, and then they are all three naughty."

Spur looked out where the three children were playing and shook his head.

"I didn't think she was that bad, but I'll have a talk with her."

Clare turned to face him. Her frustration showed as she spoke.

"Spur, parenting is more than playing. You have to discipline too. And don't worry—Annie will still love you. Kids need boundaries though."

Spur stared at Clare. He frowned as he looked again toward the children. *I didn't think they were that bad. A little loud, maybe. Guess I had better raise my standards.*

"Clare, are you ready for your checkup? We will have you in and out in a jiffy." Father Ravalli signaled for Clare to follow him. He hurried across the mission grounds to his combination office, clinic, and ride-up pharmacy.

Spur started to follow. He stopped as he looked toward where the children were playing.

"We'll take the kids, Spur," Maggie called to him. "Come on over for dinner when Clare is done. Stub, you and Tuff come too."

Spur waved to her as he followed Father Ravalli toward his little office. He waited outside while the priest doctor checked Clare. Both Clare and Father Ravalli were smiling when they came out, and Spur relaxed.

"Now, Spur, I would like Clare to have her baby here if possible. I, for sure, want to be present. Don't wait too long to bring her in or send for me.

"And Clare, I want to see you in two weeks. If that little one hasn't turned, we'll go ahead and turn him then." He smiled at both before he looked again at Spur.

"Clare is young and healthy. This should be an easy birth. Enjoy your day." The priest made the sign of the cross over them and hurried back to the church.

Spur was quiet as he helped Clare into the buggy. He finally asked, "If everything is fine, why does he want to see you so soon? And what does turning a baby mean?"

"He doesn't think it is any big deal. The baby is bottom down instead of head down. Father wants to turn him. He said if he turns him too early, the baby could flip around again, so he is going to wait two weeks. Lots of times, they turn on their own though." Clare shrugged and smiled at Spur. "Father Ravalli said he has turned babies many times. .

"He is still a little worried about the scar tissue. That's why he wants to be there for the birthing. Just a precaution he told me.

"I'm not going to worry about it. Like I said before, I feel fine."

"I think that is one more reason to get moved down to Chas' house as soon as possible. We could get to town faster than coming down our mountain. We could have some nasty weather by time that little fellow is ready to come." Spur's eyes were serious as he looked over at Clare.

She sat still a moment before she smiled at him.

"If I like the house, we can start moving this week. Kit can help me clean. Once that is done, we can move in."

CHAPTER 38

CHAS' HOUSE

CLARE WAS QUIET ON THE RIDE TO CHAS' HOUSE. SHE twisted her hands together and Spur finally squeezed them.

"Just relax, Clare. You don't have to do this. I know it feels like I'm pushing you, but we can keep things the way we are doing them right now. Afterall, it's working. You can even stay with Maggie as you get closer. That will put you right in town. We'll make it work." He pulled the buggy up to the front door and jumped down.

"Here we are. Let's check this out so we can get back home."

Clare stared at the quiet house. She stepped up on the wraparound porch and opened the door. She caught her breath at the sight of the curved staircase, and she touched the red pump that was mounted by the wash area.

Spur leaned against the kitchen wall and watched her with a smile.

Clare carefully touched everything, from the large kitchen table to the chairs in the sitting room. Her eyes were wide as she looked at Spur. She said nothing as she mounted the stairs.

The beds were made in all five bedrooms. The large rugs needed to be beaten, but the floors were clean. She looked around at Spur in surprise.

"Who cleaned? I thought you said the upstairs hadn't been used in some time."

"I did sweep a few floors. I'm sure it's not cleaned as deep as you would, but it's passable. 'Course, Chas was a neat man, so there wasn't much downstairs to clean up. Just a little dust and some pieces of mud under the desk." He grinned at her and winked as he added, "A feller has to do something at night when he can't sleep, just thinking about his wife.

"So what do you think, Clare? Think you could handle living here?" Spur's dark eyes were sparkling with excitement.

"You really want to live here, don't you?"

Spur shrugged. He looked around and slowly nodded.

"It would be easier for me for sure. No being away from my family during the week or long trips to and from. Like Tuff said, it's more central to our operation now. It's pleasant here and out of the wind. The view is nice, and the house is large. It has more conveniences for you too.

"It's an easy decision for me, but I don't have the emotional ties you do. My decision would be all about practicality."

Clare's blue eyes studied his face. They were a little watery.

"I want to walk around outside for a bit before I decide. Show me the garden. You mentioned last night that there was a tunnel between the barn and the house. I'd like to see that too."

The kids came racing down the stairs. Annie grabbed the railing and was about to climb on when Spur called to her.

"Nope. Not in your britches. Maybe in your nightgown." When Clare glared at him, he added with a grin, "Or maybe not."

Clare was quiet as they looked around outside. All three children were excited to see the tunnel and immediately wanted to explore it.

Spur nodded somberly as he looked at each of them.

"Just remember, this is not a place to play. It was built for safety purposes, and we need to keep it that way. We'll follow it to the house, but you never use it unless we give you permission. The doors on each end are heavy. An adult needs to open them. If you were to be locked in there, it might be some time before we would find you, let alone get you out." He looked around at the three excited little faces as they bounded toward the barn. "Deal?"

Zeke looked at him seriously. "It might come in handy in the winter if the snow gets really deep. We could use this instead of scooping ourselves out."

Spur grinned at him and tousled his hair.

"We could but that would only be if we couldn't get out the door—and I hope that never happens. No, it was built for protection, and we need to keep it that way.

"You don't talk about it to other people either. This is our family secret. Someday, we might need to use it, and the fewer people who know about it, the better."

"Do Stub and Tuff know about it?" Zeke's eyes were big as he stared up at Spur.

Spur shook his head. "Not yet, but I will let you show them if we move here. As far as I know, the only hand here who knows about it is Cookie.

"I don't think Chas had been down there in years. I had a heck of a time getting the doors to even open. I greased them but that's another reason I don't want you in there. They might swell with moisture and be even harder to open."

"Can we tell Auntie Maggie and Grampa Ike? I think they might like to know."

Spur chuckled as he looked down at Zeke.

"You can but your Grandpa Ike is the one who told me about it. He was out here when Chas was building this house. He helped lay up some of the stone in the tunnel. Shoot, he can probably tell you more stories about it than I will ever know."

Spur slid aside a tool chest against the wall in the barn. The floor underneath didn't look any different than that around it. A large ring was just barely visible next to the wall. It was standing upright and fit into a circular slot in the wall. Spur folded the metal ring back and pulled on it. A large door in the floor slowly opened.

Clare gasped as she stared. Rock steps led down into a stone tunnel. Spur walked carefully down the stone stairs and lit the lamp that was hanging on the wall. He reached up his hand.

"You kids come down one at a time before I help your mother down."

Once Clare was down, Spur handed her the lamp. He pulled a ring on the door and carefully lowered it. He pulled another ring, and they could hear something sliding.

"That's the tool chest. It is on a metal runner. It can be pulled back in place once the door is closed. That old dusty rug is hooked underneath it. When you pull it closed, the rug covers the rails." He pointed at a heavy latch on the underside of the door.

"That locks the door in place, but I don't want it used unless there is an emergency. If you couldn't get it unhooked, we'd have to tear the door out to get in here."

Candle stubs were spaced about every twenty feet in notches in the rock. The tunnel was rounded on top. The side walls were straight. Both the walls and the floor were made of round rocks set in clay. Clare's breath was coming quickly, and Spur took her arm.

"Don't worry, Clare. I haven't seen a single rat or snake down here… yet." He grinned at her, and she slid closer to him.

The children were running ahead. Their voices ebbed and flowed as they ran back and forth.

"Why would Chas build this? It was obviously important to him as much time as was taken on the construction." Clare's voice was full of surprise.

Spur looked around with a frown. He shrugged.

"I would say it was for protection. It was built after the War Between the States, so it had nothing to do with hiding slaves. Besides, we are too far west for the Underground Railroad.

"There might have been a little trouble with the Blackfeet, but Chas wouldn't have left the house and buildings unprotected. I'm just not sure." Spur's voice was soft as he added, "There are lots of things about this place I would love to ask him.

"I know Chas got his start mining but even Ike doesn't know where his mine was. He must have taken more than a little gold out of it because he built this operation with that as seed money. Of course, land didn't cost much when he started. Some was even free.

"He filed deeds for everything he owned, and they are at the bank. Those land deeds show ownership for twenty-five thousand acres, and they show he paid cash for most of it. Chas' land runs south quite a ways. It runs up in the mountains a bit too. He owned more grass than us, and since it butts right up to our ranch, it's a nice setup.

"Most of his land was purchased after he married Agnes. Maybe her family had money—I don't know." He grinned down at Clare and drawled, "I always hoped to meet a nice little gal with money. 'Course I figured she'd be homely, and I'd have to keep my eyes focused on the ranch rather than look at her." He squeezed Clare and whispered, "I sure didn't think I'd marry a gal as pretty as you."

Clare looked up at Spur and laughed out loud.

"Spur, I would be willing to bet you never courted a homely woman in your life, and I doubt you cared if she had money. You didn't intend to stay around anyway."

Spur chuckled. "You've got me there. Still, there are lots of things I don't know about Chas. I have read through all his papers in his desk and in the bank too. Nothing in there mentioned this tunnel.

"If it was anyone besides Chas, I'd wonder if he was part of an outlaw gang. Chas was too honest for that though. Besides, the way this tunnel is fortified, it was for someone he loved, not for a bunch of outlaws to run through."

They arrived at the end of the tunnel and once again, Spur pulled on a large ring. Something slid over them and he pushed open the large door. He blew out the lamp and set it in a holder by the door. When they reached the top, they were in Chas' office.

The runners on the floor beneath the desk were made of metal and they went all the way around the room. They looked like an accent around the baseboards. They blended in with the variety of colors in the grain of the wood on the walls.

"I worked in this office for nearly a week and never thought a thing of that metal runner down there. I just thought it was part of the trim."

Clare studied the desk. She touched the old wood and slid her hands over the rough finish. She smiled as she looked up at Spur.

"Chas was a kind man. This office tells so much about who he was." She pointed at the full bookshelf. *Tennyson's Poems* sat in the middle of the top shelf.

"I find that an interesting book to be in Chas' collection."

"'Tis better to have loved and lost, Than never to have loved at all," Spur quoted.

Clare stared at him. "'In Memoriam' is a long poem. You read the entire thing?"

Spur scratched his head and grinned at her. "I tried but that poem is ninety-nine pages long. I knew what line I was looking for though, so I just read the last word in each line until I found it." His grin became bigger. "I thought it might benefit me to be able to quote it someday."

Clare's eyes were sparkling as she watched Spur talk. When he finished, she laughed.

"Spur, you are a mess." She lifted the large book down and flipped through it.

"Tennyson left the love of his life after becoming engaged. He was worried about his ability to support her—that and his concern that he might have epilepsy.

"He eventually went back to her. By then, he was more financially secure. His previous diagnosis of epilepsy was incorrect, and they married. I read that his wife picked the name of this poem, 'In Memoriam.'"

Clare set the book back on the shelf. "Such a story of love and loss. Confusion too."

"I'd sure be confused if I wrote a poem that long. I wouldn't be able to even remember what I was blabbing about three pages before let alone ninety-nine." Spur scratched his head as he pointed toward the book.

"A fellow I knew used to keep a little book of Tennyson's poems in his saddlebags. He read them to us in the bunkhouse on cold nights. Some of the riders enjoyed them.

"I did a few of them, but mostly, I just went to sleep. I do remember the last line of his poem, "Ulysses." 'To strive, to seek, to find, and not to yield.' I think that is fine advice.

"You look around a little more. I am going to head back down to the barn. I want to make sure the door down there is hidden well. I'll scatter a little hay over it.

"We can head home as soon as you are ready. We'll have to take the long way around though because this buggy will never make it over the trails in that short-cut."

The little ones talked excitedly on the way home before they finally fell asleep. Spur was whistling softly. Clare waited for a time before she looked over at him.

She eyed him cautiously and asked, "You aren't going to ask me what I decided?"

Spur grinned at her. "Nope. I reckon you will tell me when you are ready—but I'll back the wagon up to the house before I leave in the morning."

Clare stared at him. Her eyes sparked as she commented dryly, "Quite sure of yourself when it comes to me, aren't you?"

Spur chuckled and shook his head. "Nope, you keep me confused most of the time, but I can usually tell when you like something. You liked Chas' house. In fact, you liked his entire place—maybe because you liked old Chas. Whatever the reason, you decided to move there before you ever went outside." Spur's smile was big as he looked over at Clare.

"If the weather stays nice, we'll move this week. And I don't want you to load that wagon. You get one of the hands.

"I'll send Caine down to pick up Ike's wagon. That should give us enough room for everything. Once you ladies are done, we'll load and start hauling things over there."

"I hate being so predictable." Clare sighed deeply as she took Spur's arm. "You are right though. I loved the house. I can feel Chas there, and I liked that too. He was such a kind man. So gruff with such a gentle heart." She looked up at Spur.

"Would you mind if I polished Chas' desk? It looks like it could use a good oiling. The grain of the wood is so beautiful. It would show more if it was polished."

Spur looked at Clare in surprise.

"I have no secrets from you, Clare. You can polish the desk if it needs it, and you can go through all his papers. You can even read my mail." He added, "Just don't move my piles. I know where everything is." He grinned at her and bumped her shoulder.

"Now if you just had some mail I could read, why I might be able to figure you out a little better."

Clare studied Spur's face. "Why? Because I am the only girl who wasn't dazzled by your charm or fawned over your compliments?"

Spur laughed as he looked down at Clare. His eyes were intense when he spoke. "I have sure flirted in the past, but you are the only girl I've ever really loved. One time I was maybe just a little close, but I ran.

"Not with you, Clare. There is something about you that makes me want to stick around. I want to know all about you. I want to know what makes you happy and what makes you sad. I want to know what makes you the Clare you are." He put his arm around her and gave her a little squeeze. "And I reckon I have the rest of my life to figure that out."

Clare was quiet. When she looked over at him, she had tears in her eyes.

"I have pushed you away, Spur, and you just keep coming back. I don't know why you think you love me. I have given you nothing to make you hope I will ever return that love."

Spur's smile was soft as he looked down at her. "Because you're worth it," he said simply as he removed his arm. Then he winked at her and added, "Besides, I think I'm wearing you down."

He was soon whistling. Clare frowned. *Is he wearing me down or am I just getting used to having him around? He makes me comfortable and he makes me laugh. Could that ever be love or is that just friendship?* She shook her head. *Life is so confusing* she thought as she once again took Spur's arm to keep from bouncing around on the buggy seat.

CHAPTER 39

Too Many Ghosts

SPUR WAS GONE BY THE TIME CLARE AWOKE, BUT THE wagon was parked in front of the house as he had promised. She had struggled to sleep the night before with all the planning going through her head. Now she had overslept. She rushed to the bedroom where all three of the children were sleeping.

"Wake up! We are making a trip today to Missoula to pick up a friend of mine. Hurry now. I overslept and we are going to be late."

Clare laid their clothes on chairs in the kitchen and rushed around fixing breakfast. She almost jumped when she heard a tap on the door.

"Morning, Clare. I just wanted to let you know I am ready to leave when you are."

Clare looked up quickly and nodded. She looked again.

Stub's blue eyes were brilliant against the black of his hair and the beard that was just starting. His shirt was blue and the black vest he wore was brushed. His boots were clean and polished to a shine. Clare's eyes opened wide and she laughed.

"Why, Stub. You look absolutely dapper. Kit will be so taken by you."

Stub shuffled his feet and looked down at the floor. When he looked up, he was grinning.

"I figured I had better make a good impression. Once she gets back here, I'll have more competition than I can handle."

Clare hurried over and kissed his cheek. "Only Tuff can make as good of an impression as you, Stub.

"I am going to pack the children their breakfast to go, and I'll add a little extra for us. We will be ready to leave as soon as they are dressed." She turned away and clapped her hands as she hurried towards the bedrooms.

"Chop, Chop. Chicken mop! You can have a picnic with your breakfast in the buggy on the way." Three sets of little feet came rushing into the kitchen. They were soon dressed and loaded in the buggy. As Stub drove down the lane, the three little ones were discussing what they wanted to trade as they ate their breakfast contentedly.

A pretty girl with dark hair and large, brown eyes sat in front of the stage station. Several cowboys had stopped to talk. Her bright eyes and friendly smile drew them in. She glanced up when the buggy pulled to a stop in front of her. She jumped to her feet with a squeal and ran toward the buggy.

"Clare! Oh, I am so excited to see you. Zeke—my, how you have grown!" She studied the two girls. "Now, you must be Annie and you are Nora." She smiled up at Clare. "What delightful children."

Stub sat on his seat and stared. Clare waited a moment for him to help her down before she climbed out of the buggy.

"Stub, would you mind helping Kit with her bags?" she asked dryly.

The other two cowboys quickly grabbed Kit's bags and carried them to Clare's buggy. One tipped his hat to Clare and nodded.

"Miz Beckler. Good to see you." He looked down at Kit and grinned.

"It was nice to talk to you, Miss Saunders. Guess we know where to come calling now." Both cowboys were still smiling as they tipped their hats to Kit. Their grins grew larger when Stub glared at them. They chuckled as they walked away.

The tallest one turned around and hollered, "Durn, Stub. Y'all look like a dandy, an' ya still plumb lost yore tongue. We'll see ya next week when we pick up those cows. Might even come a day early."

Stub waved and snorted as he climbed down off the buggy seat. He hurried around to where the two women were talking.

"Do you ladies want to go anywhere here in Missoula? I can give you a tour if you want. Or we can turn this buggy around and head for home."

Clare looked at Stub in surprise.

"I would love a tour, Stub. I have only been to Missoula a few times and have never spent much time here. How about you, Kit? Would you like a tour of Missoula?"

Kit nodded eagerly. Stub gave her a hand up. He helped Clare in next and she was laughing. "Very smooth, Stub," she whispered. Stub grinned and blushed. He was still grinning when he walked around the buggy.

Stub pointed with his whip at the various businesses as they drove down the busy main street.

"The Salish Indians first called this area Nemissoolatakoo. A loose translation of that is river of ambush or surprise. That's about right because it was a rough area. Of course, few Whites could pronounce it and the name of the area was shortened to Missoula.

"This town was founded as Hellgate Trading Post nineteen or twenty years ago in the early '60s. Some folks called it Hellgate Village, but mostly, it was just called Hellgate.

"Once it started to grow, the city fathers got together. They wanted to pick another name, one that would be more inviting to ladies such as yourselves." Stub grinned over at Kit, and she responded with a quick smile.

"In '66, the settlement was moved upstream five miles, to the east of where the first settlement was. The founders wanted to build a sawmill and a flour mill. They did and folks started calling it Missoula Mills or just Missoula.

"The Mullan Road was started in '59. It was finished in '60 but it's been moved in several places because of washouts. That road connects Fort Benton here in the Montana Territory with Walla Walla on the coast." He looked over at Kit and added, "The stage you took from Helena likely followed part of that route." He pointed in front of them with his whip.

"With that road going through Missoula, it allowed the army to move troops and supplies easier. Fort Missoula was built in '77. With the fort and the mills, Missoula became an important trading area. I suppose if we ever get rail service this far, a line will go right through here." He smiled at Kit.

"Shoot, in another few years, you will be able to visit more often since travel will be easier."

Kit was quiet for a moment. She looked over at Clare as she spoke softly.

"I don't plan to go back to Helena. I am going to try to find work in Stevensville. If I can't find anything there, I'll look for work in Missoula."

When Clare looked at her in surprise, Kit shrugged.

"Too many ghosts, imaginary and real. I need a change."

No one spoke for a moment and Clare squeezed Kit's hand.

"You stay as long as you want. I have enough work to keep both of us busy until spring. You can look for a job then.

"So how are Sisters Casimir and Rudolph? Did they get their hospital built? And Big Dorothy?"

Stub was quiet. Kit's comment hit him, and he understood how she felt. *Ghosts. Yeah, I need to put some ghosts to rest too. I think I'll bury that metal box today. The weather is as nice as it will be for some time. This thaw might have softened the ground enough for me to dig a hole. I think I'll put it up in Rock's little cemetery.*

CHAPTER 40

BURYING OLD MEMORIES

ONCE THEY WERE HOME, BOTH WOMEN HURRIED INTO the house. Stub walked to the barn and pulled the old metal box off a shelf. He stared at it a moment, grabbed a shovel, and headed outside.

Kit came out of the house. She looked around the yard. She hurried toward Stub when he walked out of the barn, staring in surprise at the shovel.

Stub nodded at it. "I have some old memories that need buried too. After listening to you talk, I decided to do that today."

Kit watched him a moment before she asked shyly, "Do you mind if I help you? Clare was so tired that I told her to lie down. The ride must have worn her little ones out because they didn't argue when she said it was nap time.

"I'm not tired. I thought I'd go for a walk, but helping you sounds more interesting. What can I do?"

Stub handed her the box. "You can carry that. I don't have a marker yet, but I can make one later."

Stub's voice was soft as they walked up the hill toward the cemetery.

"A Reb soldier handed me that box when I gave him a drink of water. I was a sergeant in the Union Army, and we had just won a hard battle at Peach Tree Creek in Georgia." He shook his head. "It was a bloody mess.

"We weren't supposed to pick up any enemy soldiers who couldn't walk. We weren't even supposed to help them." Stub frowned. He was quiet a moment before he continued.

"A young fellow grabbed my leg when I got down to fill my canteen. He wanted a drink.

"He was just a kid, even younger than me, and for sure too young to be in that war. There he lay on the ground, surrounded by dead and dying men. He'd been shot in the stomach, and he knew he wasn't going to make it. I knew I shouldn't give him water, but the kid was dying. I handed him my canteen and we talked for a bit.

"He had a kid sister and he wanted me to find her. He asked me to give her that box." Stub pointed toward the metal box Kit was carrying. "He told me her first name, but he died before he could tell me his last name. There are some letters in there from his sister but no last name on any of them." Stub's eyes were bleak as he looked at Kit.

"I failed him. I have been carrying that box around for fifteen years, and I haven't found a hint of who he was. I even took it to Cheyenne with me when we picked up Rock's cattle. I was going to ask some of the cowhands down there if they knew anyone who could help. They were mostly Southerners though and didn't think much of Yankees. I decided it best to keep my mouth shut.

"I think it's time to bury this box. Maybe my nightmares about that war will stop."

Kit had tears in her eyes as she listened. She looked at the box and then put her hand on Stub's arm.

"But you helped him. You gave him water when you weren't supposed to help any of them. You showed kindness to a stranger, Stub, and an enemy at that. You have nothing to be sorry for.

"I'll help you bury this box." She looked out over the little cemetery. Her eyes were full of tears when she looked back at Stub.

"I lost a brother in that war. In the last letter we received, he said he was headed to Virginia. The Battle of the Wilderness was fought there in May of '64. We never heard from him after that. We always assumed that's where he was killed." Kit smiled softly and her eyes took on a faraway look.

"We lived in Texas when the War Between the States started. My brother and some of his friends enlisted. They thought it would be a great adventure.

"When he didn't come home, my mother was devastated. Our family was poor, and the cattle market in Texas crashed. My father was a rider, and he lost his job. We decided to move.

"We joined a wagon train headed north. Father hired on as a scout. Mother did laundry and cooked for the men who weren't married. She wanted to go back to Georgia, and Father wanted to go west.

"He said we would go north for a time. We could decide later where we'd go." Kit's voice broke as she looked at Stub.

"We didn't make it far. Lots of people became sick. Mother was the first to die.

"Some outlaws spotted our wagon train shortly after that. We were close to No Man's Land, down south in the Indian Territory. They shot Father before they attacked the wagon train. We lost more men in that fight. Father hung on for several days before he died.

"I went on with a nice old couple in the wagon train as far as Nebraska. They settled there. They invited me to stay, and I lived with them until they died. Then some people who claimed to be relatives came in and claimed their land. They threw me out and I was on my own." Kit's voice was bitter when she continued.

"I was thirteen years old, and I had no skills."

"At first, I was in charge of the laundry for a traveling troupe of actors. We hit all the cow towns and mining camps. I even did a little singing. When we arrived in Bannack, here in the Montana Territory, that's when it all changed.

"A woman there forced me to go to work for her. It was the same woman who claimed those old people's land. She said I needed to earn my keep and she…well…that was the beginning." Kit looked away before she looked directly at Stub. She added sarcastically, "There is always one thing a girl can do regardless of how old she is.

"We ended up in Helena. After a year, Big Dorothy became my madam. I'm not sure how that came about, but Big Dorothy had a lot of power up there. My life was better after that.

"Big Dorothy was kind. I know that sounds strange, but after what I had lived with for the past two years, she was a welcome change. She knew I didn't want to be there, so I became her errand girl. I still had to work in her cribs but not as much as the other girls.

"Clare was my first friend outside Big Dorothy's. She helped me to get a job at Delmonico's where she worked as a waitress.

"They all loved her there, and she had influence with the man who owned it. We have been friends ever since.

"Once she left though, that job wasn't the same. Some of the men who had been my customers at Big Dorothy's wouldn't leave me alone. I decided to make a change and here I am." Kit sucked back a sob as she looked at Stub.

"I never intended to tell anyone what I was. I didn't want that life to follow me. I don't know why I told you."

Her hands shook as she held the box and Stub put one of his hands over hers.

"I don't reckon what we have been matters near as much as what we are." Stub's face was kind as he looked at her. "Your secret is safe with me, Kit."

Kit sank down on the ground. She pulled the box up to her chin and sobbed.

Stub cursed softly as he knelt beside her. He wasn't sure what to do. He finally hugged her.

"Don't cry, Kit. We'll bury this box along with our memories. It can be a new start for both of us."

Slowly Kit's sobs became further apart. She stared at the box in her hands and looked up at Stub.

"Would you mind if I open this before we bury it? I would like to know his name. If his family is gone, then two people will remember who he is."

When Stub nodded, Kit lifted the lid. As she stared at the contents, she caught her breath. She lifted out the tattered letters with shaky hands and began to cry again.

Stub tried to take the box. "You've had enough sadness for today, Kit. Let's bury this. It's too hard on you to take someone else's pain."

Kit pulled the box back and shook her head. She was smiling as she cried.

"This soldier is my brother, Stub. You helped my brother!"

Stub stared at her in shock. He pointed at the letters. "But her name was Addie. She had to be older than you would have been. Those letters were written in cursive."

Kit smiled as tears ran down her cheeks. She wiped them with the back of her hand.

"My name is Adeline Kathleen. Zeb always called me Addie. After he died, I wouldn't let anyone call me that.

"My father always said I was his sweet little kitten and the nickname stuck. When I worked, I never used my given name." She smiled at Stub. "And so, I became Kit." She held up the letters.

"After Zeb left, I so wanted to write him letters. I couldn't write yet, and a neighbor girl who was a little older offered to write for me. I told her what I wanted to say, and she wrote it down. She was just learning cursive, and her mother thought it would be good practice for her."

Kit hugged the box to her chest. Tears ran from her eyes, but she was smiling.

"Thank you, Stub. Thank you for finding my brother and for giving him a drink. Thank you for keeping this box for fifteen years. And thank you for trying to find me even though it caused you pain." She leaned forward and kissed his cheek.

"You are a kind man, Stub." She gave a laugh that ended in a sob. "And you don't have to dig that hole. I will be keeping these." Kit smiled at him again.

"If you don't mind, I will sit here and read them."

Stub nodded and slowly stood. He stood awkwardly for a moment. He commented softly, "I'm glad Zeb was your brother, and I'm glad I never buried that box all the other times I intended to."

He walked down the hill toward the barn. He looked back once, and Kit was reading one of the letters. She had one hand on her heart, and it looked like she was crying.

Stub shook his head and kept walking. "I think I'll go find the men and see what needs to be done yet. I've had about as much emotion as I can handle for one day."

CHAPTER 41

SAYING GOODBYE

MAGGIE ARRIVED ON TUESDAY TO HELP. CLARE looked at her in surprise when the older woman climbed down from her buggy. Maggie laughed.

"Talk to Spur. He told Ike Monday morning on his way to Chas' that you had agreed to move.

"And no, he didn't ask us to help. We wanted to…and when we leave this evening, we are going to take those children home with us so you and Kit can finish by Thursday. Spur said he was hoping to haul everything down the end of this week."

Kit, Clare, and Maggie packed and sorted. After Maggie left with the children that evening, the other two women worked even faster. By Thursday morning, the little home echoed with emptiness.

Clare looked around the cozy house. Her heart felt tight as she looked at the curtains. They were the only thing in the house that had not been packed. She clutched the edge of the wash area and took a deep breath as she tried not to cry.

Spur poked his head through the door. The smile left his face when he looked at Clare. He walked over and put his arms around her.

"Hey, it's all right. We'll come back any time you want. Don't cry, Clare. Please don't cry."

Clare let him wrap her up as she sobbed.

"Rock bought that curtain fabric for me the day we married. He told me later he never understood why women liked curtains."

Spur listened to her quietly. When she stopped crying, he calmly took down the curtain rods. He rolled the curtains around the rods and put his arm around her.

"They can go with us. Every house needs a little color. I'm not sure if Chas hung any curtains in his house—I guess I never noticed. We'll take the rods too so we'll be prepared." He smiled down at her.

"Stub already left with the first wagon, and Kit went with him. Tuff has the buggy. He is in front of Stub.

"This wagon is loaded if you are ready to go. Once we get it unloaded, I'll come back. I'll load the chickens and tie on the milk cow. They will be the last things to go down to Chas'.

"We aren't taking much out of the barn other than the runners for the sleigh—unless you can think of something else in there you want me to take along."

Clare shook her head. She let Spur help her into the wagon. He frowned as she sat down.

"I should have sent you with Tuff. That buggy would be a smoother ride for you. Faster too."

Clare shook her head. "No, I want to ride in the wagon. I came here in this wagon and that's how I want to leave. Besides, it's slower so I can look around."

Spur jumped up beside her. He was still a moment as he looked over at her.

"Do you want to say anything to Rock? We aren't in such a hurry that we can't stop."

Clare looked up at Spur. Her lips trembled as she whispered, "I would but I would like to go by myself."

Spur nodded. He drove the wagon up the hill toward the little cemetery and stopped close to Rock's stone. He helped Clare down before he walked to the opposite side of the wagon. He leaned his back against it and chewed on a piece of dry grass. *This is so hard for Clare. Still, I think it's best. I sure hope I'm right.*

Clare wasn't gone long. She smiled at Spur as he helped her into the wagon. She slid over next to him when he jumped in.

"Thank you for stopping and for bringing my curtains." She gave a low laugh. "They probably won't even fit the windows. I think I'm an emotional mess today."

Spur patted her hand, and they turned down the trail toward the valley floor.

CHAPTER 42

SPUR'S SUGGESTION

CLARE WAS QUIET AND SPUR DIDN'T SPEAK FOR ABOUT a half mile. Then he began humming and was soon singing. When he finished "Red River Valley," he was smiling.

He looked over at Clare.

"I have been thinking."

Clare cocked an eyebrow and watched Spur suspiciously.

"I was wondering if you would like to get Rock a more permanent marker. You know, like a headstone."

Clare stared at Spur. She gripped her hands together tightly and nodded.

"I was just thinking of that today when I told him goodbye. His cross has already faded. A new marker would be wonderful."

Spur nodded and tapped the backs of the mules with the lines.

"They have some new markers available now. They are made of zinc. Folks call them white bronze.

"I saw one several years ago. I was headed back to Cheyenne on the train. We were held up in Salt Lake in the Utah Territory for a couple of hours. I ran into an older woman there. She looked like somebody's grandma." Spur smiled as he looked over at Clare.

"We both had a little time, so we visited for a bit. She said she had been back East visiting family. Her husband had passed while she was gone. She decided to buy a marker for him. Picked it up right at the factory and brought it home with her."

Spur frowned before he continued.

"He had been buying cattle on the West Coast, and they didn't find his body for a time. Shoot, they weren't even worried until he was about five days late. He had planned to be gone for two weeks. By the time they found him, he had been dead nearly a week. Her hands brought his body back to the ranch. They had to bury him right away though. They couldn't wait for his wife to get back.

"She was a sweet woman. She said they had been married for nearly fifty years. Her family was from Bridgeport, Connecticut.

"That was where his marker was made. She just went down to the factory there and told them what she wanted.

"The marker was in a box, but she opened it and showed it to me. It was mighty pretty too. It was almost a blueish white. It was unusual because it was hollow inside." Spur's voice was soft when he added, "She said she bought it because she could take off the front plate and leave little messages for her husband in there." Spur looked over at Clare. Her face was pale. He cleared his throat as he put his hand over hers.

"I thought maybe you would like one of those for Rock. You and the kids too.

"She gave me the name of the company and I wrote them. I just received pictures of what they offered last week. Things were kind of hectic, so I didn't say anything until now.

"Their information is on my desk over at Chas' house. I can show it to you later if you want."

Clare's sob caught in her throat. Spur squeezed her hand. He held it for a moment before he let go. He faced forward and waited for Clare to speak.

"It was very kind of you to contact that company, Spur. Yes, I think that marker sounds like a fine idea. Maybe we can look them over tomorrow night."

Spur nodded. "Maggie is familiar with them too. She said she had seen them in several different cemeteries." He frowned. "I didn't think to ask her where, but she said she would be glad to help you fill out the order once you decide what you want. Maggie called them zinkies." He glanced over at Clare.

"Now that I know what they look like, I have seen a few of them scattered around the country. I knew they looked different than the rest of the stones, but I didn't go up close to look them over." Spur squirmed a little in his seat and turned red. He finally cleared his throat and looked at Clare directly.

"I never have liked cemeteries. They make me uncomfortable. I like to remember folks as they were when they were alive."

Clare looked at Spur in surprise.

"Why, George Spurlach. I can't believe you just said that! I truly didn't think anything could bother you."

Spur grinned at Clare.

"You bother me, but you I don't avoid. I just keep hanging around to be bothered more."

Clare slowly blushed and Spur chuckled.

"How about you tell me what song you want me to sing? Let's have a little music since we still have another hour to go. Or we can talk. You know I do love to talk."

Clare didn't answer right away and Spur smiled. *I think that visit to Rock's grave was good for Clare. She seems almost contented. I'm happy too. The weather is fine, and it won't be too dark when I head back for that last load. Yep, this turned out to be just a darn pleasant day.*

CHAPTER 43

A New Home

THE NEXT TWO WEEKS WERE A BLUR OF ACTIVITY. Clare and Kit cleaned the house from top to bottom. Every time Clare drew water from the inside pump, she felt a thrill of excitement.

I had no idea what a convenience this pump would be.

The windows in the kitchen were too large for Clare's curtains. Besides, there were only two curtains and the large kitchen had four windows.

Annie and Nora begged for them to be put in their room. They only covered the bottom half of the two windows but both little girls were delighted. Annie called them Papa's curtains, and Nora thought they were beautiful.

Clare looked around her new home. Everything was clean. The women had applied linseed oil to the woodwork. It took some time to dry and soak in, but the results were beautiful. Once it was no longer tacky, they polished the wood until it was glossy, allowing the wood grain to show.

She stared at her hands. They had been rough and dry. Now they were oily and looked dirty. She lifted the kettle out of the fireplace and poured some into her wash basin. She washed her hands and left the water there as she began to prepare dinner.

Clare smiled as she looked out the window. Another cowboy had come calling. He wanted to take Kit to the Harvest Dance in Stevensville that evening.

"Poor Stub," she murmured. "He just keeps disappearing more and more. He refuses to compete for Kit's attention, and now he's grumpy all the time."

Kit came in with a smile on her face.

"Going dancing tonight?" Clare asked with a smile.

"I hope so. I told Buzz I already had a date. If that darn Stub doesn't ask me, I am going to ask *him*. And he had better say yes."

Clare's eyes widened and she laughed. "You might have to go find him. He has been working late nearly every night."

Just then, Stub rode into the yard and Kit darted out the door. Clare couldn't see Kit's face, but she could see Stub's. He stared down at Kit and slowly began to smile. He finally nodded and turned his horse to ride home.

Clare stepped to the door as she called, "Stub, you can use our buggy this evening. We aren't planning to go in."

Stub grinned and waved. "Thanks, Clare. I'll see you afterwhile."

Kit rushed back into the house with a smile.

"I am so excited! Stub has barely talked to me since he gave me Zeb's box. I was beginning to think he was avoiding me."

Clare tried to keep the laughter off her face, but it bubbled out of her.

"Of course he's avoiding you. There has been a steady stream of cowboys in and out of this ranch since you moved in. Stub didn't want to compete, so he backed off.

"Poor man. He is lovesick and you didn't even notice. My, has he been grumpy!"

Kit stared at Clare in surprise. She glanced toward Stub's departing back as she giggled. "I'll pretend you didn't tell me that.

"All the attention has been fun, but it is just entertainment. Stub is different. He is thoughtful and kind. He is a deep thinker. He's interesting, and I like an interesting man."

Kit dashed up the stairs. She called back down as she ran, "I am going to find something to wear. I'll be down to take a bath in just a bit."

Clare smiled as she pulled out the wash tub. "I'll put this in Spur's office so Kit can have some privacy." She glanced out the window and paused to watch Spur talk to Zeke. The little boy followed him toward the barn and Clare smiled.

"Spur said he was going to teach Zeke how to milk the cow today.

"Rock hated to milk cows, but Spur doesn't seem to mind at all. They are different in so many ways.

"Both of them want the kids to learn though, and they both believe in chores."

Clare reached for the kettle of water, but Kit gently pushed her away.

"I can draw my own water, Clare. You sit down for a bit. You have been on your feet all day, and I know your back is hurting.

"Here, let me put this stool under your feet. Now you sit there a bit." She handed Clare a book from Chas' bookshelf and closed the door.

Clare read for a while. She laid the book down and closed her eyes.

"I *am* exhausted. Maybe I will take a quick nap." She slowly climbed the stairs and sank down on her bed. She sighed as she pulled the heavy quilt over herself.

"Just a quick nap before I fix supper," she whispered as she dozed off.

It was dark when Clare awoke. She rushed downstairs. Spur was washing the dishes and the children were nowhere to be seen.

He looked around at her with a smile.

"Hello, Sleepyhead. You slept right through supper. I saved some back in case you woke up." His smile became bigger, and he nodded toward the door.

"Stub took Kit to the Harvest Dance. He came home early to ask her. He was hoping he wasn't too late."

Clare laughed. "He would have been, but she turned Buzz down. She told him she already had a date. Then she asked Stub. Good thing he said yes!

"Thank you for fixing supper. I guess I was just worn out."

Spur grinned at her and winked.

"It's all right," he drawled. "I like to wear a fancy apron from time to time. You have quite a few so I had to try lots of them on before I found the perfect one." He lifted the corners of the yellow apron he was wearing and bowed to her.

"Would you dance with me, Mrs. Spurlach? I would sure like to take a turn around the kitchen with you."

Clare laughed and Spur swung her around as he sang, "I'll Take You Home Again, Kathleen." He held her for a moment after the song ended before he released her.

"You sit down here and eat. Then let's talk about Thanksgiving."

Clare looked at Spur in surprise.

"What about Thanksgiving? Do you mean you want to have people over?"

"I think we should feed all the hands. A few will ask for the day off, but most will be right here working. We have the room, and I can help you cook. What do you say?"

Clare laughed as she looked at Spur.

"You are excited! Have you ever been to a big gathering?"

"We always had them when I worked for the Rankins. I love big gatherings with lots of friends. 'Course, I never did anything like that until I moved in with Sister Eddie. Now those were big. I think every lost kid in town came.

"It will be some work, but I think it would be fun."

Clare watched Spur as he talked. She finally laughed.

"I have never seen a turkey around here, but we have some chickens we can fry. We had a setting hen this summer and some of her hatches were cockerels. I'd like to get those young roosters out of my chicken house, and they are certainly big enough to eat now."

"Fried chicken it will be. I'll tell the men tomorrow and we'll see who all wants to come." He grinned at her. "I am guessing all of them. Good thing Kit is around. Of course, Maggie will want to help too. Shoot, this kitchen will be so full, I won't have to help at all."

Clare rolled her eyes and Spur chuckled.

"I'll see if I can round up some potatoes. There was a fellow in town who wanted to sell some last month. I'll see if he has any left."

"Peeling them will be your job. We are going to need about thirty pounds so get your knife ready." Clare's eyes were sparkling, and she tried not to laugh.

Spur frowned and scratched his head.

"Now there is another one of those rules I just don't understand. Why do folks peel potatoes? Why do we think we have to take the skins off when we mash them? Is there something wrong with the skins?" His dark eyes twinkled, and he grinned at Clare. "I guess since I'm in charge of the potatoes, I can peel them or not…I think I will go with the not." He grinned at her again as he pulled out his knife.

"Besides, I know where this knife was used last. That won't bother me, but you might not want to know." He chuckled when Clare stared at the knife and frowned.

"Now eat up, Sweetheart. Your supper is still just a little warm."

CHAPTER 44

A THANKSGIVING FEAST

GOMER ARRIVED ON THANKSGIVING MORNING AND the children were delighted. The little donkey walked into the house and turned around several times. He followed the children to the base of the stairs when they ran up. He snorted and looked around at Clare.

"You stay down here, Gomer. If you are going to come in this house, we are going to have some rules." He brayed and Clare laughed.

"I will see if Spur can put straps on the door so you can come and go as you please. Now go over by the fire and behave."

Maggie and Ike had come the day before, and the big house was a flurry of activity as food was prepared.

Clare looked up as Kit hurried back into the house. Her face was flushed. Stub was just riding out of the ranch yard and Clare laughed.

"Spur told me he might move Nudge up to the other place as foreman. Looks like the Nudge and Stub might be trading jobs," she commented dryly.

Kit's eyes sparkled and she giggled. "Well, this place is closer for Stub, you know."

"Yes, and so are you."

Kit paused as she pulled off her coat. Her face was serious when she looked at Clare.

"I enjoy spending time with Stub. Actually, I don't call him Stub. I call him by his given name, and that is Steve.

"I never intended to share my past with anyone, but I told Steve the first day we talked. That was the day I found out he was with Zeb just before he died.

"Steve never condemned me for how I lived my life before we met. He said he doesn't believe in dwelling on the past. Between talking to him and Father Ravalli, I feel like I have shaken off some of my dirtiness." Her brown eyes were full of emotion when she hugged Clare.

"Thank you for letting me come here," she whispered. "This has been such a wonderful change. I feel like a new person."

Clare hugged her back. "And I am happy to have my best girlfriend here. You stay as long as you want. You do so much work though, you are making me lazy."

Maggie hurried into the house carrying a crock of cooked pumpkin.

"I invited Father Ravalli to come out. He said he would try. He had to check on a woman having a baby so it will depend on how that goes.

"He dropped off a couple of large pumpkins yesterday, and I cooked them up. We can't have a Thanksgiving feast without pumpkin pie, you know."

Ike brought in the butchered chickens followed closely by all three children. Annie had her nose almost inside one of the carcasses as she described the process to Clare.

"And then Grandpa Ike show us the craw and the gizzard.

"Aunt Kit, did you know chickens don't have teeth? I can go get one of their heads if you want to see."

Clare stopped her before she ran back outside.

"Why don't the three of you clean up that chicken mess. Carry it out into the trees and dump it. That smell will draw coyotes in tonight, and I don't want them up in the yard. And try to get the feathers off in one of those snowbanks before you wash your hands in the horse tank."

Clare watched them from the window. Annie had chicken heads in her hands. She was waving them in the air and trying to make them bite Zeke.

Nora didn't want to touch anything. She screamed when Annie pointed the heads at her. She tripped over the bucket of water and feathers as she ran to get away.

Spur finally came out of the barn and settled everyone down. Clare could see him pointing and soon all three children were headed up the hill with buckets of offal and feathers. She watched him for a moment. She was smiling when she turned away from the window.

She blushed slightly when Maggie smiled at her.

"I can make the pie crust if you want, Maggie. I can't wait to have pumpkin pie. I don't know when I ate it last." Clare hugged Maggie quickly. "Thank you so much for coming out. I don't know what I'd do without you."

Maggie said nothing as she hugged Clare tightly. *I hope our Clare finds love again. I think Spur is growing on her. I like that man. I sure never dreamed he would adjust to being a father so easily—and to being a husband too.*

Spur poked his head in the door.

"You ready to start on the potatoes? I have a few volunteers who are going to help."

Clare looked up in surprise and then hurried to the window. Ten cowboys stood there talking. Some were sharpening their knives while others held large knives in their hands.

Spur grinned at Clare.

"You surely didn't think I was going to cut up thirty pounds of potatoes myself, did you?"

"I should have guessed when you volunteered that you had a plan," she replied dryly.

"They are on the counter. Some of the skins do look nice so I don't think they all need peeled. And show them how to take out the eyes so they don't lose half the potato." Clare was smiling as she spoke. She laughed when Spur stuck a potato in his mouth. He grinned around it as he lifted the heavy tub and headed for the door.

"Put them in this bucket when they are cut." She followed him to the door and called, "Thank you! We appreciate you men."

Some of the men had obviously done this type of work before while others had no idea where to start. Caine began whittling and before long, his potato looked like a pig.

Clare sighed and shook her head.

"I'm afraid they will waste at least five pounds. I hope we don't run out."

The meal was finally ready, and Clare called the men in. Twenty riders pulled off their hats and left their boots by the door. Those who didn't find a seat at the table sat on the stairs.

Cookie had brought over his plates and utensils, so there were enough for everyone.

Clare smiled at the shy group of riders.

"Spur and I want you to know how much we appreciate all of you. We certainly couldn't run this ranch without you. As soon as he leads us in grace, bring your plates over here and we will fill them for you. And please, eat until you are full."

The meal was quiet at first but became noisier as the men became more comfortable. However, when Maggie cut the pumpkin pies, the room became almost silent.

One of the riders looked from the pie to the women and shook his head.

"Ladies, if word gets out about this here party, you are gonna have a lot more men to feed next year." More men nodded in agreement as they wiped their plates with large slabs of bread.

When the meal was over, little food was left. Spur ate the last piece of pie and rubbed his stomach.

"My new favorite pie. I don't believe I ever had it before today, but I sure hope to eat it again."

After the men had said their thank yous and filed outside, Maggie pushed Clare into a chair.

"You sit down. That baby is due in just a few weeks, and we don't need it to come early."

Clare didn't argue. Her back hurt and her feet were tired.

"I can help dry if you want to hand me plates."

Kit chattered as the women worked. She finally looked at Clare and asked, "When does Father Ravalli think your baby will come?"

"He said sometime the first or second week of December, but I guess it will come when it wants."

It wasn't long before the kitchen was back in shape. Maggie and Ike were preparing to go home. She sent the children upstairs.

"You play quietly or take a nap. If you fight, I will give you work to do."

Clare stood up. She had one hand on her back and the other under her stomach.

"I think I will go lie down. My back hurts and I'm tired." She hugged both women. "Thank you, both of you. This was so much fun. We certainly couldn't have done it without you."

"Take the downstairs bedroom, Clare. Spur hasn't slept in there since you moved in."

"No, I'll go upstairs. The kids will sneak outside in a little while and it will be quiet up there."

CHAPTER 45

A Fast Trip to the Mission

MAGGIE WATCHED CLARE SLOWLY CLIMB THE STAIRS. She thought a moment before she turned to Kit.

"You tell Ike we are going to spend the night. I think Clare might be in labor. If Spur has to take her to the Mission, we will be here to help. If not, I can help you prepare supper, and we will go home in the morning."

Maggie finally went upstairs. She was with Clare for a time before she hurried back down. She drew some water and pointed at the door.

"Have the men find Spur. Clare is in labor."

It was over an hour before Kit saw Spur racing toward the house. His horse was lathered and one of the riders grabbed it as he jumped off. He threw his hat on the floor as he rushed into the house.

Maggie called to him from the top of the stairs. "You'd better hitch up that buggy, Spur. You need to take Clare to the Mission."

Spur stared at Maggie a moment. He charged back through the door and raced toward the barn, hollering at the men as he ran. He quickly reappeared. A team of horses was hitched to the buggy, and it was quickly tied in front of the house.

He raced up the stairs, taking the steps two at a time. He looked down a Clare for a moment before he scooped her up. As he headed for the stairs, he called back to Maggie.

"Grab some blankets. The temperature dropped and this is going to be a cold ride."

He smiled down at Clare and kissed her cheek.

"Don't worry, Sweetheart. We'll be at the Mission in no time. The next time you take a ride in that buggy, it will be with a baby in your arms."

Spur lifted Clare into the buggy and then jumped up beside her to wrap the blankets around her. He started to sit down, and Clare pointed at his head as she groaned.

"Your hat, Spur. You forgot your hat." She sucked in her breath sharply as Spur raced back into the house. He pulled on his hat. He was barely in the buggy before he had the horses racing down the lane. He reached over and patted Clare.

"I sure am glad you agreed to move down here. We can make this trip to town in about half the time it would have taken us before."

Clare didn't answer and Spur looked over at her in concern.

"So how does this work? Do I keep talking or do you want me to shut up? You don't seem to want to have a conversation."

Clare took a deep breath and then clenched her teeth as she groaned.

"Go faster," she panted, and Spur did.

He hauled the team to a stop in front of the Mission and grabbed Clare. He could feel wetness when he picked her up. He raced for Father Ravalli's little office. He banged on the door with his elbow.

"Padre! Clare's in labor!"

Father Ravalli was in his quarters, and he rushed over. "Lay her down there, Spur." He looked at the nervous man and patted his arm. "I can use your help if you want to stay. If you think you will pass out, then wait outside."

"I can help. Tell me what to do."

"I want you to sit by Clare. If we can keep her relaxed, this will be easier for her. There is a pitcher of water there. Put a little water on that cloth and keep her face cool.

"Now, Clare, we are going to get rid of some of these clothes so I can see what's going on. It looks like your water has broken already.

"Spur, unfasten her dress and slip the skirt down. I want to check her and we'll proceed from there."

Spur's hands were trembling as he unfastened Clare's dress. She had her eyes closed and she was gritting her teeth. Suddenly, her eyes opened and she gripped his hand.

"Don't you leave me, Spur. Don't you run away."

Spur looked down at Clare in surprise. He laughed softly. "I'm not going anywhere. I have to get your dress off though. I am going to put my hands under you and pull on it. You are all wet and it is stuck." He gently loosened her hand and began to work her dress down.

"Everything from her waist down has to come off. Bloomers and all." Father Ravalli was washing his hands and barely turned around.

Spur finally had everything off. He looked at Clare's stomach with concern. "Lordy," he whispered. "She looks like she could split wide open."

Father Ravalli's eyes twinkled and he whispered, "Don't say things like that too loud, Spur. That's not what she needs to hear."

The priest quickly checked Clare. He was smiling as he moved up by her face.

"Clare, your baby is coming. He is head down so that is good.

"Now, I want you to squat on the floor. My Salish friends have shown me an easier way to birth babies. Spur can help you down. You push when I say, and don't worry about your little one. I will catch it.

"Spur, you help her out of bed. Hang onto her. They call this labor for a reason.

"That's it. Okay, now push. Good one. Push again. Stop now and let me adjust something.

"You hang onto the bed, Clare. I need Spur to help me here." The priest's voice was urgent.

"You hold the baby's head, Spur. Hold him close so I can work this cord."

Spur stared in horror at the head and neck of the baby in Father Ravalli's hands. The umbilical cord was wrapped tightly around the baby's neck, and the tiny child was almost blue.

"Hold him, Spur. Closer. Hold him higher." The priest's voice was sharp.

"Clare, go ahead and push again."

The baby slid the rest of the way out and the priest quickly worked to unwind the cord. When it was unwrapped, he motioned for Spur to lower his hands. The baby wasn't moving.

"Keep your hands under him." The priest lowered his mouth and blew air into the tiny boy's mouth. The priest patted the baby's chest and blew air again. Spur was barely breathing as he watched.

Clare had collapsed against the bed. She was sobbing.

"Get me a quilt off the table, Spur. He is coming around. And help Clare up."

The baby gave a choking cry and screamed loudly. Father Ravalli kissed his cheek and made the sign of the cross over him. He handed Clare her little boy.

"You have a beautiful son, Clare. He's a long fellow and quite the fighter. There is no quit in him." He winked at Spur. "I think you have another Annie," he added with a chuckle.

"Now you let Spur help you into that bed. Don't worry about the sheets. They will wash.

"I am going to get you back up in a moment though. We want to make sure everything comes out that is supposed to." His smile was large as he added, "And there was no problem with that scar tissue."

Before long, Father Ravalli took the baby.

"You help her up, Spur. Ease her down to the floor. Just like that. Now you hold this baby, and we will deliver that afterbirth."

Spur watched in amazement as the afterbirth slid out. He had seen this process in cattle and horses many times, and the birth of a new animal was always incredible. The birth of a child was a new level of joy though. He gave Clare his arm to stand. Once she was in bed, he handed her the baby.

"He's beautiful, Clare. Perfect in every way. Well, other than that one missing toe. He has nine other ones though, so he should be fine."

Clare gasped and pulled the quilt back. She pulled up the little feet that were tucked next to the baby's stomach and checked them. She glared up into the face of her laughing husband.

"I declare, Spur. You have a terrible sense of humor."

"Ah, come on, Clare. Would you have loved him any less?"

Clare kissed her nursing baby. She smiled up at Spur.

"No, no I wouldn't have. And thank you, Spur. Thank you for getting me here in time and for all your help too." A look of concern crossed her face as she looked toward the priest.

"Father Ravalli, you don't think he will have any problems from the cord being wrapped like that? Problems later, I mean."

The priest patted Clare's arm.

"He is perfect, Clare, right down to his toes." The priest's kind eyes twinkled as he added, "Although I just about checked his feet myself when Spur made that comment.

"Now you two enjoy a little time before I send Spur home. Young mothers need rest." He smiled at Spur.

"I am guessing Clare is worn out from that big celebration today. Add a birthing to that and she needs some sleep."

"Your family may come tomorrow to see you, Clare. You might even be ready to go home if they come in the afternoon. We'll see by then." He pulled a blanket over her and patted her leg. He blessed the little family and hurried out of the room.

Clare stroked the baby's face. She had tears in her eyes when she looked up at Spur.

"I was so afraid when he didn't cry." Clare's voice was a whisper and it cracked as she spoke.

Spur kissed the baby. He kissed Clare's head as well.

"I was too. The cord was so tight around his neck. He was blue and he wasn't breathing. That padre never flinched though. He breathed air into him. He breathed *life* back into him. I can't believe that worked.

"No wonder everyone around here loves that priest so much."

Spur looked down at his hands and stood. He washed them in Father Ravalli's basin before he dropped back down beside Clare.

"Now I can put my arm around you." He kissed her cheek and smiled. "That was amazing, Clare.

"I sure thought you were going to pop though when I looked at your stomach. And I thought you might split in half when he was coming out. He—"

"Stop talking, Spur. I want to think pretty thoughts, and you are ruining my moment."

Spur chuckled as he looked down at her. "It for sure was incredible. New life has always amazed me, but I don't think I have ever been part of anything that could top this." He kissed her cheek again and grinned.

"Thanks for making me marry you."

Clare's blue eyes were wide when she looked up at him.

"I'm glad you were here," she whispered.

Spur lit the lamps on the side of the buggy and drove it home in the dark. "I sure am pleased we moved before that little fellow came. That trip to the Mission would have taken too long….and this trip home would have been a difficult one too."

Lamps were shining in Chas' house when Spur pulled up. Stub came out of the bunkhouse to take the horses. He gave Spur a quizzical look and the new father grinned.

"Little boy. Everything is good now. I liked that priest before, and I like him even better now."

Stub let out a deep breath. Tuff had followed him out of the bunkhouse and they both smiled.

"Tuff, since you are up, help me with these horses.

"You just as well get on in the house, Spur. Everyone is up and waiting on you." Stub slapped Spur on the back and grinned.

"Congratulations, Pa!"

Spur was smiling as he pushed the door open. His friends were watching the door and they began smiling when they saw his face.

"It were a boy, warn't it? I told Maggie Mae it were a boy but she was convinced it'd be a little bitty girl."

Spur nodded. "A boy. Father Ravalli said he was a long one. He looked pretty little to me, but I don't know as I have ever seen a newborn baby before. I guess I'll take his word for it. The little fellow has a good set of lungs for sure."

He added quietly, "It's a good thing we made it to the Mission in fast time. The cord was wrapped around his neck, and it didn't look good for a time there.

"I don't think that padre ever gets rattled though. He just unwound it and breathed life back into that little boy.

"I'm headed to bed. I'll tell the kids in the morning."

Ike called after him, "Did Clare pick a name?"

Spur paused and looked back in surprise. He frowned and shook his head.

"She never mentioned anything, and I didn't think to ask. I guess we'll find out when we go in tomorrow. Father said she might be able to come home if we wait until the afternoon."

Spur walked slowly to the back bedroom. He almost stumbled. "I sure am tired and if I'm tired, Clare has to be beat." He peeled his clothes off and fell into bed.

Maggie looked after him with a smile. She could hear him snoring and she slipped back quietly to shut the door.

CHAPTER 46

A New Pa

SPUR AWOKE TO THREE LITTLE FACES SMILING AT HIM from the doorway. When he grinned at them, they rushed into the bedroom and jumped up on the bed.

"Tell us! Tell us! Is our baby a boy or a girl?" Annie's face was excited as she bounced on Spur's stomach.

Zeke looked soberly at Spur. "I hope it's a boy. We need more fellows around here. There are just too many girls."

"I don't care if our baby is a boy or a girl. I am going to hold it all day long," Nora stated calmly. "It will be *my* baby."

Annie immediately began to complain, and Spur chuckled.

"Our baby is a boy. We can all hold it, but only Mama can feed it." He looked seriously at the three little faces. "And that is important because if you feed it anything but Mama's milk, it will get sick.

"Now let me get dressed. As soon as you finish your chores, we will go see our baby."

The three kids slid off the bed and ran screaming into the kitchen. Spur grinned as he listened to them tell Maggie their plans. He found some clean britches and was still tucking in a fresh shirt when he appeared.

Maggie's eyes were glinting as she looked at him. "Not waiting until this afternoon?" she asked dryly.

Spur grinned. "Nope. I reckon I am as excited as the kids are to get in there. We'll all go in this morning, and I'll go back this afternoon if the padre says she can come home."

Maggie handed a package of food to Spur.

"Take that in with you. If Clare hasn't eaten, that will save the priests some extra work. If she has eaten, leave it with them." She thrust a second bulky package into his arms. "And that is a fresh dress. I'm sure Clare is ready for a change of clothes.

"I want to give the girls baths first. They can ride in with Ike and me. Now you hurry on in there."

Spur nodded. He pumped water into his shaving basin. He had shaved and was almost done eating when Zeke rushed inside with eggs and a bucket of milk.

"Tuff milked the cow this morning. He said he can do it faster than me. That way, you and I can leave sooner.

"The girls are going to ride with Auntie Maggie and Grandpa Ike." He whispered to Spur, "Grandpa Ike promised them some candy!" Zeke's brown eyes were shining as he talked.

"Can I drive the team this morning since the girls won't be along? I have been practicing hitching them up and standing up in the buggy. Sometimes I drop the lines, but I'd like Mama to see me drive."

"That would be fine, Zeke. Now you get on a heavy coat and grab a couple of blankets." Spur looked over at Kit.

"You want to come along? Ike and Maggie's buggy will be full with two kids in it. You can ride in with me if you want. We just as well make it a family affair."

Kit blushed slightly as she shook her head.

"No, I am riding in with Stub and Tuff after dinner. I can clean up here so all of you can head out."

Spur grinned at her. "You seem to be spending a lot of time with that sawed-off cowboy. I'd say you like him or something."

Kit blushed furiously. A blast of cold air filled the room as Stub opened the door. He looked around before he spoke. Ike and Spur were laughing, and Maggie was trying not to.

Stub's eyes settled on Kit's pink face. He looked back at Spur. The ornery cowboy winked at him. A slow grin filled Stub's face and he stepped up beside Kit.

"Now don't you go scaring Kit off just when I am working up the courage to ask her to be my girl. If you go and run her off, why my old heart will be plumb broken."

Kit stared at Stub in surprise and her face turned a darker red.

Stub pulled Kit a little closer to him and whispered, "What do you say, Kit? Will you be my girl?"

Kit's body went still. She looked up at the grinning Stub and she finally laughed. "I will think on that. Maybe if you talk sweet to me."

Maggie clapped her hands excitedly and Ike grinned. Spur shook his head.

"I don't know. I have been coaching that feller on moving a little faster. I was about to give it up. Ol' Stub finally came through." He grinned at Stub and gave Kit a quick hug.

"Let's go, Zeke. Your Uncle Stub was so kind as to hitch up our team. Let's get on in town and meet that baby brother."

"Climb up here and take hold of these lines. Sort them through your fingers like this.

"Now stand between my legs." Spur crossed one leg over the other.

"Keep a firm grip on those lines but don't jerk them. And stand straight. I will catch you if you start to fall."

Zeke turned the buggy around slowly and guided the horses out of the yard. He drove quietly for a few miles. Finally, he looked around at Spur.

"When our baby can talk, will he call you Pop?"

Spur looked at the little boy in front of him in surprise. He finally nodded.

"Why, I reckon he will. I will be the only pop he'll ever know."

Zeke was quiet a while longer before he looked back at Spur again.

"At first, Rock was my uncle. When he married my mama, I got a new pa. I liked having a pa." Zeke's eyes were serious as he talked. He turned back around to watch the road before he continued.

"Since you married my mama, that kind of makes you my pa. Do you think it would be alright if I called you Pop too? I think I'd like to do that."

Spur looked at the serious young man in front of him. A knot formed in his throat, and he swallowed. He nodded and answered quietly, "I'd like that too, Zeke. I have never had any kids of my own, but I'd sure like to be your pop."

Zeke looked back quickly and grinned before he faced forward again. He snapped the lines on the backs of the horses.

"I reckon the girls will want to talk to you about that too. We have been discussing it some." He stood a little straighter.

"Giddy up, you durn horses. We're wastin' daylight."

CHAPTER 47

A New Baby Brother

CLARE WAS STANDING BY THE WINDOW WITH THE BABY over her shoulder when Zeke turned the team into the lane that led to the Mission. She almost gasped. When she saw the pride and excitement on his face, she laughed softly.

"Zeke, you are growing so quickly. Where did my little boy go?"

Spur jumped down with the lines in his hands and waited for Zeke. Then he handed them to the little boy and showed him where to tie the team.

Clare knocked on the window and Zeke looked around in surprise. When he saw his mother standing there with a smile on her face, he puffed himself up and strutted a little.

Spur was grinning when they knocked on the door of the little office. Father Ravalli had a smile on his face when he opened the door. Spur pointed behind him.

"The whole clan will be here in a little bit, Padre. We are all mighty excited about this baby."

Father Ravalli laughed and pointed them toward the door behind him.

"Clare is up and around. She thinks she is ready to go home but I want her to wait until later today. She promised me she would take it easy, but I know how that works with young ones."

Clare opened the door when Spur knocked. She was smiling as she leaned toward Zeke.

"This is your little brother, Zeke. Isn't he beautiful? Look at all that curly hair."

Zeke touched the baby's soft cheek. "He sure is little. I reckon it will be some time before he is ready to play with us.

"Can I hold him?"

Clare sat Zeke down in a chair and handed him the baby. "Keep one arm around his body and the other one under his head. He can't hold it up by himself yet."

The baby squirmed and frowned but settled down when Zeke leaned back in the chair.

"Hello there, Little Brother. You sure took your time getting here. You are so darned little that you aren't going to be much good for some time.

"Since Spur will be the only pop you'll ever know, you can go ahead and call him that. I'm going to call him Pop too. He said it would be all right." He looked up at his mother and smiled.

"I like him, Ma. I think we should go ahead and take him home. No sense in him staying here just because you need to."

Clare looked at Zeke in surprise and Spur chuckled.

"Now we had that conversation about eating, remember? This little guy is attached to your mother for some time. Since she stays, he stays."

He looked over at Clare with a smile and asked, "So did you pick a name?"

Clare's eyes were soft as she looked at her two sons. "I was thinking maybe we would call him Chas. Chas Worthy Spurlach. Rock's name was James Worthington and he hated it. I think he would like Worthy though." She smiled up at Spur as tears glistened in the corners of her blue eyes. "Then he will be named after the three most important men in his life."

Spur squeezed her hand and nodded. He cleared his throat and dropped down beside Zeke. He lifted the baby's tiny hand and little fingers wrapped around his. Spur stared at his hand for a moment.

He spoke softly, "Welcome to the family, Chas. I think you will like it around our place. You probably won't get much sleep, but you will always have someone around to hold and play with you." He kissed the little hand and stared at the sleeping baby a moment before he stood. He cleared his throat and handed Clare the packages.

"Maggie sent some food in case you hadn't eaten. Some fresh clothes too." His dark eyes sparkled as he looked her over. "You know, this is the first time I have seen you that you weren't pregnant." Clare frowned at him.

Spur chuckled as he added, "And you look just as good now as you did before."

Clare blushed slightly and Spur winked at her. "You don't think I sat beside you accidentally on that train ride to Blackfoot, do you?" He shook his head. "No, sir. I have always made it a point to sit by the prettiest lady I can find when I ride a train.

"Of course, now when you and I travel, I won't have to work so hard at it."

Clare sputtered a couple of times and Spur laughed again. He nodded toward the window.

"Here comes the rest of your loud family. I had better see if the padre has a few more chairs."

CHAPTER 48

JUST BE HAPPY, CLARE

SPUR MOVED CLARE'S CLOTHES DOWN TO THE LARGE bedroom at the back of the house. He had the room ready for her by the time she came home.

Father Ravalli had kept her an extra day. Clare wouldn't tell Spur why, but Father Ravalli explained his reason.

"Women bleed for a time after a baby is born. Clare is bleeding more than I like. I want to keep her one more night to keep an eye on her. It shouldn't be a problem, but it's best to be safe.

"Make sure she has plenty of rags and have her take a soaking bath every night." He stared at Spur as he added, "And I mean every night. Childbirth is a little bloody, so she is going to be tired for a time. A soaking bath will help her uterus to contract. It will help her to relax as well." He patted Spur on the back. "Besides, she will feel better if she can bathe."

Clare was quiet on the way home. Spur whistled for a time. He waited for Clare to speak. When she still didn't talk, he cleared his throat.

"I moved your things down to the large bedroom. I thought that might be easier for you rather than running up and down the stairs."

Clare said nothing but Spur could see a tear in the side of her eye. He patted her leg.

"Clare, I'm not coming to your bed until you ask me. I'm fine on the cot. When I get tired of that, I can sleep upstairs. The big room is yours.

"I hope someday you will be ready to share more of yourself with me. If not, well, that's the way it is."

Clare stared down at the baby in her arms and a sob escaped her.

"I'm sorry, Spur. You have been so wonderful.

"Annie and Nora told me they want to call you Papa. You have kept up your end of this contract and have received so little in return."

Spur stared at Clare in surprise. He frowned as he shook his head.

"So little? I have a family, Clare. I've never had that before. I have a beautiful wife who loves her children so much that she is willing to sacrifice her happiness for them. I have a ranch and I know who my father is.

"I have more than I ever dreamed. If you can't love me because you gave your heart away to a good man, then I'll deal with that." He shook his head. "No, I think I'm the winner in this deal."

When another sob came from deep in her chest, Spur put his arm around her. He kissed her tear and whispered, "Don't cry, Clare. You can't control your heart any more than you can control the wind in the trees or the moonlight. You just be happy. That is good enough for me."

Clare let Spur pull her close. She soaked up his warmth and slowly relaxed. Chas snuggled in closely to her and stirred a little in his sleep.

CHAPTER 49

A Few Questions on the Ride Home

SPUR SANG SOFTLY FOR A TIME. WHEN THEY WERE about three miles from Stevensville, he looked over at Clare.

"I was thinking maybe we should give Chas' ranch a name. It is going to be confusing to have a ranch and a little fellow with the same name. What do you think?" Spur looked down at Clare as he spoke.

Clare looked up in surprise. "What are you thinking? You want to change the name of the /B as well?"

"Not necessarily, although I think all the cattle should eventually wear the same brand. I'd like to register a brand for you and me. I was thinking of a double spur. It will look more like two connecting U's side-by-side with a leg on the bottom of each. An actual spur would have too many contact points. Double Spur Ranch. What do you think?"

Clare was quiet a moment. She finally nodded and smiled up at him.

"I like it. Maybe we could keep the /B registered though in case one of the children wants to use it as his or her brand."

Spur gave Clare a squeeze and nodded. "I'll get our brand registered this week. We'll start to brand everything next year with the Double

Spur. Of course, the cattle that are branded with the /B will stay that way. We'll gradually phase that brand out, but it will take a while to make a complete change."

He winked at her and bumped her with his elbow.

"Shoot, by then you might decide that you like me enough to add a few more kids to this family."

Clare pulled away and turned a deep red.

"You are so bold, Spur. Good grief. Is there anything you won't talk about?"

Spur scratched his head.

"Now that you mention it, there are a few things I do have questions about. Do women cycle every month? I mean every female animal I know of comes into heat. Do women do that?"

Clare stared at him. She moved to the opposite side of the wagon seat.

"I am not discussing that with you."

"You brought it up. I mean you did say, 'Is there anything—'"

"I was being sarcastic!"

"And I'm being honest."

Clare glared at him for a moment before she responded.

"Yes, women cycle but that is all I am going to tell you."

"Now with cattle, you wean the calves to make sure the cows come into heat. 'Course some cows are already bred by the time we pull the calves off. How does that work with women?"

Clare sputtered as she glared at him. "I am not talking about this with you anymore."

Spur's dark eyes were twinkling and he laughed. "All right. I'll behave myself. I do have more questions though. Like, what if a woman has twins, one boy and one girl. Is the girl a freemartin like a heifer calf twin is?"

Clare's confusion showed on her face.

"The heifer is sterile. Would it be the same for a little girl?"

Clare stared at Spur for a moment before she asked, "Do you just sit around and think of this stuff? Why on earth would that be a concern to you?"

"My old buddy Rusty and his wife down by Cheyenne, they had twins. One was a girl and one a boy. I was just wondering if that little girl will be able to have babies.

"It would be a shame if she couldn't. Little tiny red-headed girl with curls everywhere. She'd make some mighty cute kids."

Clare laughed and she shook her head.

"Cows and women are not the same. She should be able to have babies. And if you promise to not ask me any more personal questions, I will slide back over beside you. It is cold over here."

Spur's face lit up in a grin. He put out his arm and Clare slid over. He hugged her tightly and whispered, "Now what if—?"

Clare's elbow slammed into his side and Spur grunted as he laughed.

"That was the reaction I thought I'd get. You sure are fun to tease, Clare Ann Spurlach.

"All right, I'll give you some peace. How about you tell me what song you want me to sing, and I'll serenade you the rest of the way home."

Clare smiled up at him. "Sing me 'The Bonnie Banks O' Loch Lomond.' I loved that song the first time we danced to it. I love it even more since it is a part of you and Chas. Sing that song to me."

CHAPTER 50

STUB'S QUESTION

DECEMBER BROUGHT LOTS OF SNOW. THE COWBOYS put in long days moving cattle around to where grass was easier to find. The ponds were covered with ice and holes had to be cut. Even some of the fast-running creeks iced over in places and had to be broken open.

"Less than two weeks until Christmas. I have so many things to make before then," Clare murmured as she hurried to finish preparing supper. She watched through the kitchen window for Spur. Every day he made it home gave her a sense of relief, and today was no different.

She looked over to where Kit was working on a dress.

"The men are home. It is snowing again so I am guessing Tuff and Stub will spend the night in the bunkhouse. Why don't you see if they want to eat with us?

"I mended a pair of britches for Tuff. He is growing so fast that he is blowing out the crotches of everything he wears. Help me to remember to send them home with him."

Kit was already headed out the door before Clare finished talking. She smiled after her friend.

"So young and so in love. I wonder when they will be getting married. Kit has said nothing, but she smiles a lot.

"Of course, Stub shows no expression. You have to watch his eyes to know what he is thinking. They are such a cute couple.

"Probably in the spring. Spring is always a fine time for a wedding."

Clare watched out the window as Stub paused his horse beside Kit. He listened to her and nodded. They were both smiling when he put his hand down. Kit grabbed it and Stub swung her up in the saddle in front of him. They were laughing as he turned his horse toward the barn.

Clare smiled again. She could see Zeke and Annie carrying the milk bucket. They were arguing and slopping the milk as they hurried. Nora was close behind with a bucket of eggs.

Spur had moved the chicken coop into the barn shortly after Chas was born. He added a window so they would have light during the day. He told the kids the chickens would quit laying if it was too dark. He had even built the coop up about two feet off the ground so it would be easier to clean under.

The snow fell in large flakes and soon piled up in the low spots. The wind wasn't as strong here as it was up on the mountainside. Once again, Clare was pleased that Spur had convinced her to move.

She stirred her stew and admired the new kitchen stove Spur had brought home that week. "He totally spoils me," she whispered. "He does so much and expects so little in return."

Clare thought about the new shirt and vest she was making for him as she set the table. She tried to work on them in the afternoons when the house was quieter. She was making Zeke a matching set. She hoped they would both like their Christmas surprises.

The kitchen door slammed open, and Clare hurried to grab the milk. She hated the mess the spilled milk made on her floors.

"You kids leave your boots by the door. I don't want that snow tracked all over this house. And we are all taking baths tonight. I am hoping we will be able to get out for church in the morning, and I want you clean."

Annie glowered and muttered under her breath. She looked toward the barn and her frown disappeared. She began to giggle. She whispered loudly, "Stub was kissing Aunt Kit in the barn. He asked her something. She said yes and started crying. I don't think she was sad though because she was smiling."

Clare studied the three little faces as she frowned.

"Were you hiding in the barn to spy on them?"

"We weren't hiding, Mama. They just didn't see us. When they started kissing, we sneaked out. I was picking up the eggs. Annie and Zeke were playing with the kittens." Nora's face was serious as she spoke, and Clare hugged all three of them.

"You all wash up and one of you may hold Chas while I finish dinner."

Nora finished first and was seated on the floor with Chas on her lap when Spur came in. Annie raced to meet him and grabbed him by the legs.

"Stub was kissing Aunt Kit in the barn and we saw them. I think they are in love!"

Spur chuckled and lifted her up. "Oh, you think so, do you?" He rubbed his mustache on her face and neck until she was giggling and trying to get loose.

"Do that to Mama. Make her laugh when you tickle her with your mustache, Papa."

Spur's eyes glinted and he sauntered toward Clare. She backed up and he grabbed her. Soon Clare was squealing and telling Spur to stop as she laughed. He kissed her cheek and set her back down. He grinned down at her.

"Hello, Little Darlin'. Something smells mighty good." He reached down and lifted Chas.

"How's my little cowboy tonight? One of these days, I'll have you out there moving cattle around and *I'll* be snug in the house." He winked at Clare and added, "All cozied up close to your mama."

Clare lifted the baby out of his arms. "Wash up, Spur. I invited Stub and Tuff to stay for supper. And afterwards, I want everyone to take baths."

Everyone turned around as Kit and Stub walked through the door. Stub's smile almost split his face. He had his arm around Kit, and she was smiling too.

Spur pretended not to notice but Clare laughed. "You two look like you have a secret and are dying to tell it."

Tuff came through the door just then. His grin was large. Stub grabbed his younger brother and pulled him up beside them.

"Tuff and I have been talking. We decided I should ask Kit to marry. I asked tonight and she said yes. We are getting married the day after Christmas."

Clare caught her breath. She looked over at Spur and his face was nonchalant. *He so knew about this*, she thought. *Still, that is soon.*

Clare hugged both Stub and Kit. Her eyes were shining as she looked at them.

"I'm so happy for both of you! You will marry at the Mission? You have talked to Father Ravalli already?"

Stub nodded. "I talked to him this afternoon when I went into town.

"I picked up the mail too. There was a letter for old Chas, so they sent it with me." He held out the letter to Spur.

"Just lay it on my desk. I'll look at it later. Right now, I just want to eat.

"You fellows get washed up so that stew doesn't get cold. Although, with Clare's new stove, I guess that's not a problem anymore." Spur looked around the room with a grin.

"Some cowboy went out and bought my wife a fancy stove. I think he has taken a shining to her. I will have to say it does a fine job of keeping food warm though." He winked at Clare and she smiled.

CHAPTER 51

AN EVENING SERENADE

BATH TIME AND BEDTIME WERE ALWAYS HECTIC. Clare was exhausted by the time the three children were bathed. She groaned as she sat down.

"Those kids were filthy. Would you mind dumping that water? I'll drag it into your office and take a bath in there. It won't be so far to carry, and I'll still have privacy."

Spur nodded and grinned at her. "That will be fine. I was thinking of doing some bookwork this evening. That will add a whole new dimension to it."

Clare stared at him and then blushed furiously.

"Honestly, Spur. I never know what will come out of your mouth."

Spur chuckled and carried the tub outside. He dumped the dirty water and rinsed it with snow before he carried it into his office. The water was boiling, and he filled the tub.

"Sure is nice to have that pump in here, isn't it?"

Clare nodded as she looked around the kitchen. "And a kitchen stove too. You spoil me, Spur."

"Making your life a little easier isn't spoiling, Clare. Besides, I like a happy wife."

Clare smiled at him and then glanced toward the living room where Stub and Kit were talking.

"You knew Stub was going to ask Kit tonight, didn't you? I'm guessing you even knew the date they were planning to marry."

Spur chuckled. "No point in waiting around if you know it's right. Just ask my wife." His dark eyes glinted, and he sat down across from Clare.

"Stub has been head over heels for Kit ever since she came. It took him longer to work up the courage to ask her to be his girl than it did to know he wanted to marry.

"They are good for each other, and that means they will be happy." He patted her hand and added, "Besides, now you will have a girlfriend to talk to and spend time with. And one who will be living just a few miles away."

Clare nodded. "I am going to miss her when she moves out though. She has been so much help." She handed Spur the sleeping baby.

"If you'll hold him, I will take a bath."

Spur nodded. He watched Clare walk across the kitchen and close the door to his office.

"You sure have a pretty mama, Chas. Just looking at her makes my heart tingle." He kissed the sleeping baby and whispered, "I think I am softening her up. She might even be starting to like me some."

He stood and danced around the kitchen with the baby as he sang to him. "Oh, Shenandoah, I long to see you/ Away, you rolling river/ Oh Shenandoah, I long to see you/ Away, I'm bound away/ 'Cross the wide Missouri."

Clare listened to Spur's singing and smiled. "Serenaded while I take a bath. Yes, I certainly am spoiled."

CHAPTER 52

MADAM BELLA

SPUR FORGOT ABOUT THE LETTER STUB HAD delivered for over a week. When he finally took the time to do some office work on December 21, he found it.

The writing was a woman's and Spur frowned as he studied it. It looked familiar but he couldn't place it.

"Chas isn't around to read this, so I guess I will read it for him." He tore the letter open and stared at it in shock. It was from Maebeline, and she obviously didn't know that Chas had passed away.

Dearest Charlie,

You have been on my mind of late and I have decided to come see you. I have often wondered what your ranch looked like.

I'm sorry your Agnes passed away although she surely wasn't a suitable mate for you. She was always so frail. Too bad you were not able to have any children with her.

I lost track of your son fifteen years ago. He ran away when he was thirteen or fourteen, and I never saw him again. Oh, some of the girls mentioned that they had seen him over the years. Those who knew you said he was as tall as you. They said he even wore a mustache like you did when we first met—maybe you still do. His hair was black though. It was so curly when he was little. He took after my side that way, I guess.

The last news I heard was that he had helped take a herd of cattle up the Bozeman Trail right into your valley. A man died on that drive and the woman who shared the story with me thought it was our son. Not that she knew you were the father. I never told anyone you were. She knew our boy though, and she was sure it was he who died.

It is just you and me, Charlie. That's why I am coming to see you. I want to get out of this business. Maybe you and I can build a life together.

I have a business in Helena, so it won't take me long to get there. If the weather is good, I plan to come for Christmas. I will be in Stevensville by December 23. If you cannot pick me up, I will hire a driver to bring me out.

I am looking forward to seeing you and to catching up.

Love, Madeline

Spur looked at the calendar.

"Three days! Madam Bella will be here in three days!" He read the letter again as he frowned. "Has she really changed or was this a ploy to trick a wealthy rancher into marrying her? I'm inclined to believe the latter.

"I guess we'll never know. Chas is dead and she is not staying here. I don't trust her around my family."

Spur carried the letter into the kitchen. He was frowning. Clare looked up with a smile. It left her face as she watched Spur.

"Bad news?"

The shock still showed when Spur looked up.

"Madam Bella is coming here. She expects to arrive on the twenty-third, and she thinks Chas is still alive." Spur's face became angry, and he threw the letter down.

"She thinks I'm dead and she wants to reconnect with Chas.

"I don't trust her though. She has been vicious and conniving her entire life. I'm guessing she thinks Chas is rich, and she wants his money."

Clare stared at Spur a moment. She put her hands on his shoulders. Her voice was soft as she looked up at him.

"But what if she isn't? What if she really has changed? People can change, Spur."

Spur shook his head bitterly. "Not her. Tigers don't change their stripes. And I don't want her staying here. I don't trust her…and I sure don't trust her around people I love."

He knocked the letter off the table and kicked it before he pulled on his hat.

"I'm headed into Stevensville. I'm going to talk to Ike to give him a head's up. Who knows what she will do when she finds out Chas is dead."

Clare jumped when Spur slammed the door, and the baby began to cry. She picked the letter up and laid it back on the table. Then she lifted the baby and talked softly to him as she walked to the window. Spur slammed his fist into the hitching rail as he walked by and stormed on toward the barn.

Stub had just arrived. He watched his boss and turned to look toward the house. He slowly dismounted and followed Spur into the barn. Before long, he was back out with a saddled horse. He mounted and raced his horse down the lane.

CHAPTER 53

OLD HURTS AND BAD MEMORIES

K IT'S FACE WAS BRIGHT AS SHE HURRIED INTO THE kitchen. She stared at Spur's uneaten breakfast. Her eyes moved to the letter on the table. When she saw the name at the bottom, she gasped and clutched the side of the table. She picked up the letter with shaky hands and held it toward Clare.

"What does Mae want with Spur? She's not coming here, is she?" She fell into a chair and began sobbing.

Clare hurried to the table and sat down by her friend.

"Kit, what's wrong? Do you know Maebeline?"

Kit wrapped her arms around her shoulders. She was shaking as she spoke.

"She is the one who forced me to be with men when I was thirteen."

Clare's face went pale. "Oh, Kit. I am so sorry."

Kit walked to the window. She stared out for a moment before she turned to face Clare.

"My father was a cowboy. He was a small man with a large personality. He laughed all the time, and I loved him so much.

"Mother was frail when they met. She had come from New Orleans with her family. She never told me anything about her life there. She just said anything was better than where she had been.

"They met at a barn dance around San Antonio and fell madly in love. Father was a $30 a month cowboy, but he was a hard worker. He was soon offered a foreman's position on a large ranch there, and things weren't so tight.

"Then the War Between the States came. When it ended, cattle in Texas were worth nothing. Lots of ranchers went broke. Some even said the more cattle you owned, the poorer you were. Father lost his job. My parents had to leave Texas."

Clare put her arm around her friend and Kit continued.

"We headed north with a wagon train. Somewhere in Indian Territory, Mother became terribly ill. Soon other members of our wagon train were sick. We stopped and were camped there for nearly two weeks. When we started again, Mother and five other members of our party were no longer with us. We buried them on the prairie in unmarked graves. There was no wood for campfires let alone for markers.

"We hadn't gone much further when we were attacked by outlaws. Father was away from the wagons, but the wagon master managed to organize our party. We beat them back and the wagon train prepared to continue on.

"I was angry and upset. I couldn't believe they were just going to leave without my father. The wagon master tried to tell me that we didn't have the men to search for him, but I didn't care.

"It was true there weren't many men on that wagon train. There were not enough to start with—too many widows. Then we lost men to sickness plus more in the battle with those outlaws.

"Still, it wasn't right to leave him. I think some of the folks silently agreed with the wagon master. Thankfully, the outspoken families refused to go on until we searched for Father.

"Father's horse came back to camp that night. There was blood on his saddle, and I was terrified. One of the young men backtracked it and found Father. He had been shot in the back, but he was still alive.

"Father only lived a few days. We didn't have a doctor in our group, and no one wanted to take the bullet out of his back. It was too close to his spine. There was nothing anyone could do for him.

"I rode with him in our wagon. I took care of him as best I could and we talked." She smiled at Clare. "I so loved my father, and I will always treasure those two days." Kit began crying and Clare hugged her.

"My father was a wonderful man." She smiled through her tears at Clare. "I know he would have loved Steve. They are alike in so many ways." She wiped her eyes as she looked out the window. Her voice was sad when she continued.

"A nice older couple took me in. They had put a little money aside and were one of the few in that party who had adequate supplies. They shared what they had, and we finally made it to the Nebraska Territory.

"They homesteaded there and bought more land. They loved the land and they shared all they had with me.

"It was so beautiful. The grass grew over those sandy hills and just went on for miles." She smiled at Clare. "Miles and miles of grass." Her voice caught in her throat.

"They broke a little of the bottom ground out and planted a few crops. It was a peaceful life, and we were all happy.

"The summer I turned thirteen was extremely dry. A fire started on the prairie and there was no way to stop it. Those nice folks sent me to the creek with the fastest horses. They were following with the plow horses and the milk cow. I made it and they didn't." Kit's voice was brittle when she finished.

Her brown eyes were angry when she looked at Clare.

"They had no heirs and they had left everything to me. Then a woman no one knew showed up with a will. Folks around there tried to contest it, but the bank deemed it legal.

"That woman took over the ranch and kicked me out." Kit walked back to the table. She picked up the letter and studied it a moment before she threw it down. "She fooled everyone.

"I took a job with a troupe of traveling actors. I did their laundry and even sang a little. I was afraid at first, but I enjoyed the singing. We hit cow towns and mining camps." She laughed as she looked at Clare. "I was so small that everyone thought I was much younger than thirteen. Sometimes I made as much as $5 a night just with the coins or bags of gold dust that were tossed on our stage. Of course, I couldn't keep anything since I was dependent on them.

"Everything was fine until we got to Bannack here in the Montana Territory. *She* was there—Maebeline—the woman who stole those old folks' ranch. Oh, she used a different name in Nebraska, but it was her.

"She had a traveling wagon of women, and she claimed I was her daughter. The troupe I was traveling with didn't want any trouble. They kicked me out and left in the middle of the night.

"I had never been with a man, but Mae had me taking three to five customers a night." Kit pointed at the name on the letter.

"Her name was Maebeline but everyone there called her Mae.

"She is a horrid woman, Clare. She wins people over with her charm and her beauty, but she is evil. If she is coming here, it is because she wants something." Her voice dropped to a whisper. "And she will try to kill me because I know who and what she is."

Clare stared at her friend in horror. She pulled Kit close as the young woman sobbed. "Don't cry, Kit," she whispered. "Stub and Spur would never let anything happen to you." Clare's heart clutched with fear. *No wonder Spur despises her. What a terrible woman. He is right to be angry she is coming here.* Her blue eyes were hard and cold when she looked at her friend.

"You and I are going to prepare for this. We will make sure all the guns are loaded. We can put them in places where we can get to them easily. Gomer will warn us if a stranger comes so we can be ready.

"This house has a tunnel that runs from here to the barn, and we are going to use it. If Mae does come, we will hide you in there. She won't even know you are on this ranch.

"Now let's see if we can lift the door to the tunnel without the men helping us. I don't want the children around when she comes either." She paused and looked over at her sleeping baby. "In fact, let's have you call when you get in there to see if I can hear anything up here. If I can hear you, I might have to keep Chas with me."

It took all their strength to slide the desk and pull the tunnel door up. Clare carried a candle down the steps and lit the lamp that was there. She blew out the candle and handed the lamp to Kit.

"Now walk through this tunnel. Stop and call out from time to time. I will go back upstairs and see if I can hear you."

Clare was out of breath by the time she closed the heavy door. She listened closely and could barely hear Kit calling. She looked over at her sleeping son in fear. "He will have to stay with me," she whispered. "If he cries, they will be found." She hurried into the office. After three tries, she was finally able to pull the heavy door up.

Kit's eyes were wide, and her breath was coming quickly as she climbed out.

"What is that place? Why is it here?"

"We don't know. Spur found it before I moved in, but there is no mention of it in any of Chas' papers." She took a small gun out of Spur's desk and handed it to Kit.

"This is mine. I want you to keep it with you. It will be accurate up to four feet and it only holds two bullets." Her eyes were intense as she looked at her friend. "Use it if necessary and don't hesitate. You might not have a second chance."

Kit stared at her friend and slowly nodded.

"What about you? What if you need protection?"

Clare smiled and pointed at a heavy stone crock in an upper cabinet that read "Provisions." She reached behind it and pulled out an old pistol. The hammer was back, and Clare held it carefully.

"The children don't know it is there. The crock is too heavy for them to move and there is nothing in that cabinet they are interested in." Her eyes were sad as she looked at Kit.

"Maebeline is Spur's mother. I'm not sure how he will react if something goes wrong. We must be ready.

"Now let's go to the barn and I will show you the other opening."

CHAPTER 54

ANTICIPATION

DECEMBER TWENTY-SECOND AND TWENTY-THIRD passed quietly. Spur finally rode to town on the morning of Christmas Eve. Ike had neither heard about nor seen any strange woman.

Snow was falling when Spur left Stevensville. He smiled as he rode home with the large flakes drifting around him.

"She is late. Hopefully, this snow will keep her from coming."

By that evening, the snow was deep. Spur walked to the window and looked out. He was smiling when he turned toward Clare.

"We'll see how bad the drifts are in the morning. If they are deep, we might not even be able to go to Christmas Mass.

"How about we have Santa come tonight? That way if we can go, there won't be so much chaos in the morning." He grinned at Clare.

"I was thinking we might have Stub put bells on the horses and drive the sleigh up the lane. We'll have him holler, 'Ho, Ho, Ho!' as he drives. He can pull right up by the house, open the door, and toss a bag of goodies in.

"If he does it during supper, we'll have a reason not to let the kids get up and look out the window." His eyes were sparkling, and Clare laughed.

"Spur, you are as excited about Christmas as the kids are!" She pointed toward her bedroom.

"I have everything finished and wrapped. Bring in one of those feed bags from out in the barn and I will put the gifts in there. After dinner, I'll take the children upstairs for a story and you can sneak them out.

"You'd better hide it well though. Annie has been snooping everywhere for weeks."

Her blue eyes were wide as she whispered, "What about Maebeline?"

Spur shook his head. "If we can't get out, she can't get in. I think I'd almost rather meet her in town with lots of folks around anyway. She might not be so likely to try to pull something." He pulled Clare in for a quick hug.

"Let's relax and enjoy this Christmas."

Dinner was chaotic. The children were excited for Christmas. Spur looked around at them seriously.

"You know, all this snow has made it hard for Santa to get everywhere he needs to go. I'm thinking he might be here a little early this year, maybe even tonight."

Three sets of eyes went wide as they listened. Zeke was the first to speak.

"You really think so? I thought maybe it would slow him down. And how does he come down a chimney anyway? Ours will be full of smoke, and he would land right in the fire."

Spur grinned as he winked at them. "Now nobody has really seen old Santa, have they?" Three heads shook as they watched their father.

"Well, maybe he sneaks in through the door. I mean everyone would be asleep so no one would hear him."

"Gomer would hear him, and he would let us know," Annie stated confidently. "Gomer wouldn't like anyone sneaking in the house."

Spur nodded soberly. "That's true. Maybe we should make Gomer sleep in the barn tonight."

Nora shook her head. "No, he can sleep with Annie and me. He has been upstairs before anyway."

Clare stared at them in surprise while Spur filled his mouth to keep from laughing.

"We all had to take naps and Mama took one too. Gomer was lonesome so he came in the house. We all sneaked down and showed him how to climb the stairs. Zeke even pretended to be a donkey." Nora was very matter-of-fact as she explained.

"It worked too." Annie gave Spur a glorious smile. "Gomer climbed right up the stairs. He even took a nap with us. He woke us up when he wanted to leave, and we all sneaked outside before Mama woke up.

"We love Gomer."

Clare frowned at them. "We all love Gomer, but I still don't want him upstairs. Now finish your dinner. We are all taking naps this afternoon just in case Santa does come tonight.

"If he does *and* if you take naps, I'll let you stay up a little later tonight."

Zeke frowned. "But how is he going to come when we are all here?"

Annie looked at her brother and sister. She whispered loudly, "Maybe he will come while we are taking our naps!" All three children stared at each other with large eyes and raced upstairs.

Clare read them several stories including "Twas the Night Before Christmas." She finished with a story of the Nativity told from a donkey's viewpoint, and the children loved it.

"I think that donkey was Gomer's grandpa. Gomer would give Jesus' mommy a ride, wouldn't he, Mama?" Nora's eyes were serious as she stared up at Clare.

Clare laughed and nodded her head. "I believe he would. Now you all lie down and go to sleep. If I have to come up here to quiet you, I will leave a note for Santa telling him that."

The upstairs was completely quiet when Clare left. She smiled as she walked down the stairs.

She leaned down and looked at the steps. Sure enough, donkey hooves were scored into the wood in several places.

"Those kids," she whispered. "And, Gomer, shame on you."

CHAPTER 55

CHRISTMAS AT THE DOUBLE SPUR RANCH

THE CHILDREN TOOK LONG NAPS. OF COURSE, WHEN one awoke, all three were up. They rushed downstairs and were disappointed that Santa had not come while they were asleep.

Clare sent them outside to do their chores.

"Build a snowman too. I think Santa might like that."

She took the milk from an excited Tuff. "I'm helping Stub tonight," he whispered. "We hid the gift bag in the tunnel just inside the barn entrance. No one will find it there." He helped the children put the large round head on their snowman and then strolled back down to the barn.

Clare smiled as she watched him go. *Tuff is getting so tall. He is nearly two inches taller than Stub, and he is certainly not done growing.*

She finally had all the children washed and seated for supper. They were antsy as they waited for the adults to be seated.

Spur took an unusually long time to wash up and shave. He casually glanced out the window and Clare saw him wave. She looked away and tried not to smile. *Spur has had so much fun planning this.*

Conversation was lively. Suddenly, Zeke looked up. His eyes opened wide.

"I hear sleigh bells!" he whispered.

The table became quiet and then a loud "Ho, Ho, Ho!" broke the night.

All three children covered their mouths. Their eyes were wide with excitement, and they tried to get up. Spur shook his head and put his finger over his mouth.

"Santa doesn't like to be seen, remember? We have to be quiet. He will only stop if he thinks were are gone or asleep." He looked over at Clare and whispered, "Blow out the lamp and let's pretend we are all asleep."

The table became completely silent, and the sound of the sleighbells drew closer. The "Ho, Ho, Ho" became louder until there was a rustling at the door.

Annie put both hands over her mouth. Her eyes were huge as she stared at the door.

The door opened just a little. It stopped and then opened wider. A mitted hand tossed a bag in through the door before it closed. The sounds of the sleigh disappeared quickly into the night. Gomer brayed and the children stared.

Clare quietly lit the lamp. For a moment everything remained quiet. The children screamed as one when they saw the packages that had spilled out of the tossed bag. Supper was over. They almost fell out of their chairs as they raced toward the bag.

Spur pushed back his chair with a chuckle.

"You kids grab that bag. Drag it in there by your mother's tree and let's see what old Santa brought you.

"Now you all sit down, and I'll pass these out. That's what a father does—or so I'm told." He grinned at Clare as he dropped down on the floor.

He picked up the first package and squinted his eyes. He turned the package several different ways. Clare finally sat down beside him.

"How about I help your father read these names? I think his eyes aren't working so good tonight."

Nora's package was the first to be handed out. It was a beautiful doll with curly, reddish-brown hair. Spur lifted up a piece of hair and stared at it. He looked at Clare and again at the doll.

"How much did you cut off to make that doll?" he asked quietly.

Clare refused to meet his eyes and she handed Spur the next package. "For Zeke."

Zeke opened the package and a deep red shirt plus a black vest fell out. He stared at it a moment. "I wanted a bow and arrow, not darn clothes," he whispered to Spur.

Spur winked at him, and Zeke sat up a little straighter as he watched his mother pull out more packages.

Annie received two new pairs of britches. "Yay, no dresses! I get to wear britches!" she hollered in excitement.

Clare handed Spur the next one. He stared at it a moment as he looked at Clare. "Old Santa outdid himself. I didn't think fathers received gifts."

He pulled out a black vest and dark red shirt. He held them up and finally put the black vest on. He flexed his shoulders a couple of times before he took it off.

"Now that is a mighty fine vest. I don't know that I've had a new one in over ten years, and certainly not one so nice." He winked at Clare and whispered, "I think I'll have to find a way to thank old Santa. And his missus too. She probably had to help him make these."

The next package was a small one. Clare started to pass it to Spur. She paused when she looked at it again. She looked up at Spur in surprise.

"It has your name, Sweetheart. Don't be passing it over to me."

Clare opened it. It was a beautiful piece of purple glass with a tiny lilac inside. The chain was gold and the filigree around the stone was intricate. Clare turned it over and cut into the glass were the words, "For Clare, Love Spur."

Clare's hands shook as she held it and there were tears in her eyes. Spur lifted it out of her hands.

"Turn a little and I'll hook it on you." When he finished, he kissed her cheek. "A beautiful necklace for a beautiful woman. It suits you, Clare."

Clare touched the stone and smiled up at Spur. "Thank you, Spur. It is lovely."

Zeke was bent over, looking in the bag. "There's more in there! Hurry up, Ma!"

The rest of the gifts weren't wrapped and Spur dumped the bag on the floor. Zeke squealed and grabbed the bow with a quiver of arrows. There were two doll dresses and Nora picked them up reverently. Annie stared at the cowboy boots with a yoyo tucked inside. She grabbed them and hugged Spur.

"Look, Papa! Now I have boots like a boy!"

The last things in the bag were three boards. They had holes cut on each end. Each had a child's name engraved in the smooth wood.

"Who knows what these are?" Spur's eyes were sparkling with excitement as he looked at the three children.

No one knew. Spur chuckled as he looked over at Clare. "How about you? Want to guess?"

Clare studied the boards and finally looked up at Spur. "A seat for a swing?"

Spur nodded and the kids screamed in delight.

"We can't put them up until the weather clears, but you will each have your own swing. And when Chas gets a little bigger, maybe Santa will bring him one too."

Spur looked in the bag and pulled out a soft package wrapped in brown paper.

"Why there is no name on this. I wonder who it's for? We'd better have your mother open it."

Clare slowly opened the package. A purple and white dress tumbled out. She stared at it a moment. She stood and held it up as she studied it. The flowered bodice was fitted and was attached to a full skirt. The bottom of the skirt and the cuffs of the sleeves were solid purple. Both the sleeves and the neckline were edged with purple, tatted cotton lace. Small buttons ran down the front, and a large sash tied in the back.

Nora's eyes were large as she touched the dress.

"Santa made you a dress, Mama!"

Clare nodded. "It appears so." She glanced over at the grinning Spur. "It seems he even knew my size." She touched the soft fabric as she smiled at the children. "It's lovely. We must all find a way to thank Santa Claus."

CHAPTER 56

HONEST ANSWERS

THE CHILDREN RACED UPSTAIRS TO PLAY WITH THEIR toys and Spur leaned back on his hands. He grinned as he looked over at Clare.

"Now that was just downright fun. I've never had a Christmas so exciting." He picked up his new shirt and vest. "And new duds to boot. I'll wear these tomorrow."

Clare laughed softly. "Zeke's clothes are just like yours. He was so concerned about getting his bow and arrows that he didn't even notice." She fingered her necklace and smiled up at him.

"The necklace is beautiful, and the dress is too. I will wear them tomorrow." She touched the fabric again and laid the dress out as she looked over at Spur.

"How did you get the correct size? And who made this?"

"Sadie Parker did. You met her when you were in Cheyenne back in July. She's quite the sewer and she had your measurements. I guess you had a dress or something made because when I wrote her, she knew what size you wore.

"I told her I wanted a purple dress with little flowers on it. She took it from there." Spur's voice was quiet when he added, "I know you

293

love that little lilac cove Rock built so I figured you'd like a dress with purple flowers."

Clare was quiet. When she didn't answer, Spur spoke again. His gaze was intense as he looked at her.

"Can you let your hair down? I want to see how much you cut off."

Clare stared at him a moment. She removed some pins, and her hair dropped down several inches below her shoulders. She laughed at Spur's frown.

"It's just hair, Spur. It will grow back. Besides, Nora will love her doll even more since its hair is the color of hers."

Spur picked up a lock of Clare's hair and let it slide through his fingers. "Like bronze silk," he whispered. He tipped her head back and kissed her lightly on her lips.

Clare didn't pull away. She didn't kiss him back though.

Spur chuckled as he relaxed on his side. He leaned on his elbow as he watched her.

"What am I going to do to stay warm this winter, Clare? I have a soft, warm wife sleeping all alone in a bed we should be sharing. Here I am, huddled on a little cot, shivering and shaking with cold."

Clare pulled her knees up to her chin and stared at him.

"Tell me about some of the places you have been, Spur. I was never out of the Montana Territory until Rock took us to Cheyenne this past summer. That trip was long. Some parts were difficult and other parts were beautiful. It was all exciting though." She picked a piece of lint up off the floor before she continued.

"I grew up in a shack about three hours from here. I lived in Stevensville for a time and after that, Helena. I didn't see much of the town though. I mostly worked. I love this little valley and it will always be my home, but I have hardly been anywhere."

Spur watched Clare for a moment. He rolled over on his back as he thought. He finally sat up and grinned at her.

"Now, Clare, you have to remember that my traveling took me places where rough men like to go. I didn't spend much time in cities, and for sure no time with refined women such as yourself." Clare rolled her eyes and Spur chuckled.

"I trailed cattle from Texas north on six or seven drives. Maybe more. I didn't keep track. We delivered them to towns scattered around the back half of Kansas, towns like Ellinwood, Dodge City, Ellsworth, and Newton. Abilene too, but I only took one herd there.

"I think one of the towns I enjoyed the most was Ellinwood. It was a unique little berg built along the Santa Fe Trail. It had lots of wagon traffic in the beginning. The large herds of cattle followed later. Both of those things brought a rough element to town."

When Clare looked at Spur in question, he added, "The Santa Fe Trail was a freight trail in the beginning. Settlers used it to move west as well but the freight went first. The discovery of gold in California as well as up here added lots of traffic. Of course, the cattle drives started after the War Between the States. That added more traffic.

"Cattle in Texas weren't worth anything, but they brought good money in Kansas. You just had to trail them north. There wasn't much for railroads in Texas or through Indian Territory until later. For sure not any that ran north very far."

"Those Germans who came to Kansas were always quite the problem solvers. They knew how to build too. They put a whole town under Ellinwood's main street. Two blocks of businesses underground and on both sides of the street. A series of tunnels connected those underground businesses to each other.

"Up above, the women kind of ran the town, and a fellow could have gotten fat on that food. Those ladies could cook. Below, it was a man's world."

"If the food was above ground, how did you find out about the tunnels and the businesses under the street?"

Spur laughed. "Well, food was only part of what we were interested in. We all needed baths and haircuts. The saloons were down there too.

"I went down there the first time because I needed to get my saddle fixed. See, the harness shop was down there too. I had ridden a borrowed saddle all the way up from Texas, and I had the saddle sores to show for it."

Clare stared at Spur. Her voice was dry when she asked, "How in the world do you break a saddle?"

Spur laughed. "I knew you'd think I was goofing off, but I wasn't. I broke it working. What I was trying to do was mighty risky though, especially for a fellow who wasn't so good with a rope." He leaned forward and rested his chin on his knees for a moment as he watched Clare. Then he turned his head and looked at the fire as he talked softly.

"We were crossing the Brazos River down in Texas. A steer was bogged down. I could rope some and I figured I could pull it out. Well, I roped it all right except the saddle girth broke and my saddle came off with me in it. Threw me right down in the water with my feet still in the stirrups." He grinned at Clare as he added, "I was being jerked across that river, riding a broken saddle through a herd of spooky longhorns hooked to a mad steer who was bucking and lunging all the way!" Clare's eyes were wide as she stared at Spur, and he chuckled.

"I was in a heck of a fix. My feet were tangled up and the saddle was sinking. I thought I was going to drown. I was seventeen years old, and my life looked like it was ending that day.

"Those longhorns started to spread out since I wasn't there to keep them bunched. They were headed for me, and I couldn't even keep my head above water. I thought I was a goner.

"That's where I first met Angel and Miguel Montero. Their family made a living moving herds across the Brazos. Their father was a heck of a rider. Those two boys were too even as young as they were then. I'd guess Angel was around twelve or thirteen at the time. Miguel was a little younger than him.

"They charged their horses toward me. Angel cut my rope loose from the steer and I immediately sank. Miguel pushed his horse between the cattle and me. He bunched the cattle that were spreading out and drove them back toward the rest of the herd. Angel dove in the water. He cut one stirrup off to get me loose from my saddle. Then he hauled me out of there. I was coughing and choking. He left me in the shallows, tossed my stirrup up on the bank, and headed back to the river. He dove under water and came up a little later with my saddle. Even wet, I knew it was mine because it was missing one stirrup. He swam through that river dragging my saddle and hauled it up on the riverbank. He grinned at me and whistled for his horse.

"Before he mounted, he said, 'I think, señor, you should not try so hard to stay in your saddle. Perhaps you should work harder to teach your saddle to stay on your horse.' I just stared at him.

"I drug myself up the bank and the wrangler handed me the reins to another saddled horse.

"You can bet I made a point to thank those two fellows when we were done. There is not much to Angel now so you can imagine how little he was then. He was strong and wiry though." Spur chuckled and shook his head. "They just laughed when I thanked them. I don't think it was any big deal to either of them. They were tough then and even tougher full-grown.

"That was the drive that ended in Cheyenne. I had never been up north until then. I was so tired of trailing cattle that I decided to stay put when we hit town.

"I took a riding job with Lance Rankin. You would have met him. He's Rowdy's brother.

"I got tired of the cold though after four years and headed back down to Texas. I worked for several outfits before I took a foreman job with the Millet brothers. They were a rough outfit." Spur was quiet a moment as he leaned back on his hands.

"Angel is a good man. We became friends after I headed back south. I was pleased to see him in Cheyenne when he moved there last summer. I was even happier we were on Rock's drive north together."

Clare listened quietly. She finally asked, "So tell me about this underground town."

"Well, that's where all the businesses were that catered to men. The bath house, the laundry, the barbershop. I think there were ten or eleven saloons down there." Spur's eyes twinkled as he added, "I thought I was in heaven. All that fun in a two-block area. The tunnels outside the businesses were as wide as a man could reach when he stretched out his arms. I always thought that was so a fellow could keep himself upright as he walked from one saloon to the next one."

"The baths were fifteen cents for clean water but...you could take one for five cents in third water. That meant you were the third fellow to use the water before it was tossed out...and every tub of water was used three times.

"Shoot, we all opted for third water. A beer was five cents too, so we could drink two more beers if we used the third water."

The disgust on Clare's face was evident and Spur laughed. "Yeah, I don't think you would have liked me much back then. I was a little wild. I'd try just about anything once."

"Did they have brothels down there?"

Spur squirmed a little and finally nodded. "They did. There were two of them. Like I said, it was set up for everything a man could want. We all took a bath, got a shave and a haircut, bought a new shirt, and we were ready for a night on the town.

"That harness maker, he wasn't any dummy. He made me pay up front. He knew I wouldn't have had the money later."

"Have you ever been with a woman before, Spur?"

Spur frowned and looked at the floor. His face was agitated when he looked up at Clare.

"What kind of a question is that? No matter how I answer it, I lose. Either you won't believe me or you'll be mad."

"Answer it honestly."

Spur was quiet a moment. He looked toward the fireplace. When he looked back at Clare, his face was earnest.

"After Sister Eddie died, I went kind of wild. By the time I was eighteen, I was walking a fine line between an outlaw and an honest man. The men and women I associated with lived on the wrong side of the law, and I did a lot of things I'm not proud of.

"So yes, yes I have. I cleaned up my act about five years ago, and I have been flying straight ever since. I'm twenty-nine years old and I haven't been with a woman since I was twenty-four."

"What made you change?"

Spur picked at the floor before he looked up.

"It was the girls on the line. I watched how hard it was for them. Some of them died from the sicknesses they caught. It was hard too when they became pregnant. Shoot, I knew what my life was like, and I didn't want to pass that on to any other little kids.

"I helped a couple of them find homes for their babies, and I helped others bury theirs. I held those women while they cried because they knew they would never see their little babies again. I realized that what brought me pleasure brought pain and suffering to someone else. That was when I decided I didn't want to be responsible for someone else's hard life or sadness. After that, I was a friend to any of them who needed help, but I didn't go upstairs. It wasn't easy, but it was the right thing to do.

"I always hoped the right girl would come along sometime—that I would meet someone and fall madly in love." His eyes were intense as he added softly, "I just didn't know it would be you."

CHAPTER 57

WHY ME?

CLARE'S BLUE EYES SEEMED TO PEER INTO SPUR'S SOUL, and he sat up. He watched her quietly and waited for her next question.

"Why me, Spur? What made you fall in love with me? There are hundreds of girls out there, lots with not nearly so much baggage or as many kids. What made you fall in love now?"

"When I climbed in that train car beside you on your trip down to Cheyenne, I watched you with your kids. I was sure they couldn't all be yours because they were too close in age, and you were too young. Still, you were a great mom. I admired you for that.

"Then in Blackfoot, you rescued little Rollie. I saw him every time I passed through there for nearly three years. I noticed but I did nothing to get him out of that life.

"Oh, I gave his ma a little money when I passed through to help her out, but I did nothing to change her life—his either. You met him one time and made that change.

"When we were at the party the Rankins threw before the drive, I watched all you married folks. That was the first time I realized that the people I admired most in this world were all married and married happily. Something hit me that night.

"I realized I was lonesome—that I wanted a fuller life than the one I was leading. I wanted a wife and a family. It surprised me but there it was.

"The next morning when Stub and I caught up with the four of you—Gabe and Merina, you and Rock—I realized what lucky men they were." He smiled at Clare.

"You and Merina are a lot alike. You are both tender and tough. You both love fiercely, and you both were willing to sacrifice your happiness for your family.

"You know I courted Merina for a time four years ago, and you know when things began to get serious, I ran. I didn't make any attempt to contact her for four years. I could have, but I didn't. I was surprised when I ran into her in Cheyenne. By then, she was Gabe's girl. I didn't know that though.

"I wanted to pick things up where we left off, but she wasn't interested. It had been a long time with not so much as a note from me, and she had moved on. The funny thing was, I wasn't really all that upset. A little sad, but not all torn up.

"We parted as friends which was what we all wanted. Gabe was my pard for a time, and I didn't want to lose his friendship. I kept waiting for my heart to break but it didn't.

"Then you made me marry you. I was furious at first. Even drunk though, I knew Sister Eddie would have approved of you.

"And I would have run if we hadn't married. I wanted to go with the boys when they left that morning. It was all I could do to not pack my horse.

"When I was in Helena, I thought about running again. Then I got the message you were in danger. I headed home as fast as Beau could take me." Spur's voice was soft as he added, "In Helena, I finally admitted that I was in love with you.

"I never planned it. Shoot. At first, I was just hoping we wouldn't kill each other, that we would remain friends no matter what happened."

He touched Clare's cheek with the back of his hand. "You are a rare woman, Clare. Life has dealt you some hard knocks, but you keep getting up.

"You give all of yourself to your family." He lifted up a curl of hair and dropped it. "Just like cutting your hair. You don't see it as a big deal. To me, it is though.

"I admired you when first I met you, and now that admiration has turned to love." He leaned back on his hands again as he watched her.

"I just hope someday you will be able to share a little bit of your heart with me."

Clare said nothing but a single tear slid out of her eye. It hung on her cheek for a moment and slid slowly away. Her eyes were full of pain when she looked at him.

"Spur, I—"

"Shhh. Just be happy, Clare." He put his arm around her and pulled her close beside him.

"Let your heart go," he whispered. "Quit trying to boss it around and let it be free. If you do that, your heart will decide, and you won't have to agonize about this.

"Maybe you'll love me and maybe you won't. Let your heart be the one to make that choice."

He stood and reached his hand down to her. "We'd better get those little hooligans of ours in bed…and me too. Morning will come mighty early."

Kit slipped through the door just as Clare was standing. Spur looked over at her and laughed.

"How was Christmas at the <u>S</u> Ranch? Ol' Stub has been planning this evening for weeks."

Kit's eyes sparkled. "It was wonderful. He is so thoughtful. I just hope we can get out of here by Friday.

"And I think you have started a Christmas tradition with that sleigh and Santa Claus," she added with a laugh.

"Steve said to tell you the lane isn't passable. He didn't think it would be safe to drive under some of those hanging snowbanks, and the lane had drifted so bad that we would have to. It looks like we will all be staying home tomorrow."

CHAPTER 58

A Message From Rock

CLARE WAS TIRED BUT SHE COULDN'T SLEEP. THEY HAD let the children stay up way past their bedtime to play with their Christmas gifts. The upstairs was quiet now, but it had taken them some time to calm down.

She rolled from side to side in the bed. Finally, she lay on her back and stared at the ceiling. The moon was bright, and the shadows of the trees danced on the walls of her bedroom.

"I miss you, Rock," she whispered. The wind blew the tree branches against the house and more snow floated softly to the ground.

Clare climbed out of bed. She pulled her light wrap around her nightgown and stared outside. The moon was bright, and the snow glistened in its light.

"I am going to visit your grave tomorrow, Rock. I am going to our little flower nook and sit on the stone bench. I know the flowers are gone but that is where I feel you."

"Read my letter, Clare. Read my letter before you go out in this storm." Rock's voice came clearly to her. Clare waited for Rock to speak again, but she only heard the sound of the wind. It increased in intensity and howled as it swept through the trees.

Clare turned and looked toward the front of the house. "Maybe Spur is still awake. I will ask him for it," she whispered. She pulled the wrap closer to her body and tiptoed toward Spur's small office in the front of the house.

The door was open. She could barely see the outline of his body on the cot against the wall. Spur pulled one long, hairy leg back under the covers and asked quietly, "What are you doing up, Clare?"

Clare's voice caught as she spoke.

"I—I think I am ready to read Rock's letter. I was wondering if you would get it for me."

Spur was quiet for a moment. He sat up and pushed his hand through his hair. The moonlight outlined Clare's form in the doorway. He looked closely at her face as he sat on the edge of the cot. He cursed under his breath. *If she reads that letter this late, she won't get any sleep at all.*

He nodded and stood up in his cut-off long johns. They were unbuttoned halfway down the front and dark, curly hair showed on his chest. He opened a drawer in Chas' desk and pulled out a sealed envelope. The only word on the envelope was Clare's name.

Rock's letters hadn't been in envelopes when Little Bear took them from inside Rock's shirt as he was dying. Spur had added the envelopes and put a name on each one.

Blood had soaked into Clare's letter where it had pressed against Rock's chest. Spur had tried to wipe it off but the blood smeared. Now there was a dark stain on the paper. He held the letter in his hands for a moment before he handed it to Clare.

"You want me to stay up while you read it?"

Tears sparkled in the sides of Clare's eyes as she looked at Spur. She nodded. "I think I would like that."

Spur followed her to the kitchen. He lit the lamp before he walked back to his office.

Clare's hands trembled as she opened the letter. They shook even more as she began to read.

Spur leaned against the doorway to the office. He cursed softly under his breath and looked away. When he looked back toward Clare, she had one hand over her heart.

Spur resisted going to her. *She needs to read it, and I need to let her do it on her own time.*

My beautiful Clare,

We just left Butte City and are headed across the prettiest valley you ever did see—almost as pretty as ours. I had to rent grass for us to have passage through here but that's all right. Now we can take it slow.

We lost a rider last night. A miner beat one of Gabe's hands to death in a saloon. His name was Rufe. He stepped in when that miner hit a woman. Rufe knew he was outnumbered, but he tried to stop it anyway. Gabe's riders got him out and they holed up in a house of ill repute.

The rest of us headed for town when we got the news. Gabe pistol-whipped the miner who stomped Rufe. Then we all helped to burn down the saloon where he died. Old Gabe can get quite the mad on when he is pushed too far. Spur too. I never saw Spur lose his temper the entire drive—until Rufe was beaten.

We are ten days from home now. The young men have done great. Tuff is quite the worker, and he has enjoyed being around other young fellows. Overall, it's been a good drive. I don't think I'll do it again though. I shouldn't need to since we are bringing in a nice group of breeding stock. More than that though, I don't like leaving you and the kids. I can't wait to get home.

I love you, Clare. The Good Lord knew what he was doing when he put us together.

Love Rock

A second page had been added, and Clare began to cry silently as she read it.

Clare—If you are reading this, I didn't make it home. Please don't be sad. The Good Lord decides when it is our time to leave this earth. I guess mine came early.

I know you will work hard to hold our family together. Don't try to do it all alone though. Let Maggie and Ike help. They love you like a daughter. And keep Stub and Tuff on. Just because Stub has a little land doesn't mean he won't still want his job as foreman. Let him decide. Both Tuff and he love you so don't push them away. Besides, you are going to need Stub more now than ever.

I had a long visit with Father Ravalli before I left. We talked about all sorts of things including death and eternity. I'm not sure why or how that conversation came up since I was just there to deliver some cattle. It did though and I have thought a lot on this trip about what he said. He's a wise man if you ever need to talk to someone.

I want you to find love again, Clare. Keep your heart open. If I hadn't let go of Suzanna, you and I would never have married. You move me over in your heart like I did her. Don't hang onto me. That will only make your heart sad. And for Pete's sake, don't become a drunk for six months like I was!

I know the children are your first concern and that makes me love you even more. It breaks my heart to know that I won't be there to watch them grow up or to meet that little one growing inside you. But then, I guess I will see them anyway according to that padre, I just hope you don't sacrifice even a small possibility of love for the security of a father.

Maybe you can talk Spur into staying on to run things. I spent quite a bit of time with him on this drive and he's a fine man. He has a lot of management experience as well as good cowman knowledge.

He knows his horses too. He could help you get that breeding program we wanted to start off the ground.

I love you, Clare, and I always will. Now let me go. Move on with your life. Don't let your heart shrivel up and get hard from bitterness. You smile and you remember all the things we laughed about together. Then you find someone else who makes your heart happy.

Goodbye, Clare. Goodbye, Sweetheart.

Love Rock

When she finished, Clare sank down in a chair and began to sob. Spur pushed away from the doorway and strode across the room. He pulled her up and held her in his arms while she cried.

Finally, Clare looked up at him. Her eyes were a brilliant blue.

"Your chest hair is tickling my nose."

Spur stared down at her and then rubbed his mustache on her neck. "Well let's tickle your neck then too." Clare's laugh was cut off with a sob. She looked up at Spur for a moment. Her voice was soft when she spoke. "If I asked you to hold me tonight until I fell asleep, would you do it?"

Spur stared at Clare for a moment. A rush of emotion went through him. He finally shook his head.

"I don't think that's a good idea. You don't have on enough clothes, and my willpower is shot to hell. No, I think I'd better stay right here."

Clare's breath caught and she looked down at her open robe. She pulled it shut and started to speak.

Spur took her shoulders in his hands and spoke quietly.

"Clare, it's Rock you are missing. You want his arms around you. I won't come to your bed until I know it's me you want. I won't pretend to be him."

Clare pulled away. She stared at the man in front of her for a moment and blushed.

"Good night, Spur. Thank you for—thank you for being a gentleman."

CHAPTER 59

PROBLEMS AND EMOTIONS

SPUR WATCHED AS CLARE HURRIED DOWN THE HALL. He groaned as he turned back toward his cot. "That woman has no idea how easy it is to see through that thin nightgown—or how hard it is to not look.

"'No' was the right thing to say but it sure wasn't easy." He sat down on the bunk for a moment. He scratched his head and cursed softly.

"I just as well get up. I won't be getting any more sleep tonight. I guess I'll go split some wood. That dead tree we pulled up by the house needs to be chunked into firewood."

Several of the hands rubbed their eyes and went to the window of the bunkhouse to see what the banging was outside. They stared for a moment at their boss splitting wood in his shirtsleeves.

"Think we should go out and see if he needs help?" asked Dack.

Handy shook his head. "Nope. Any man who is chopping wood at three in the morning has problems we can't solve—and they usually involve a woman."

Neither man talked after that. They watched a bit longer before they crawled back under their blankets. They heard the chopping continue for another thirty minutes before they finally fell back asleep.

Spur was gone when Clare woke the next morning. His blankets were laying on the floor and she frowned. *Spur always makes his bed.* She folded the blankets over the cot. She blushed again as she thought of what she had asked him.

"He was right. It was Rock I was missing. Poor Spur. This has all been so unfair to him." She closed the door and hurried to prepare breakfast. She glanced out the window and then looked again.

The large tree the men had drug up by the house the day before was gone. The chunks of wood were split and stacked neatly against the house. She stared at the large pile for a moment.

"Goodness, the men must have run out of wood. That was a large tree to cut up before breakfast. I wonder who all helped do that so early?"

Spur came out of the barn and talked to the men. They nodded and headed for the corral. He glanced toward the house but turned toward the camp kitchen. Clare watched him a moment before she turned away from the window. Her emotions were still raw from the night before.

Chas began to cry, and Clare lifted him from his cradle.

"Good morning, Little Sweetheart, and Merry Christmas. Are you ready for some breakfast? Let's rock a bit and enjoy this quiet house."

The house was incredibly quiet, and Clare dozed as Chas nursed. Spur poked his head in the door. He slowly backed out. Clare never stirred.

"I reckon we will both be mighty tired today," he muttered as he headed for the corral.

CHAPTER 60

A Snowy Christmas

"NUDGE, SPLIT THE MEN UP AND HAVE THEM BREAK ice in the ponds and creeks. I want at least two men in every group in case there's trouble." Spur pointed toward the south as he talked.

"They can haze any cattle they see toward the winter graze. Be sure to push them off that burned area if any are there.

"I want six riders replacing those men in the line shacks. Two to each shack. Send the men who are there back home." He grinned at his foreman. "They can draw straws for that job. The rest of the men can take the day off once chores are finished." Spur handed Nudge a stack of envelopes.

"Clare wanted to give the men a Christmas bonus this year. You can pass them out. The envelopes that have stars on them are for the men headed to the line shacks. She thought they ought to have a little more." He chuckled as Nudge stared at him.

"Don't even bother to ask me how much. This was all Clare. I wasn't consulted.

"I want everyone home tonight though. We'll start earlier tomorrow. Since Stub is getting married, some of the boys might want to go." Spur nodded over his shoulder toward the ranch kitchen.

"Have the riders headed to the line shacks take packhorses. Supplies will be getting low by now. Cookie said he'd have three packs ready this morning." He looked over to where the men were saddling their horses.

"I told Cookie to put something special in them since they'll be out over Christmas."

"I'm going to ride over to the north place and see if Stub needs any help. I should be back by dinner."

Spur waved toward the men as he called, "I'll see you boys later. Merry Christmas to all of you!"

Nudge watched Spur ride north. He held the envelopes as he headed toward the barn. Several cowboys were leading their horses out and they stopped beside Nudge. Handy nodded at Spur's departing back.

"Everything all right? Dack and I saw the boss chopping wood around 3:00 this morning."

Nudge frowned at the man. He turned to look toward the house. His eyes moved to the pile of wood and he shrugged.

"What goes on in that house is none of our business. He seemed fine to me.

"Tie those horses up. We need to have a little meeting." He nodded his head toward the barn and hollered at the men gathered in front of it.

"Meet me inside. I have some Christmas bonuses to hand out!"

CHAPTER 61

I WASN'T EXPECTING THAT

STUB WAS ORGANIZING THE MEN WHEN SPUR RODE into the yard.

"Morning, Boys. Stub have you all lined out?"

Stub stared at Spur and answered before the riders could respond.

"Sure do, unless you have other plans."

"I was thinking maybe the boys would like a little time off today since it's Christmas. I want all the ice broken in the ponds and creeks, but they should be able to get that done this morning.

"Figure out who is going to drag those dead trees up here for firewood. When they're done, they can take the rest of the day off—as long as they are back tonight." He grinned as he looked from Stub to his riders.

"I'm guessing you'll want to go to your sour, sawed-off foreman's wedding tomorrow."

The men laughed and nodded as they milled around.

Stub glared at Spur. When Spur's grin became bigger, he chuckled.

"Shoot, I'll cut up the wood if the boys get it drug up here. I have no reason to go to town."

The men perked up as they waited.

Spur nodded and held up a handful of envelopes.

"Clare thought you fellows needed a Christmas bonus. Be sure to thank her because I had nothing to do with this." He grinned at the men. "I think my wife is a softie when it comes to you boys."

The men stared from Spur to Stub. When they realized Spur wasn't joking, they began to grin.

"Split into groups of two or three. No man by himself." Spur looked seriously at the cowboys. "I don't want to fish anybody out of a creek because he decided to take a winter swim."

"Anything else you want done, Boss?" Stub watched Spur as he waited. *I think the boss has something else on his mind.*

Spur nodded. "I thought maybe you and I would chop ice on your place. I'd like to talk to you anyway."

"I'll get my horse and we can head down there."

The two men rode slowly toward Stub's little ranch. Neither talked until they were out of the ranch yard. Spur finally looked over at his foreman.

"What do you want, Stub? Where would you like to take your ranch now that you're getting married?"

Stub was quiet a moment before he answered.

"First of all, I didn't buy that ranch. It was given to me when my best friend died. That plumb makes me sad when I think on it."

Spur listened and slowly nodded. "That's true but it was gifted to a good man and a loyal foreman. When you think of it that way, you did kind of earn it."

Stub frowned and shrugged. "Maybe.

"Kit and me have been talking. Maybe we will give it back to you and head down to Wyoming. Tuff is itching to get closer to his friends. I wouldn't mind a change either."

Spur stared at Stub in surprise.

"That sure isn't the answer I expected. I was going to offer you a partnership on some cows."

Stub nodded. "I thought maybe you were. Things have changed though.

"I was content to work for Rock. We had been pards a long time. It rattled my chains when he died.

"When Kit and I decided to marry, things changed again. I realized it wasn't just me and Tuff making decisions. Now there would be three of us." Stub blushed slightly, "And probably some kids down the road too."

CHAPTER 62

GIFTS AND CHARITY

"LAST WEEK, I RECEIVED A LETTER FROM WILLIAM Sturgis down by Cheyenne. You know him." Stub glanced over at Spur as he spoke.

Spur nodded and Stub continued.

"That day last summer when you and I rode up there, I talked to Sturgis alone for a time." Stub's neck turned red as he continued.

"I knew Sturgis' son. We all called him Curly Joe. I even rode with him for a time. In fact, I had met Sturgis several times.

"I was one of the fellows who helped kill Curly down in Cheyenne. We caught him stealing horses. I wanted his pa to know I was sorry for taking his only son.

"Old Sturgis remembered me. He didn't hold it against any of us for killing a horse thief, but he was still sad his son was gone.

"He said the little gal his son had been sweet on had married. Her name was Andy, and Sturgis liked her a lot.

"Anyhow, he was telling me he didn't have anyone to pass his ranch onto now since his only child was dead. I told him he ought to make Andy's husband his foreman and maybe partner on some cattle. I said that would guarantee he could have grandkids. Just 'cause they wouldn't be blood didn't mean he couldn't claim them.

"Well, it seems Andy inherited a ranch from an uncle out in the Idaho Territory last fall. Her folks passed after she married and her only sister lives out there." Stub looked toward his ranch before he continued. "Anyway, she and her husband are moving out there in the spring."

"That left Sturgis looking for a foreman." Stub's voice was soft as he added, "He offered the job to me with the possibility of working up to a partnership with him."

Spur stared at Stub in surprise as he smiled.

"Well good for you, Stub. That sounds like a heck of a deal."

Stub nodded. "He said I can even run some cattle with his right away if I want." Stub was quiet for a moment before he continued. "That would give Kit and me a new start." He looked over at Spur and his mouth hardened down.

"Some of the boys on a ranch north of Stevensville remember Kit from when she worked at Big Dorothy's. They have been running off at the mouth about her past.

"We can leave or I can shoot them. Kit would rather leave."

Spur chuckled and nodded. "Kit's probably right, but my first instinct would be to shoot them too."

Stub laughed ruefully. "Yeah, Kit's talked me out of it several times." He looked over at Spur and shook his head.

"Kit has been through so much and is still just the sweetest little gal ever. I sure am glad she came down here to visit Clare."

Spur nodded. "And Clare is going to be broken-hearted when she leaves.

"If you decide to leave, we can buy your place back. Then you'll have a little nest egg. You can invest that in cattle."

Stub stared at his boss. He shook his head as he turned red.

"I won't sell back land to the person who gifted it to me. That wouldn't even be right."

Spur was quiet as they rode for a time. He finally looked over at Stub.

"I have spent a lot of time going over Rock's books. That ranch was gifted to him by a man named Darby McCune, a brother to old Badger down in Cheyenne.

"Darby set Rock up and gave him a good start, right down to a gold mine. According to Rock's records, Darby picked around in those mountains for years. He finally discovered gold not long before he died." Spur chuckled.

"He had gold buried in the floor of Rock's house. Rock found it when Badger helped him replace the floor. Badger had gone there to visit his brother. He didn't know that old Darby had died.

"Rock always appreciated the generosity he was shown, and he gifted more money than folks will ever know. If he was here, he would never let you give that land back. It is yours free and clear.

"If you decide to leave, that land is yours to sell. I'd like first dibs to buy it back, but you sure aren't going to give it back to us." Spur looked over at the quiet man riding beside him and he chuckled. "Old Rock would likely come out of his grave and smite me down if I let you do that."

Stub was quiet as he stared at Spur. He shook his head and muttered, "Don't seem right."

Spur laughed. "What about me? Shoot, what did I do to earn the right to be part of all this?" He waved his arm around at the land around him. "I was a durn tumbleweed before I married Clare." He was quiet a moment before he looked over at Stub again.

"Do you have a ring? I found Agnes's ring in Chas' desk. I'd sure give that to you if you want it."

Stub's face showed his surprise. He frowned before he looked away. "I don't have one, but I won't take charity. I told Kit we'd get one once we had a little money set aside."

Spur pulled his horse to a halt.

"Stub, it's not charity. It's a gift. That ring has been setting in Chas' desk most likely since Agnes died. It could use a new home. It's mine to give, and I'm offering it to you. Besides, Agnes had tiny fingers and so does Kit. Take the ring."

He grinned at Stub and pointed toward his house. "Otherwise, Annie will find it, and who knows what animal she will try to put it on."

Stub chuckled and nodded. "That Annie is a case, isn't she?" His face was serious when he looked over at Spur.

"I'm glad you married Clare. I thought it was a bad idea in the beginning, but you have kept her from becoming hard.

"Clare has a tender heart, but she has a streak of iron in her too. I was afraid she would dam everything up and become a bitter woman."

"Especially after she fired you as soon as you returned from the drive."

Stub chuckled and nodded. "Yeah, there was that."

"You have a way of calming her down though. You quiet those rivers she has running hard and fast inside her.

"Rock did that too. Funny how you both accomplish the same thing but in such different ways." He looked over at Spur.

"You are good for her, Spur. I'm glad you signed onto this ranch."

Spur was quiet as he listened to Stub.

"I hope so. I'm head over heels in love with her, and she's still in love with Rock. It's kind of a hard row to hoe sometimes."

"And I'm glad you are the one hoeing it. Still, you and her were friends before Rock died, and that's not a bad way to start a marriage." Stub's eyes were sincere.

"Clare likes you. She's just struggling to let Rock go. When she does, she'll see you."

CHAPTER 63

AN UNWELCOME GUEST

THE TWO MEN VISITED AND CHOPPED ICE ALL morning. They were headed back to the Double Spur shortly after noon when they saw a sled coming up the lane. It was glossy black, and the runners were red. Two large white horses were pulling it.

Spur let out a low curse and kicked Hell Fire.

"Get up now, Boy. We need to beat that sleigh to the house."

Stub was startled, but he spurred his horse to catch up.

Hell Fire jumped and bucked drifts until he was on the flat. He was willing to run, and Spur let him. They slid to a stop in front of the house just as the sleigh swung around.

Spur looked coldly from the man who was driving it to the woman sitting beside him.

"Don't bother to get out. You aren't welcome here."

The woman stood and glared at Spur. "I am here to see Chas. No one in town would give me directions. Luckily, we ran into a young man who works here, and he told me where to go." Her eyes narrowed down, and she stared at Spur closely as she caught her breath.

"And just who are you to give me orders? Now move aside. I want to see Chas."

Spur pointed toward the cemetery.

"He's right over there. And even if he wasn't dead, I doubt he'd want to see you.

"You turn this sleigh around and head right back to Helena. You aren't welcome here, Maebeline, not even for a visit." Spur's voice was hard, and his eyes were angry as he gritted out his words to the woman in front of him.

Stub looked toward the house and caught a quick glimpse of Kit's frightened face before it disappeared from the window. His face pulled down in a frown as he studied the beautiful woman in front of him.

Spur certainly doesn't like her. I wonder what she did that makes him hate her so.

Maebeline's eyes opened wide, and her voice was almost a purr when she spoke.

"George! It is you. I heard you had died, and I was just devastated. What a joy to see my only son standing right here in front of me.

"Did you marry? If so, I would love to meet your wife. Do you have a family? I'm sure old Chas loved having children around. And I would as well. Children are so precious.

"Now please. Invite me in. We drove a long way. Rom and I both need to rest a moment before we return to Helena." Her eyes were calculating as she added, "I had no idea Chas had passed. What caused his death?" When Spur didn't answer, Maebeline waved her arm around the ranch yard.

"I'll just bet you have children. That means I have grandchildren! I never dreamed I'd get to see you again let alone be a grandmother." Maebeline's eyes were cunning as she watched Spur.

Stub felt a chill go through him. *That woman is evaluating Spur like a big cat would its prey.*

The woman reached her hand out to Spur. He hesitated but instead, shook his head. He had just grabbed for the horses' heads to turn the sleigh around when Clare appeared in the doorway of the kitchen.

"Spur, the children are not here, but bring your mother in. I would love to meet her." Clare stood tall and slim as she smiled at them. "Do come in, Maebeline. I have looked forward to meeting you for as long as I have known Spur." Clare's voice was sugary sweet, and her wide eyes gave her face the appearance of innocence.

"Just for a few minutes. Then you be on your way." Spur's voice was hard.

Maebeline reached behind her. "I brought some cookies. Let me get them."

The coldness was back in Spur's eyes. "The cookies stay there. Unless you want to feed one to that hulk beside you. Better yet, you can break a piece off each one and eat it yourself."

Maebeline's eyes narrowed almost to slits, and Stub saw pure, unadulterated hate in them. He spoke up quietly.

"Boss, I've got my gun pointed at her through my coat. You just give the word, and we'll bury them both right here."

Maebeline glared at Stub a moment. Her face changed quickly as she looked toward Spur. It was once again smooth and beautiful.

The man beside Maebeline lifted her down and she turned to Spur with a bright smile.

"So tell me—how long have you worked for Chas? When did he pass? Surely he was still alive when he received my last letter. We have kept in touch, you know. He was such a wonderful friend."

Spur didn't answer. He opened the door and walked through, not waiting for his mother. Once again, Stub saw the fury in her eyes.

"Keep moving, Lady. You might be Spur's kin, but to me, you are just another unwelcome visitor. And we have a passel of them buried all over this ranch."

Maebeline looked back at Stub again and glared. She turned to the man beside her.

"Rom, would you bring my satchel in? I have some papers in it I need to show George."

Maebeline swept into the house. Her eyes seemed to inventory everything in the kitchen. They lingered the longest on the desk in Spur's office.

"So you moved into Chas' house when he passed? I guess that would make sense since he had no heirs that you knew of." She looked at Clare.

"Tell me about yourself. How long have you and George been married?"

CHAPTER 64

A SILLY WOMAN

CLARE REACHED FOR SPUR'S ARM AND GAVE IT A squeeze as she laughed. She looked up at him and batted her eyes before she looked back at Maebeline.

"Long enough to have four children. I actually knew Chas before Spur met him. We were quite good friends. I used to take him on picnics."

Maebeline's eyes narrowed as she studied Clare's face. Clare could feel herself shrivel inside, but she kept up the façade.

"When Chas died, he left his ranch to me. Of course, I couldn't run it alone. Spur and I married to be respectable. Now he runs everything.

"We moved into the house several months ago. Chas had no children or living relatives whom he was close to. When he gifted the ranch to me, I was quite surprised. But of course, I said yes.

"I'll just bet you did. Well, I hate to break it to you, but Chas left this ranch to me."

"Impossible! Chas would have told me on one of our picnics."

Spur was trying to keep the surprise off his face. Clare was baiting his mother and the evil woman could barely contain her fury.

"Oh yes, very possible. You see, Chas and I are, I mean were, extremely close. He considered me one of his oldest friends." She dabbed her eyes as she added, "We even had a child together. He died, poor little thing. He fell from a horse and broke his neck. I was devastated. He was such a precious little fellow."

Her eyes were cunning as she added. "And then George came along. He was the love of my life.

"I was so lost when you ran way, George. I cried for days." She turned her eyes back to Clare when the younger woman spoke.

"I don't think that is right. The Chas I knew would never have cheated on his wife. He was only married one time and that was to Agnes." Clare's voice was emphatic as she shook her head. "She was the love of his life, and he was to her as well."

Maebeline leaned forward triumphantly. "We were together for nearly two years. He only married Agnes to gain stature in this community." She dabbed her eyes again. "She was so frail. She just couldn't give him the children he wanted. I often told him she was not a suitable mate. She was wealthy though, and Chas was all about money and power."

Spur slowly straightened. Clare could see and feel the fury leaking from him. He reached behind his chair for his shotgun and pointed it at Rom.

"Take off your coat and drop every weapon on you. Make a false move and this scattergun will tear you apart."

He glanced at Maebeline. "I suggest you tell him to do as I say. At this distance and two barrels, you aren't going to survive that blast either."

"Now, George, there is no need to be so abrupt—"

"Tell him!"

Maebeline turned angrily to Rom. "Take off your coat and drop your guns on the floor. Kick them over toward George."

Spur moved the shotgun up higher. "That arm gun too." He grinned suddenly.

"Go ahead, Rom. If you think you can slide that gun down and shoot it faster than I can pull these triggers, do it. I'm up for a challenge."

Clare's stomach tightened as she watched Spur. She saw the reckless man she had heard stories about. He was prodding Rom, daring him to shoot.

When Rom dropped his sleeve gun, Clare hurried forward and picked up all the guns.

"My goodness, you certainly carry a lot of guns, Rom. It must be quite dangerous where you live. I'll take the bullets out of these. Our children should be home soon, and I don't want the littlest one to be injured if she finds them." Clare smiled brightly at Maebeline and Rom.

"We have taught our children how to handle guns. We want them to be acclimated with them in the event they would need to shoot a predator or something. Wolves and mountain lions are prevalent out here, you know."

Maebeline was working hard to calm down. She turned to Clare and asked sweetly, "How old are your children? You look quite young to have four of them."

Clare laughed prettily. "The oldest is six and the youngest is just a few months old." She giggled and whispered, "Your son is extremely virile."

Spur almost choked and Stub had to look away for a moment to keep from laughing.

Maebeline could barely conceal her contempt or her fury.

"You are a silly woman, but you are pretty. Obviously, you are giving him what he wants. What all men want.

"Keep it up. You'll probably have a dozen of the little monsters before you're done."

Clare giggled. "I don't think so. I have limited Spur to once a day now that we have four. I read in a magazine that helps reduce my chances of getting pregnant." She smiled brightly at Maebeline.

Once again, Stub had to look away and Spur laughed out loud. "That's my girl," he said with a chuckle. His dark eyes danced, and he winked at Clare.

Maebeline snorted. "Where in the world did you find her? She has absolutely no sense at all."

"I met her on a train and followed her down to Cheyenne," Spur drawled with a grin, "and I have been following her ever since."

CHAPTER 65

THE SNAKE ROOM

MAEBELINE SHRUGGED HER SHOULDERS AND ROLLED her eyes. She took the case from Rom and set it on the table. She opened it and took out an official-looking document.

"You can see here that Chas left this place to me. Of course, I don't want to be rude. You will have a day to gather your belongings and your children. After that, you will need to contact me before you visit."

Clare leaned forward and stared at the will. Her blue eyes were wide as she looked up at Spur.

"Spur Darlin', that looks like the will Chas gave us. You know the one you showed that lawyer man in town before you took it to the bank? That is so strange.

"We should probably take this one to the bank and compare them. I wonder why Chas would make out two wills?" She squinted her eyes. She shook her head as she pointed at his signature.

"No, this one is messed up. Chas always signed his legal papers as Charles Rutlege Boswell. This one says Rutledge."

Maebeline looked quickly at the paper. She glared at Clare. "Charles Rutledge Boswell was his legal name."

"I know! It was the strangest thing. Someone misspelled his middle name on his birth certificate, so he always signed his legal papers with that wrong spelling." Clare giggled again. "It's so silly to get all twisted up over the spelling of a name. I mean some folks spell mine Clare, Clarey, Clare Ann—it doesn't matter. I am still the same person." She gave Maebeline another wide-eyed smile.

Spur grinned. If Maebeline hadn't been so dangerous, he would have enjoyed this exchange even more.

Clare looked over at Spur.

"She should probably take that will in and show it to your banker friend. Isn't his brother the sheriff? Oh, never mind. My mind just sidetracked.

"They won't be open today, but there's a nice boarding house in town. You can show it to them first thing tomorrow." Clare's eyes became wider as if she had just thought of something.

"Spur Darlin', we have an extra bed! You know the one that you cleaned the snake nest out of?" She looked at Maebeline and continued confidentially.

"Old Chas never used the upstairs. He locked it off and we had the most terrible infestation of snakes when we moved in. We have gotten rid of most of them, but they keep coming in through a hole somewhere. They climb right up the wall of the house just looking for a warm place to sleep. Then they crawl out at night and slip in bed with you. Bodies are warm you know." She gave Spur a wide-eyed smile and giggled. "They really like to get in bed with me. Spur said that's because my body is so—well, I can't say what he said, but they like our bed for sure!"

Stub coughed and Spur grinned widely.

"I told the kids not to worry. Those old snakes won't hurt them. Just make sure they don't coil around your neck. That is just not good.

"That's why I let our donkey sleep in the house at night." Her eyes lit up with excitement.

"Say, I'll call him. Gomer is usually real friendly. Well, unless you try to hurt one of the kids or something. Why, I can barely spank them. And trust me, they need spanked."

Clare hurried to the door and called, "Gomer! Come boy!"

She looked back over her shoulder and gave Maebeline a brilliant smile.

"You will love Gomer. He doesn't smell so good, but he is the friendliest fellow. He will just rub all over you. He loves to be petted, especially around his tail. Don't stand behind him though. He wants to be looking at you all the time or he kicks."

She opened the door wide. "There you are, Gomer! Now come in here and meet Spur's mother and her friend. They are going to sleep in the Snake Room tonight. You can stay in there too. They might need a little protection."

A little donkey rushed into the room. He brayed and then turned his tail to Maebeline. She backed up as she stared at him, and he farted loudly. Then he bucked and brayed again before he pushed the door open and raced outside.

Maebeline glared around the kitchen. Her plan to steal this ranch wasn't working as easily as she hoped. She stared at Clare, and the simple woman gave her a huge smile.

"Would you like me to show you to your room? Oh, look there, Spur Darlin.' It's a snakeskin. Now I wonder where that snake is?"

Clare lifted a large snakeskin one of the riders had given to Zeke. It was supposed to stay in the barn. However, Zeke brought it in the house all the time much to Clare's irritation.

"I find snakeskins just fascinating. And to think the reason a snake sheds it skin is because it grew too large!" She squinted at the skin. "I think this one belongs to Harold. He isn't the biggest snake in here but he's close.

"Now come. I'll show you to your room."

Maebeline was already moving toward the door.

"No, thank you. We will spend the night in town." She looked at Spur and almost purred, "Perhaps you can meet me at the bank tomorrow morning at ten?

Spur shook his head. "Nope. I have chores to do around here first. The earliest I can make it to town is noon. And I only have fifteen minutes so it won't be a social call."

He followed his mother and her driver to the door and Clare called, "Now y'all come back and see us! We love having company!"

Clare was still waving when the sleigh drove out of sight. Spur began laughing. Stub joined him while Clare giggled and fanned herself.

"Why I just about wore myself out with all that foolishness!"

Spur grinned at her and gave her a squeeze.

"Clare, that was quite the performance." His smile became larger and he whispered, "I sure learned a lot of things about you I didn't know before."

He looked around the room. "Where is Kit? And all the kids?"

Clare hurried to the office. "They are in the tunnel. We didn't want Maebeline to see Kit since they have a history."

The men quickly slid the desk aside and pulled open the door. Kit's anxious face stared up at them. Stub reached down his hand and pulled her up. She was trembling, and he hugged her until she quit shaking.

Spur lifted Nora and Zeke up. He leaned down and called, "Come on out, Annie. I don't think you want to sleep in there!"

Annie came racing toward them. "I went exploring and I found some secrets!" Her face was excited, and Spur chuckled.

"I'm sure you did." He held up the snakeskin and pointed at Zeke.

"This stays in the barn. Get it out there. And then let's eat. All this talking wore me out."

Clare looked at him and rolled her eyes. "You barely said anything. I'm the one who should be tired."

Spur grinned at her. "Well, not as tired as I'm going to be since we've limited our playing to once a day."

Clare looked away as she blushed. "That sounds so crass when you say it that way," she whispered.

Spur threw back his head and laughed. "It was mighty bold the way you said it. Come on, Wild Girl. Let's eat so we can get these kids back outside."

AN EVIL WOMAN

KIT WAS QUIET DURING DINNER. ONCE THE CHILDREN were outside, she picked up the plates. She paused and looked at Spur with a frown on her face.

"Mae used to keep one fingernail filed to a point on her left hand. Did you notice if she still does?"

Spur frowned and slowly nodded. "She did have one fingernail that was longer than the others. I wouldn't have noticed, but she didn't bend it much."

Kit's face became paler.

"That is her poison finger. She has a deadly potion she dips it in. I'm not sure if it is snake venom or if she created something. If she pokes or even scratches you with it, you will most likely be dead. She probably carries something to reverse it, but I have never heard of her using it."

Spur stared hard at Kit.

"How do you know so much about her?" Both men were watching Kit as they waited for her to answer.

A sob caught in Kit's throat. She moved her eyes from Spur to Stub. "She is the one who forced me to sell myself at thirteen. We knew her as Mae, and she is pure evil. Somehow, Big Dorothy got me away from her in Helena." She smiled briefly at Clare.

"That was when I met Clare." Kit's eyes reflected her fear, and her voice was almost a whisper when she spoke. "I know too much about her. If she finds out that I'm alive, she will have me killed. That's why I hid in the tunnel with the children."

Stub stood. He stared at Kit a moment and kicked the corner of the table. "I should have shot her when I had the chance." His eyes were hard as he looked over at Spur.

"She won't give up. She intends to have this ranch." His voice was harsh as he ground out, "Let me kill her. I can put an end to this."

Spur frowned as he looked down the lane. He shook his head.

"I can't let you do that. I probably should, but I can't."

Everyone looked up as a rider raced into the ranch yard. He was yelling and pointing excitedly when Spur jerked the door open.

"That fancy sleigh that was here was caught in a snowslide. The feller is dead, and that woman is trapped under it. One of those big white horses is dead too. We need some more hands to help dig her out!"

Stub looked hard at Spur and headed for the door. He slowed as he looked around at the men clustered around the rider.

"Where's Tuff?"

"He offered to stay with her. She asked for someone to talk to her. Tuff is the best talker among us. He was telling her all about you and Kit and the wedding—"

Stub was rushing for his horse before the man finished talking, and Spur was right behind him. Clare pointed down the trail as the men stared in surprise at the running horses.

"Go. Take your ropes and pull that sled off, but don't get close to that woman. She is evil. Now go!"

Clare was breathing quickly, and Kit started to cry.

"If something happens to Tuff, it will be my fault."

338

Clare shook her head. "He is a wise young man. Let's say a prayer he doesn't get too close. Come. Let's do that now." She led Kit back into the kitchen and closed the front door with a shaky hand.

CHAPTER 67

SPUR'S MOTHER

STUB WAS WITHIN SHOUTING DISTANCE OF THE overturned sleigh when he saw Tuff lean over the woman.

He hollered as he raced his horse toward them.

Tuff started to turn toward his brother and the woman grabbed his coat with one hand. She swung her other hand, and Tuff fell back with a look of surprise.

Stub slid off his horse and ran to his brother. He jerked him up by the shoulders.

"She poke or cut you anywhere?" His body went still as he touched Tuff's forehead. "Did she do that?" Stub's voice was shaking.

Tuff felt his head and looked at the blood in surprise.

"I don't think so. I hit a tree branch earlier when I was riding through the timber. I didn't think it drew blood, but I guess it did."

Stub began to look Tuff over. He found a long cut in the boy's coat across his ribs.

"Take your coat off. I need to check you."

Tuff's face turned pale. "She grabbed my coat. I thought she was just afraid."

Stub didn't answer as he began to pull off all the layers Tuff had on. He finally grinned and let out a shaky breath.

"A heavy coat, a vest, two shirts, and longhandles. Were you cold when you woke up this morning?"

Tuff slowly grinned. He looked down at his clothes as he nodded. His heavy coat and vest were both cut through. One shirt had a small cut but neither the second shirt nor the long underwear were damaged.

Stub glanced over at Spur. He cursed softly as he strode to his horse. He pulled off his rope and walked over to the angry woman.

"My name is Stub. Tuff here is my little brother, and Kit is to be my wife. You are going to get a dose of your own medicine, and we'll see how you like it."

He dropped the rope quickly over Maebeline's hands and jerked them over her head.

"Get my piggin' string off the saddle, Tuff, and a pair of those heavy gloves." When Tuff returned, Stub paused and looked at Spur.

"You want to hold this rope, or you want Tuff to?"

Spur's face was pale as he stepped forward. He shook his head.

"I'll hold it. Tuff, you get on back to the house. Get some warm clothes on." Spur grabbed the rope and pulled Maebeline's hands higher over her head. She was screaming and calling the three of them every name she could think of. Some they understood while others only Spur knew since they were in French.

Tuff was staring from the woman to Spur and back toward his brother.

One of the hands grabbed Tuff and pushed him toward his horse.

"You get on out of here. You don't need to be helping with this." The man's voice was gruff as he spoke.

"Go, Tuff! Get out of here!"

Stub's voice was brittle, and Tuff ran for his horse. He raced it up the trail and glancing once over his shoulder.

Stub turned to Spur. "When I tell you, give that rope a little slack. Then pull it tight.

"Now!"

Spur relaxed his hold and Maebeline jerked her left hand out of the loop that encircled both hands. She lunged at Stub and Spur snapped the rope tight pulling his mother's right hand behind her head. She fell back on the ground, screaming and cursing.

Stub dropped the loop of the piggin' string he was holding over Maebeline's left hand. He handed the end of his short rope to Spur. "Keep that tension tight and stay back." He pulled on his heavy gloves and paused as he looked down at Maebeline.

"Now would be a good time for you to apologize to your son for the Hell you put him through as a child. And for all the men and women you have killed or cheated over the years."

Maebeline's eyes were slits in her face, and she spat at Stub. He didn't understand the words that poured in torrents from her mouth, but he understood what they meant. He shrugged and grabbed her left hand. He sliced her face with her pointed fingernail, first on one side and then on the other. He did it so fast that the cluster of riders didn't realize what had happened until Maebeline began screaming.

Spur dropped the ropes and stepped back.

Maebeline's face was bleeding and she touched it with her free hand. For the first time, true fear showed in her eyes.

Spur stared down at his mother. He backed away and mounted his horse. He rode it slowly toward the ranch without looking back.

CHAPTER 68

A POISON FINGER

STUB'S VOICE WAS COLD WHEN HE SPOKE.

"You just sliced your last man, Mae."

The rest of the riders watched in horror as the woman began to grab her throat. Stub looked around at them.

"She had poison on that fingernail when she tried to slice Tuff. And that's what it would have done to him."

Maebeline slowly quit moving. Her hands no longer grabbed at her throat. Her face and neck were dark, almost black in color. The poison had worked in less than two minutes.

Stub pointed at the dead horse. "Take his harness off and pull him away. The wolves can clean him up.

"Pile brush on her and that sleigh too. I want the whole works burned.

"Make that fire hot. I don't want any of that poison to affect an animal that might be scavenging. Once the fire burns out, I'll bury anything that doesn't burn."

Stub grabbed Tuff's coat and vest along with the shirt that had been cut. He tossed them on top of the broken sleigh. Soon, Maebeline's body was completely covered.

Several of the men drug in dead trees. One pointed at Rom's body. "What about him?"

"Toss him on top of the sleigh. Who knows what he has hidden in his clothes?

"You boys get that fire started and get on out of here. I'll come down later and add more fuel if I need to." Stub turned his horse up the trail and pushed it to a lope. He wanted to catch Spur before he reached the ranch.

The fuel was piled high when the men quit and lit the fire. It exploded into an inferno, and they backed away.

One rider looked at the man beside him. "You ever seen anyone die like that before?"

The other rider shook his head.

Another man spoke up. "I knew an old woman down where I grew up. She could cure just about anything. Word was she could kill just about anything too with the concoctions she made up.

"I saw her healings, but I never did see her kill anybody." He was quiet for a moment and then added softly, "I don't reckon I want to ever see anyone die like that again." He tossed a few more branches on the fire and backed away.

"I think I'll go talk to that padre. I ain't never been to confession, but this here might be a good time to start. I ain't never burned no one before."

Stub caught up with Spur about a half mile from the ranch. Neither man spoke as they rode.

Spur finally looked over at Stub and cursed. "She never was a mother to me, and she was mean as could be. Still, I don't take any pleasure in what we did today."

Stub looked at his friend. He commented softly, "When you have a rabid polecat, it isn't hard to put it down. But when that skunk bites your favorite horse, you have to shoot something you love. That's a whole lot harder.

"Your ma went bad a long time ago. I'm sure she had plenty of chances to get herself right with the Lord. She chose not to. And like a rabid dog, she had to be put down." He reached over and squeezed Spur's shoulder.

"I'm sorry you had to help with that. Thanks for holding that rope. Tuff is too young to have today's memories let alone have a hand in that. Those other riders too."

Spur shook his head. "She tried to kill Tuff. And for what? He's just a kid!"

"Because Tuff told her Kit was marrying me, and I'm his brother. It would have been the last hurt she could have put on Kit.

"You shouldn't feel bad, Spur. If she hadn't put poison on that finger, a cut like that would have never killed her. It was her own poison that killed her—not you or me."

Neither man spoke the rest of the way to the ranch. Tuff was coming out of the bunkhouse with an old coat on as they rode into the yard. He took Spur's horse and the two brothers headed to the barn.

Spur walked up to the little cemetery. He squatted down in front of Chas' grave. He took off his hat and pushed his hand through his hair.

"She's gone, Chas. I should feel relief. Instead, I feel sad. Not sad that she is dead, but sad for all she represents. She despised me as a baby and as a little boy. Still, I cried and wanted to go home after Sister Eddie took me in. It was just a messed-up deal.

"I want to make sure those kids down there know they are loved. I don't want them to know anything about the childhood I experienced." He frowned and shook his head. "Or Clare's for that matter. She hasn't talked much about it, but I don't think she had much of a home either. Still, look at what a great mother she is. Why I think she'd tear a man apart if he tried to hurt one of those kids." He stood and patted the wooden cross.

"I wish you were still around, Old Timer. I'd like to chew the fat with you."

Spur pulled his hat on and headed down the hill to the house. He could smell the pies before he reached the door and he smiled.

"I reckon we all had a rough start. Things are looking up now though."

CHAPTER 69

A MATCHED PAIR

CLARE LOOKED UP WHEN SPUR OPENED THE DOOR. His face looked sad when he dropped down at the table.

"That pie sure does smell good. I could almost taste it when I walked through the door." Spur looked down at his hands. He stood and walked over to the wash basin. He stared at his face in the small mirror. The man looking back at him had laugh wrinkles around his eyes. The large mustache hid his upper lip, and his face showed just a touch of sadness. *I think I'll take a bath tonight. I feel dirty all over, and I haven't even worked that hard.*

Clare set two pies on the table. One was chocolate and the other was apple.

"Tell me which one you want a piece of and I'll cut it. Kit is taking two pieces of apple out to Stub and Tuff." She paused and added softly, "We saw you ride in."

Spur stared at the pies for a moment. "I'll have apple too. That is the one I smelled all the way to the house."

Kit grabbed a cloak and hurried outside with her pie. Clare set a piece of pie in front of Spur. She handed him a fork and and sat down across from him. Her hand was warm on his arm.

Spur's eyes were sad as he looked at her. "Maebeline was a terrible mother. She never liked me. She told me all the time what a bother and an inconvenience I was. But today, it hurt me to know she was going to die." He shook his head.

"It makes no sense to me. When I think about my childhood, most of my thoughts for the last fifteen years have been about Sister Eddie. The pleasant ones for sure. I hardly thought of my mother at all.

"Even today when she was here, I didn't think it would bother me to pull the trigger on that shotgun. When it came down to ending her life though, I could barely help. I held a rope so Tuff or some other cowboy didn't have to." He pushed at his pie before he looked up. "Stub cut her face with her own fingernail. She had tried to slash Tuff just as we rode up. Luckily for him, he put on lots of layers this morning. Her fingernail cut through his heavy coat, vest and one shirt." He frowned.

"Stub burned Tuff's clothes. He was afraid you would try to mend them."

Clare touched his hand. "I'm sorry, Spur. I know how hard that was for you." She stood and walked to the window. She looked out for a moment. She turned to face him as she leaned against the wash basin.

"My father was hung last year for shooting my younger brother, Silas. That brother was Nora's father. I wanted Silas to come and work for us, but Pappy killed him. That was when we took Nora in." Her face paled a little. "It was on our wedding day. Rock had left his guns in the wagon. I had my derringer and I wanted to kill Pappy that day. Rock convinced me to let the law take care of things." Clare glanced out the window before she looked back at Spur. "Rock pushed me aside. Pappy was trying to shoot me." She laughed dryly. "It looks like we had a matched pair when it came to parents."

Spur slowly smiled. "And yet, look at the mother you are. I'd hate to come between you and a child of yours." His smile became bigger.

"Easy calver, good milker, great mothering instincts…if you were a cow, you'd be a keeper because you have all the desirable traits."

350

Clare stared at Spur a moment and finally laughed.

"Except I'm not a cow. So how do I rank among human mothers?"

Spur pushed his chair back. He pulled Clare up and wrapped his arms around her as he grinned down at her.

"You'd rank darn high. In fact, you'd be clear at the top in my book."

Clare let him pull her close. She put her arms around his back.

"I was so afraid when you and Stub rushed out of here. Kit was crying. She just knew Tuff would be dead. She said it would be her fault."

Spur said nothing but he hugged Clare tighter. He finally relaxed his arms.

"I do like hugging a soft woman," he whispered. "Especially one who is sweet…and meek…submissive too." He laughed when Clare glared at him.

"I sure am pleased you made me marry you, Clare Ann Spurlach."

"When you let them go, Tuff was ready to ride south. Steve said he couldn't go alone because he was too young. Then you hired them both back.

"Three or four weeks ago, Steve received a letter from Mr. Sturgis." She glanced at Spur before her eyes returned to Clare. "He is the man Rock bought his black cattle from.

"Mr. Sturgis offered Steve a foreman's job with the opportunity to partner with him on some cattle." Her voice was soft as she added, "He has no heirs. He is looking for someone to pass his legacy on to."

Clare stared at Kit a moment before she hugged her friend. She had tears in her eyes as she exclaimed, "That is wonderful, Kit! I am so happy for you. What an incredible opportunity."

Kit nodded. "It is, but it means leaving you. These last few months have been wonderful." Kit's eyes were misty as she looked at her friend.

"We will write. We'll have to visit too. When Rock and I went south last summer, they were slowly building the rails north. In another year, they should be much closer." Clare bumped Spur with her shoulder.

"Besides, Spur has been on the move most of his life. If I don't let him out to travel from time to time, he just might shrivel up and die."

Spur had been quiet, but he grinned over at the two women.

"Makes a difference when you have a family to come home to. I'd hate to be gone now as much as I used to be."

The children turned around when they heard a horse rushing up behind them. They stood up and called when they recognized Tuff.

He was grinning as he slowed to ride beside the sleigh.

"I heard those bells and knew you were in front of me. I thought I'd ride down with you.

"Stub isn't far behind me. He is so nervous he can hardly breathe. He's kind of grumpy too."

Spur laughed as he looked over at Kit.

"I think it's a fine opportunity although I hate to lose Stub. And Tuff too. That kid is a worker."

Tuff looked up when he heard his name and grinned at Spur's compliment.

"Of course, once he gets down there and runs wild with those two fellows, he might not be worth a darn."

Tuff's eyes shined and he held up a letter.

"I wrote Nate and told him we were moving. I assumed it would be in the spring.

"I can't wait to see Sam and him again. We had so much fun on that cattle drive. You should have seen Sam conk that fellow over the head in Butte.

"They were a rough bunch, but Gabe set things right." His eyes clouded as he added, "I liked Rufe. He was nice. He was funny too.

"All those fellows treated us like hands. They didn't treat us like kids.

"We were sure happy to get our riders out of that town. Gabe pistol-whipped the man who killed Rufe. Beat him to death and then left him in the street. The old gal who ran the sporting house where our boys were holed up said she would tell the law she did it. It didn't seem to worry her at all.

"That was a darn rough town, and I was glad to leave."

Clare's face was pale, but she smiled at Tuff.

"Rock was proud of you, Tuff. He said you did a great job on that drive. He just knew you were going to grow into a fine man. Although it will be a great opportunity, we will miss all three of you."

Smoke showed ahead. Tuff and Kit both looked that way. More fuel had been added to the burn pile. The flames snapped and popped loudly over the sleigh as they rode by.

Clare's face paled as she glanced toward the pile of burning brush. The smell was nauseating. Spur said nothing. He didn't even look that direction. Clare glanced back toward the children, but they were playing and didn't notice.

"Are you going to talk to the sheriff today?" Clare asked.

Spur shrugged. "I haven't decided. Maybe someone will ask about Maebeline. Then again, maybe Rom and she will just fade away.

"I might talk to the padre though. I feel like I need to tell him what we did." He reached over and squeezed Clare's leg.

"Let's talk about something else. It's a happy day for Kit and Stub. Let's keep it that way."

CHAPTER 71

A Wise Priest

THE WEDDING CEREMONY WAS A SIMPLE ONE. MAGGIE offered to keep the children. Only the four friends were in the little church. The crew had opted not to come after the altercation with Maebeline. They went to the saloon instead.

Stub's face was pale, and he kept tugging at the top button on his shirt.

Spur finally leaned over to him. "Just unbutton it, Stub. We don't need you passing out. Tighten up your bandana and no one will know the difference."

Kit looked beautiful in a green and white dress. She and Clare had made over one of Kit's nicer dresses. They had taken lace and trim from another dress which they added to the one Kit was wearing. The result was beautiful.

Stub was almost tongue-tied. Kit finally slipped her arm through his.

"Relax, Steve. Today I am marrying the most handsome man I have ever known, and I would like him to be smiling." Kit's voice was soft, and her eyes reflected the love she felt. She could feel the tenseness drain out of him.

Stub pulled her closer and nodded at Father Ravalli. "Let's get this deal started. Kit might change her mind and then I'd be one sad case."

Father Ravalli's voice was soft as he performed the wedding ceremony. When he asked for the ring, Kit squirmed.

Stub gripped her hand tighter, and Spur pulled a ring out of his pocket.

Father Ravalli blessed it, and Stub placed it on Kit's third finger. She stared at the ring in surprise and Spur winked at her.

When the ceremony was over, the priest beckoned to the two men.

"Come on back here. I need to talk to you." He sat down in the back pew and patted the seat in front of him. "Sit down there and tell me what happened."

Kit and Clare had followed them to the back of the church.

Stub looked up at the women and shook his head. "I don't think they should hear this."

Kit's eyes glinted. "It involves the men we love, and that means it involves us."

Father Ravalli said nothing, but his eyes twinkled. "Please. Sit down. The four of us will talk." He looked from Spur to Stub and back to Spur.

"I understand that two people were killed on the road leading to your ranch yesterday. Tell me about it."

Both men were quiet, but Clare spoke up.

"The woman was Spur's mother. She had come to our home with a will. She claimed that Mr. Boswell had left the ranch to her.

"We hid Kit and the children after she arrived. Spur was concerned for the children's safety and Kit…Kit knew that woman from her past."

Kit blushed and looked away as Clare continued.

"We were finally able to get her out of the house without any shooting. Shortly after she left, one of the hands rode in. He said there had been a snow slide. The driver was killed, and the sleigh was crushed. Spur's mother was under it."

Spur looked away and Clare added, "She tried to kill Tuff by slashing him. She had one fingernail she had dipped in poison." Clare paused before she added softly, "She tried to cut Tuff, but Stub arrived in time to save his brother." Clare looked at the two men sitting quietly beside her. She sat up straighter and gripped Kit's hand.

"Maebeline died from her own poison finger. Had it not been poisoned, the small scratches she received would not have killed her."

Father Ravalli was quiet as he looked at the four people in front of him. Several of the riders had been in to see him. The story they shared verified what Clare said.

The priest looked from Stub to Spur.

"Did you give her an opportunity to seek forgiveness? We must remember that no sin is too great for Our Lord to forgive."

"I did ask her about that." Stub's voice was hard and angry. "She cursed me and spit at me. Then I sliced her cheek with her own fingernail.

"I didn't want to bury her for fear something would dig her up. I'm not sure what that poison was, but it was fast and ugly. I had the hands pile brush on top of everything, and we set the whole works on fire.

"More brush was added this morning and it's still burning. I'll bury what bones I find when the ashes cool."

Spur said nothing. When Stub began to talk about the burning, he stood and walked to the other side of the church.

Father Ravalli nodded slowly. "I will go out today and bless their bodies. We never want to assume that someone is damned. Redemption must always be prayed for." He glanced toward Spur and added, "Why don't the three of you go on outside. Let me talk to Spur alone for just a moment."

The priest waited until everyone left before he approached Spur.

"Is there something you would like to talk to me about, Spur?"

Spur turned toward the priest. He wiped the back of his hand across his face before he spoke.

"Maebeline was a poor excuse for a mother. She never wanted me, and she reminded me of it every day when I was small. An old nun took me in when I was around six and raised me until she died. I was fourteen when Sister Eddie passed.

"I don't understand my sadness. I've barely thought of my mother these last fifteen years. Suddenly she shows up with all the blackness and evil she's always carried around, and I'm sad she's dead."

Father Ravalli put his hand on Spur's shoulder.

"Those feelings are natural, Spur. A child wants to be loved. Children are *born* to be loved.

"When that doesn't happen, children sometimes hang onto the hope that maybe someday, their parents *will* love them.

"You are one of the lucky ones. Your Sister Eddie lifted you out of the darkness you were born into. She gave you a new life.

"Your mother wasn't able to make that change. Perhaps because she couldn't or maybe she didn't want to. We don't know that.

"You must pray for her soul. Say a prayer of thanksgiving too that you were not sucked down into that blackness."

He smiled at the tall man in front of him.

"The Good Lord made you, and He doesn't make mistakes. He has a plan for you and has had from the beginning. Here you have been given the opportunity to be the parent you always wanted.

"Go and be a good father to Clare's children. Be the father you never had, and give those little ones the love you always wanted." He made the sign of the cross over Spur's head.

"Go with God, my son."

Spur stood and smiled at the priest in front of him. He gripped his hand and squeezed the priest's shoulder.

"Thank you, Padre. I knew I'd feel better if I talked to you." His step was lighter as he strolled out of the church. By the time he reached his friends, he was whistling.

"Let's head over to Maggie's and pick up those kids. I might have Tuff spend the night with us. I can send him over to the /B in the morning, so I don't have to ride over there." He waved over his shoulder to where Kit and Stub were talking. "I'd send my foreman but he's a little preoccupied at the time." Stub never looked up and Clare laughed.

"Besides, I think I smell pie in this sleigh and I'm guessing there is enough for everyone."

Stub had his horse tied behind the sleigh. Spur turned around with a grin.

"Now keep it proper back there. I don't want to get embarrassed." He leaned over to Clare and whispered, "Of course we might see something you and I should try—especially now that I know you like to play every day."

Clare said nothing. Her face and neck slowly turned red, and Spur chuckled.

"Slide over here, Sweetheart. Cuddle with me a little. Let's don't let them have all the fun."

CHAPTER 72

A Sad Little Girl

CLARE PUT THE CHILDREN IN BED EARLY AND followed soon after. Spur took a soaking bath and fell asleep easily. He awoke suddenly to the sound of sobbing. He listened closely and then headed upstairs taking the steps two at a time.

Nora was sitting up in bed. She had the letter Rock had written in her little hand and she was crying.

When Spur sat down on her bed, she sobbed, "My papa died and then I had a new papa. Now he is dead too, and I don't have a papa."

Spur picked her up and held her while she cried.

"Here now, Nora. Don't cry. I'll be your papa. The Good Lord sent me here just for that reason. Now don't you be sad." He pointed at the crumpled letter.

"Would you like to read that letter from your second papa in Heaven?"

Nora stared at the letter and then held it out to Spur. "Be careful when you open it. I don't want it to get all messed up."

Spur shifted Nora on his lap and carefully opened the letter. He turned it so the moonlight shined on the writing.

My sweet little Nora,

I'm guessing you didn't read this letter when the other two kids read theirs. Why I'll bet you slept with it for two or even five months. I'm happy you are reading it now though.

You know how you like to look at the statue of Jesus's mommy in church? Well, I am going to live where she lives! I didn't get to finish the cattle drive or come home to you and Mama. Instead, I am going to my new home, way up high in Heaven.

I know how much you love flowers and I want you to plant a whole bunch of them on my grave. Shoot, plant them on all the graves out there in our little cemetery. You always helped me with the flowers, and I want you to keep doing that. And watch for butterflies. When you see one, you will know that I am there helping you.

I'm sorry I won't be home to kiss you goodnight or to tickle you. Just know if I can figure out a way to do it from up here, I will.

Now you smile for me and be the happy, sweet girl I have always loved. And if your mommy marries a new papa, you give him hugs and kisses like you gave me.

I love you, Nora.

Love your Papa

Nora was quiet a moment. Her eyes were serious as she looked up at Spur. "You are my papa now, aren't you?"

Spur hugged her. "I sure am. I will be your papa as long as you need one."

Nora frowned at him.

"Kids always need a papa. And when they get old like Mama, their papas become their friends. I think Grandpa Ike is Mama's papa. He's my grandpa, and he's Mama's friend.

"That's why I'll always want you to be my papa." Her eyes were serious as she added, "But I don't want you to scold me."

Spur chuckled and Nora smiled. Then she took Spur's face between her hands and rubbed her nose on his. She smiled shyly at him and giggled.

"That is how my papa kissed me every night."

Spur could feel his heart get squishy. He rubbed his mustache against her cheek and tickled her.

"Did your papa tickle you like this?"

Nora giggled and curled up in a ball. Spur continued to tickle her until she could barely breathe.

She smiled up at Spur as he covered her with blankets. "I'm glad you are my papa. I asked God for a new papa, one that was as nice as my last one. I'm glad he sent you." She was quiet a moment before she continued.

"Annie found a treasure map in the tunnel. She wanted to keep it, but Zeke made her put it back. Annie said we had to promise we wouldn't tell anyone. We all promised but I crossed my fingers. That means it's all right if I tell you.

"It's all wrinkled and torn in places. I don't think it's a toy. I told Annie that too."

Spur could feel a chill go down his back. He looked at Nora in surprise as he asked, "How did Annie find it?"

"She was trying to run up the wall to see if she could jump from one side to the other. When she kicked one of the big rocks, it fell out. We could see things inside the hole. The map was one of them." Nora's eyes were big as she spoke. "I told Annie she broke the wall, and I was going to tell on her. She said if I didn't want to get a spanking, I had better not tell." Nora frowned at Spur. "I don't want a spanking."

Spur chuckled. "You aren't going to get a spanking, Nora. Now tomorrow, I want you kids to show me where you found the treasure map. And you are right—it is really old. It belonged to Grandpa Chas, so we have to be very careful of it."

Spur kissed Nora and rubbed his nose on hers again.

"You go to sleep now. I'll put your letter back under your pillow and we can read it anytime you want. Sleep tight and don't let the bed bugs bite."

Spur walked slowly downstairs. He glanced back at Clare's bedroom. It was still quiet. He shook his head.

"Rock, you left some mighty big tracks to fill. I'll do my best, but I sure don't know much about being a father. You may need to send some advice from time to time."

CHAPTER 73

A Night Ride

SPUR HEARD A RIDER RACING INTO THE YARD. HE looked at the clock on the mantle. *Eleven o'clock.*

"What in Sam Hill is wrong now?" He jerked on his britches and boots. He grabbed his hat and rifle as he headed for the door.

He pulled the door open and Handy almost fell into the house.

"Sorry to wake you up, Boss, but we have a problem.

"When Buck and I got to the south line shack, we saw Jake's and Caine's horses in the corral. We were kind of surprised that they'd be done breaking ice by ten in the morning. Still, we weren't really expecting trouble.

"Then some fellers in the house cut loose on us. They spooked the packhorse and Buck's horse bolted. I hollered for Buck to head back home and get help.

"They shot me in the shoulder. Had me pinned down all day. When dark came on, I slipped down to the horses.

"My horse was eating hay through the corral fence. I got him to come to me, jumped on him, and took off out of there. The clouds were slipping back and forth over the moon, but I had a little light. I came across Buck's tracks in the snow. His horse has little feet and I picked them out.

"I could see where two riders came up behind him. Further along, there was some blood on the ground. After that, his horse was being led. The moon went under some clouds, and I lost the trail about four miles from the line shack.

"I could see campfires down below in the valley though. There were four fires, so I figured there were too many of them for me to fight alone. That's when I headed back up here." His eyes were bleak. "I couldn't find Jake and Caine, but that horse Buck was riding—he raised it from a colt. He wouldn't let another man take that horse without a fight."

Spur listened quietly and then pointed at the table. "Sit down over there so we can patch you up." He looked out the window and thought for a moment.

"I think there is enough moonlight tonight to take a night ride. We'll pay a visit to the fellows in the line shack and then ride down to that campsite."

Several riders had come out of the bunkhouse and others were looking through the door. Spur hollered at them.

"Saddle up, boys. Grab your rifles and plenty of bullets. We are taking a night ride.

"Tuff, you ride over to the /B and gather the boys. Tell Nudge to leave a couple of men there to keep an eye on things. Send the rest toward the south line shack.

"And saddle Hell Fire for me."

The bunkhouse came alive with a rush of activity. Spur looked back toward Clare's bedroom and then lifted the kettle onto the hook above the fire.

"Take off your shirt, Handy, and let's see where you were hit."

The wound was jagged and was going to be slow to heal. However, the bullet had gone through.

Spur had just torn some rags to clean the wound when Clare hurried out. Her hair was down, and it looked like she had just dropped her dress over her head. He motioned toward Handy.

"Outlaws hit the south line shack. We are headed down there to clean them out. Three of our boys are missing too.

"Bind him up and keep him in the house. He can sleep on the bunk in my office."

Handy started to protest but Spur shook his head. He stated quietly, "I need you here, Handy. We don't know what we are going to find. This might be a decoy to get everyone away from the ranch. I don't want my family left unprotected.

"And Clare, you load every gun in this house. You be ready. Don't let any strangers get close. Put Gomer out. He will let you know if a stranger rides in."

Spur strode out the door. A rider handed him Hell Fire's reins and the Double Spur riders were gone in a rush.

Clare found some whiskey and poured it onto a clean cloth.

"I'm sorry to hurt you, Handy, but we have to clean that wound."

Handy's mouth clamped down in tight line as Clare applied the whiskey. When it was clean, she made a poultice from dried herbs and packed those into the hole. She smeared honey over the wound and bound his shoulder. She pointed at the cot.

"Go lay down for a bit. I am up now. I'll load the guns and get things ready here. You rest awhile. I'll call you when I get tired."

Handy frowned and started to speak, but Clare shook her head.

"I am too nervous to sleep now, and I need you fresh." She smiled at him and patted his arm.

"Don't worry. I'll wake you soon enough."

CHAPTER 74

A Land Grab

THE MEN WERE QUIET AS THEY RODE. THEY SLOWED down as the snow became deeper. Spur looked around at his riders.

"Who is the best shot in this outfit?"

All eyes swung toward a young man with a big smile. He grinned at his friends and drawled, "The fellers call me Squirrel 'cause I can shoot one jumpin' in the trees. I can hit those little buggers that dig in the ground too.

"I ain't gonna say I'm the best, but I hit what I aim at." His grin became bigger and he added, "Back in Tennessee where I growed up, bullets was in short supply. My Pappy wanted an accountin' of ever' one we used. He expected us to come back with five varmints if'n we used four bullets."

When Spur stared at him in confusion, Squirrel grinned. "If you's lucky, some critters 'ill line up one in front of t'other. Two meals an' one shot."

Spur chuckled and the men laughed.

"Who is the fastest? I'm thinking we might want to shove a snowball in that chimney. I need someone to sneak across that open area, climb up the side of the line shack, and drop it in the chimney without getting caught."

A lanky cowboy who looked to be all arms and legs pointed to himself.

"I'll do it. I put pegs on the side of that shack, an' I can climb up there in the dark. Shoot, I might stay there. I'll have a clean shot when they come runnin' out."

"You do that, Ladder."

Spur looked around at the riders. "I want to try to take them alive if possible. We need to know how wide this deal is. Is this just a few outlaws looking for some horses or is this about something else?

"Not likely to be cattle thieves in the middle of winter—too hard to get them out of this valley. A big group of men makes me wonder though what else might be in the planning."

The men were quiet as they thought about what Spur said. One of the riders toward the back whispered to the man beside him. "What's the boss talking about? What else could it be besides rustling cattle?"

The second man was quiet a moment and then pointed his thumb to the west.

"I was up in the Idaho Territory some time ago. It was a rough area, but it had some good grazing. The long valley where our ranch was located was just full of grass.

"A fancy fellow came riding in. He had a bunch of deeds that he said gave him ownership to most of the grass in that valley.

"Some small ranchers had claimed the land on the northern end and up into the foothills. A big cattleman claimed the rest. He had filed on some, but he didn't own everything he used.

"That fancy fellow had some gunmen working for him. They called on those small ranchers, one by one. Usually, the menfolk weren't home when they arrived, and they terrorized the women. Made all kinds of threats.

"It worked on some of them. Several families packed up and left. Most stayed though and that's when the trouble started.

"Those ranchers started dyin'. Stampedes, fires, runaway horses.

"That big rancher did nothin'. I think he was maybe just a little happy. He figured when it all blew over, he'd end up with the whole valley.

"Those outlaws came for him one day when his riders were all out on the range. Killed him and stampeded the cattle right through the ranch yard. His wife ran out to get their little boy, and both of them were killed.

"There wasn't any law and that land thief thought he'd gotten off scot-free. Him and his crew just moved in and took over.

"One of the cowboys who worked there didn't see it that way though.

"He gathered the hands who rode for that big ranch, those who hadn't quit. He sent them up into the hills. Then he rode all through that valley and met with the small ranchers who were tryin' to hang on. He said he had a plan. They agreed to meet at the big ranch on a certain night.

"Those little ranchers and their hands surrounded those outlaws about midnight. The young man who was organizin' things slipped into the barn and turned the horses loose. The rest of his crew kept firing on the men in the bunkhouse and the big house. When they wouldn't come out, an order was given. Flames sprang up all around the bunkhouse and barn.

"Those outlaws poured out of there like rats off a sinkin' ship.

"That feller who was in charge was abrupt. Any men who could be identified as outlaws were hung on the spot.

"Two men were released and told never to come back. No one could identify them, and they claimed to be innocent.

"The top dog in the big house was given no such chance. They burned that house down and him with it." He looked over at the younger man beside him. "That there is a true story. I know because I was one of those two young men who was released." He stared through the murky night toward Spur and nodded.

"Yessir, I think the boss suspects a land grab, and he's goin' to be ready."

The rider who had been listening was quiet a moment. "What about the feller who organized all that. Did he take over?"

"Naw. Turned out the boss man had him a spinster sister. She showed up and took over. She offered that feller a job, but he turned it down. He just rode away. I never saw him again.

"I heard he finally settled down around Cheyenne. His name was Rankin. I don't recall his first name.

"I remember his eyes though. They could drill into a man. Made a feller nervous even if he wasn't guilty."

"Rankin wasn't much older than I was at the time. I don't know if he ever married. All I know is I don't never want to cross him. I don't reckon he'd give me a second chance."

"Did the spinster lady ever marry?"

The cowboy who had told the story chuckled. "Don't know. 'Course she'd be old enough now to be your grandma in case you're thinkin' on sparkin' her."

"I was thinking if that spinster woman married, maybe she had a granddaughter. If she had a granddaughter, they'd for sure need some hands. I could spark the granddaughter. We could fall in love, and I'd have that ranch I always wanted."

His friend chuckled.

"Duke, you'd better quit your dreamin' and get your head back where it's supposed to be. This is goin' to be a long night, and you need to have your ears lined up with your eyes."

CHAPTER 75

An Early Morning Surprise

THE DOUBLE SPUR RIDERS ARRIVED AT THE LINE shack around three in the morning. All was quiet. Clouds scuttled across the sky changing the night from light to dark as they passed over the moon.

Ladder slid off his horse. He made a large, hard snowball and stuffed it into the flour sack Spur handed him. He ran soundlessly across the packed snow to the side of the shack and was quickly on top. He shoved the sack into the chimney and squatted down beside it. The men scattered out around the shack and waited.

Before too long, smoke began to pour from under the door of the shack. That was followed by coughing and cursing, along with the sound of feet hitting the floor. The door to the shack flew open. Three men clad only in longhandles and boots fell through the doorway coughing.

Ladder's voice carried clearly through the still night.

"Evenin' boys. Nice of you fellers to come outside to greet us. Now just kneel on down in that snow and put your hands in the air. Or make a run for it, and we'll cut you all down. Life is full of choices."

The men tried to look around and Ladder cocked his shotgun. He had a smile on his face but the shotgun he held wasn't joking. They dropped to their knees and stared as the Double Spur hands surrounded them.

Spur's face was hard as he stared at the men kneeling in the snow.

"We are missing three hands and we had better find them alive. If we don't, we'll hang every man jack who's involved.

"Now you can start talking or I am going to let Shiloh here start cutting off little pieces of you until you become more agreeable."

A smiling cowboy slipped off his horse and sauntered toward them. He lifted a large knife from inside his shirt and slid it along his finger. His eyes glittered in the moonlight as he spoke.

"Ah, señors, my knife is lonely tonight. You see, she has not been able to prick anyone in some time and she is thirsty. My grandfathers among the Apache talked often of how to keep a man alive for hours. My mother, she was the daughter of a bandito down in Mexico. The blood I have running through my veins is not so peaceful, I think."

The men stared at Shiloh for a moment. Two remained quiet but one threw out his arms.

"Have mercy, fellers! We were told this was a ridin' job. We were supposed to stay at this line shack an' run off anyone who showed up."

The riders surrounding the men on the ground said nothing, but several of them pushed their horses closer.

Spur stared at the men in front of him and asked sarcastically, "And you thought this was open ground with all the improvements here? This isn't exactly a run-down line shack with broken corrals. How did you explain away those slept-in cots?"

One of the kneeling men cursed and stood up.

"Just shoot us now and be done with it. We knew this was a rawhide outfit, and we took the job anyway. All we had to do was stay here for a week and run off anyone who rode up. We were told this deal would be over in less time than that. We'd get a month's wages and then we were to head out.

"We figured with $30 each, we could make it far enough south to stay shy of the fellows who hired us."

"You kill my riders?" Spur's voice was hard as he growled out his words to the men in front of him.

The man shook his head. "We were supposed, but we're broke cowhands, not killers. Your boys came in the night before last. It was late and they were tired. They put up their horses and walked right in on us.

"We took their guns and sent them on their way."

A growl began to grow among the riders and Spur asked quietly, "You sent them outside with no shelter and no guns?"

"You had better hope they live. If any of them are missing toes or fingers, we'll take that from each of you before you hang.

"Tie them up, boys. Ladder, do you think you can rig that shotgun to go off if they try anything?"

Ladder grinned and the outlaws were bound together. They said nothing as they were laid on the floor. Ladder attached the shotgun to the door and ran a rope from the trigger down to one outlaw. When he was satisfied with the tension, he cocked the shotgun and Spur's riders slipped out the window.

They quickly remounted. Shiloh led off and they followed the slim rider southwest toward the valley floor. They were about a mile from the shack when a man rose from the ground beside them. His rifle covered Spur who was the closest to the standing man.

"You boys just ease on back. I have the big fellow dead to right, and my partner has you covered from the other side."

Spur put his hands on the saddle horn and grinned. "Jake, what are you doing? Taking a stroll in the moonlight?"

Jake lowered his gun barrel with a happy curse. "Boss? Are we happy to see you fellers! Caine, come on out from under that snow.

"You boys back your horses up and we'll pull out the rope we buried to trip you up in case you tried something."

Caine laughed and rose from the other side. He pulled his lariat up as he walked toward his friends.

"It's about time you showed up. We figgered you were part of that crowd down by the river. Thought maybe we'd have to take on all of you, and then clean out those fellers down by the fires all by ourselves too." He grinned at his friends.

"Now who is going to give me a ride? I've done all the walking I intend to do for some time."

Each man was given a hand up behind another rider and Spur led off.

One of their friends asked, "You boys spend the night outside? Anything frozen on you?"

"Naw. We found a cave the last time we were up here. It had a little wood stacked inside and we packed some more in. We weren't really planning on trouble, but since it was handy-like, we figured we could make it more comfortable.

"You kill those fellows who kicked us out? We didn't hear any shots."

Spur listened as the men visited quietly. He finally looked around and spoke in a low voice.

"I don't want any more talking. We can see their fires and sound carries across this snow. Keep it quiet."

Shiloh had been scouting ahead and he eased back to ride beside Spur.

"We might want to get a move on. They are fixing to hang Buck."

Spur cursed under his breath and slipped off his horse. They crawled through the brush until they could look down on the fires below. He leveled his rifle at the group of men surrounding Buck and swore as they kept moving around. He swore again when he saw that the rope around Buck's neck was attached to the tree branch above him.

Squirrel dropped down beside Spur.

"Let me handle this, Boss. I can make that shot."

Buck was mounted on his own horse. His hands were tied behind his back. A man was holding the reins to his horse and another man held a whip in his hand. That man laughed as he raised the whip.

"Say your prayers, Boy. Your friends aren't going to get here in time to save you. Shoot, they are probably scared anyway."

Squirrel fired. The rope was sheared in two and the horse Buck was riding bolted. Buck leaned low over his horse. He talked to it and guided it with his knees as it charged through the camp, scattering men and supplies. He raced out into the night.

Spur yelled at his men, "Cut 'em down! Keep shooting until nobody moves."

The battle was over in minutes. The men who were still alive threw their hands in the air. One tall man seemed to be uninjured, and he slowly stood.

He looked around the destroyed camp. He gave a cold laugh as he stared at the ready guns held by the riders who circled his camp.

"You must be George's outfit. It's a little early for visitors, but come on in, George. I'll put some coffee on, and we can have a little confab."

CHAPTER 76

You Can't Choose Your Relatives

THE MEN OUTSIDE THE CAMP WERE QUIET. SPUR finally answered. His voice was hard, and he ground his words out.

"I don't see there is much to talk about. Your men ran two of my riders out of my line shack, shot a third one, and you just tried to hang Buck. Plus, you are camped on my land, eating my beef. Just one of those things would be enough reason for me to shoot every sidewinder here. All four give me reason to hang you.

"Nope, I don't reckon we have anything to talk about."

"Was Buck the name of that fellow who just ran his horse through here? We were just funning him. He came busting in here earlier today. Couldn't control his horse. A man could tear up a lot of supplies riding into a camp like that.

"Now come on in here and let's talk. I've never met you before and I'd like to meet Mae's only kid." He gave a low humorless chuckle. "I never thought my sister would tolerate motherhood. You must be special."

Spur stared in surprise at the tall man. As he dropped off his horse, he spoke softly to Squirrel.

"You keep your rifle trained on him. If he tries anything, drop him."

Spur walked slowly up to the fire. He stared at the tall man in front of him and almost sucked in his breath. The resemblance between them was uncanny.

Both were tall with broad shoulders and narrow hips. Both had thick black hair that curled from under their hats. Their dark eyes studied each other, and the older man laughed.

"Well, I'll be." He put out his hand, but Spur didn't change positions.

He studied the face of the man in front of him, and he didn't like what he saw. The man's eyes were cold, almost dead. His hard mouth was twisted into a sarcastic smile. The planes of his face were drawn tight, and he held himself with an arrogance that Spur didn't possess.

In contrast, the man's hands looked soft. It was obvious he did not make his living doing anything that required physical labor. Spur also noticed the way the older man kept his left hand free. Since his six shooter was on his right side, Spur knew the man carried a sleeve gun in his long, black, tailored coat.

When Spur didn't take his hand, the man gave a low laugh. He slid a tree stump closer and sat down by the fire, facing the direction from which Spur had walked.

"See? I'm giving your sharpshooter there a full view of me. Now sit on down here and let's talk about why I'm here." He motioned toward another stump on the opposite side of the fire.

Spur looked around. His neck hairs were standing on end. Everything about the man in front of him felt deadly. He watched as the Double Spur hands moved through the camp disarming the rest of the outlaws. He looked toward the direction Buck's horse had run, but he saw no sign of the rider or his horse. Finally, he dropped down on the stump. He refused the coffee he was offered.

Spur's eyes were cold as he spoke. "This isn't a social call."

Irritation flitted briefly through the other man's eyes before he smiled.

"My name is Andrew. I'm your mother's younger brother. We had a plantation in Georgia before the War Between the States. Mae didn't like working with her hands so she left home at sixteen. She said she knew other ways to make money that were less taxing." His eyes glinted as he smirked at Spur.

"And so she did."

Spur felt a surge of anger go through him. He motioned toward his uncle's hands.

"Looking at your hands, I'd say you did too." Spur's voice was sarcastic, and fury registered on Andrew's face briefly before he hid it with a smile.

He waved his hands dismissively.

"We lost the plantation during that war. Things have been difficult since then." He leaned toward Spur as he attempted a friendly smile.

"And that brings us to you.

"It seems you have settled on land that belongs to Mae. We are terribly sorry, but you see, that land is not yours. You will need to move."

Spur stared at the man. The fury that went through him showed on his face.

"And you have talked to Mae since our meeting?"

Andrew shrugged his shoulders as he shook his head. "No, but she showed me the documents. Everything was in order."

"And since all was in order, you assumed you could run off my hands and even hang them?"

Andrew's eyes narrowed down. Spur had not reacted as he expected, and his irritation was plainly visible.

"Look, George. Mae was given that land by Chas Boswell. She has the papers to prove it. She filed those papers with the bank after she left her meeting with you. I'm sure this is a sudden surprise to you, but such is life."

Spur stood and looked down at Andrew as he answered quietly, "Mae didn't make it to the bank, Andrew. Rom drove too close to an overhang of snow. There was a slide, and the sleigh rolled. Rom and Mae both died.

"We burned the sleigh and everything in it. Your sister and your fake documents are gone. This steal is over."

Spur turned to walk away, and Buck charged his horse between the two men. Two rifles sounded at the same time followed by a third shot.

Andrew slid to the ground holding his throat. He was gasping and trying to talk as his life drained away.

Buck fell from his saddle. He was shot low in his chest. He was dying as well.

"There are more," he gasped. "Father and son. Mae…Two more… Clare. Save your family—they…" Buck gripped Spur's coat as he smiled up at him. "For Clare. I did it for Clare." He fell back with a sigh. Spur stood motionless for a moment as he processed what Buck had said.

Ladder touched his shoulder. Spur jerked away as he whirled around.

"Boss, you need to get home. Now. We'll clean things up here. Go take care of your family."

Spur was already running toward his horse before Ladder finished speaking.

Ladder pointed at Caine and Jake.

"You two each grab a horse and come with me. We'll go back to the line shack. We need to cut those boys loose. Once we're done there, we'll head for the ranch to back up the boss." He pointed toward more men.

"Six of you head for the ranch as fast as you can to back up the boss. The rest of you boys, tie up anyone left alive. Pull the guns off those dead men and drag their bodies over to that ditch. This ground is too hard to dig a hole so just pile some rocks on them. Put those wounded men on horses and head for the sheriff's office. Take those extra horses with you.

"Squirrel, you fill out the report. Don't leave anything out.

"If any of you meet Nudge and his men along the trail, turn them around. Tell them to hightail it for the Double Spur.

"Now get moving!"

CHAPTER 77

FOUR MEN DOWN

SPUR TOOK THE BACK WAY TO THE RANCH AND
pushed Hell Fire as hard as he dared.

"Just a few more miles, old fellow. We've got to get home fast." Some
of the snow drifts were deep. Spur watched the sun and shook his head.

"Maybe I would have made better time if I had taken the usual trail.
This is slow going."

Hell Fire finally crested the last hill and Spur looked down on the
quiet ranch. Clusters of trees grew near the back of the house, and Spur
rode as close as he dared without being seen. He stepped down and
ground-tied his horse.

"Now you stay here. I'll be back for you as soon as this is all over."
The horse nuzzled his shoulder and Spur slipped away.

He was almost to the house when he heard men's voices. He didn't
hear the children and he smiled grimly. "Clare got them in the tunnel.
I hope they stay there." He opened a back door that led into the house.
He slipped inside and pulled off his boots. Clare kept a rug there and
Spur set his boots on it. "I can walk quieter in my sock feet," he muttered
softly as he eased into the hallway.

As he drew closer to the front of the house, he could hear a man talking.

"So, this is how it's going to be. Either you tell us where your kids are, or we are going to shoot that man over here. It's your choice."

"Let them shoot me, Clare. Don't you tell them where those kids are." Handy's voice was angry. It was followed by the sound of a shot, and something crashed to the floor.

Spur heard Clare gasp and he cursed under his breath.

"Look, Lady. This ranch is already ours. We just want to know where your kids are so we can put all of you in the sleigh. You are leaving here one way or the other."

Clare's voice was clear and strong when she answered.

"I will die before I tell you where those children are. Besides, they have nothing to do with this. I've seen the deed for this place.

"Spur found Chas when he was dying. They had time to talk a little." She added quietly, "Spur is Chas' son.

"You are too late. The only name on that deed is Spur's." Clare's voice was angry and hard. "He filed that deed weeks ago. It was certified by the lawyer in town. This place is his fair and square." Her voice was dripping with distain as she added, "You are nothing but killers. This place will never be yours. And when you die, we'll burn your bodies like we did Mae's."

One of the men slapped Clare. She said nothing as she staggered and almost fell.

"Take her in the back, William. Teach her some manners and have your fun. Don't kill her though. I want her alive when we kill George."

William grabbed Clare by the arm and drug her down the hall.

"You and me are going to have a little fun, and then I am going to beat you. I don't like a sassy woman. You won't be so proud or so pretty when I get done with you."

Spur wrapped an arm around William's neck as they passed the doorway where he was hiding. He slid his knife between the surprised man's ribs. William couldn't speak and Spur put his hand over the man's mouth to muffle his gasps. He pulled William's falling body into a bedroom and slid him to the floor. He knelt beside the dying man as he wiped his knife on his shirt.

"Look long and hard, Boy. This is the last face you'll see. I'm Mae's son, but that is all you and I have in common. Be glad I need to be quiet, or I'd make you suffer longer for touching my wife." Spur's voice was low and hard as he stared down at the man.

He stood quickly and reached for Clare. She was trembling and Spur held her for a moment. They could hear the second man talking in the kitchen.

"Now don't take too long, William. I know those kids are in that tunnel along with the map to Chas' gold mine. Mae is sure it's hidden in there. As soon as we find that map, we'll get rid of the kids and be out of here." His voice was silent for a moment and then he called back with a mocking voice.

"I hear your children, Clare. I hear that baby crying. As soon as I find the opening to that tunnel, I'm going in there.

"Now you be nice to William and maybe we'll let them live a little longer." His voice was quiet as the sound of books hitting the floor echoed through the room.

"You know why Chas built that tunnel? It was to protect his pretty little wife. Mae almost got to Agnes in St. Louis.

"She hired a fellow to follow Chas after he ran out on her. The man reported back to Mae that Chas had a new woman and was getting married. As you can imagine, Mae was furious. She contracted one of her men in St. Louis to kill Agnes.

"Agnes and her father were traveling with a group of Indians, and one of them killed the man Mae sent. They pulled out of St. Louis in a hurry and Agnes escaped.

"Mae never caught up with them again. In fact, she didn't even know Agnes had died until a few years ago. A drunk cowboy in Helena who used to work here told Mae all about Chas and him losing his wife. He told her about that tunnel too.

"She tried to get him to tell her where the opening was, but he clammed up. His buddies got him out of town before Mae could find out any more."

Silent tears appeared on Clare's cheeks and Spur held her tightly for a moment.

He kissed her cheek and whispered, "Clare, I want you to go outside. Go through the trees and come into the barn through the side door. Open that tunnel and get the kids out. Take them up in the loft. There's a shotgun under the seat of the sleigh. Take it with you. If anyone comes up that ladder, wait until his shoulders appear before you pull the trigger. And only shoot one barrel in case you need the second one."

Clare's eyes were wide, and her breath was coming quickly. Spur touched her cheek.

"Go!"

When Clare was out the door and headed for the trees, Spur walked up the hallway. He made no effort to be quiet. *Hopefully, that fellow will think that I'm William.*

The other man was in the office. He had his back turned when Spur eased into the doorway of the kitchen. The man spun and dropped, firing as he turned. Spur staggered but fired three quick shots.

The man dropped his gun and fell to the floor. He started to lift his left hand and Spur kicked it. A small gun flew across the floor.

The man on the floor was breathing hard. He gasped as Spur looked down at him.

"Got ya, didn't I? The way you're bleeding, you'll be meeting your maker tonight too." He gasped again and held his stomach.

"I told Mae this was a bad idea, but she wouldn't listen. She said, 'Of course it will work, Victor. I have pulled this swindle many times. You don't think I became wealthy on my brothel alone? A woman always needs a backup plan.' Guess she was wrong."

He squinted at Spur's face.

"You are a combination of Mae and Chas. He was the only man she came close to loving." He tried to chuckle, but it was more of a cough as he added "Close for Mae, but that's not saying much.

"She was going to poison him and take his money the night he ran away. I don't know how he found out. Someone must have warned him.

"She sure was mad when he disappeared. Not as mad as when she found out she was pregnant with you though." Victor took a shaky breath. "Sure would like to shake hands with you before I go."

Spur staggered a little and backed up. "I reckon not. You likely have a poison finger like Mae had.

"Nope. I'll stay right here." Spur staggered again and bumped into the table. The man on the floor laughed viciously.

Spur started for the door. He tripped and almost fell. He finally pulled the door open. "Have to get to Clare. The kids—have to find them—aren't safe." He whistled loudly for Hell Fire and fell across the door sill.

CHAPTER 78

LOTS OF GOOD HELP

ELL FIRE CHARGED THROUGH THE RANCH YARD AND
up to the house. He nuzzled his owner and nickered loudly.

Clare heard riders racing into the yard. She pointed at the ladder as
she struggled to keep her voice calm.

"You children climb down and wait for me. Our riders are back so
we are safe now."

She heard Nudge yell, "Spade, get down to the Mission and bring
Father Ravalli up here. We are going to need him." She hurried down
the ladder and shoved the shotgun under the seat of the sleigh. The
children were clustered in the doorway of the barn. Several men were
lifting Spur up and Clare ran toward them with little Chas in her arms.
The three older children followed her.

Tuff grabbed Annie and swung her around.

"How about we have a snowball fight? Maybe even build a snowman.
I'll let you use my hat and we can get a cigar from Cookie."

The three children looked toward the house. They watched the
cluster of men worriedly before they looked back at Tuff. He knelt in
front of them with a smile.

"All those adults in there aren't going to want a bunch of kids underfoot. Let's play awhile and then pester Cookie for some treats."

Annie frowned. "I think we should check on Papa. Mama is real worried."

Tuff nodded soberly. "She is but old Spur is a tough one. Cookie will fix him up. After that, Father Ravalli will come."

"I think we should stay out of the way. Now come on. Let's go have a snowball fight. And if any adults come back here to see what we're doing, we'll throw some snowballs at them."

Annie laughed excitedly. Both she and Zeke ran after Tuff. Nora watched them. She looked back toward the house with a worried look on her face. She ran up to the door and slipped through the adults until she was beside Spur.

She looked up at Clare with big eyes. "Is our new papa going to die, Mama? I don't want him to die."

Clare's eyes were red, but she smiled and shook her head. She knelt beside the serious little girl. Chas was squirming and fussing in Clare's arms.

"Father Ravalli is coming, and he will make your new papa all better. How about you take care of Chas for me? You go into the living room and rock him." She kissed the little girl's face and whispered, "I want him to sleep. Will you help our baby to go to sleep?"

Nora nodded and took her little brother. Her little voice could soon be heard singing. Nudge peeked through the door and laughed.

"Nora is quite the big sister. That little fellow is just watching her. She is singing her little heart out."

Clare didn't answer. She was watching Spur and tears were sliding down her cheeks.

Cookie patted her arm.

"Now don't you worry none, Miss Clare. I got that bleeding slowed. That priest doc will be here afterwhile, an' he'll have that bullet out in no time.

"Ya just sit here an' hold his hand. I reckon that's the best fer both a ya." He walked out into the kitchen and snorted.

"Handy, if yore head weren't so durn hard, you'd a been dead fer sure. Now sit still whilst I bind that crease in yore big skull where that bullet notched ya.

"You'll have a headache fer a time but ya ain't dyin' today."

CHAPTER 79

BODY AND SOUL

SPADE WAS BACK IN TWO HOURS WITH FATHER Ravalli. The good doctor had been making a house call and the cowboy had tracked him down.

The priest hurried through the door. He checked Handy quickly and nodded as he handed him a bottle.

"You keep that clean now. Put this medicine on it twice a day. And I want a clean rag around that every other day." He blessed the surprised man and hurried back to the bedroom where Spur lay. His hands went still as he checked the unconscious cowboy. He nodded over his shoulder.

"You men clean that table off. Clear everybody out but Clare and three of the strongest men.

"Clare, you scrub that table down. I need to get this bullet out immediately."

As Clare hurried to scrub the table, Father Ravalli gave more orders.

"Lift him carefully. Don't pull on his arms. I don't want that chest wound to bleed any more than it already is. Lay him down right there. Yes, that's good. Now all of you but Clare—out of here."

When the kitchen emptied, Father Ravalli smiled at Clare.

"Are you able to help me, Clare? This is going to get bloody. With the grace of God, I will get that bullet out."

Clare nodded as her throat closed. She scrubbed her hands and took a deep breath.

"Just tell me what you want me to do."

Father Ravalli scrubbed his hands and quickly laid out his surgical instruments. When he was ready, he looked over at Clare and smiled again.

"You just hand me the instrument I need when I tell you. They are laid out in the order they should be used. Let's both pray the Good Lord will guide my hands and keep them steady."

The priest put a cloth over Spur's nose and the big man quit tossing around. His breathing was soon even and deep.

Father Ravalli said a quick prayer over Spur and blessed him. Then he began. He didn't talk for the next hour and a half except to tell Clare what he needed.

Even though it was terrifying for her to watch, Clare could feel a sense of peace. The priest surgeon's hands were quick and steady. He seemed to sense problems before they happened and moved quickly to remedy them.

Finally, Father Ravalli stood up. His lips moved as he said a prayer, and his hands formed a cross again over Spur. He flexed his back and smiled at Clare.

"Clare, you are wonderful help. Perhaps someday, little Nora will be as excellent of a nurse as her mother.

"Call in a couple of men and we'll move Spur back to that bed you had him on.

"And tell them to wash up before they come in here."

CHAPTER 80

SHARE YOUR HEART, CLARE

NUDGE AND TWO OTHER RIDERS LIFTED SPUR TO move him back to Clare's bedroom. Nora was no longer in the living room and Clare ran upstairs.

Both Nora and Chas were asleep in Nora's bed. The little girl's arm was around the baby, and he was snuggled close to her. Clare's breath caught in her throat as she watched the two of them.

"I am so blessed," she whispered as she hurried downstairs.

The men had Spur in bed. Nudge pointed at the longhandles rolled down around Spur's waist. His face turned a little red as he commented, "Those should probably come off but I'm not doin' it. Reckon that will be up to you."

Clare blushed and nodded.

"Thank you, Nudge. Please thank all the men for me. I will let you know when he comes to."

She watched Spur a moment before she hurried to the kitchen. Father Ravalli had cleaned everything and was packing his instruments. He pointed at the pump mounted on the cabinet.

"You are living in the lap of luxury here, Clare. What a blessing to have an inside pump for your water."

Clare nodded and laughed. Her eyes went toward the bedroom where Spur lay.

"I am. I was just thinking that when I checked on Nora and Chas." Her hands went still, and she added softly, "Spur has been wonderful. I couldn't have picked a better husband and father if I had tried."

Father Ravalli laughed, and his eyes danced.

"I believe the Good Lord has a sense of humor." His face became more serious as he added, "Now I want Spur to lie still for several days. That bullet was deep, and his wound needs to heal. I will be out tomorrow evening to check on him if the weather permits.

"Give him this if he wakes." He handed Clare a bottle as he spoke seriously, "I don't want him to have much of it because it is an opiate. Only give it to him if you can't keep him still." He handed her a second bottle. "Give him this as well. It will help keep the infection away.

"I want him to take it three times each day. Give him one dose tonight and another dose if he wakes before morning.

"That wound needs to be kept clean. Bathe it tomorrow morning and tomorrow night." He patted her shoulder and smiled at her again as he turned to leave. His eyes were twinkling as he added, "Now you tell Spur I have my eye on some of those black cows. The longer he stays down, the more of them he is going to owe me."

Clare's blue eyes opened wide and she laughed.

"I think we owe you quite a few already. Thank you, Father." Her breath caught and a sob slipped out. "I don't want to lose another husband," she whispered as she looked toward the bedroom.

Father Ravalli put his hands on Clare's shoulders. His eyes were kind, and his voice was soft as he spoke.

"Clare, I can't make you any promises. Only the Good Lord knows when it is someone's time to go. I can tell you though that the surgery went well. Spur is young and strong. He should be able to recuperate."

Father Ravalli dropped his hands and picked up his valise. His eyes were twinkling again when he added, "Besides, Spur has five strong reasons to get well—and one of those reasons is in front of me.

"Don't be afraid to share your heart, Clare. Love between a husband and wife is a wonderful thing. Open yourself to the love inside you. Embrace it and be happy."

He took a rag from the table and poured something on it. He wiped the blood off the floor, checking carefully to make sure all was removed.

Clare walked to the window and watched the priest as he hurried outside. He spoke to several of the men. He followed them over a sidehill. It wasn't long before he was back. He mounted his mule and headed down the trail.

She turned her head to follow the sound of children squealing and laughing. Tuff ran around the house calling behind him. He was dodging snowballs and was followed by Zeke and Annie. Most of the riders were throwing snowballs too. Clare smiled and walked back to the bedroom. She scooted a chair close to the bed and watched Spur sleep for a moment. When she remembered what Nudge had said, she blushed again.

"I just as well get your longhandles off, Spur. Your back will feel better without that lump under it."

Clare pulled the blanket back and began to ease Spur's long underwear down over his hips. She had them almost to his knees when Spur spoke softly.

"I've been trying to get you to take my britches off ever since we married. Now here you are doing it and I can't move."

Clare's hands went still, and her face turned a deep red. Her voice was calm when she answered though.

"They need to come off because they are bunched up under your back. Now lie still while I finish." She refused to look at his face as she pulled his longhandles the rest of the way down. Once they were off, she pulled the blanket back over him. She glanced at his face, but Spur's eyes were closed.

Just as she turned away, Spur opened one eye and grinned at her. "I'd be more comfortable if you were in this bed with me. In fact, I think I'd heal a lot faster."

Clare sputtered and pointed at the bottle beside the bed.

"You stop talking or I am going to give you some of Father Ravalli's medicine to knock you out. He doesn't want you moving around—and that includes talking."

Spur stared at Clare for a moment and he frowned.

"Just one little kiss and I promise to go to sleep." He puckered his lips and Clare laughed in spite of herself.

"I don't think so. If I kiss you, you will grab me." Her eyes sparkled as she added, "No, I think I'll wait until you are asleep to kiss you."

Spur stared at her and clamped his eyes shut. He took several deep breaths and then groaned at the pain.

"You are a cruel woman, Clare Ann Spurlach. Just a cruel woman."

Clare slipped a small amount of Father Ravalli's medicine into his mouth and Spur fell asleep with a smile on his face.

CHAPTER 81

HE WON'T STOP TALKING

STUB AND KIT ARRIVED THE NEXT MORNING. THE foreman glared around at his men before he spoke.

"You boys took long enough to let me know Spur was shot. Just because the boss gave me two days off was no reason to keep that from me."

Nudge grinned at him and winked at Kit.

"We did it for Kit. We knew you'd leave your bride all alone, and we figured we could get along without you for a day.

"Besides, Clare doesn't want anyone talking to Spur. She is having a hard time keeping him quiet."

Several of the men started laughing and Stub grinned.

"Yeah, old Spur does like to talk. I'm guessing Clare has a full-time job just keeping him shut up." The hands all laughed again. He lifted a quart jar of brown liquid carefully out of his saddle bag.

"Badger McCune gave this to me down in Cheyenne before we left on that drive. He said it helps if a fever comes up. Knocks them out too.

"I think I might just give some to the boss." Stub helped Kit down and followed her to the house.

He turned and growled at the men who were standing around, "Now don't be hanging around here. Get out there and break that ice. Just because the boss is laid up don't mean work stops."

The riders grinned and mounted their horses.

Clare met Stub and Kit at the door.

"The men didn't tell us until just a while ago or we'd have been here sooner." Kit hugged her friend as she spoke.

Clare laughed dryly. "Well, since this all happened yesterday, you aren't too late." She smiled at Kit as she sank down onto a kitchen chair.

"I'm so glad to see you. I barely slept at all last night. Spur won't stay asleep and the medicine that Father Ravalli left is addictive. He doesn't want Spur to have much, but the small amount I am giving him isn't working." Her face colored as she added, "And he won't stop talking."

Stub laughed out loud. He held up the jar in his hand.

"Let's try some of this. I'm guessing Father Ravalli will want to know how to make it when he sees how well it works.

"It smells bad, but a cup will knock him out for half the night. It will kick a fever as well. Shoot, between this and any medicine that priest left to fight infection, Spur will be up and going in no time at all." He paused and looked at Clare. "He did leave medicine to fight infection, didn't he?"

Clare nodded. "Yes, Spur is to take it three times each day. He told me this morning that he isn't taking any more until he eats, but he is to have no food until this evening."

She looked at her friends and whispered, "I'm so tired. Spur is a terrible patient and…and I'm so worried about him." Clare's hands shook as she clasped them in front of her.

Kit stood and took Clare by the arm.

"You are going to bed. I will run this house today. You get rested up and then we'll work together." She looked back at Stub as she led Clare toward the stairs and added, "Fill that cup completely full. Let's knock him out until this afternoon."

Stub chuckled as he filled a large cup to the brim with the brown liquid. He gagged when he smelled it and held it away from himself.

"I don't know what all is in this, but looking at some of those floating seeds, I can guess. I'll tell Spur I sneaked him a little bad liquor and see if he'll drink it."

CHAPTER 82

BADGER'S POTION

SPUR LOOKED UP WITH A GRIN WHEN STUB POKED his head through the door. Stub held out the cup as he walked toward the bed.

"I brought you a little rotgut whiskey. It doesn't smell so good, but it has a kick and it will give you a buzz." He looked toward the door furtively and whispered, "I had to wait till Clare left to bring it in here. Now drink it up fast. She'll have my hide if she finds out."

Spur grinned at his friend and took the cup. One eyebrow went up when he smelled it. He eyed it ruefully and shook his head.

"I'd like a drink, but that stuff smells terrible."

Stub shrugged and pushed the cup toward Spur. "You'll like the kick though. Drink it up before Clare gets back."

Spur lifted the cup and drank it down. His eyes were becoming glassy as he stared at the empty cup. Stub grabbed the cup as it started to slip from Spur's hand.

"That does have a kick. Why I don't feel nothin' but just warm all over." Spur stared down at his hand as he tried to lift it.

"I cain't even lift my hand. I ain't been this drunk since Clare made me marry her." His smile was wide and loose as he added, "Ain't she somethin'? I don't want to go to sleep. I'd rather talk to her." Spur closed his eyes and his voice slurred.

"You tell Clare to come back in here. You ain't near as purty to look at and I…." Spur began to snore, and Stub chuckled as he left the room.

"You durn sidewinder. That ought to shut your mouth down for at least five hours. Now we can all have a little peace and quiet around here."

Spur didn't wake until nearly 2:00 that afternoon and he began shouting, "I need to take a leak, and someone stole my britches!"

All was quiet upstairs when Kit hurried back to the bedroom.

"I'm the only one here. I'll help you to the back door and then you are on your own." She pulled Spur's blanket up higher.

"Now swing your legs over the side of the bed and put your right arm over my shoulder. Lean on me as little as possible. Father Ravalli doesn't want you to put any strain on your left side or on your arms."

Spur growled as he tried to hold the blanket.

"There is going to be some straining going on or else I am dropping this blanket—and I don't think either of us wants that to happen."

Kit put her left arm around Spur and grabbed the edges of the blanket.

"Let go of that blanket so I can hold it up. Keep your left arm across your stomach and lean on me."

They finally made it to the back door. Kit turned her back and unwrapped the blanket. She held it behind her and calmly stated, "Get it done. I don't want to stand behind you all day."

Spur glared at her over his shoulder. When he finished, he growled again, and Kit wrapped the blanket back around him. As she eased him down in the bed, Spur glared at her again.

"Where's Clare? I'm hungry and now I'm hungover from whatever Stub gave me to drink. Can I at least have a little something to eat?"

Kit tried not to laugh as she looked down at him.

"I'll bring you some broth. You can have it after you take your medicine."

She was back quickly with some hot broth and a glass of water. Spur's stomach growled loudly. He stared at the broth and opened his mouth for the medicine.

He was drinking it when Kit left and he yelled after her, "It sure is lonely back here. I don't think much of being stuck back in a corner of my own house. I'd at least like to be around my family!"

Kit didn't answer and Spur muttered to himself, "One more night back here alone and I'm leaving. I'll sleep on that lounge thing in the living room. At least I'll have someone to talk to."

He rubbed his head. "Durn, my head hurts. I haven't had this bad of a headache from whiskey in more years than I can remember."

The broth warmed his stomach and Spur began to relax. He fell asleep and slept until Father Ravalli arrived that evening.

CHAPTER 83

A Terrible Patient

CLARE LOOKED BRIGHT AND REFRESHED WHEN SHE met Father Ravalli at the door.

"Come in, Father. Won't you stay for supper? I can have one of the men take you home in the sleigh. Spur put lanterns on the sides so we can travel in the dark. Of course, the horse knows his way by now as well."

Father Ravalli smiled and nodded.

"How is our patient? Trying to get out of bed?"

Clare looked at the priest and shook her head.

"Spur is a terrible patient. He refuses to sleep, he talks all the time and yes, he now wants out of bed. He said he hates being back there by himself. He wants to be 'where the action is,' so he says."

Father Ravalli chuckled. "I will look in on him. Spur is quite social. He might behave better if you put him in your living room."

Clare looked at the priest in surprise. "I thought you wanted him where it was quiet."

"I would like him to stay down, but we might have better luck doing that if he could be around people."

Clare rolled her eyes and Father Ravalli laughed.

"We all heal in different ways, Clare. The Good Lord had lots of fun creating us. And some He made more social than others.

"I'll look in on him and we'll talk at supper."

Father Ravalli tapped lightly on Spur's door. He heard a stir of activity followed by the creaking of bed springs.

"Come in," Spur growled. He looked up in surprise as Father Ravalli stepped through the door.

The priest's wise eyes twinkled as he looked down at his patient, but his voice was serious.

"You need to stay in bed, Spur. I put quite a few stitches in you, and there is a chance you will pull them out if you get up and around too soon."

Spur frowned at the priest.

"I don't like it back here by myself. There is no one to talk to. And if that's not bad enough, I'm not supposed to get out of bed and my as—I mean my tail end hurts from laying around on my back."

Father Ravalli studied Spur's frustrated face. "What if we move your bed into the living room? Would you stay down for a time then?"

Spur nodded slowly.

"I would. For sure longer than if I have to stay back here. I don't like being locked up, Padre. It makes me antsy."

Father Ravalli unwrapped the bandage around Spur's chest. "Your Clare is a fine nurse. She learns quickly and repeats what I show her. She did an excellent job of wrapping your wound—although I'm guessing you complained the entire time." The priest's voice was bland as he studied the wound.

Spur blushed slightly. "I reckon I haven't been an easy patient." He grinned at the priest. "I told her I'd stay in bed if she'd stay with me. That's when she left, and she hasn't been back for nearly two hours."

Father Ravalli tried not to laugh. He gave Spur his medicine and sat down on the edge of the bed. His kind eyes were serious as he looked at his patient.

"You gave Clare a terrible scare. That bullet was deep, and she helped me with my surgery to remove it. She is trying to be brave. There is a part of her though that is terrified you are going to die.

"Now you can use your time in the house to make her life easier, or you can continue to be difficult and make things harder for her. I'm sure you don't want to do that, so let's talk about what we can do to help you become a better patient."

Spur was at first surprised and then remorseful. "I'm sorry, Padre. I didn't intend to make things hard for Clare. I guess I wasn't thinking." His face was hopeful as he asked, "If I promise to behave better, will you move my bed to the living room? And when can I have some real food?"

Father Ravalli's face broke into a smile.

"I want you to stay in bed for three more days. Starting Friday, you may get up every four hours. I only want you up for an hour though. When you get tired, climb back in that bed. That means four hours down, one hour up. No picking anything up. Clare can hand you the baby, but you can't pick him up yourself.

"No lifting the older children either. I want you to pretend that your left arm isn't there and that your right arm is broken.

"Now come out to the kitchen and sit down while we move your bed. You can visit just a little, but then you need to lie down.

"And I'd like to know more about that drink you were given. I hear it calmed you right down and helped you to sleep."

"It did do that. It also packed a heck of a wallop. My head hurt for three hours after I woke up. It smelled terrible, but it warmed me all the way through.

"Stub said he brought it back with him from Cheyenne, so now I know what I drank. A fellow down there by the name of Badger McCune makes it. I've seen him give it to men before, but I never had any myself until this morning."

Father Ravalli smiled at the mention of Badger's name.

"Ah, yes. Mr. McCune. He came to see me a few years back. An interesting man. In fact, he wrote down the ingredients in his 'potion' as he called it.

"I believe I will make some of that. I do remember him telling me its medicinal qualities. As I recall, it is excellent for fever as well."

He felt Spur's forehead. "You certainly don't have a fever. I believe we will have you drink another cup of that when everyone retires for the night. If we can avoid infection from setting in these next two days, I think you will be up and ready to move around some in a week."

Spur's stomach rumbled loudly, and Father Ravalli laughed.

"We'll get you some supper as well. Yes, Spur, I believe you are on the mend."

CHAPTER 84

A BETTER MAN

SPUR'S ATTITUDE CHANGED WHEN HE WAS MOVED TO the living room. He was quieter and better behaved although when Friday came, he stayed up for much longer periods than he was told. Kit had gone home earlier that day and Clare was cleaning up after supper.

"Father Ravalli said you should only be up for an hour. Now go back to bed. It has been three hours already! Besides, the kids are in bed, and I need to go too."

"I will if you'll come with me. Come on, Clare. Lay with me for a bit. Bring Chas along and nurse him if you want." His dark eyes glinted and he added, "I know I'll sleep better if I can look at your pretty face for a bit."

Clare started to shake her head but as she looked at Spur's mournful face, she gave in.

"All right but not for long. Chas is already asleep. When he cries, I am taking him upstairs. And you'd better behave or I'll leave."

Clare helped Spur back to bed. She looked over at him suspiciously several times. He was leaning heavily on her, and his right hand flopped around. When he was finally in bed, she walked to the other side. She slipped off her shoes and lay down on the edge of the bed.

413

Spur rolled carefully on his right side and grinned at her.

"It only took me three months, but I finally have you in my bed."

Clare stared at Spur and sat up. "I'm going to get up. I knew you couldn't behave."

Spur groaned and rolled over on his back. "I think you are perfectly safe. I can't lay on my side let alone do anything else.

"How is Handy? His head healing all right?"

"It is. Father Ravalli told him not to ride for three days. It pained him awful but unlike you, he did what his doctor said. It's been five days now and Stub just let him ride out with the men."

Spur was quiet a moment before he looked over at Clare.

"I'm thinking of making Ladder foreman when Stub leaves. He's sensible and doesn't snap under pressure. The men like him too. What do you think?"

Clare laid down and pulled a blanket over herself. "I like Ladder. He would be a great foreman." She watched Spur a moment and asked softly, "You remember those men you tied in the line shack with the shotgun pointed at them? They escaped."

Spur looked over at her in surprise.

"Ladder told you that?"

"No, Caine did. He took Father Ravalli home Monday night in the dark. I made him a pie the next day as a thank you and we visited a little. He told me Ladder must have known they'd be gone because he walked right into that cabin without worrying about the shotgun.

"All three men were gone. One man wrote a note and signed it 'Snake.' He thanked Ladder for the grubstake and said they were headed south, back to the Territory.

"Caine said Ladder laughed when he read the note. Ladder told him Snake earned his name because he could worm his way in or out of anything.

"Caine remembered Ladder tying that rope specifically to one man. Ladder leaned over him and touched his shirt before he left. Caine thought at the time Ladder was checking the rope. He thinks now that must have been when Ladder gave Snake some money." Clare's eyes were bright as she looked at Spur.

"You had just paid the men and Ladder is broke. I'm guessing he gave Snake his full month's wages."

Spur laughed softly. "I'm glad. Those boys were just cowboys. They were broke and took the wrong job. Maybe they will learn from this."

Clare was quiet as she pulled the blanket closer around her body.

"That is why Ladder will be a good foreman. He has a kind heart. He's tough but fair. He's actually a lot like you."

CHAPTER 85

HAPPY NEW YEAR, DARLIN'!

SPUR ROLLED SLOWLY ONTO HIS SIDE. HIS EYES WERE intense as he asked, "Does that mean you like me too?"

Tears filled Clare's eyes and she whispered, "I was terrified when I saw you lying on the floor. You were bleeding so badly. The man you killed had his hand stretched toward you, and he had a metal piece over one of his fingernails. I think he had a poison finger like Mae did.

"I was afraid he had cut you."

"What about that finger? Did you bury it with him?" Spur was watching Clare as he spoke.

"No, Caine told me that Father Ravalli removed it. They showed him where they had drug the body. He wrapped it up and took it with him. He poured something on the rag he wiped the floor with too. I could smell it after he left, but I don't know what he used."

Spur carefully reached out his left arm. He touched Clare's face and wiped away the tears.

"He said he was my uncle. He asked to shake hands when he was dying but I refused. He was as evil as Mae was." He smiled as he watched Clare.

"I'm glad Chas didn't fill that tunnel in. He built it for his family, but it saved mine." Spur was quiet for a moment.

"Come closer, Clare. Lay up next to me. Let me hold you tonight, at least until that little guy wakes up."

Clare stared at her husband for a moment. She slowly slid across the bed until she was next to him.

Spur kissed her. He kept his right arm under her and wrapped her up closer.

"I have wanted to hold you for so long," he whispered as he looked down at her.

"I can feel your heart beating." He was still for a moment and then added, "You heart is beating faster than mine."

"That's because I never know what you are going to do. You have me nervous all the time."

"But you still like me."

"Maybe a little. I just don't trust you."

Spur chuckled. "I don't even trust me, not where you're concerned." He rolled over on his back. "You are safe tonight though. I can hardly cuddle, and I've never had trouble doing that before."

Spur's eyes slowly closed and soon he was snoring softly. Clare raised up to look at him. "He is asleep. I thought he was pretending." She lay down against his side. "I'll just stay here for a moment. When Chas wakes, I'll get up."

Chas didn't wake until it was nearly morning. Clare picked him up and placed him in bed with Spur. The baby nursed and they both fell asleep.

She was still asleep when Spur awoke. Chas lay on his back between the two of them. His little mouth was open slightly and he made sucking movements as milk leaked from the corner of his mouth.

Spur leaned over to stare at his son. He studied the little round body and full cheeks.

"Your mother is a good milker, little man. Life right now is about as good as you can ask for."

Spur slowly rolled out of bed. He felt better this morning than he had in what seemed like a long time. He carefully pulled his britches on over his longhandles and headed to the kitchen with his shirt in his hand.

When Clare awoke, he had bacon cooked and eggs frying.

Clare touched her hair. "I can't believe I slept all night in my clothes. I'm a mess."

Spur grinned at her. "I think if you had been in that thin nightgown last night, I might hurt a lot more this morning."

Clare blushed a deep red. "Spur, you say the boldest things. Now shush before someone hears you."

Spur chuckled and pointed at the bed. "I think that can go back in the bedroom. I am done laying around. Something must have happened last night. I believe I am durned near healed.

"Happy New Year, Darlin'. It's the third day of 1880!"

CHAPTER 86

THAT MAN SHOWS UP
EVERYWHERE

THE HANDS MOVED SPUR'S BED BACK INTO THE bedroom that day. He stayed in the house but was up most of the day.

By Sunday, Spur was outside. When he returned several hours later, he held onto the porch rail as he walked up the stairs.

Clare met him at the door with her hands on her hips.

"Father said for you to take it easy for two weeks. It has barely been a week. You are going to rip those stitches he put in you, and then you'll be bleeding inside. Now you get back here and lie down."

Spur grinned and kissed her cheek. He washed his hands and sauntered back to the bedroom.

Clare heard him call out, "Sure is lonely back here," but she ignored him.

The following Friday, he was outside most of the day. His face was pale when he came in around five.

"It sure felt good to be up and around. I didn't do much but sit around and give orders, and I'm still worn out.

"I'm going to rest a little before supper."

Spur tripped a little as he walked down the hall. He sat down heavily on the bed and was soon fast asleep.

Clare called him an hour later for supper, but he never moved. She walked back to the bedroom and called again. When he didn't answer, she pulled his boots off. He still didn't move so she loosened his britches. Watching him carefully, she slid them down and off his legs. She pulled the blanket over him and quietly closed the door.

Chas was fussy that night and Clare brought him downstairs around two in the morning. "Why are you fussing? You have eaten and you're dry.

"I think you just want to play. Maybe I'll put you in with Spur. He's probably ready to play too as early as he went to bed."

Clare knocked softly on Spur's door. When he didn't answer, she opened the door quietly. She couldn't hear him breathing and she put her hand on his head. It was cool and she breathed a sigh of relief.

A strong hand suddenly grabbed her arm and Clare gasped.

Spur awoke and stared at her. "Clare! What are you doing? I almost punched you!"

"Chas won't sleep. I thought maybe you would take him. I'm tired and you should be rested as early as you fell asleep."

"That will be fine. Lay him down. I'm going to go wash up a little. I'll be back shortly."

Clare lay down on the bed beside her kicking baby.

"You little stinker. You just keep playing. Your father will be back soon, and he can deal with you."

When Spur came back, Clare was asleep on the side of the bed and Chas was cooing in the middle. Spur picked him up and walked down the hall talking to him. Chas slowly wound down. After fifteen minutes of singing and rocking, the little boy was fast asleep.

Spur took him into the bedroom and lay him down beside Clare. He stared at his wife for a moment before he looked away.

"If I lay down here with your mother in that flimsy nightgown, I won't get any sleep. Then I'll wake you with all my tossing around." He looked down at Clare one more time. He shook his head and climbed the stairs to her bedroom.

Clare woke early and sat up. Spur was gone and Chas was still asleep. She slipped out of bed and hurried upstairs to change her clothes.

Dawn was just breaking, and Clare dropped her nightgown on the floor. She slipped her dress over her head and was buttoning it up when she heard someone stir in her bed.

She clapped her hand over her mouth to keep from screaming when she recognized Spur's long leg hanging over the side of the bed. He rolled onto his side as Clare slipped out the door.

"That man shows up everywhere. We just as well share a bedroom. He is always around anyway."

Spur's voice sounded behind her, and he was laughing.

"To be fair, you came into my room last night. Still, I wouldn't have moved when I did, but I got a cramp in my leg. And sharing a bedroom would be mighty fine with me." He climbed out of bed and sauntered by her to lope down the stairs, whistling low in his chest.

Clare watched Spur a moment. She frowned as she followed him. *That man makes me so mad!*

CHAPTER 87

A New Foreman

CLARE WAS FIXING BREAKFAST AND SPUR WAS WORKING in his office when there was a knock on the door.

Ladder stood there with a smile. He held a letter in his hand and offered it to Clare.

"This came for you, Miz Clare. Fellow at the express office give it to me yesterday when I was through town." He looked over at Spur and grinned.

"Good to see you workin' again, Boss. I was startin' to wonder if you'd retired." The cowboy's eyes were glinting with humor and Spur chuckled.

"Come on in here, Ladder. There is something we want to talk to you about."

The smile left Ladder's face. He pulled off his boots and Spur pointed at the table.

"Have a chair. This won't take long."

Ladder dropped down on a chair and looked at his boss quizzically.

"I understand you let those three cowboys go that were tied up in the line shack."

"Now lettin' 'em go ain't exactly right. They got loose is all. They was gone by the time we made it back up there."

"That Snake fellow a pard of yours?"

Ladder looked from Spur to Clare and slowly turned red. His eyes were clear though when he looked back at Spur.

"Yeah, I knew Snake. We was pards a long time ago down Texas way. He was always wild, but he was honest.

"Those boys was just cowboys. They didn't kill Jake an' Caine like they was told to do—they shot over their heads. They shot high on Handy too, an' they only hit 'im 'cause he just kept a comin'.

"An' as far as turnin' those fellers out in the weather, ever' rider who has stayed in that line shack knows about that cave." His eyes glinted as he grinned at Clare.

"Snake got his name a long time ago. Even as a little kid, he could worm his way out of any rope you tied around him. I don't know how. He just could.

"When we rode together, we used to get our Saturday night drinkin' money takin' on dares. Sometimes, Snake was tied on the floor of a saloon. Other times, he was in the bottom of a water trough.

"I recognized his horse when we rode up. I sure was irritated he was part of such a lowdown outfit. I guessed he just needed a winter ridin' job an' I was right.

"I tied the three of 'em together an' tied that shotgun to 'im. I knew if I made those ropes long enough, Snake could get loose without pullin' the trigger on that shotgun."

"And then you gave him a grubstake. Likely all you had been paid."

Ladder squirmed in his chair.

"Those boys was goin' to have to leave on the run. I just gave 'em a little travelin' money. I have a good winter job." He looked carefully at Spur and his face lost a little color.

"I did have a job anyway. If I lost it, I reckon I'll head south too… but I won't apologize for helpin' a friend in a bad spot."

426

Spur studied the serious rider in front of him and he laughed. He gripped Ladder's shoulder and nodded toward Clare.

"We called you in here because we want to offer you a foreman job.

"Nudge gave me his notice yesterday. He's been hanging around with a little gal down south of here. Her pa has a big ranch in the Idaho Territory. He wanted to stick around to get his share of what Chas offered, but she finally convinced him to quit.

"Stub will be leaving when the weather breaks and we need a foreman."

Spur's eyes were serious as he added, "And we want one who is level-headed. One who will think around problems. You came up with a way to get around killing, and I like that.

"Clare and I talked it over. We think you are the man for that job."

Ladder stared at the two of them. The color came back into his face, and he let out a long breath.

"You ain't gonna fire me?"

Clare smiled at him and laughed as she looked over at Spur. "No, we want to keep you on. Once you start, you may stay in the Slash B house."

Ladder stared at the two of them and slowly grinned. He put out his hand to Spur and nodded.

"I'd be proud to help you ramrod this operation, Boss. You too, Miz Clare. You just tell me when I start an' I'll be ready to go."

They visited a while longer and Ladder headed back outside. He had a little swagger in his walk, and Clare laughed as she watched from the window.

Caine met him in the yard and Ladder grabbed the younger man. He acted like he was going to swing at him. Then he looped one long arm over the shorter man's shoulders and the two of them headed to the barn.

Clare turned around with a smile still on her face.

"So you are going to let Nudge come back this spring and help gather his cows?"

Spur looked over at Clare in surprise. His face colored a little as he chuckled.

"Maybe. You have a problem with that?"

Clare laughed softly and she shook her head.

"No, Nudge is a good man. He is doing what he thinks is best for his future wife. A man should never be punished for putting family first." Her eyes sparkled and she added dryly, "Caine told me that too."

"That Caine seems to be just full of information. Maybe I should have a talk with him."

"Don't you dare. He is just a lonesome young man. He cares about the men he works with. Everything he told me made someone's life better." Clare's blue eyes were sparking, and her hands were on her hips.

"You leave him alone."

Spur laughed as he watched her, and he shook his head.

"All right. I'll do that. You just ply him with pie from time to time, and maybe I'll get a better handle on what's going on around here."

Clare rolled her eyes and turned back to her cooking. She jumped when Spur put his arms around her.

"You are a sassy one, Clare Ann Spurlach. I sure am happy you made me marry you. You just slip into my bed any time you want. And lose your clothes too. That will be fine with me," he added with a whisper.

Clare swung the spoon she was using at Spur, and he jumped back laughing. He walked over to the crib where Chas was cooing and picked him up.

"I wonder what kind of a little man you will be. You sure have a feisty mama."

CHAPTER 88

A Letter From Rollie

CLARE HELD UP A LETTER AFTER BREAKFAST. SHE looked around the room at three expectant little faces.

"Guess who wants us to visit this summer?"

Clare laughed as the children guessed. "Who wants to see Rollie?"

Spur grinned as the table became loud and Clare continued.

"Gabe and Merina invited us down. Rollie misses you. He calls you his cousins." She held up a piece of paper that was included in the envelope.

"Merina is teaching him to write. She included this. He had stuck it on his door one morning." Clare laughed softly.

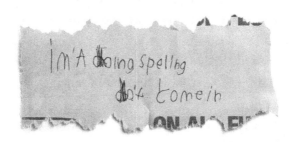

"Rollie wasn't excited about school in the beginning, but Merina said he is doing much better. He might even be able to write his own letter next time."

Clare frowned slightly as she looked over at Spur. "Merina said Angel and Miguel didn't come home with the rest of the riders after they finished the drive. She said they had some business to take care of, but she didn't say what it was."

Spur listened closely. "Who knows where Miguel might sidetrack, but Angel is responsible. She didn't say if they made it home? When was that letter written?"

Clare scanned the letter again.

"Merina didn't say any more about them. She wrote this letter October 20 so Gabe and his hands wouldn't have been home long.

"It took nearly three months for this letter to get up here." She studied the envelope a little longer and commented softly, "Too bad they can't put some kind of mark on these envelopes so we can see where all they go before they arrive. Who knows where this one went?"

The children were running around the table, shrieking and laughing. "Cousin Rollie! Cousin Rollie!"

Spur pointed at the door.

"You three get out there and get your chores done. Those bucket calves will think you forgot them."

As the three children bundled up and tumbled out the door, Clare called after them, "Don't forget to break the ice for the chickens and check on that cat Father Ravalli gave you. She might have had her kittens by now."

Spur laughed as the kids fell through the door. They were arguing about who would be able to hold the first kitten and what their names were going to be.

"That old cat isn't stupid. She had those kittens last week. She hid them up in the loft. She knows how much they'll be handled."

CHAPTER 89

A New Year On
The Double Spur

CLARE WAS QUIET AS SHE LISTENED TO SPUR. SHE finally turned around to face him.

"I think it's time we move my clothes downstairs."

Spur nodded. "I'll do that today. No need in me taking that bedroom anymore. I'm just about healed."

Clare's face turned pink as she continued.

"I want to clean your office today." She paused and her face turned pinker as she added, "I thought we might move your things into the downstairs bedroom as well."

Spur listened quietly. He almost started to tease her, but he was silent instead.

"Annie asked me yesterday why you and I don't sleep in the same room. She was concerned that maybe you don't want to be her papa or that I was going to send you away."

Spur stood and walked over to Clare. He put his arms around her and hugged her tightly.

"You think you're ready for me to be around all the time?"

Clare looked up at Spur. Her eyes reflected what looked like fear.

"Yes. Maybe. I don't really know. I know I want you to hold me, and I haven't slept as soundly in a long time as I did with you last night.

"You make me laugh and you confuse me. Sometimes, you just infuriate me. In spite of all that, when I look at you, I get happy inside."

Spur pulled Clare closer and kissed her. His eyes began to twinkle.

"Now, you do know if you wear that thin nightgown you like, I'm not staying on my side of the bed."

Clare blushed furiously and tried to pull away, but Spur hugged her tightly as he laughed.

"Come on, Clare. You haven't left much to my imagination."

Clare dropped her eyes and looked away.

"I declare, Spur. You are so bold. You have no muzzle whatsoever. You say things just to embarrass me and I—"

Spur cut her off with a long kiss. Clare's breath was coming quickly, and she tried to step back. Spur shook his head.

"Huh uh. We're married and we can do whatever we want. No need to be all shy, Mrs. Spurlach. You kiss me back now. You started this conversation."

Clare stared up at him. She finally wrapped her arms around Spur's neck and as she smiled. The next kiss was longer.

Spur nuzzled her neck and whispered, "You are going to have to be gentle though, Clare. If you get too wild, I might break my stitches."

Clare jerked back and glared up at him.

"Good grief, Spur. I never know—"

Spur was late getting out of the house that morning. He didn't care though. His grin was big, and his step was just a little jaunty as he strolled down to the barn.

It was a new year on the Double Spur Ranch.

Made in the USA
Monee, IL
31 May 2024

59122196R00256